THE
SILVER
WOLF

J. C. Harvey is the fiction pen-name for Jacky Colliss Harvey. After studying English at Cambridge, and History of Art at the Courtauld Institute of Art, Jacky worked in museum publishing for twenty years, first at the National Portrait Gallery and then at the Royal Collection Trust, where she set up the Trust's first commercial publishing programme. The extraordinary history of the Thirty Years War (1618–48) and of 17th-century Europe has been an obsession of hers for as long as she can remember, and was the inspiration behind the Fiskardo's War series, which begins now with *The Silver Wolf*, marking her fiction debut.

THE
SILVER
WOLF

J. C. Harvey

ALLEN&UNWIN

First published in Great Britain in 2022 by Allen & Unwin,
an imprint of Atlantic Books Ltd.

10 9 8 7 6 5 4 3 2 1

A CIP catalogue record for this book is available from the British Library.

Hardback ISBN: 978 1 83895 328 7
Trade paperback ISBN: 978 1 83895 329 4
E-book ISBN: 978 1 83895 330 0

Printed in Great Britain by TJ Books Ltd

Allen & Unwin
An imprint of Atlantic Books Ltd
Ormond House
26–27 Boswell Street
London
WC1N 3JZ

www.allenandunwin.com/uk

This one is for Nick, who started it.

Contents

Author's Note

—∽⊙∽—

Gentle reader, hello.

The events in *The Silver Wolf* stand in much the same relation to the events of the Thirty Years War as a tapestry does to its support: in other words, with just enough points of connection, I hope, to bear the weight. Every writer of historical fiction has to decide where the needle dividing the two, the historical and the fictional, comes to rest, and in the case of this book, and the two to come, I have played fast and loose with documented history, opening real historical doors onto landscapes and happenings that never existed until I made them up. Then again, all too often, I would hit the horrid truth that no matter what I might create in my imagination, the actual events of the war would be worse: stranger, crazier, even more hideously comic; more incredible, more appalling. And if all history is a matter of interpretation, that of the Thirty Years War is so, as much as any and more than most; a consequence of its vast geographical spread and of the number of opposing forces it drew in. Alliances formed and were dissolved in the time it took a messenger to gallop from one stronghold to the next; under the banner of a religious war, of Catholic versus Protestant (or rather, of Catholic versus Calvinist, Lutheran and Anglican), any number of ancient grudges and territorial disputes were brought out and brandished anew. Everything, in this war, was happening everywhere at once. The following is very broad brush therefore, but if the Thirty Years War is unfamiliar to you, and some background would be useful, well then – now read on.

In the early seventeenth century there were members of the Habsburg family on the thrones of three of Europe's great powers; in Spain itself and to the east, in the Holy Roman Empire, that enormous chunk of central Europe including Austria, Bohemia and most of what is now modern Germany, there was the Emperor Ferdinand II. Catholic, Lutheran and Calvinist rubbed up against each other throughout the states of the Empire, but in the rest of Europe Habsburg dominance was both feared and mistrusted; especially by the people of the Valtelline in northern Italy, who had endured Spanish troops marching through their territories, up to the Spanish Netherlands, for years; especially France, even though France had its own Protestant religious dissenters, the Huguenots, to deal with; and especially the Dutch United Provinces, who had been at war with Spain for decades.

The Thirty Years War began in the Bohemian capital, Prague, a little after 9 a.m. on 23 May 1618, when three men – Vilem Slavata, Jaroslav Borita von Martinitz and Filip Fabricius – were ejected from a summit meeting of the Bohemian nobility in Hradschin Castle via one of the castle's windows. All three somehow survived their seventeen-metre drop into the moat; all three were loyal to the Holy Roman Emperor; and all three were Catholics. Those ejecting them were not, and the men they had thought to throw to their deaths were, they said, 'enemies of us and of our religion'. Drunk with its own daring, Bohemia then invited the Calvinist prince Frederick, ruler of the Palatine in Germany, rather than the Holy Roman Emperor to occupy its throne. Disastrously, Frederick accepted the invitation. Very shortly after that, an Imperial army overran Bohemia and decorated Prague's lovely bridge with the heads of the Emperor's enemies. Then Ferdinand moved in on Frederick's kingdom in Germany. Frederick, now in exile, beseeched his father-in-law, James I of England, and every other Protestant ruler for assistance, and thus brought into being a tatty coalition of

English and Scottish mercenaries and the rulers of Brunswick, Saxony, Prussia, Brandenburg, Hesse-Kassel, and, on the pretext that Ferdinand was threatening the Baltic, Denmark, where Christian IV of Denmark coveted the role of Protestant champion every bit as much as did Frederick himself. And then there was Sweden, where King Gustavus Adolphus had been quietly honing his talents and his armies in wars with Denmark, Russia and Poland since 1611. The Emperor, for his part, could call upon all the wealth and all the men of his empire, all that of Philip IV of Spain, and upon all the greatness of the Catholic grandee Maximilian of Bavaria, too. Meanwhile, manoeuvring against both Emperor Ferdinand and Philip of Spain (and with an eye over his shoulder to England and the Baltic to boot) was Cardinal Richelieu of France, and his monarch, Louis XIII.

Thirty years later, when the war finally ended with the signing of the Peace of Westphalia on 24 October 1648, it had claimed the lives of twenty per cent of the then population of Europe – some five million individuals. Some estimates put that figure as high as twelve million. There were parts of Germany where sixty per cent of the population was lost. Towns were decimated, trade and industry destroyed, villages wiped from the map. A century's worth of population growth, of people, simply disappeared. There were over a quarter of a million men in arms in Germany by 1635, and if the violence they brought with them didn't kill you, the plagues and famines that inevitably followed in any army's wake would, even more easily and in even greater numbers. Every statistic, where the Thirty Years War is concerned, is hideous and/or incredible, in equal measure.

This is especially true where its finances are concerned. We're used to Europe having a single currency, the euro, but in the seventeenth century it had guilders, florins and marks, *kreuzers* and *pfennigs*; French *livres* and francs; Swiss *finfers*; Dutch (and German) *stuivers*; Italian *lire*, *ducats* and *soldi*; Spanish *pistoles*, *escudos* and *reales*. And there was the Imperial thaler, of course, which, if you are reading this book in North America, is where the word 'dollar' comes from. So long as your coin was gold or silver, someone would take it, but as war progressed and the structure of society rotted away, counterfeiting and inflation galloped forward hand-in-hand. Vineyards and fields were stripped, marched over or burnt out by invading troops; military encampments decimated supplies for miles around but could make suppliers rich; the wandering masses of refugees walked through crops ready to harvest and put an enormous strain on the resources of any town where they came to rest. Where there was no-one left to sow or harvest crops, land had no value; and if land had no value, nor did anything else. Leipzig, for example, was bankrupt by 1625, just seven years after the war began; while the town of Marburg in Hesse took *two centuries* to pay off the debts it incurred during the war.

Unsurprisingly, even at the time, those living through the war seem to have understood that what they were enduring was without compare in terms of the horrors it inflicted upon them, and they responded by writing their experiences down – in diaries, journals, letters and accounts of all sorts; some to inform friends, some aimed at descendants, some as a record of atrocities and outrages aimed at what you might call the court of time. One such was Hans Heberle, a shoemaker from the village of Neenstetten, whose description of the beginning of the war I make use of in Chapter Six of Part One. Hans had to flee from his village to the nearby town of Ulm no fewer than thirty times between 1634 and 1648.

Equally unsurprisingly, such dreadful times gave rise to tales of magic and monsters; of men who could raise mists and miasmas with their breath or by scattering dust on the wind, and hide themselves therein; of the Devil walking abroad and striking pacts with the unwary; and, of course, of the hard man, the merciless warrior who had gone beyond the power of iron or lead to harm him. One such hard man has come down to us by name. 'Captain Carlo Fantom,' John Aubrey informs us, in his *Brief Lives*, 'a Croatian, spake 13 languages... was very quarrelsome and a great ravisher.' Carlo Fantom would move from the Thirty Years War to the English Civil War, where 'Sir Robert Pye was his Colonel, who shot at him for not returning a horse... The Bullets went through his buff-coat and Captain Hamden saw his shirt was on fire. Capt. Fantom took the bullets and said he, "Here, Sir Robert, take your bullets again." None of the soldiers would dare fight with him; they said they would not fight with the Devil.'

Reading Aubrey's description was one of the moments when I felt the inescapable clench of a plot coming into being. I owe Hans Heberle and his contemporaries much in the way of inspiration for *The Silver Wolf*. I owe John Aubrey and the two volumes of his *Brief Lives*, also; but Aubrey would be most surprised to discover he had ever written a third, or that one Jack Fiskardo should feature in it, first as Carlo Fantom's helpless victim, and then as his sworn foe.

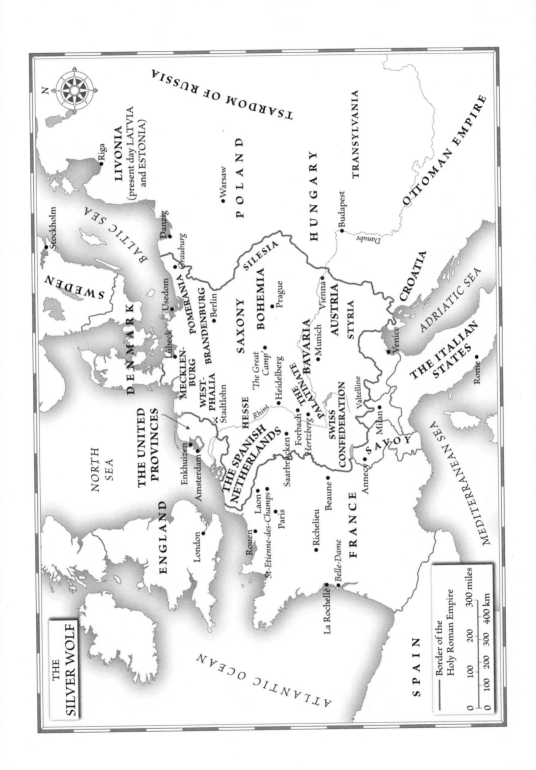

Cast of Characters

PART I

In Amsterdam

Mungo Sant, a Scottish mariner, captain of the *Guid Marie*

Jack Fiskardo, a thirteen-year-old vagrant, living rough on the docks as best he can

'Ringle-Eye', a dockyard gang-lord

'Copperknob', his second-in-command

Yosha Silbergeld, a wealthy merchant, Sant's business partner

Zoot, Yosha's housekeeper

Cornelius, her son

Paul, Yosha's steward

Beatrice, Zoot's maid

Yosha's household servants, including:

    Old Jan, a gardener

    Master Nicholas, a schoolmaster and tutor of fencing

At the Carpenter's Hat, on the road to Annecy, Savoy

Reinhold Meier, landlord

Tabitha, his daughter

Captain Balthasar, 'the Shadow Man', one-time scout in the army of King Henry IV of France

Ravello, an army intelligencer. A spy.

In the village of St-Étienne-des-Champs, Picardy

Robert, landlord of the Écu de France
Mirelle, his sister

On the Bergstrasse, heading toward the city of Heidelberg in Germany

Walther Kleber, a carter
Hartmann, a horse-dealer, sadly now deceased
Oleg, Hartmann's hired hand
Deaf Peter, a military courier
Jo-Jo, his lackey

In Hertzberg, a town in Saarland, Germany, a mustering place for the Imperial army of General Tilly

Fat Magda, a tavern-keeper
Paola, her partner
Ilse, their serving girl, Jo-Jo's sister
Gotz, a gunnery sergeant
Luckless, his newest recruit
Eberhardt Rauchmann, a brewer
Rufus, a headsman of the Roma
Yuna, his wife
Emilian, his son
Benedicte, his brother, a seer
Carlo Fantom, Croat mercenary and hired assassin

PART II

In the village of Belle-Dame, near La Rochelle, Poitou

Jean Fiskardo, one-time captain of cavalry in the army of King
    Henry IV of France

Sally Arden, his English wife

Monsieur Gustave, a wealthy farmer

Anne, a widow, newly returned to the village from Paris

Marguerite, her daughter

The villagers, including:

    Madame Marthe

    Salty Pierre

    Didier-France

    Pastou

    Séraphine

The children of the village, including:

    Claude

    Sebastien

    Didier-Marie

    Adèle

In Paris, at the palace of the Louvre

Concino Concini, an Italian mountebank, now ennobled as the
    Marquis d'Ancre; advisor to Marie de'Medici, widow of the
    late King Henry IV of France

Armand du Plessis, Bishop of Luçon, Secretary of State, later
    Cardinal Richelieu

Nicolas de L'Hôpital, Marquis de Vitry, captain of the royal guard

PART III

In the army of General Tilly

Cyrius, a one-time miller, now an army sutler
Agetha, his beloved
Squirrel, her daughter
The scouts:
 Aesop
 Holger
 Titus
Korbl, a blowhard

Somewhere within the forests of Lower Saxony

Christian of Brunswick and the rebel army of Frederick of Bohemia

In the great camp

Bronheim, colonel of an Imperial cavalry regiment
'Herzog Heinrich', one of his captains
Heinrich's crew:
 Hans
 Gunter
 Stuzzi
 Matz
Gretchen, Bronheim's whore
Bertholdt, leader of Bronheim's crew
Officers in Bronheim's cavalry, including:
 Captain Mannfred
 Lieutenant Eickholz

In the town of Grauburg on the Polish border

Torsten 'the Bear' Bjornson, captain in the army of Gustavus
   Adolphus, King of Sweden, wintering above Grauburg with
   his regiment
Zoltan, his ensign

On the island of Usedom, off the coast of north Germany

Zoltan, now Jack's second-in-command
The men of Jack's company, including:
   The Executioner
   The Gemini
   Ziggy
   Karl-Christian von Lindeborg (Kai), Jack's ensign

He was left orphan very young, which (said he) determined all the course of his life; for having fought to live, so he grew to the taste of it, and lived to fight. He was first made Captain in the army of Gustavus Adolf, the Swedish King, and coming back into Germany with the said King's troops, had such skills in the bearing of arms that it was said he had purchased them of the Devil, in especial, that he was a Hard Man, so could not be put down by bullets nor by steel; and that he carried with him always the silver token of a wolf, such as the Hard Men use, so that one may know another. Yet being asked if he was indeed proof against shot or blade, he gave a great laugh and answered: those that say it, they should see my scars.

His father was a gentleman-at-arms under King Henry of France and there was much black work, as the soldiers say, in his father's death, and in his mother's too. For many years he set himself to uncover those accountable; whether he did so or no I cannot discover...'

John Aubrey, *Brief Lives*, Volume III

PROLOGUE

June 1630

A ND AWAKE. Heart banging at his breastbone like a fist upon a door, the dream unravelling, pulling back down into its hole, the light of a midsummer morning filling the room with its unholy brightness, and the girl patting his face.

'*Was ist?*'

She peers at him, narrowing her eyes. For a moment the shape of a body – wholly shrouded, even the face – had hung there behind her, like a chrysalis on its thread. *No. You're here. Not there.* Sweat, cooling on his neck. Outside, the squeal of gulls; their shadows dive across the bed. He closes his eyes.

'*Du skrek ut,*' he hears her say. '*In sömnen.*' Her tone is offended. It can't be welcome, to have your bedmate yelling in his sleep.

A riffle through the languages now waking in his head: French, English, German, shreds of Dutch, bits of Polish... Swedish, that's the one. The dream has muddied his thoughts, the way it will. We are in Stockholm, we speak Swedish, and this evening (more's the pity), this evening we embark. He takes her hand. '*Tack,*' he says. Thank you.

Her face is still unsure. She's dark for a Stockholm lass, with something snub about her; small and neat and dark and, at this moment, just a little wary. Though she'd been full of spark and pepper the night before, come jouncing across the room and hauled him to his feet announcing, 'Now, I fuck the devil!'

'The devil has a handsome cock,' she tells him, now. She manages to make this sound almost prim. 'But, he has bad dreams.'

He feels like asking her, *What did you expect?*

The sound of a door banging open downstairs and footsteps – bootsteps, rather – out into the cobbled yard. 'Your men,' she says.

'I know. I recognize their dainty step.' A shout – Zoltan, chivvying the rest. The *hur-hur-hur* of laughter. 'Not to mention, their angel voices.'

She props herself up on one elbow, the small weight of her breast against his arm. She still wears her shift, yet has somehow contrived to remove every stitch of clothing he'd had on him. His boots are one in one corner of the room, one in the other. His breeches on the floor. His coat on the bedpost. His shirt hangs like a trophy from the corner of the tester up above their heads. She says, 'Your men are very proud of you. They paid for me.'

'They did?'

She nods her head, lays her fingers to her upper lip and mimes the extravagant curl of a moustache. 'This one. He paid me. And I cost a lot.'

Zoltan.

'And they tell me about you.'

He pushes himself up to face her. 'My men,' he tells her, 'are a bunch of shameless, murderous liars. Don't trust a word that comes out of 'em.'

'They say the Devil taught you how to fight, until you beat him, too.'

'For sure he did. You should see me with a pitchfork.'

A snort of laughter. 'They say you sold your soul,' she says. Growing bolder now. 'They say all those who stand against you die.'

'Sweetling, soldiers tell tales. They make up stories. It's what they do.'

'They say five Polish troopers emptied their pistols at you, one after another. And not one bullet grazed you. And that you killed them all.'

'First,' he says, 'two of 'em shot at each other, all I had to do was duck. The third unhorsed himself; I doubt he's more than bruised. The fourth I took out the saddle and yes, he, I'd say, was done for. The fifth turned tail and ran. Although they did annoy me somewhat, true.'

Her eyes are wide, wide open now. 'And the King,' she says. 'You saved the King. And he made you a captain, on the battlefield.'

'My firm belief is he mistook me for another.' It does have that feel to it, even now, an episode from one of those soldier's tales perhaps: sunset, the small space opening, the back-wash of smoke, the little crowd, the two figures. In his remembrance of it he'd been down on one knee, like a suitor.

She shakes her head. 'I believe your men,' she says. 'I think they have you right.'

Over the rooftops, out from the quayside, out from where the great ships lie at anchor, the sound of a drum. At once the shout goes up from the yard below: *'Domini!'*

'Listen to them,' he says. 'Why would you believe that pack of dogs and not me?'

She leans toward him. 'Because they say that you are shy with women.' Her lips brush his forehead, as if giving him a blessing. 'And you are.'

Not shy with them, he thinks, *but bad for them*. Perhaps being taken as diffident is better.

The one drum is now two. Another shout. *'Domini! Wo sind Sie?'* Where are you?

She watches as he dresses, a cool appraisal, as expert in her territory, he supposes, as he is in his. 'Are you scared, to be going into Germany?'

'Not yet. But then I was there before.' He nods toward the

window. 'They are, I think. They wanted to stay in Poland. With the Polish girls.'

A sniff of disdain. 'Polish girls are all bones. Like cows.' She bangs her knuckles together. 'Bomp, bomp, bomp.'

His sword hangs under the coat. He lifts it over his shoulder, buckles the belt about his waist, and as he does so, her face makes that same small change he's seen so many times before. She asks, 'When were you in Germany?'

'It was one of the places.' A weight pulling down one pocket, tiny but heavy, so gold. A Polish zloty, perhaps. He sits back down with her, boots at his feet. 'First there was Amsterdam – No –'

No, there was not, any more than in reality there had been the kindness of a shroud. '*First*, there was France. Then there was Amsterdam, which is a city with a port, like to this.' Working on the boots now, stamping to get his heel down. 'Then there was Germany. Then there was Poland. Then there was here.' He stands up. When she comes to pull the bed straight, she'll find the zloty slid between the sheets. 'Will I do?'

'Tell me,' she asks. 'When you call out, what gives you bad dreams?'

Bold as you like, this one. He thinks, *I will remember you.* 'What's your name?'

'Lilla,' she says.

'Lilla. I dream of my father, because I never saw him dead. And I dream of my mother, because with her, I did.'

'They were killed?'

He takes her hand. 'They were killed.'

Her fingers tremble. The smallest tremor, but they do. For all her boldness, her gaze has slid to the little silver pendant, there on its cord at his breast. 'Who killed them?' she asks.

He lifts the fingers to his lips. 'A ghost.'

PART I

May 1619–December 1622

CHAPTER ONE

The Dock-Rat

'The clouds gather thick in the German sky…'

Thomas Frankland, *The Annals of King James and Charles I*

MUNGO SANT, born Dundee, more years ago than he cares to remember, stands on the foredeck of the *Guid Marie*. A fine wind spanks her forward, her sails are full, and her bowsprit is aimed straight at the future like a lance. What times these are.

Beneath the bowsprit the Guid Marie herself (a hideous little totem, distorted as driftwood and black as a shrunken head) has what Sant would think of as a smile within the crack that serves her for a mouth, and the chisel marks that are her eyes, like her master's, are fixed on the horizon, where a grey smudge has become visible, a thickening in the sea.

There comes a thump from underneath her decks, some twenty feet down from Sant's right boot.

Sant hears the thump, assesses then dismisses it. He lets the lids of his eyes fall shut – *closing mah ports* – and relishes across them the strum of wind and warmth and sun. Gold. It is Sant's favourite colour.

Sant calls himself a trader, but the names smuggler, pirate, sea-wolf (or perhaps in his case a sea-fox – wily, cunning, nose ever-lifted to the breeze) would do equally well. Dame Fortune may have been a little slow to smile on Sant, but she's smiling now, oh yes. He can smell it. He can feel it in the lifting of the sea. And all because of one man: the Golden Jew.

My Golden Jew, thinks Sant, and smacks his lips. Simply saying the man's name is like the opening of a treasure chest: Yosha Silbergeld, my Golden Jew. Now there's a fox, if you like. It has taken Sant years to get within the business ambit of the Golden Jew, but he's in there now, by God he is.

Another thump. Sant heaves a sigh. All those years of readiness and waiting, and what's his cargo? A horse. One single horse. Even Noah was trusted with two.

Ah, but... that one single horse is the Buckingham mare. Bedded easy, so Sant hopes, remembering the thump, on three soft feet of golden hay, still fragrant from the Norfolk meadows. Two hundred guineas' worth of equine perfection. Her tiny, shiny hooves. Her Arab face, dished and curvaceous as a viola. The rolling globes of her rump, gleaming like polished walnut. And somewhere outside Stockholm, in a pine-fringed field, a stallion stands waiting for her, a stallion with a two-foot prick curved like a stick of giant coral, and all across Europe the horse-riding nobility eagerly await the progeny resulting from their union.

And Sant is carrying the Buckingham mare into Amsterdam because Yosha Silbergeld is brokering the deal. There's some God-damned uppity new powers come into being recently under the Northern Lights, flexing their Protestant muscles, and trade with them requires both subtlety and skill.

Sant opens his eyes. The smudge of grey has broken free of the horizon and is taking shape: masts and cranes and warehouse gabling. *It's a braw time to be a man o'business*, thinks Sant: the line of ships waiting to get into Amsterdam must stretch back a mile into the sea.

Yosha Silbergeld's factotum is waiting for them on the quayside. The usual bunch of urchins, urgent as gannets, surround the man, entreating *Myn heer! Myn heer!* The man claps a hand to his hat and locks an elbow over his purse; Sant, looking down from the foredeck, permits himself a smile. The man calls up:

'You haf her?'

'Aye, aye,' Sant calls down. 'Any news?'

'Ah!' says the man. 'Bo-hem-yah has new king!'

'Oh aye?' Bohemia. The arse-end of Europe, and landlocked to boot. 'Who's that, say?' Sant enquires, but only to be polite.

The answer is so unlikely that for a moment he doubts his hearing. 'Freedreek ov Heidelberg!' comes the cry.

'Frederick of Heidelberg?' Sant leans out over the rail. 'What, he as wed Elizabeth Stuart? *That* Frederick?'

'*Ja, ja!*'

'And what's the Emperor had to say to that?' In the chequerboard of European faith, Bohemia's neighbour, Imperial Austria, is more Catholic, some would argue, even than her cousin Habsburg Spain. 'Frederick's a Calvinist!'

Yosha Silbergeld's factotum pulls himself up a little taller, on his own stiff, Dutch, Calvinist dignity. He steadies himself for a bellow.

'BO-HEM-YAH HAS CHOSE!' he declares proudly. 'ISH WILL OF GOD!'

Predictably, one of the urchins takes this moment to pull at the man's pocket. The man takes off his hat and uses it to beat the boy about the head. '*Myn heer* Sant, be so good,' he calls up imploringly. 'Ve unload our lady-horse, *please*.'

*

Below the deck, the Buckingham mare gives a gentle whicker to herself. Odours fill her nostrils, flood her brain: mud, coal smoke, people. But the Buckingham mare is plucky. She has stood the voyage; now she stands the strange sounds from above her head and the appearance before her of the *Guid Marie*'s first mate. She lets herself be led forward under deck, tolerates the explosion of blue sky as the hatch is levered up, even the constriction of the canvas cradle round her belly. She watches with keen interest as the square of hatch rotates beneath her swinging legs and is replaced with wooden deck. When the first mate reappears beside her and tugs on her rope she understands, and trots obediently forward. Now she is on the gangplank. Her velvet nostrils gape.

And then – what was it? Did a circling gull scream too loud? Did a sail flap, just too close? The Buckingham mare throws up her head, the rope flies out of the first mate's grasp, there is a scrabble and a scrape and the Buckingham mare, in reverse, collides with the *Guid Marie* and comes to a stop with her rump wedged up against the creaking rail; three legs on the gangplank, rigid with panic, and one, hind right, hanging in thin air.

Two hundred golden guineas, poised to slip into the mud of the Zuyder Zee and so be lost for good. 'You mosh DO something!' the factotum booms.

'*You* bloody do something!' counters Sant. 'Yon's your bloody horse!'

The Buckingham mare dips her head to her knees. On deck and off, Sant's crew surround the gangplank and consult.

'Pull 'er 'ed.'

'You pull 'er 'ed, she'll pull you over with her!'

'Smack 'er arse.'

'Smack 'er arse? You mad? Look at her – one wrong step, and she's gone.'

The first mate moves a hand toward the rope. The Buckingham mare rolls up her lip at him and he retreats. What the bloody hell was it, wonders Sant (*whit the bluidy hail*), that set her off?

There's quite a crowd now, on the docks. And out of the crowd there comes a boy: hair like pulled taffy, like frayed rope, scabbed and ragged as a beggar; and he squints up at Sant and announces, 'I'll get her.'

And he speaks English. That in itself would make him stand out. And maybe a bit of Gallic in there too, some tell-tale cadence in the boy's speech, and maybe that's no more than Sant's imagination. Sant surveys this little dockyard offering. 'You'll get her?'

'Two gulden,' the taffy-headed one replies. 'You gimme two gulden and I'll bring her down safe.'

Two gulden. It's a ridiculous amount. But make a bollocks of this, thinks Sant, and that'll be that for any further dealings with his Golden Jew. 'Two shilling,' he says. 'You bring her safe down here, I'll give you two shilling.' If anyone is going into the drink with half a ton of horse on top of them, better this little dock-rat than one of his crew.

'Done,' says the boy. He walks slowly up the gangplank, rubbing his hands together. The tide is rising still, the angle now a good twenty degrees. Sant hears his first mate query, 'Where'd he come from, then?'

The Buckingham mare watches the boy; three legs on the gangplank, one held quivering in space. The boy clucks his tongue, and her ears swivel to the front. He rubs his hands together one last time, holds them out to her, and she licks and nibbles over his palms. ('What's that about?' asks Sant's first mate.)

Cautiously, the boy picks up the dangling rope, puts it between his teeth, and, with the nose of the Buckingham mare buried in his palms as in a cup, leads her down the gangplank, docile as a lamb.

'I'll be buggered,' says Sant's first mate.

Sant and the boy conclude their business at the quayside while Yosha's factotum checks over the Buckingham mare. 'A shilling,' says Sant.

'Two,' says the boy, in the weary tone of one who had expected this.

'One and sixpence,' counters Sant.

'English or Scots?' the boy says, holding out his hand.

English coin is worth twelve times as much as the Scots variety. 'English, you little punk,' snarls Sant, digging out his purse. Damn it, even the blasted dock-rats have become a walking Bourse.

The boy bites each coin to be sure they're true silver before buttoning them into the little bag hid under his shirt. 'What set her off?' Sant asks, as he makes to walk away.

'Sunlight,' the boy calls back. He has a wary eye on the small posse of his kind lurking at the back of the crowd. 'It's the sun on the water. They don't understand it. Don't know what it is.'

A shilling and a sixpence for a bloody sunbeam. Sant watches the boy, hightailing it down the quay, posse in pursuit. *Long may you live to enjoy it*, he thinks, viciously.

MUNGO SANT STANDS in the first-floor chamber of the house of the Golden Jew, on boards not one whit less sturdy, wide or scrubbed than the deck of the *Guid Marie* (and considerably better polished – the floor is like black ice), and waits for the tiny creature bunched up on the far side of the table to cease shuffling through the many papers piled before it and acknowledge his existence.

'A good crossing?' Yosha Silbergeld has half-a-dozen languages at his disposal, depending on his listeners and his mood: English for Sant; Dutch for his neighbours; French when he is feeling louche; Russian if lugubrious; Latin, which never fails to impress, if he finds himself in a tight spot; and if angry or upset, nuggets of Yiddish surface in his conversation like fruit in a batter.

'Easy,' says Sant, proud. 'Four days, there and back.'

A squeaking noise. Yosha gets from one end of his office to the other by pulling himself about in a burgermeister's chair. Think first a laundry basket, only made of oak, most vigorously carved and comfortably upholstered, and cut away at the front. Then put it on eight curved wooden legs, each with an ebony caster. There. A burgermeister's chair.

Yosha's own legs dangle out the chair's cut-away front, shapeless and jointless as those of a rag doll. Is there anything in those stockings at all? Sant wonders, uncomfortably. Does the man have legs?

Yosha speaks. 'I have another cargo, coming out of Lübeck on the twenty-eighth. Would you be interested?'

Lübeck. So what would that be – timber? Barley? Furs? No matter. Knock out a few of those bulkheads, it can all be slotted in. 'Aye, sure,' says Sant, game as ever.

A gentle scritching at the door. It opens, and Zoot, Yosha's housekeeper, enters, bearing a tray.

Sant has a tender secret passion for Zoot, has had ever since he first clapped eyes on her. *This*, he thinks, watching her approach, *is what a woman should be.* Blue-eyed. Comely. Mothersome. In charge. He looks for the small shadow of her son, who is usually to be found hiding somewhere there behind her, but this time she's alone.

'Now,' Yosha says, 'we drink.'

A moment's trepidation on Sant's part. Yosha, who spent his youth an onion-skin above starvation, has in his riches developed a taste for exotics, and a mischievous penchant for trying them out on his guests. The last time Sant stood in this room, business had concluded with an invitation to taste a drink from

the Americas, so Yosha assured him, referring to the substance
as 'toclet'. It came in a dullish darkish plug, which Zoot had first
to grate, then whisk with boiling water, strain and pour. The
resulting concoction was nonetheless gritty as mud, poisonously
bitter, and with an abiding aftertaste that left Sant's teeth and
gums strongly in mind of the odour of fresh caulking – a fine
smell, but not one as you'd wish to have in your mouth. This
time he is relieved to see that on her tray Zoot bears no more
than two Venetian glasses and a bottle of Dutch gin, clear as
water and so gloriously spirituous that for hours afterwards Sant
will hesitate to light his pipe.

'The Buckingham mare,' says Yosha, raising his glass. 'Tell
me. Is she as pretty as they say?'

LÜBECK IS BARREL after barrel of stinking pitch. The crew hold
their noses. Then as the last wagon empties, the shipper takes
Sant to one side. There is a second cargo, or there could be. 'You
make port in Amsterdam, I'll have my agent collect,' the man
says. 'But you keep this one to yourself. You can do that, hey?'

Thirty crates of sword-blades, finest tempered steel: the
blades as long and thin as barracudas, and as deadly. Their
weight lowers the *Guid Marie* in the water in a manner that has
the first mate sucking his misgivings through his teeth. 'Where
are these headed?' Sant asks, hoping to God it's nowhere he
knows, but the shipper answers only, 'What do you care?'

It almost sinks his boat. Rounding the tip of Denmark,
halfway home, the *Guid Marie* runs head on into a yellow squall.
The squall becomes a storm, and nowhere, in Sant's experience,
can do a storm like the Baltic. Foremast cracked, rats foaming
up from the bilges and the pumps working round the clock, the
Guid Marie finally wallows into Enkhuizen three weeks late.
Sant is forced to endure first the sight of her, dismasted like

a hulk; then the worse indignity of watching her being towed down to Amsterdam; and lastly, on his own, beset by Furies, pay for his cargoes to be loaded onto carts (the carters drunk, as all Dutch carters always are) and suffer with them the bumping four-day voyage overland. Sant returns to that house on the Prinsengracht with his purse as flat as a eunuch's ball sack, raw with the misfortune of it all.

And finds himself proclaimed a hero. A second Ulysses. A dozen ships lost in the tempest for sure, yet Sant not only brings the *Guid Marie* safe home, but Yosha's cargo too. Zoot makes up a bed for him, a bed with linen sheets of such purity and whiteness a man might go snow-blind, and in the morning she shaves him, bending across his face to afford him such sensations as might otherwise only be known to a sailor in a last coddled embrace with a mermaid. And Yosha, who had thought the *Guid Marie* so surely lost that he has written as much to Lübeck (though he does not share this with Sant), does share with him, at breakfast, the notion that the *Guid Marie*, as so weatherly a craft, and Sant, as so stout-hearted a sailor, perhaps deserve some reward. The *Guid Marie* might be strengthened, new pines found for her masts, her holds cleaned out, rebalanced, and he himself, he modestly suggests, would pay. No, not a loan; let's call it a partnership. Perhaps Sant might care to meet his shipwright?

Sant would. Squalls and storms and the misgivings of his conscience are nothing, mere pebbles in his shoe; now this is something like. No mere carrier he, no hired hand, but a partner with the Golden Jew.

The shipwright knows his business. He walks about the *Guid Marie* and lays his hands upon her swollen timbers in the tender manner of an accoucheur; then has her towed into dry dock under Sant's watchful eye and the gables of Yosha's newest, largest warehouse. Her masts are levered out, her keel scraped, the interior of the ship, which had so recently slopped with salt water, still admixed with a little hay, becomes dry and sweet and piled with wood shavings. Her exterior becomes a camp: ropes and tarpaulins, cauldrons of tar, ladders and scaffolding; a camp populated with timber-merchants, carpenters, sailmakers...

Dock-rats. They steal the ropes, they steal the tarps; they steal the workmen's lunches out their laps – gone in a twinkling. They'd steal, so Sant's first mate opines, the hairs from your head if you left off your hat, and then they'd take your hat and all.

Patience, says Sant.

Within a week, the workmen and the dock-rats reach a truce. The dock-rats work the bellows for the forges, heft the awkward loads, and the workmen pay them in copper and iron – the same copper and iron, Sant notes, as should be going into the timbers of his ship; but a man can now put his hammer down without finding it gone when he next reaches for it, and the dock-rats can loiter round the camp without some enraged carpenter laying into them with a length of rope.

Yosha is philosophical. Pennies and ha'pennies, phut.

The men work about the *Guid Marie* like ants clearing a carcass. Day after day the hammers ring, the saws squeak and rasp, and every evening Sant goes back to the house on the Prinsengracht and that clean white bed with a dust of hemp fragments from the ropes over his head and shoulders.

Rivalries break out between the boys. The generalissimos of the dockyard gangs fight for the best jobs, battering each other into bloody and uneasy and short-lived quietude, then dole them out amongst the younger boys, taking a cut from each. It's a foolhardy soul seeks to set up for himself. Sant watches two such of the older lads – one damn near full-grown, with a staring eye and nasty feral twist to his face, plus another, with that fierce Dutch red to his hair – in furious consultation, with their gesticulations suggesting that the subject of their exchange is a third boy, who's sat surrounded by wooden deadeyes, rubbing them smooth with rottenstone. Sant isn't close enough to hear the conversation, and wouldn't understand it even if he was, but if he could, he would hear this:

'I told him, I said, it's you in charge of who gets what round here, and he said no man was in charge of him, least of all some pissant scut like you, and what he got was his.'

Outrage. 'He said that? I'll fucken scuttle *him*.'

Sant, his attention wandering, peers over at the lad sat there with the deadeyes, intent on his task. Why, it's his Taffy-Head.

And the boy has grown. Not quite up there with the redhead (whom Sant christens Copperknob), and certainly nowhere near the size of Generalissimo Ringle-Eye, but he'll be a bruiser, this lad, should he live so long. Look at the size of those feet!

To be honest, his chances do not look good. Ringle-Eye marches up on Taffy-Head and sends him sprawling. The boy picks himself up, regards the back of his attacker with his head to one side. Measuring him up. *Good for you*, thinks Sant.

The shipwright interrupts his musings. 'She coom along goot, *jah*?' the man calls out, in that extraordinary looping Low Countries accent. From breaking down, now they are building up. Next day a new mast hangs above the deck, ready to be lowered into place, two more are taking shape down in the yard even as Sant watches, and men hang on ropes about the sides of the *Guid Marie*, raking out the old stuff between her planks, ready to stuff in the new – and oh, look at that. There's Copperknob.

Sporting a black eye.

Sant locates Taffy-Head at the stern of the *Guid Marie*, human counterweight to a pair of blocks being lowered into place for a handy little cannon. Sant wonders if his Dutch is good enough to risk a joke – something about sterns and farts and fire-power – and decides that on balance it probably is not. Instead he indicates the boy, swinging above their heads, those promising feet planted against the side of the *Guid Marie*, marching across her like a crab as the men on deck direct the operation. 'Doing a good job, is he?' he enquires of the shipwright.

'*Jah*, so,' the man replies. 'Ish qvik, ish strong, does vot ish told.' And at the man's words the boy twists his head round like an owl, and he flashes Sant a sudden, wide and unexpected smile.

Sant turns to the shipwright. 'What's that one's story, do you know?'

The shipwright makes a face, raises his hands. 'One day ish here. Koom oop on *aak*.'

'*Ark*?' Sant repeats.

The shipwright's brows are knitted with effort. 'Wit men of barsh.'

Ah, a *barge*. 'Where from?'

The shipwright gives a shrug. He looks up, following the boy's progress as the men on deck haul him in over the rail, as if pondering the mystery of his origin. 'But ish good boy. Not like you, you thieving little snot,' he continues abruptly, breaking into his mother-tongue and lashing a brushful of hot tar in the direction of Copperknob, who's loitering just out of reach. 'Get out of it!'

It would appear Copperknob got the best of the fight. Sant's Taffy-Head, once back at ground level, displays a split lip, a cut to his forehead and a bit of a hobble when he walks. But all the same. Laid a keeker on him. Nae bad.

A DAY LATER, and two fishermen have found a body floating beyond the dock. They're hauling it from the green waters as Sant and his first mate approach. It comes up star-fished, legs akimbo. It's obvious it is the body of a child.

There, thinks Sant. He feels obscurely cheated, as if his care of Taffy-Head (which was what, exactly?) has been thrown back in his face. Also he is pierced by something almost as pure as grief – Jesus, such a little life. Who'd it have hurt, to let it continue a while longer?

Nae sae bluidy tough then after all. A bitter, an almost angry regret.

The body breaks the waters. The boy's hair is red.

They lay the body down upon the quayside. Water leaks from it, running between the stones. At the back of the boy's skull is a soft concave declivity, the dint that a spoon makes, tapping an egg. "Ee 'it the 'ed,' says one of the fishermen, explaining, to Sant. 'So, ish drown.'

'Look at his hands,' whispers Sant's first mate.

The knuckles of one hand are discoloured and swollen, of the other split down to the bone. 'Christ,' the first mate says. Back in Folkestone he has two boys of his own not much older than this. 'Christ, they're a savage bunch of little shits round here.'

And Taffy-Head has disappeared. Gone; vanished; not to be found.

Sant spends the morning watching the new mast go in with the words *good for you* appending themselves to the boy's image, whenever the latter pops into his head; the afternoon in company with the same but now with a coda hanging off them: *whir'iver the hail ye'are.* The shipwright, seeing him distracted, takes him in the evening to a beer-house by the docks, from which Sant emerges hours later with a gait that would do him more credit on a sloping deck in the Roaring Forties. Zigzagging to the water's edge he pisses like a horse, and the relieving of the pressure on his bladder makes him all the more aware of the uneasiness lurking in his thoughts. The boy. Where the devil is he?

If he were dead, Copperknob would still be alive. If he were whole, he'd be making himself as visible and acting as much the innocent as he could.

Therefore he's hiding, and he's hurt.

Foxy Sant surveys the yards behind him, all his foxy instincts on alert. So. If I were small and hurt and hiding, where'd I be?

Not round here. Not Yosha's warehouse, far too close to the scene.

He starts with the warehouse next door, and a pair of guard dogs comes flying at him like chain-shot. So not that one, either. At a loss, he looks down the long line of the quay, stretching out before him into indigo and star-speckled darkness, and the moon on the water catches his eye and gives him a wink, as if to say *that's right*.

He walks along the quay, sheds and warehouses on one side, growing smaller in size and fewer in number, and on the other boats and smacks and little craft, all knocking on the tide. Tarps and crates, a flotsam of timber and rope – hiding places innumerable, and not that easy to negotiate either, not with six pints inside you. He's coming up to the end of it, that long, stone arm. Discarded piling. A nest of barrels. He pushes against them, thinking to force himself a path, but there's one barrel in there weighted with something. There is a canvas draped across its mouth. It has, in fact, every appearance of a den.

Experimentally, Sant reaches into the barrel, up to his oxter. 'God *damn!*'

He dances backwards. At first he thinks he must have caught himself on some sharp hidden edge, but bringing his hand to his nose, he sees the cut is straight as only a blade could make it. Something in there is armed with a knife.

Ye wee son of a bitch.

He casts about for a solution. There's a pile of sacks close by, such useful stuff as is often left about a docks. Sant takes one up, splits it, wraps the sacking round his hands; thus muffed, goes in to try again. 'Come on, Diogenes. Let's be having you –' and plucks the boy out.

The boy's head lolls; his eyes roll back. His legs are splayed;

when Sant attempts to put him on them they will not bear his weight. He's racing with fever, and one arm, under Sant's grip, feels somehow marshy. When the boy lifts the knife again, it almost drops from his grasp.

Crawled in there. Crawled in there like the wounded thing it is.

Sant hefts the boy into his arms; bowlegged, begins to walk.

Five minutes hollering and banging on Yosha's grand front door with the boy growing limper by the second in his arms. Then that burly factotum cracks the door open, demanding, '*WIE IS HET?*'

Sant sticks his boot in the crack. ''Tis me, ye baw-heid.'

Once in the hall, the man blocks his way forward. The women peer down from the stairway, safe above. Sant holds the boy out to them, as Abraham with Isaac.

'I have here a wee friend o'mine,' says Sant. 'In need of a bit of help.'

It is Zoot who finds the child a bed, snips off his filthy clothes. Thus also Zoot who discovers the wound an inch below the arc of his ribs, crusted with pus, like the fissure in a geode. Thus also Zoot who summons the doctor.

The doctor says the boy will die. 'No he won't,' growls Sant, the good faery at the christening, nay-saying the curse.

Zoot, in her nightgown, hair in a loosening plait, strokes at the boy's face. He lies between them on the bed, respiration hardly moving the sheet. The bulkiest thing about him that splinted, bandaged arm.

Sant knows no more of medicine than how to get a fish-hook out your palm and the extraordinary area a man can cover if hit amidships by a cannonball, but in this case he is right. The boy hangs for a week – one-handed, one assumes – ready to drop off into darkness, then begins the slow climb back toward the light.

On the third day of the second week, Yosha has himself

carried, burgermeister's chair and all, up the stairs to the first floor of the attics in his six-storey house, where the boy is being tended. He pushes himself to the bed, and receiving no reaction from its occupant, bursts out, 'What are we to do with this?'

Zoot, measuring a trembling quarter-drop of laudanum into a tiny glass, ignores him. Sant, in calling her a housekeeper, has done her a disservice; Zoot is far more than that. For instance: Yosha, as a Jew, even amongst the unheard-of liberalities of the United Provinces, is still forbidden from employing Christians in his house; therefore nominally all his servants work for Zoot and all household expenses are paid from her purse. (It is also forbidden for a Jew to make love to a Christian, which explains much of Zoot's careful chaperoning of her son.) Zoot has had fifteen years with Yosha; they have left her plenty wise enough to distinguish those moments when he expects an answer from those when all he requires is an audience.

'Are we meant to take it in?' The wheels of the chair squeak round the bed. 'Little *yungatsch*. It could be anything. From anywhere. For all we know, it is poxy. Or it has the plague.' Yosha glares at the boy; glares too at the silver pendant Zoot had taken from about the boy's neck and placed carefully on the table where, should his eyes open, it will be the first thing he sees.

This is a child, Zoot intones to herself. You feed it, keep it warm, and watch it grow. Simplicity itself.

'Is this what we are meant to do? No – it is impossible.' And in his apparent fury, Yosha catches a wheel of the burgermeister's chair against a leg of the bed, and jolts it, and its occupant, who has a nice sense of timing and a mature appreciation of dramatic effect, not to mention the sense to have kept his eyes tight shut throughout, lets forth a tiny moan. Zoot rushes forward, Yosha scoots back. Voice a-quiver with remorse, he asks, 'Did I hurt him?'

HE'S IN HIS BOAT, that's where he is, it's rocking on the waves. He must be very small, because Maman can fit into his boat as well. Her knees rise up like mountains either side of him and her hand on his forehead is warm as the sun. She smiles at him. 'Maman has a secret, Petit Jacques.' He reaches up to touch her face. Her eyes close. Her skin grows chill beneath his touch. She is high above him; she is swinging out of reach. *Maman… Maman…*

He opens his eyes. The dream-world drifts and fades, and seems to vanish down the sides of the room.

There is another boy standing by his bed.

The boy is smaller than him, but has all the glossiness of those habitually well fed. He is immediately jealous. Also the boy wears the most absurd, complete, adult suit of clothes, all the seams intact and no dirt on it anywhere. Most puzzling of all, the boy is clutching to his midriff a small cat, barely out of kittenhood.

'*Goedemorgen,*' the boy says, bobbing a quick half-bow. He has the eager manner of one anxious to please, and he speaks the kind of careful, simple Dutch this most polite of nations reserves for those they think won't understand. 'My name's Cornelius. Who are you?'

'Jack,' says the boy, uncertain if this is another dream or not. But communication is established. Cornelius (who also has the fluttery pulse and clammy palms of one who knows he shouldn't be there in the first place) tries a nervous smile. 'D'you want to see my Turkish cat?'

The Turkish cat is Yosha's latest exotic. It has one yellow eye, one blue, and other than a pale apricot tail it is, of course, a piercing, blinding white.

Cornelius puts the cat on the bed, where it sniffs at Jack's fingertips, turns itself upside down and starts to purr. Jack smiles. 'It looks like it's got the wrong tail,' he points out.

'Her name's Catarina,' Cornelius announces. 'She goes swimming. In the canal.'

Jack shakes his head. 'Cats don't swim.'

In fact Catarina does swim, with every appearance of enjoy-
ment, almost daily, but her owner decides to leave this to one
side. Cornelius has had to glean his knowledge of this mysterious guest from hiding under tables while the adults talk above,
and he has a request of his own. 'Can I see it?' he asks. 'The
place where you were hurt?'

The mysterious guest seems to find nothing unreasonable in
this at all. 'Sure, if you want,' he replies, and pushes back the sheet.

Cornelius had primed himself to expect something fearsome,
but perhaps not quite as fearsome as this. He had not expected
stitches to be so prosaically stitches, for a start, sewing, through
the skin. He had brought his head down close for the inspection, now he jerks upright and backs away. Catarina, startled,
jumps off the bed and darts through the open door.

'It's all right,' says Jack, seeing his discomfiture. 'It don't hurt
now.'

Cornelius is round-eyed. 'Did it hurt when it was done?'

'Well, it hurt then. For sure it hurt then.' He regards the
wound as if he were almost fond of it, although touching it still
makes the sick feeling rise in his throat.

'What was it like?' Cornelius asks.

'Like a punch,' Jack replies, authoritatively. 'Then it got hot.
It burns and stings.'

'They said—' Cornelius begins, but at that moment a voice
drifts up the staircase: 'Oh, that accursed cat!' There is a clatter,
as of large and heavy-laden maidservant with small cat getting
underfoot. Then the voice says, and is sharper now, as of maidservant putting two-and-two together: 'Cornelius? Are you up
there? What did your mother tell you? Come down this minute!'

He opens his eyes again. He has another visitor. The man from
the docks. The man with the horse. 'Well now,' the man says.
'How's it with you?' And adds, 'Me laddie.'

'What am I doing here?' Jack demands.

'You don't remember?'

He does, and he doesn't. He remembers the fight, and staggering forward, the stone quayside flying up to meet him, and the pain in his arm like a bolt being shot across a door. He remembers hugging the arm to him, and thinking how he must not pass out, then seeing his enemy coming at him again. He remembers kicking out with his legs as the only weapon he had left. What had happened after that?

Sant, seeing the wandering look on the boy's face, sits himself carefully down on the bed. 'You had a fight,' says Sant. 'You and yon red-haired lad.'

And that, he sees, the boy does remember. A sharp beam of anger. 'He stole my money, fuck him,' the boy says. Sant is taken aback. His gaze lights for a moment on the little silver token of the wolf, propped up there on the table. It seems an odd thing for a child to have about its neck, a distasteful thing, if Sant is honest – the graphic modelling, the red enamel (eyes, teeth, bulb of the phallus) – astonishing that such malevolence can be concentrated in something less than two inches high, but it seems to be almost the only possession the boy has. Other than that equally alarming, business-like knife.

'Aye, well,' says Sant, 'he'll no' be trying that again.'

The boy is watching his face – reading it, it seems to Sant. His eyes are notable: light centred (very light), dark ringed around the iris, very dark lashed. He lifts the arm, in its splints. He says, 'I didn't start it.'

Sant is touched. 'Of course you didnae.' He stands, and walks about the room. 'It was I, brought you here. You know where you are?'

'No,' says the boy, keeping his eyes on Sant the while.

'This is the house of Yosha Silbergeld. You've heard of him, no doubt.'

He thinks, *The old man who was carried up here in that chair.* He answers, 'No.'

'Ah,' says Sant, disappointed, and the boy, as if in compensation, offers, 'There was a boy like me.'

'Cornelius.' Sant is amazed. It seems wildly unlikely Zoot would let her darling come up here. 'Part of the family.'

'His grandson,' the boy suggests.

'Aye, sure,' says Sant, who's far from certain. And changing the subject, asks, 'So I hear the name is Jack, that so?'

The boy nods.

Sant glances back at the knife. An ivory hilt, Adam carved to one side, Eve in her snake-dance on the other, and a spring-loaded button (Sant has tested it) that sends the blade out the hilt with the speed of a striking cobra. And most intriguing of all, the silver knop engraved not with a J, but with the bold flourish of a B. 'And where might you hail from, young Jack?'

For the first time, the boy's gaze tracks from Sant's face. He points, seemingly at random, out the window. 'Back there,' he says.

It occurs to Sant that he is being mocked. He peers at the boy suspiciously. 'So how'd you find yourself in Amsterdam, eh?'

'I worked a boat,' says the boy. And for a moment Sant finds himself wondering if that pointing arm was indeed aimed at random; it's just possible the boy had checked the position of the sun, got a bearing from it, and given his answer.

'And what boat was that?'

Something within the boy's eyes becomes just a little opaque. A ghost of the laudanum, thinks Sant.

'The *Sally Arden*,' the boy says, vaguely.

The *Sally Arden*. It raises a vague tolling in Sant's mind, as of a buoy above a wreck. Indeed of a buoy above a wreck. There was a *Sally Arden*, out of Gravesend, mooring at Dunkirk, that nest of piracy; Sant knows it well. He knew the *Sally Arden*, too. From behind an upturned tavern table, Sant once watched the master of the *Sally Arden* lay out four men one after another, surging from the wreckage all about him like a bull. He remembers the man's fists, tattooed with open fangs across the knuckles, like the twin mouths of hell. But didn't man and boat go down off Finisterre? This, Sant decides, is a goose-chase. 'So now you're here,' he says. 'What do you think to it?'

'It's pretty good,' says the boy, cautiously.

'A'cause there's an idea downstairs as they might make a place here for you.' He waits. 'Think you might like to stay?'

The boy sits upright, as if the conversation has suddenly become serious. 'I don't know,' he says. He looks down at himself. 'I mean I'm not going about *nakit*. Where's me clothes?'

The clothes – quivering with vermin – have been burned. And the minute the splints come off his arm, Jack is plunged into a copper bath before the kitchen fire, and has Zoot going over him with a scrubbing brush. No protests are enough to hold her back. She clips at his hair with a pair of iron scissors, revealing triangles of white behind each ear that never saw the sun, and scrapes through what's left with strong soap and a nit-comb. She puts him in a decent suit of sober black, and a shirt with a collar wide as an open book, while his feet are hidden in a pair of good buff-leather boots. The boy stands on one leg then the other, like a stork, to admire them. Zoot makes him face about, and there he is, revealed – good wide brow, well-set shoulders, that lift to his chin and those clear eyes – *that's not a bad-looking lad, that*, thinks Sant.

One last pulling straight of his collar, one last patting down of his hair, and off Zoot sends him, for his interview with Yosha.

Jack enters at one end of the room; Yosha propels himself forward from the other. The light is again behind him. He brings himself to a halt. The boy's expression is one of curiosity.

'So,' Yosha says. 'You decided not to die. You like to make the doctor look an idiot.'

Jack says nothing.

'So now we must decide what happens to you next,' says Yosha. He reaches out, and takes Jack's chin between finger and thumb. Children dislike this, he knows. His own Cornelius cannot endure it.

His visitor has a very steady gaze. Instead of discomfort, or even fright, Yosha finds he is staring into a perfect mirror of himself, two twin reflections, and moving under them the passage of the boy's thoughts: *Old. Can't shift for himself. But he's got this big house. Not met his type before. Let's wait and see what he does next.* Yosha is impressed.

'What happened to your legs?' Jack asks, breaking the silence.

'Burned them,' says Yosha. 'In a fire.'

Jack looks around the room – the marble pillars either side of the chimney-breast, the whiteness of the ceiling – as if for signs of damage. 'What, here?'

'No. Another place,' Yosha answers, short. 'And a long, long time ago.' Changing the subject, he asks, 'So. You like to stay here, yes?'

Jack has given this much thought. Being under a ceiling is strange, and sleeping in a bed again, all tangled up in sheets and blankets, is plainly ridiculous, but there are advantages: he's fed, he's warm, and then there are his boots… 'I might,' he says.

'So. In this house, everyone works. In this country, everyone works. If you stay here, what can you do?'

'Well,' says Jack, 'I can run errands. I can fetch and carry stuff; I've done that. I can deliver messages and get them right. I can do knots and ropes.' He pauses, counting how far he's got in his list of accomplishments. 'I can sail a little boat, and I can fish. I can find places, not using a map. I can make a fire without a tinderbox.' Another pause. 'And I can ride.'

'What can you ride?' asks Yosha, sensing the unlikelihood of this. He is reaching for the bell.

Back comes the answer. 'Anything.'

Paul, Yosha's factotum, reliable as always, quiet as ever, there in the doorway. 'Ah, Paul,' says Yosha. He rocks back and forth in the chair. 'Up, up. We are going to see Prince Maurice.'

Prince Maurice is fourteen hands high, and a handsome chestnut. A thick streak of Schleswig Kaltblut in his ancestry has given him magnificently feathered legs, but if you look very closely, and know what you are looking for, it is still possible to discern, somewhere in his profile, a trace of Barbary stud. He is occasionally harnessed to a cart, to carry Zoot on forays into the countryside; Cornelius is periodically threatened with being made to learn to ride him. Other than that his main purpose has been to allow Yosha to exercise his quirky sense of patriotism: Prince Maurice, after Maurice of Orange, Stadtholder of the Dutch Republic and thorn in the Spanish backside.

'So,' says Yosha. 'You can ride that?'

As befits the house, the courtyard is large too. Prince Maurice wears a woven halter, but he has neither saddle nor bridle on him, and the mounting block is yards away. Paul makes as if to help the boy, but Yosha waves him back. In silence, as Paul waits, puzzled, Jack steps forward. He's rubbing his hands together. He holds his palms out flat toward Prince Maurice.

'What is that?' Yosha demands. 'This thing you do with your hands – what is that?'

'You rub your hands together, it brings up the salt on 'em. Horses like salt.' Prince Maurice is working his muzzle over the boy's hands like a washcloth. 'It's how you make friends.'

He rubs Prince Maurice on his nose, then slowly walks around him, smoothing a hand against the horse's flank as he does so. Prince Maurice leans against the hand and blows out a lengthy sigh. Jack kneels, taps a back leg and has Prince Maurice rest the hoof in his lap. Then he goes around the other side and does the same. Paul finds he must fight down a smile: the boy could hardly be making more of a meal of his inspection if he were going to make Yosha an offer on his horse.

'Well?' Yosha demands.

'I could ride him,' Jack says, finally. 'I could, but he's got a limp.'

'A limp?' exclaim Paul and his employer, simultaneously.

'There,' says Jack, having Prince Maurice raise the back hoof again. 'You can feel it. Must've banged his leg.'

Yosha is squinting up at Paul in mock, or mock-ish, outrage. 'You let my horse have limps?'

Paul crouches down beside the boy. 'See?' Jack says, guiding his hand, and there it is, unmistakable, a little swelling and a little heat under the horse's skin. '*Myn heer,*' says Paul, standing up, 'I do not know how this can have happened.' There is still a suggestion of unsteadiness about his mouth.

'Might just have done it now,' says Jack, magnanimously. He is holding Prince Maurice's head, letting the horse huff at his neck. 'They're none too clever, horses. Though he's a nice enough old fella,' he adds, as if the horse might be offended, 'ain't you, hey?'

'So,' says Yosha, giving Paul his most acute, side-angled stare, 'you think you can find a place for this boy? This boy who can tell if my horse has limps?'

'Oh yes,' says Paul, gravely. The cheek of the little beggar! 'Yes, *myn heer.* We can find a place for him.'

So. He assists Paul with Prince Maurice. He helps with the endless chopping of logs for the house's many fireplaces, sweeping up the debris after good as can be. He's energetic filling jugs and pitchers at the pump; he'll peel parsnips and potatoes without complaint. 'Handy with a knife, ain't he?' as the cook remarks. A chicken, brought dead in a basket, miraculously revives in the heat of the kitchen, and when the maids run shrieking as this half-plucked, half-dead thing leaps squawking round the room, the boy catches and dispatches it as fast and with as little hesitation as if he were twisting the green part off a bunch of carrots. He runs errands to the market. He runs errands for Yosha. Yosha sends him down to the docks with twelve silver gulden to pay off the sailmaker (not an enormous sum, by Yosha's standards, but a fortune for a dock-rat) and the boy returns, at the expected time, and with a receipt. 'So,' says Zoot, standing quietly in a corner of Yosha's office, 'you are satisfied now?'

'I am satisfied *so far*,' Yosha answers.

Zoot finds Jack seated at the top of the flight of stone steps that lead from the kitchen down into the courtyard. The cook has put a hunk of cheese in one of his hands and an apple in the other, and he is munching through them in alternating bites. He turns – Zoot, in passing, had been unable to prevent her hand from cupping the round of his head, and as he stares after her, astonished, for a moment his face drops apart. It was Zoot just went past behind him, wasn't it?

The people in your head are safe; he knows that now, he understands. It doesn't matter how hard it is to keep them there; it's just a thing that must be done. You lock a door on them; then no-one can hurt them. And nor can they hurt you.

And when the *Guid Marie* – remasted, rebalanced, remade – is relaunched, he's there as well. Standing on the quayside, to the right of Yosha's chair, with Zoot, Cornelius, and all the rest of them.

SANT'S FIRST COMMISSION, in his remade ship, should be the transport of those barrels of pitch up the Thames to the royal docks at Deptford. But there's a mean wind blowing all the shipping in the Channel south-south-west, and Sant might either spend the next two days tacking down and up, like a thread being run through a hem; or he might put into Dunkirk, say, and wait for more favourable winds to take this one's place.

Dunkirk is not a place where questions are welcome. Nonetheless, Sant finds a likely spot, an old watering-hole of his, and two likely old lads sat inside the door, sucking beer through their moustaches. One sounds as if he comes from Hull; the other has the unmistakable sharp-pitched tang to his speech of the London Basin. Listening to them grumbling in duet is like listening to a shanty for a bassoon and a piccolo. Sant sits himself down beside them and opens the conversation with a 'Been a whiles since I was here,' but gets no answer.

'Looking for a boat,' he continues, lying smoothly. 'The *Sally Arden*. Her master, Josh Arden – he had a mooring here. Any idea where I might find her?'

'Oh aye,' says Hull, with relish. (His companion still has yet to say a word.) He points, with his pipe-stem, out toward the sea. 'Straight oot and straight down. Crab-food.'

'No!' says Sant, feigning horror, shock, dismay. He lets a little more Scots come back into his voice, as one might under the influence of strong emotion. 'You dinnae say.'

'Her and every soul aboard,' Hull says, and sticks the pipe back in his mouth as if plugging a leak. There is silence for a moment. Then the whippet-like snap of the Cockney breaks in with 'Friend of Josh Arden, were yer?'

'Wouldn't say a friend,' says Sant, cautiously. 'But I remember his boat.'

'Aye,' says the other, shortly. 'Many do.'

Sant beckons to the publican, indicates their tankards – his, Hull's, the whippet's – and holds up three fingers. Hull and the whippet take note, and the atmosphere between the three becomes rather smoother-edged.

'So when did she go down?' Sant asks, once the round has arrived.

'Must be – oh a good twelve year ago now,' says the whippet.

'More than that,' says Hull.

So if Josh Arden left some poor bitch fresh in whelp before he went to feed the crabs, reckons Sant, that might just fit. Mentally he swings the legs of a compass over the boy, measuring likelihood… yes. Josh Arden would have been old to become a father, but that wouldn't have stopped the man, not as Sant remembers him. 'He have any family you ever hear of?' queries Sant. 'Any children?'

'Had a daughter,' says the whippet. 'Named his boat for her.'

Indeed? In his head, Sant swings the legs of the compass back on themselves. Josh Arden. Not the father then, the grandfather. Hull has put his head against the wall and let out a long luxurious sigh. 'Bonnie lass, was she?' Sant enquires, remembering the boy and those dark-lashed eyes. There's a nice rose-tinted bubble coming into shape now in Sant's head with the image in it of himself and the boy – grown, washed, hair cut, in his decent clothes of good Dutch woollen – and some braw rose of a woman, fulsome with teary gratitude as Sant returns her son to her.

'Knock your eye out,' Hull replies. 'How old Arden fathered her God knows.'

'Not all he tried to do to her, I heard,' says the whippet, and there is a wettish splutter from Sant, which might only be a mouthful of ale gone down the wrong way, or might just be the popping of a dream.

'What become of her?' Sant asks, once he's mopped himself up.

'Run off,' says the whippet.

'Died,' says Hull, in the same breath. The whippet pauses for a beat, then nips back in again. 'Run off *and* died,' he informs Sant, as the last word on the subject. 'Poor little flower. Sad.'

So a dead trail in every sense. And best left that way, by the sound of it. Sant, feeling strangely mournful, drains his tankard and gets to his feet. 'You off then, are yer?' says the whippet, whose tankard is also empty.

'Aye,' answers Sant, abstractedly, gathering his thoughts. But what, he asks himself, did he expect? Some faery-tale ending and he, Sant, the bringer-about? Not in this world, that's for sure. 'Time and tide and by your leave, friends. Good day to the both of you.'

'Tide don't turn for three hour yet,' mutters Hull, as they watch him go.

The whippet leans toward his neighbour. 'You wasn't going to tell him 'bout the Frenchie then?'

'What Frenchie?' Hull replies. 'Him what poor Sally wed?'

'No, not him, the other one. The one who come by asking questions. You remember. Little fella. Him with the rattler of a cough.'

'Give over,' says Hull, with scorn. 'No, I were *not*.' Out comes the pipe, jabbed at the back of the retreating figure. 'That's Mungo Sant. The last time Sant did anyone a favour, Moses was still in his basket. Poor little Sally. Let her rest in peace.'

In London there is English broadcloth, to go down to Bordeaux. From Bordeaux there is wine, to be carried round the Isle of Wight to Southampton. In Southampton there is lashing rain, and a delay of weeks, then a burst of sun and a deluge of ripe golden corn into the holds, like Zeus mistook the *Guid Marie* for his beloved Danae. The corn is for Göteborg. Yosha believes in having a partner show off his paces. In Göteborg there's timber, for Gdansk. Gdansk is leather and pig iron, ice alongside the ship, and more news from Bohemia – whole place gone up in smoke, so Sant's first mate informs him, breathless with the cold: the Emperor, predictably, has marched his armies in, and handsome Frederick and his English bride, Winter King and Winter Queen, are gone, gone, gone; unhappy exiles in the Hague, the pair of them. 'Could have told you,' Sant replies. 'Soon as I heard they'd chose Frederick. Now there'll be trouble.'

'Could'a told *you*,' the first mate retorts. 'Soon as folk began a-shipping sword-blades.'

The iron goes to Hamburg; the leather to Rouen, en route to the cobblers of Paris. In Rouen, there is brandy. The brandy is for Lowestoft. One day slides into the next, the *Guid Marie* floating in the rhythms of the sea, the skies, punctuated by the sudden frenzy of a port – the loadings and unloadings, the business of business, and all the usual irritations too: drunken doxies, crewmen gone missing, harbour dues and tolls. It will be fifteen months before Sant sees the warehouses of Amsterdam rise out the mists and sudden inundations of the Zuyder Zee again.

FIFTEEN MONTHS IS a lot of days. You're ten years old, and even a single day can seem as long as a prison sentence. And like a prisoner within the confines of his cell, Cornelius has mapped every place in every single one of his days where he will encounter Fear.

Fear is Cornelius's shadow. It governs his relationship with Yosha, makes him stupid, tongue-tied, when he is far from stupid, in fact. It is Fear makes him shivery and awkward when he hears people laughing behind him. When Prince Maurice is out of his stable. When a dog wants to smell his hand.

For most of his conscious life, for as long as he has been aware of Fear (and he cannot remember a time when he was not aware of it), Cornelius had thought everybody lived and felt and Feared as he did. That was why it was never spoken of. When, recently, it began to occur to him that perhaps this was not so, still it did not seem to him that he could speak of it – if Fearing as he did was peculiar to him, perhaps it was something of which he should be ashamed? In any case, what would be the point? Whatever other people's lives might be, this was his, and always would be. How could anyone else help? And who would he tell? The servants are servants, so cannot be friends; his mother is both, so cannot be either. Cornelius has grown up on a lonely island of one.

Sometimes, from the safety of his room, Cornelius looks down on Amsterdam and all the people in the streets, and none of them even knowing that he watches them, and he thinks Amsterdam is the best and greatest toy-box in Creation, a Noah's Ark of wonders and delights; and at other times he looks down and something else seizes him and he knows he is going to see something so horrible it will destroy him. Spanish soldiers charging round the corner. Catarina squished by a cart. Paul, with his face bleeding. Any one of a thousand horrors – he doesn't know how he knows them all.

There is a thing Cornelius calls the Hand of Fear. At least it feels like a hand. This dismembered item, with its shattered stump of wrist, lives in his gut. Sometimes it clutches at his insides in terror; sometimes, aghast, it raises itself on three fingers and thumb and points with quivering index at whatever source of Fear he is about to encounter, and sometimes, and these are the worst, the Hand balls itself into a fist and smashes down on his viscera to punish him for being so afraid. At such times he is flush-cheeked and feverish, and Zoot keeps him in bed. Cornelius is not a coward – it takes considerable strength of mind to live like this – but he is scared of almost everything.

Or he was. Because in those fifteen months, Cornelius has discovered the secret of joy. And the secret of joy is to live without Fear.

It is Yosha's habit, when he has some suitable errand to be run, to send for Cornelius to do it. In this way, Cornelius will start to learn the business. The errands are not a great deal in themselves: a visit to some colleague Yosha knows to be good with children, a scrip of paper to be borne home plus maybe a trip around a strong-room, but the little insights thus gleaned may of themselves add up to much. And thus far, Cornelius has always accomplished these errands successfully. (Success so far only implies to Cornelius that the next trip will be even more difficult, thus even more to be Feared. One day it will be a task of such complexity that Cornelius will get it wrong, and then what will happen to him? He will cease to exist, he imagines.)

Amsterdam in its streets is not like Amsterdam viewed from the safety of an upstairs window. It is noisy, crowded, people shove into you. There are shouts. You might get followed. You might never get home.

The task of such complexity that it is bound to go wrong is to take a fork, a sample and a rarity, to a dealer in mother-of-pearl, to be given a measurement, to take the measurement to a jeweller, to get a price from the jeweller, to take the price back to the dealer in mother-of-pearl and, depending upon what the man says, either leave the fork there, or bring it home again. The Hand is aghast. What if Cornelius forgets the price? What if he forgets the fork?

'Take Jack with you,' says Yosha, as his parting shot.

Cornelius is baffled by Jack. How can he manage such grown-up things? Lead Prince Maurice about? Deal with fires and splinters? Be left, unsupervised, with knives? The two of them depart the house together, Cornelius attempting to lead the way, and Jack sauntering along behind, as if it hasn't even occurred to him what a marvel he is.

They are halfway to the dealer's when Cornelius hears the first reedy cry pursuing them. Jew boy! Then two voices: Jew boy, Jew boy! Then more. Their followers don't shout, or some conscientious adult would admonish them; they time their cries till the street is deserted, till you almost think they've given up and gone home, then you'll hear it again. Jew boy! The Hand is clutching his innards and whimpering. Now Jack will know it too, that when Cornelius goes out he is followed, and mocked, and worse. They will make one of their darting runs and tug at his jacket, they will elaborate their cry: Where you come from, Jew boy? Who's your papa?

If Jack has heard the cries, he gives no sign. Perhaps he has not connected them with his companion. Cornelius's heart begins to beat again.

They come out of the dealer's and within a matter of paces (the street is quiet, it is noon), the cries have begun again. There can be no mistaking their object now. Jack swings about and stares down the street, and the band of boys, four of them, check slightly, and pull back.

'Why do they do that?' Jack demands, as the gang ducks into doorways, out of sight.

'Trying to make trouble,' Cornelius answers, from the depths of his despair. 'Zoot says to ignore them. Says to turn the other cheek.'

'Oh yes? Do they follow her about, too?'

'Of course not!' Cornelius exclaims, appalled.

'So what's she know about it, then?'

They make their way to the jeweller's in silence, both acutely conscious that their followers, even if mostly staying hidden, are still there.

They come out of the jeweller's, retracing their steps. The cries start again, immediately. 'I've had enough of this,' says Jack. 'Let's fix 'em.'

Cornelius's mouth falls open. 'How?'

'Get to the corner,' says Jack, pushing him forward.

They reach the corner. The cries are stronger, louder now. Any second there will be the crescendo of running feet. And then a bolder spirit, right on cue: 'Who's your friend?'

Jack turns. The boys are ten short yards away. He turns and he does something Cornelius has never seen before, yet understands the import of at once: an insult of such peerless obscenity you recognize it by instinct. Jack claps right hand in the crook of left arm, raises left hand in a fist, puts two fingers out of the fist, then thrusts the thumb between them. Fuck you, cunt.

The gang of boys recoils in disbelief, then as one comes thundering forward.

Cornelius and Jack round the corner, blood, panic, frenzy, pounding in Cornelius's ears. There is the same door they passed on the way to the jeweller's, there is the same piece of timber propping it open. 'Give me that,' Jack demands. Cornelius snatches it up; it's wrenched from his grasp as the first, fastest, boy comes round the corner. Jack swings the timber into the boy's stomach. The second gets it over the shoulders, like an axe. The third runs smack-bang into it. The fourth rounds the corner, brakes, changes gear, leaps a fallen companion and hares off down the street.

Jack throws the timber to the ground, goes to the first boy, yanks him upright, and with his fist twisted in the boy's collar, slams him against the wall. He says, 'You come after us again, I'll take your fucken head off. They'll fish you out of that canal in *bits*. You got that?'

The boy is gargling for breath. Jack shakes him. 'Got that?'

The boy manages what might just be a nod.

'Then let me hear you say it.'

The boy chokes out, 'Got it.' Jack lets him go. The boy falls to the ground, whooping. It's all happened so fast Cornelius has to replay it in his head to be convinced he actually saw it. *They were going to kill us! Now they're on the ground!*

Jack dusts off his hands, says, 'Come on,' to Cornelius, and sets off, leading the way. Cornelius has to scamper to catch up.

'So how long's that been going on for?' Jack asks, in a companionable manner, after a moment or two.

'This year. All this year. Some of last.' Cornelius should be shame-faced, but he is not. He is breathless, grinning, open-mouthed.

Jack sighs. 'Look,' he says, 'when something like that happens, you don't put up with it, you put a stop to it. Right?'

And Cornelius, dizzy with liberation, the world opening before him like a lily on a pond, essays what he will later remember as his first joke. His grin is so wide it feels as if his cheeks might split. 'Got it!' he says.

CHAPTER TWO

At the Carpenter's Hat

'WANTED – a king, run away... age: adolescent; colour: sanguine; height: medium... no beard or moustache worth mention; disposition: not bad so long as a stolen kingdom does not lie in his way; name of Frederick'

Habsburg propaganda against Frederick of Bohemia

THE CURVE OF A ROAD, the crest of a hill. Where are we now?

A long, long way from Amsterdam, that's for sure. Long way from anywhere, by the looks of it. It's inky dark and tingling cold, ringed round with yet more hills that make a rim against the starry sky, and you may well ask, *why are we here?*

That building up ahead, that's why. This, as any of its patrons might tell you, is the Carpenter's Hat.

The Carpenter's Hat was once no more than a watchtower on the road to Annecy; a stone-built block with an unkempt vineyard to one side and a tuffety paddock on the other. But Annecy stands in the territory of Savoy, and since there has been scarce a year in the last one hundred when France, Savoy and Italy haven't been squaring off, one at another, and not an army marching out or trailing back that hasn't passed this way, the watchtower on the road to Annecy has grown off their custom, as it were; while those passing armies (soldiers knowing the value of a landmark, and having no respect for anything whatsoever) took one look at the four windows poking through that ancient roof, and re-christened it, as they do most everything. The Carpenter's Hat.

And making his way toward it, leading his horse, a man cocooned in his cloak and muffled like a bandit. Despite the cold he takes a long pause as the building comes in sight, raising his head to note how the light from its windows is uninterrupted by much movement from inside. But then you live long enough as an army scout, you learn to make such observations as a matter of course – or you don't live long at all.

Business tonight at the Carpenter's Hat is clearly far from brisk. *Good.*

Here he comes, tethering his horse, opening the door. Shrugging his cloak to hang from one shoulder; removing his hat. And while he takes in the room before him, let us take a look at the man himself: slight, spare, skin of his neck a little loose, hair threaded with grey. Before him, a room with thick stone walls and low plank ceiling, a room scattered with tables and benches, with a fireplace wide as a farmyard gate, piled with glowing logs.

Roars of laughter greet his entrance. There are four men sat around the fire, legs outstretched, baking their boots, and one standing, who, it seems, has just reached the punchline of a joke. Those seated turn their heads and glance the traveller's way, but only momentarily. Not only insignificant, but sickly with it – as the warm air catches him, the traveller begins to cough. Two bright spots of colour flare into being on his cheeks. The cough is, indeed, a rattler.

'Aha!' says the joker. He bows to his audience. '*Señores, perdóneme. Mi amigo por fin está aquí.*' – My friend, it would seem, is finally here. '*Te dejo con tus pipas.*' – I will leave you to your pipes. He crosses the room, hand extended. 'Balthasar! *Bonjour!*'

Balthasar gives a final cough. 'Ravello,' he replies.

They meet at the centre of the room. 'Balthasar,' Ravello says again and, placing his palm against the other's back, conducts him to a table tucked in the embrasure of a window. 'It's been a time.' His voice is lower now. 'Are you well?'

'Do I look well?' Balthasar asks.

'You've looked worse. Here, sit,' Ravello tells him, hooking out a chair.

Ravello stands a head over Balthasar, a head under the four by the fire. He doesn't have the build of a soldier, either. 'He is, of sorts, a fellow scout,' was how Balthasar had once described him. 'But more on the – the *uncovering*, rather than discovering, side of things.' Ravello has carefully brushed-up moustaches of a gentle brown, a dab of beard, and hair as fine and upright as chick-fluff. He looks both bright and biddable, the astonished listener to secrets, not (as he is) the safe deposit for so many. Only his eyes, active as fleas, might give the game away; a hint there's much more here than you'd imagine. They hopscotch over Balthasar, take in the mud on his cloak, pause on the high spots of colour in his face. The bonhomie in his voice is nonetheless relentless. 'So. Where'd my letter find you?'

'In Paris,' the other replies, wheezing softly. 'With my cadets.' He puts the back of one hand to his mouth, forces the cough to submit. Glances about him. 'This place has changed some since we were here last.'

Ravello rolls his eyes. 'The *world* has changed some since we were here last.' There is a bottle on the table; Ravello picks it up. A pair of square-footed drinking glasses, too. 'Rousette's still good though,' Ravello continues, rotating the bottle in his hand. 'Here.'

Another burst of laughter from the men sat round the fire. 'Our friends there?' Balthasar enquires.

'Freebooters. Come up from Zaragoza. Mercenaries to a man. Oh, we're safe enough to talk in front of them,' as Balthasar raises an eyebrow. 'If they've a word of French between them I'd be amazed.'

'And what would a set of Spanish freebooters be doing here at the Carpenter's Hat?' Balthasar asks.

'On their way to Deutschland. Sharks scenting blood. If poor benighted Frederick thinks throwing him out of Bohemia was the end of it, he's another think coming.' He puts a glass in front of Balthasar, fills one for himself. 'Here. Put back what your journey took out.'

But Balthasar shakes his head. 'News first.'

'Ah, that,' says Ravello. He leans forward. 'Now this may be nothing—'

'But nonetheless, you wrote.'

'But nonetheless, I wrote.' A moment while Ravello seems to gauge the temper of his audience. 'It's Rufus,' he says. 'Rufus believes he has found something for you. Something significant.'

'Rufus,' Balthasar repeats. There's a suggestion as he says it that the name don't taste quite as it should. 'And what would that be, I wonder?'

'Can't tell you,' comes the reply. 'Whatever it is, he'll pass it on in person only. But then again, whatever it is, it has to be more than you've got.' He fills Balthasar's glass, and lifts his own. 'Here. Drink. To Jean Fiskardo.'

'To Jean,' echoes Balthasar.

'And Sally, may God look mercifully upon her. And their poor boy.'

Balthasar puts down his glass. 'I will never accept that woman destroyed herself,' he says. 'Don't ask me to drink to that. And until I see a body, as far as I'm concerned, their boy is still alive.'

The men by the fire are trying their hand at a song. They stamp their booted feet to mark the time:

War is my homeland
My armour is my house
And fighting is my life.

Ravello gives them an approving smile. Under cover of the noise he leans in. 'Balthasar—' he begins.

'Oh, I know. You think I'm lying to myself, don't you?' says Balthasar.

Run, peasants, run, exhorts the chorus by the fire.
For we are in the field
Girl, bring the jug
Hey! Girl bring the jug.

There is a girl at the Carpenter's Hat; she is indeed bringing a jug. She steps around the singers and their groping hands with practised ease and an expression on her face of absolute contempt. Her shawl is bound criss-cross over her bodice like an extra layer of protection, but to Balthasar it's clear the groping hands are for form's sake only; these men are far more interested in keeping warm and getting drunk. He has seen many such.

'Listen, Ravello,' he begins. 'The day Sally died, there were four others in Belle-Dame breathed their last. Two little children, and one of the old village women. And a man they found out on the road with his back broke, who said some stranger ran their horse at him. That's five in one day – *five*, in a place so small you could cover it with your hand. Something, some agency, came into that village, and Sally and the rest were what it left behind. I know black work when I see it. You do too.' He waits, then he too leans forward. 'But the boy escaped. I'm sure of it, Ravello. When they found Sally's body, she had been cut down, and laid straight. Now who would have done that?

Who, other than her flesh and blood? He was alive then. I say he's alive now.'

The girl is by their table. She picks up the empty bottle. She asks, 'You want another?'

'Sweetheart, yes,' says Ravello, gratefully. He runs a hand over his face, up-brushing those moustaches; an aid to the re-dressing of his thoughts. '*Allora*. Their boy—'

'Jacques,' says Balthasar, firmly. Because you give a soul a name, it's less likely that they're dead.

'Jacques, then,' Ravello continues. 'He was how old when you saw him last?'

'Rising ten.'

'So what would he be now?'

'Rising fourteen.'

'And you're saying he's been out there all this time, fending for himself, invisible?'

'This is Jean's *son*,' Balthasar replies, with a hiss of fury. 'What am I meant to do? Forget him? Walk away?'

Ravello sits back, heaves a sigh. 'Oh, by God. You're never going to let this go, are you?'

'Not while there's breath left in me,' says Balthasar. 'Ravello, don't you understand? If I can find out what happened to Jean, maybe I can find out what happened in Belle-Dame. And if I can find out what happened in Belle-Dame, maybe I can find their boy.'

The girl is back by their table. She makes a show of wiping at it with her apron, and as she does, murmurs to Ravello, under her breath, 'That one you're waiting for? He's stood outside.'

'He is? Have him come in!'

She points a look at him. 'It's bad enough you bring them Roma here in the first place. You want to talk with him, you do it out there. He ain't setting foot within.'

Ravello, standing. Another gusty sigh. 'A moment,' he tells Balthasar, and is gone.

*

Balthasar, turned in his seat, watching through the window. It's high from the ground (this was, after all, a watchtower once) and its embrasure is easily a foot deep, so all he can make out of the two men outside are the points of Ravello's hair, catching the moonlight, and Rufus with his tasselled cap pulled over to one side, hiding that keyhole in his skull where once was his left ear. The others of Rufus's tribe will, he knows, be waiting back amongst the trees. He looks in particular for the cobweb-like waft of Rufus's crazy brother, white-gowned, white-haired Benedicte, but there's nothing. Just these two men talking, heads together, words inaudible. The bottle-glass thickness of the window panes obscures the expression on their faces too. What does he feel now, watching? What dare he feel? His heart is numb.

But then, he reflects, *I am already three parts dead.*

The girl has returned, with the bottle this time. She pulls the bung free with her teeth, sticks her thumb into her apron and wipes inside the neck. 'You came here before,' she says. A strand of hair is stuck across one cheek, and she clears it by lowering her face and touching her cheek to her shoulder, a gesture of entirely unexpected grace, as if she were giving herself a kiss. *Now*, Balthasar thinks, *now I remember you.* Of a sudden he has her name as well – Tabby, he recalls. Tabitha. You sang us a song. You'd your eye on Ravello – or half an eye, at least.

Another burst of laughter from the men sat by the fire. The girl turns about, eyeing them as narrowly as Balthasar had done himself, and as she does he sees that the curious criss-cross arrangement of her shawl is in fact a means of creating a papoose for a tiny infant, sleeping between her shoulder-blades.

'So I was. Good memory.' He tilts his glass to her.

'You had that big man with you,' she persists.

The impossibility of any woman seeing Jean and ever

forgetting him, even now. Quite marvellous. 'And you were running this place with your father. Is he still with us?'

'Upstairs. Old and fat.' A grin. 'He don't come down when it's as quiet as this.' She drops her voice. 'Your friend,' she says. 'The big man. He'd come here with that other one. You know.'

And let us marvel too at the ability of any woman to enunciate that precise quality of *with*. 'Did he?' says Balthasar, knowing exactly who is meant here, and squirming away from it like a worm from the hook.

'Her. The woman soldier. The one as everybody used to call the Moor. You know her, she was famous. Proper Amazon. The big man, that friend of yours, he'd bring her here with him and oh, how my old dad would stare.'

Over by the fireplace, one of the four is tapping his tankard with a knife. The baby, stirring at the noise, lifts from its wrappings a miniature fist, folded as tight as a bud. 'You're wanted,' says Balthasar, gratefully.

A glance behind, but it seems the tankard-tapper can wait. 'She's in this trade now, ain't she?' the girl persists. 'Same as me. Only she's got herself a place in Hertzberg, so they say.' She sighs. 'You can make a fortune in a town like that. Not like here. We're more dead'n alive here, we are.'

So we are.

'What happened to him? To your friend?'

Ravello is no longer visible outside. Rufus has disappeared as well. Balthasar feels a sort of inner bracing taking place against whatever he has left in there, mould-splotched, crumbling, rotten with disease.

'We don't know,' he says. 'We don't know. But by God I'm going to find out. Whatever it takes me, I am.'

And here comes Ravello, blowing on his hands. The girl moves away, the men by the fire calling her over. Here comes Ravello, back to his seat, seizing the bottle, filling his glass –

And the bottle tings against it. That's Balthasar's first sign. Ravello's eyes are bright, his hair seems to be sticking up more than ever, and when he goes to fill his glass, his hands are trembling. 'Well,' he says. 'That was unexpected.'

'He has something?' Balthasar hears the rising note in his own voice. There is heat about his heart, great heat, as abrupt as opening the door of a furnace on the life roaring within. 'Something significant?'

'I think he does. I think we may say that.' He lifts the glass. If you knew Ravello well enough, you'd say he was toasting himself. 'He and his Roma. They've found Jean's bloody horse!'

CHAPTER THREE

A Good Student

'These questions you are asking are profound secrets,
that must not be discoursed of.'

Sir William Hope, *The Fencing Master's Advice to His Scholar*

CATARINA LIES ON her side beneath the table in the kitchen. She is much more cat than kitten now, and here at noon has become one of her favourite places. The flagstones keep her cool in summer; in winter the heat of cooking keeps the room warm, and the table is wide enough that the feet of those seated at it don't come near enough to bother her. Tread on her glorious plume of a tail, for example, fully furred now and Magdalene red.

The conversation of a dozen people, eating heartily, buzzes in the air above her head. Seated at the table are Zoot, Paul, the cook, the housemaids (two), the scullery maid (a poor sorry creature with lank and unattended hair), the laundry maid, a carrier from Yosha's wine-merchant (who is being fed only because he happens to be there), the gardener (old Jan) and Zoot's serving girl, Beatrice, who is in love with Paul, and who whenever she leans forward to talk with her neighbours lets her gaze rest on him for one precious moment. At the far end of the table are the two boys. The meal is house-pot, a type of stew – potatoes, onions, shredded cabbage, flakes of fish (today it is salmon, both plentiful and cheap; Zoot runs a thrifty kitchen, as one might expect) – enriched with chicken livers and ground pork sausage, thickened with egg yolks, spiced with mace and sharpened up with vinegar. Mealtimes in Yosha's house are noisy, satisfying affairs; house-pot a national staple.

Catarina rises to her paws, stretches front and back, and picks her way, out of sight beneath the table, to its far end, where Cornelius is beckoning her with a piece of salmon. She takes it from his fingers and rubs against his hand to ask for more. Time was when Cornelius would dispose of almost the entire contents of his plate in this way, what small helping he allowed himself to be given. Not any more. Jack eats everything placed in front of him, so Cornelius does too. Jack belches after he has eaten, like a man. Cornelius has begun to do this as well. 'Cornelius!' his mother calls down the table, warningly, but her stern expression is not to be taken in earnest. There are some few small outbreaks of independence Zoot still counters with the greatest strictness she can ('Why can't I go to bed when I want? Jack does. Why must I have lessons? Jack doesn't'), but what she sees overall is that her son, who was small and shy and awkward, is shy no more, comes to her with scabs on his knees and roses in his cheeks, and has not had one day when he must be kept in bed in months.

Zoot's great anxiety at present – Zoot is unfulfilled without one great anxiety, heaving itself out of the mass of her daily concerns – is what, long term, is to be done with the cause of this transformation. The boy has his rough moments still

– his casual profanities horrify her, he will not learn his letters ('Because it's stupid. What do I need this for?'); and she has yet to see him shed a single tear, even when the shrieks from the kitchen brought her down to find him standing in the doorway, blood pouring from his nose ('I slipped'). Zoot reasons that time will take care of most of this – this recklessness, which in a child seems faintly mad, in a grown man would be lauded – but time will not take care of how he is to be found a future, it will only make that problem worse.

She gazes down the table, that same expression of motherly concern so dear to Mungo Sant pulling the lines of her face. Zoot knows of only one person in the world clever enough to solve its problems. As she has done so many times before, she resolves to take this one to him.

Yosha is confined to bed with a nasty case of hypochondria, an ailment in which he indulges from time to time. Zoot finds him in his nightcap and shawl, looking through a mass of papers laid across the counterpane, and since no-one is watching, and since Yosha was not always as incapacitated as he now likes to appear, greets him with a kiss.

'Yes?' asks Yosha, when the kiss is done.

'I wish to talk to you of Jack,' Zoot tells him.

'Why? What has he done now? Does he have two noses, to get them broken in a fight?'

'He did not break it in a fight,' Zoot says primly, tapping a scatter of papers into a neat square pile. 'He slipped.'

Yosha makes his *Pah!* noise. Zoot ignores it. 'I want to know what is to be done with him. If he had his own family, they would have put him to a trade by now. Instead he is here, as everybody's unpaid servant. It is not right. It is a waste of him.'

Yosha puts his papers down. 'You think we should send him to school?'

Zoot is taken aback. 'With Cornelius?' The plan to send Cornelius to school has been so long deferred that it has ceased to be spoken of.

'Certainly with Cornelius. We got someone else for him to go with? You want to send Beatrice, maybe?'

'I think Beatrice has plans of her own,' says Zoot, smiling. She considers the suggestion. Jack would look out for Cornelius at school. He would be a friend for Cornelius at school. There. Two problems solved with one masterstroke.

Yosha reaches out, and chucks her under the chin. 'So now you're happy? No more of the frowns?'

Zoot bows her head. 'Yes. Very happy.'

'Then so am I. Send a word to Master Nicholas, arrange for the lessons to start.'

Zoot stands up. She is walking to the door when Yosha calls her back. 'Beatrice and Paul, you say?' he comments, chuckling. 'Well, well.'

MASTER NICHOLAS IS tall and spare and balding, with the high-stepping gait of a water-bird. His school consists of a large unheated room in a building that also figures in Yosha's port-folio of investments, close by the Fish Market. Its curriculum is designed to tattoo upon his pupils' brains enough Latin to read a tombstone, enough history to demonstrate the perfect recti-tude of the long war with Spain, and enough geography to find your way out of the United Provinces, as even the most honest Dutchman must occasionally do. A map has been painted on the wall to help with this, a map that makes Amsterdam the bold centre of the world, with FRANKRYJK to the left, DUITZLAND to the right and ENGELAND reduced to a witch's bony finger rising from the North Sea up above. There are sorties, lesson-wise, made against algebra and mathematics;

brief forays toward rhetoric, grammar and law; then in the afternoon it teaches the bearing of arms – the skill that no gentleman may call himself a gentleman without. Master Nicholas offers tuition in rapier, fauchon, hanger, glaive. The smallest weapon in his armoury, all of which hangs neatly from racks upon the classroom walls, is a novelty three inches long that fits between the knuckles of the fourth and middle finger; the largest, a Swiss broadsword, has a blade of four feet. Armed with such a weapon, at the height of his stroke a man can attain the velocity of a slash with a cut-throat razor.

Also painted upon the walls are various targets, large and small, partnered by spider's-web geometries of lines and the tracks of shaded footprints. There are benches, where those students not being tutored may sit and view the lesson, a stuffed wooden vaulting horse, and between the two high windows, stretching from floor to ceiling, the figure of a giant, arms upraised; hands, arms, legs, abdomen all neatly gashed, displaying the nine cuts. A door beneath the giant's right foot leads to two rooms where Master Nicholas lives a life of Spartan simplicity, supported by a diet blameless as an anchorite's.

By his private calculation, Master Nicholas has been personally responsible for the deaths of eighteen of his fellow men. By proxy, through his many students, how many? The total is incalculable.

Jack and Cornelius enter with the rest of the class; as they enter, Cornelius hears Jack take in his breath. In single file, as directed, the intake of novices is each presented with stylus and wax-tablet and sits down. Cornelius sits very tight to Jack. This place, with its commands, its furnishings, and the violence by rote going on all round its walls, makes no sense to him at all.

Jack's gaze has come to rest on one of the geometries on the opposite wall. Its lines and angles plainly have a meaning, so he sets to puzzling it out. One pair of shaded footprints, and an arcing line, are marked with a capital A. He knows what an A is, there's one in his name (Zoot's lessons have succeeded that far). Round the margins of the diagram, pairs of well-dressed figures are depicted struggling with each other, and beneath one pair (the man on the right has driven his sword into his opponent's eye; his opponent, understandably, has dropped his weapon to the ground), there is another A, and a line joins the victor's weight-bearing leg to the shaded foot-prints below...

... therefore to make the lethal thrust of the man on the right, you should position your feet so, and the arcing line is the line your sword must draw in the air, first to guard you from your opponent, then to stab. Jack considers this. He reckons it would work. Eyes shining, he nudges Cornelius, who seems to be crowding him. 'It's good this, ain't it?'

He is undoubtedly the most troublesome little brat Master Nicholas has ever encountered. Always either in a daydream or a fidget; and forever sneaking up close to the racks, itching to take down one of those swords. No new pupil is allowed to so much as touch a weapon for six weeks; when they do they wear padded sleeves pulled on over their clothes and wrap-around leather stomachers, and every sword is tipped with a wooden button. Every sword in the room is always tipped with a wooden button; Master Nicholas has great respect for the safety of his pupils and the peace of mind of his pupils' parents; did he not have so much respect for Yosha Silbergeld he would send this little half-arse scapegrace home.

The great day dawns. The new intake of pupils, padded up, are facing the painted targets. 'And lunge,' Master Nicholas commands, walking down the line. 'And lunge!' What he is listening for is step, swish, stab. What he hears instead is step, stumble, *crash*. Stumble, crash, *ow*. 'Again!'

Step, swish, stab.

Straight into the centre of the target, left hand in the crook of the waist, right elbow out, wrist turned, blade straight, head level with the shoulders. It's not entirely there yet – to Master

Nicholas's practised eye the boy is aping someone larger than him by far – but *Godverdomme*, it's pretty good. 'Enough!'

The line straightens. Most of the boys grin shamefacedly at their neighbours, knowing the fools they have made of themselves. Master Nicholas taps the scapegrace on the back. 'Where did you learn?'

'Didn't learn nowhere,' the boy replies. 'I watched.'

'Who did you watch?'

Up goes the chin, as if to say that's no business of yours.

The term progresses. Master Nicholas still keeps the tail of his eye on the boy as before, but now he watches for pleasure.

He sees the boy is quick. He sees that he is strong – stronger, in fact, than some of his classmates two years older. He's a weakness for showing off and an annoying habit of pretending he's confusing left and right, but he also has faultless balance, lovely timing; all the skills you cannot teach are there in full. Master Nicholas has had enough eager little lads go through his hands to have learned to trust his instincts, and what his instincts tell him he has here is that rarest of creatures, a natural.

And, he suspects, a natural with an interesting pedigree. Master Nicholas teaches according to the writings of Don Luis of Madrid (he despises the Spanish, but it is the old story of know your enemy). He goes down the room from the oldest of his pupils to the youngest, calling out, 'First guard! Second guard! Third guard! Fourth!' and while the rest of the boys execute more or less imperfectly the workmanlike passes of Don Luis, the natural draws, lunges, guards, with a flourish, a relish that comes from somewhere else altogether. I watched, the boy said. Watching him, Master Nicholas sometimes thinks he would give his eye-teeth to know who.

—❧❦❧—

SUMMER. The windows make the classroom broiling hot, so the class moves outside to where Master Nicholas rents ground from a militia company. The curriculum expands to include archery and wrestling, at both of which Cornelius is almost as bad as he is at swordplay, and thus spends many of the lessons with the other dunces, in the shade of the trees. He doesn't mind this, not at all. It is a revelation, firstly, that there are other dunces in the world. Cornelius is making friends. It is generally a friendlier, less formal atmosphere out here than in the classroom: nursemaids walk their small charges through the fields to take the air, couples pause to watch the class, and comment, and admire, and the ne'er-do-wells from the docks come to stand at a safe distance and jeer. 'I say, he's very good, your friend, ain't he?' says one of Cornelius's fellow dunces, a small, fat, red-faced boy, whose ruby cheeks make him look as if he is forever about to burst into tears, as they watch Jack throw a gangling classmate over backwards.

'Yes,' Cornelius agrees, basking in reflected glory, 'he is.'

He and Jack walk back together in the warm dusk, Jack circling one arm in its socket in a manner that suggests it hurts and that he's proud of it, and halfway home Cornelius realizes that they are being followed. Only this time, glancing back (he cannot help himself), Cornelius receives the strong impression that it is not he who is the object of their follower's interest, but his companion. 'Jack,' he whispers.

'Yeah, I saw him,' Jack answers. 'Pretend you ain't.'

Early morning. The sun ascends over Amsterdam, the temperature is set to soar. Many a respectable citizen will today take in private to his shirt-sleeves, and the canals have acquired their ripe summer odour too. The cook is in the kitchen, irritating the sleeping fire; the housemaids, in the stifling attic, are arguing over the whereabouts of the big marble pestle and which of them had it last; and Jack is behind the house, at the bottom of the garden, fishing line in hand, bare toes in the green-tinged water. He doesn't expect to catch anything, but he wants some time to think. There is a deal of thinking to be done.

The kitchen door opens. Cornelius comes down the steps, picks up Catarina's dish, and heaves a sigh. Untouched again; his cat is off her food. He rattles the dish and calls for her. It is imperative that Catarina eat her breakfast, before it becomes a banquet for the blowflies and the cook throws it on the midden. Without this, he'll come back from school and his cat will be starved, dead.

Only she won't. He knows she won't. Cornelius watches his thoughts spiral into these tornadoes of tragedy still, but he watches them do so from the outside, he is no longer caught in the tornado with them. 'Oh come *on*,' he says, with irritation, and shakes the dish again.

Catarina suddenly appears on the other side of the canal, launches herself into the water and, head rolling with concentration, cat-paddles across its width.

It is the first time Jack has seen this. He stands up, hooting with laughter, as Catarina struggles out onto the lawn. Catarina will no more tolerate being laughed at than any other cat, semi-aquatic or no. She stalks toward Cornelius, tail aloft. 'There you are!' Cornelius calls.

And then the second cat appears. A tom-cat, rat-grey, broad of face, with ears clawed down to stumps, he races across the little wooden bridge spanning the canal, and Catarina's dignified progress becomes a sprint. Cornelius has just called out a surprised 'Hey!' when Catarina disappears into the flower-bed with the tom-cat in pursuit. The flowers shake, a stand of irises keels over to the ground, the deep red petals of a rose are knocked into the air, a single Pottebacker tulip (another of Yosha's exotics, though from rather nearer home this time) quietly folds its leaves and breathes its last, and all to the accompaniment of the most blood-curdling yowls imaginable.

Cornelius is horror-struck. Somewhere in there his cat is surely being disembowelled. 'What is he doing?' he shrieks. 'Stop him, stop him!' His face is red, there are tears in his eyes; he may have stamped his foot. Jack, pausing for a second to give Cornelius a curious glance (thinking *poor bloody cat* – there are times when he too could do with a break from Cornelius's devotion), strides into the flower-bed and comes out holding the errant suitor by the scruff. He bowls the cat across the lawn, and at a gallop, it flees over the bridge.

Catarina runs up the wall behind the flower-bed and disappears.

And does not return. No little head pushed into Cornelius's hand in the middle of the night, no warm breathing form on his feet when he awakes.

Standing at his bedroom window, Cornelius wills her to reappear. He sees a pedlar with a handcart, making his noisy way along; sees a housewife with a basket on her way to market. Sees old Jan, come from his house, pushing a wheelbarrow loaded with hoe and rake. Old Jan stops outside the courtyard gate and pauses to wipe his brow.

There are two entrances to Yosha Silbergeld's fine house: the great front door, in its maw of white stone, with the steps up to it like a tongue, scrubbed to a crystalline glitter by years of scullery maids; and the one everybody uses down the alleyway beside the house: the door in the courtyard gate. A friendly little door, which Paul has to duck his head to pass through, with its complicated lock (Paul's province last thing at night, with his heavy belt of keys: lock up the house, lock up the door in the gate), and its cheery silver-tongued bell, announcing visitors. Or, as now, announcing the arrival of a man in his seventies, who would appreciate some assistance with his heavy barrow. Old Jan plucks at the bell from outside (a handy pull of plaited leather leads through a neat hole in the door), and as Cornelius watches, Jack comes down the kitchen steps, crosses the courtyard, opens the door (the usual second tinkle from the bell as the top of the door catches it), and makes to help old Jan manoeuvre the barrow inside. And the barrow sticks. It always sticks.

The barrow is withdrawn. Old Jan steps into the courtyard. Jack goes out into the alleyway, to push.

Cornelius sees the man from the docks sidle into view where the alley meets the street.

The barrow is through. Old Jan turns it about, and trundles it off down the garden.

Jack and this stranger now appear to be in a conversation, only it doesn't get very far. Jack is already moving away, when the other abruptly steps around him, placing himself between Jack, the door in the gate and safety.

Cornelius bangs back his window. What impels him to do this he has no idea, but something in the man's rapid movement had brought to mind the wretched tom-cat, and something in Jack's uncharacteristic wrong-footedness, Catarina, too. 'Hi, you!' he shouts. Both Jack and this other look up. There is something wrong with the man's face, one eye looking off and the mouth twisted up in a way that displays his teeth like a snarling dog's. Cornelius's heart is pounding. With an effort he ignores the staring eye and hollers down to Jack, 'Don't just stand there passing the time! There's tasks for you in the house!' Then he slams the window shut, races downstairs and outside. He doesn't even have his shoes on. He has no idea what his reception will be: Jack might be insulted, thump him, never speak to him again. He has addressed his best friend as a servant, a fetch-and-carry lad, the lowest of the low. Yet the instinct that made him bang the window open is still there, solid as a seam of gold.

The door in the gate is closed. Jack is back inside the court-yard, and his face is stiff with fury. Cornelius feels his heart give a pit-a-pat of dismay. Then all at once Jack sees him, and there is that giant grin. 'Swift!' he says.

Cornelius knows what swift means, Jack has explained it to him. It means well judged, timely, an apt response to an awkward situation. Emboldened, he demands, 'That man – what's he want?'

But gets no more than a shrug in answer. 'Just trying to make trouble,' Jack replies.

This, to Cornelius, marks the point where Everything Goes Wrong. He has the entire household out looking for Catarina, and they come back empty-handed – what is the point of adults if they can't help in something as important as this? His mother's hesitant suggestion of a replacement kitten is dismissed with fury. And then there's Jack. He isn't surly (unlike Cornelius – how could she think another cat was going to make things better? That's like giving up on Catarina altogether!) but days later and he's still abstracted, quiet, unlike himself. Even the imminent return of Mungo Sant is not enough to perk him up.

Growing pains, Zoot decides. It takes some earlier than others (remembering her son and that most recent childish tantrum). And the boy has certainly grown. He towers over Yosha in the burgermeister's chair, casts a shadow like a tree. 'Do you think Jack is happy?' she enquires, as she tucks her son into bed, bends to give him his usual kiss.

Cornelius considers this, putting on his face an adult frown. 'I don't know,' he says, at last. A pang of guilt: the concealing of a secret (the man from the docks) and the act of snuggling down do not make happy bedfellows. 'I expect he's worried about Catarina,' he offers, awkwardly.

On her way to her own bed, Zoot makes a detour, up to the room on the attic's first floor. It is a very bare little room. The boy could pull on his boots and pick up his jacket, and it would

be as if he were never there. But for the fact that he is there, of
course, blankets pulled over his head and plainly fast asleep.

Zoot has never offered the occupant of the bed a goodnight
kiss, but were she ever to do so, it might be tonight.

She would be most unpleasantly surprised. The occupant of
the bed is its folded bolster. Jack is out in the courtyard, in the
dark, and is teaching himself to cross it as assiduously as a blind
man might learn his way across a room. When he's content with
his performance he will go to the stable and slip up the ladder
to the loft. Prince Maurice knows to expect him and never gives
him away; and the stable is far more restful than the busy air of
the house, full of other sleepers and other sleepers' dreams. In
any case, sleep is dangerous. When Copperknob came hunting
for him, he'd been sleeping then, woken with the other's hand
upon his throat.

He remembers that fight now, every detail. The battering he
took. The understanding that this time, it wasn't going to stop.
The being sent sprawling, and then his arm, and kicking out,
and then that one cry of dismay that wasn't his. He remembers
struggling up, holding his arm against his side, and there was
Copperknob laid out inert and helpless on the edge of the quay:
this miraculous transformation where seconds before all had
been noise and threat.

Oh yes, he's learned his lesson, where sleep is concerned.
Instead there's another place he goes to, eyes open but empty,
ears sifting any sound. He can float in there for hours. He can
come out of it in seconds.

There'll be a price to pay for this, there always is. He
remembers kneeling at the quayside after the gentle splash,
kneeling there in perfect peace, looking down as the dark waters
re-formed themselves and replaying the splash with quiet satisfaction in his mind, and it had been exactly then that he'd felt
the first warm pulse of liquid over his thigh; too thick for water
and just that bit too sluggish in its flow, even though his first

thought had been that he must have pissed himself, like some little kid. Then he had understood. Copperknob too had been armed with a knife.

Yes, there'll be a price, but it'll be worth it.

Because what do you do to an enemy?

You do what must be done.

Master Nicholas decides the boy looks jaded, and elects to move him up a year. On the face of it, it's an excellent idea. Instead, it almost gives him his first classroom fatality.

The class, in pairs, are practising passes. Two-handed grip, heave the sword up, bring it down to the right. Let the hilt swivel, heave up, and down to the left. Cornelius's partner is red-cheeked Augustus – so anxious to please, so eager to be liked, and who reminds Cornelius of some bad dream he once had of himself – and this practising of passes is heavy exercise. Within minutes Cornelius's shoulders are singing with pain, and his partner's cheeks are the colour of apoplexy. But it is exhilarating too. There is Master Nicholas, calling out the beat ('One, *left*. Two, *right*'); there is the hypnotic multiple crash of steel; there is also the delicious tremble of understanding, running throughout the entire class, that this, minus the padding and the wooden buttons on the swords, could be truly dangerous.

And there is a disturbance at the far end of the room. It comes to Master Nicholas's attention as a double echo in the rhythm of the class. He turns, Cornelius's partner turns, and Cornelius, deprived of Augustus's blade to end his own stroke on, staggers forward and almost stabs himself in the foot. Before he has recovered, Master Nicholas's giant strides are covering the length of the room a yard at a time.

What Master Nicholas saw in turning was something gone wrong in the placement of one of those pairs: one boy (Jack's partner) is standing too far back; Jack himself is clumsily close to the next boy along. Master Nicholas can reconstruct precisely what occurred the second before he turned his head: a push to show the newcomer where he now stood in the order of things, an exchange of insults. But what propels Master Nicholas down the room, what lengthens his stride into a run, is what happens next: Jack makes a curious wiping motion down the length of his blade, drops his shoulders, and begins to circle his aggressor. The class breaks backward in disarray, younger students retreating into the older, Master Nicholas surging through them all. He knows exactly what the boy has done. His star pupil, the prodigy, the little bastard, has swiped the button off his sword.

Master Nicholas lets out a roar. He is five strides away. He is four. He is three. The circling motion of the pair puts them in a line in front of him. He sees the face of the aggressor (the would-be aggressor), bleached with panic. Pathetically, the boy is trying to defend himself by repeating the passes from the exercise. Then over the other boy's head he is facing the prodigy. And the prodigy is smiling – eyes shining, and a wide, vicious, curving smile. Because this is of course what this one was made for. This is of course where all the lessons lead.

Master Nicholas's fingers make contact with the other boy's collar and pluck him away as the point of the sword comes through the space where the boy's breast had been. The attack is straight, deep, true – and straight into Master Nicholas's arm.

Master Nicholas, arm heavily bandaged, conducts his star pupil by the ear back through the streets to the house on the Prinsengracht, Cornelius scampering beside them. Cornelius is defiant to the point of hysteria: 'He didn't *mean* it!'

Master Nicholas grasps the ear more firmly. He eschews the door down the alleyway, marching his captive straight to the grand front entrance of the house. This is a public transgression, not some domestic misdemeanour. He glances down at the boy, wincing from the pressure of his grip, but otherwise resistless and resigned. But Master Nicholas is not fooled, not for an

instant. As Beatrice opens the door, he propels Jack through it:
'Oh yes,' he declares. 'Oh yes, he most certainly did.' The noise
of their return brings Zoot into the hallway, brings Yosha's
testy screech floating down the stairs: 'What is this? We got
a riot in my house, or what?' Cornelius hurls himself against
his mother. 'He didn't mean it!' But Master Nicholas's seeping
scarlet bandage and his wrath tell a different story. Hauling Jack
behind him, he is already up the stairs. 'I will not teach this boy!'
he proclaims, thrusting Jack into the room. 'I will not have him
in my class again!'

Yosha waits for the ringing echo to fade, and considers his
response. He looks at Jack, who is rubbing his ear, looks at the
bandage on Master Nicholas's arm, and, turning to Jack again,
asks quietly, 'Did you do this?'

'It was an accident,' Jack replies, steadily. He considers adding
'He got in the way', but thinks better of it.

'Accident my arse!' Master Nicholas exclaims, collapsing into
a chair.

Yosha makes a gesture of stroking, of calming, the air. 'And
have you apologized?'

'No,' says Jack.

'Then do so.'

Jack crosses the room, bows to Master Nicholas, arm at his
waist. 'I am very sorry that I hurt you. Sir.'

'Now go,' Yosha commands him.

And Jack goes, closing the door behind him. The two men
are left alone.

'Are you badly hurt?' Yosha enquires.

'No,' Master Nicholas replies. It is his pride that is smarting
now. 'Winged. But I will not teach that boy. I will not have
him back.'

'So you have said. What happened?'

'He attacked another student.'

Yosha considers this. 'Why?'

'*Why?*' Master Nicholas is out of his chair. 'Because he is an animal. He is beyond control—'

'Even animals do not attack unless provoked,' Yosha says, quietly.

Master Nicholas, checked, corrects himself. 'Very well then. There was a bit of push and shove. Another boy knocked him off balance. And your little dock-rat went for him—'

'He lost his temper,' Yosha suggests. 'That is a bad thing, and he will be punished for it.' He says this with regret, because something about the boy has snagged Yosha's liking. He knows no more of the boy's history than he did when Sant first carried him over his threshold, but he can make some guesses: loss, privation, and enough, so Yosha would suspect, of being pushed around already. It is perhaps no more than that the boy has had the chutzpah to survive at all. So he pushed back – what of it?

'He took the button off his sword, and he went for the other boy with that.'

It seems we are beyond the league of normal childhood sinning here.

'And it wasn't that he lost his temper, either. I saw his face. He was completely calm. And he was in absolute earnest. Two seconds more, he'd have stuck the other lad through like a herring.'

'He needs discipline,' Yosha suggests, playing for time. 'Zoot will tell you, he needs teaching—'

'*Teaching?*' says Master Nicholas, and varying his disbelief, continues, '*TEACHing?* I've not been teaching him. I'm merely giving him the names for what he already knows. My friend, that boy of yours – he's a marvel. He could take me on.' And checks himself again. Had the boy not, in fact, done exactly that?

And this, it seems, is news indeed. 'He is a good student?' Yosha asks, wonderingly.

The words *nonpareil, prodigy, natural* float through Master Nicholas's head. 'Yes,' he answers. 'He is very good. He is excellent. But I will not take him back. I will not have him in my school again.'

'Listen,' says Yosha. 'Let him cool his heels a week or so. Then we try again.'

'No,' says Master Nicholas, shaking his head. 'No. Listen, *myn heer*. I have seen his sort before.' He pauses. How to describe this? How to explain, to a man who lives in a burgermeister's chair? Master Nicholas leans forward, taps his temple. 'There is something gone, up here. Or something there should not be there. Not in a child. Not in a boy his age. And you cannot un-teach that.'

THE RETURN OF Mungo Sant. Not, however, Sant the jolly smuggler, nor even Sant the hardly-more-successful privateer. This is Sant the man of business, with more money in his pocket than he has ever known before, and determined everyone he meets shall mark his transformation. As means to which, and in honour of his invitation to dine that evening at the house of his Golden Jew, he has visited a barber, had the salt washed from his long-grown, brindled scraggle of hair, had his chin scraped smooth and anointed with smarting oil of bergamot, and bought himself a new shirt, of silk and cambric mix, so light and fine a man might hardly be aware that he was wearing anything at all. Here he comes, striding up the Prinsengracht, tipping his hat to the ladies: Sant the dandy, Sant on shore-leave, and at the thought of seeing Zoot again, Sant with a prickle of lechery deep in his gut, just where the hem of his shirt can keep it tickled nicely. Here he is at the door in the gate; here he is (much puzzled), reading the notice nailed upon it:

LOST

ONE QUEEN CATT

WHITE BODIED, REDDISH HINDERPARTS

ODD-EYED

REWARD FOR SAFE RETURN

He tugs the bell. The little door is opened. 'Oh, it's you,' says Cornelius, ungraciously. 'I thought maybe it was somebody with news of Catarina.'

Sant and Yosha dine alone – a minor disappointment this. There is a choice of wines, a dish of artichokes, a fish pie, cheese, and a dark and dripping side of beef, unctuous with golden fat. 'To safe returns,' says Yosha, raising his glass.

'To profits,' counters Mungo Sant, with a jovial wink, because isn't this how men of business discuss the doings of the world? 'You've heard the latest from Bohemia?'

'Ah yes, Bohemia,' says Yosha, swirling the wine in his glass. 'And now, so we are told, the Emperor will send his General Tilly to take Frederick's lands in Germany, while Frederick, they say, has commissioned Christian of Brunswick to take them back. So what was one little war, becomes two, rather larger. It is unsettling, is it not, how these disagreements have this habit of expansion?'

There is a moment's silence. 'All well in the house?' Sant asks, feeling the wink was probably misjudged. 'I see your boy Cornelius has grown.' He has a bit of a stumble over the best term to use, but then what is one meant to call him? Nephew? Young shaver? Son? To Yosha's face? Talk about grounding yourself.

But Yosha is smiling. 'Yes, he is very well indeed.'

'And how's our lad?' asks Sant, the shallows safely passed. 'I missed seeing him, when I came in.'

'Jack will be with Paul,' Yosha answers, 'and he is growing too. You will see him tomorrow. Afterwards, perhaps you and I should talk again.'

A young Hercules, is Sant's first thought. *God above, my lad's become a giant.* All that length of leg, solid with muscle now, and that squaring of his face… and then the boy's head catches the fan of sunbeams filtering through the great lights of the hall and Sant thinks, *No. Not Hercules. A young Apollo.* But then this is his foundling, and he is a little biased.

'Greetings, Captain,' says Jack, advancing, hand outstretched. 'Heard you was come home.'

'Heard you're being loaned me as my fetch-it for the day,' says Sant, and gets a broad grin in answer: 'Yeah, I guess.'

They walk together to the docks, with Sant being canvassed on the subject of whether Yosha should acquire a second horse. Sant has rarely had a more delightful conversation. *Look at the lad!* he thinks. *Listen to him! All the things he knows!* And wonders too, if those they pass might, perhaps, just possibly, take the two of them for father and son?

There are appointments with sailmakers, ropemakers, at the chandler's office, the customs house. Sant emerges from the latter, and Jack is nowhere to be seen. Outwardly unconcerned, he scans the crowd upon the quays, and spies his foundling in the shadow of a wall, and in an altercation with another, who stands with hands against the wall on either side of the boy's head. Jack sees Sant, bats an arm aside, snarls a healthy mouthful of spit and vituperation at the man and stalks away. The man watches him go. There's a twist to the man's face, familiar somehow.

And Jack's own countenance, which had been so clear, so full of enthusiasms, is stormy, very stormy. This is not a young Apollo, this is an angry little brawler, spoiling for a fight. At the same time, there is something almost girlish about so much outrage – a proper little miss, just received her first indecent proposal. Which is also, Sant supposes, not beyond the bounds of possibility. 'What was he talking to you for?' Sant enquires, seeking to make a joke of it.

'Because he thinks he can,' Jack replies, viciously.

Good answer. The viciousness is reassuring too.

The relief is short-lived. 'He said, as I'm living in that rich man's house now, can't I leave a window on the latch one night? Make sure the gate ain't locked?'

'And what did you say back?' Sant asks, ice forming in his bowels.

'Told him to go fuck himself,' Jack replies. And then he stops, considering. 'Says he knows what I did,' he mutters. 'Says I'd as better do a good big turn for him afore he tells someone else.' He kicks at the customs house wall. 'If he knows what I did, he'd do better looking out for himself 'stead of pestering me,' as if it is the illogicality of the other's argument, rather than any threat inherent in it, that angers him.

But it is hours later, the boy delivered safely home, when he is rocking in his cot on the *Guid Marie*, before Sant recognizes that strange speech for what it truly was: not the voicing of a fear, but an unvarnished admission of guilt.

Midnight. The ever-reliable Paul has done his rounds, the house on the Prinsengracht is locked up tight, and its inhabitants are all safe in their beds: Zoot, finessing further household economies in her dreams; Cornelius, with his fingers crossed under his pillow, still certain that in the morning Catarina will be there when he awakes; Prince Maurice, in his stall, dreaming of companionship (even a donkey would be something, he has known some very pleasant donkeys), head down, eyes closed.

And at the door in the gate, the lock bucks slightly, and simply disappears. There are now two neat round holes in the door.

The door in the gate creaks open by an inch, and a finger, creeping over its top edge, lifts clear the silent bell. The door

opens wider, to admit a hand, a foot, a muffled face. Ringle-Eye
enters, carrying a dark lantern – the housebreaker's illumination
of choice. Letting it emit a single beam, he allows it to find
him the direction of the kitchen stairs. On the tips of his toes
he crosses the courtyard. He puts one foot on the bottom step,
then gives a mighty start. Someone else is there.

The clouds leave the moon. A soft silver light falls across the
courtyard. 'Oh, it's you, you little arsehole,' hisses Ringle-Eye.
'Been expecting me, have ye?'

Very slowly, Jack comes forward. He'd like Ringle-Eye not
to notice that he has the higher ground. He takes his hand from
the silver wolf on its cord about his neck. He feels the weight
of the marble pestle, lodged up his sleeve, ready to drop into his
palm. He feels tucked into the back of his belt the unyielding
shape of his knife.

'Been counting on it,' says Jack.

WHAT SUMMONS SANT'S ATTENTION, as he lies sleepless in his
cabin, is not the creaking of a door, but a voice calling from
the quayside. It fills the void of trepidation with which he'd
been sharing his cot as completely as if it had been made for it:
'Captain Sant, sir! Captain Sant!'

On deck the watery light of dawn is breaking over the sea, but
the town itself is still as black as if the world were yet unformed.
On the quayside there is Paul.

'Captain Sant, you will come now, please. We have trouble.'

What kind of trouble? had been Sant's first question, as Paul led
him through the sleeping streets, but Paul had put a finger to
his lips. 'The kind we do not speak about outdoors.'

They are coming up to the door in the gate. The door in the
gate is hanging open. Sant steps through, into the courtyard,

and the first thing he sees is a broken lantern by the steps, and a splash of some dark liquid on the cobblestones. Dawn has leached the colour out of everything. Is it the dark liquid lamp-oil? Sant bends closer.

It is not. 'Ach a wae!' Sant exclaims, this time feigning neither accent nor emotion, and Paul says quietly, 'That is not his.'

Sant looks up. 'My lad's no' hurt?'

'He has a hurt here,' Paul replies, touching his cheek.

'Then who's all this belong to?' Sant demands, indicating the blood staining the cobblestones.

Paul leads him to the stable door. 'In here,' he says. 'This is who.'

The sprawled limbs, that rusty stink of gore. The blasted horse they keep in here is pulling at its halter, snorting at the smell. Someone has had the decency to put a cloth over the man's face, but on his chest there is a bull's-eye of blood round a hole so dark as to be almost black. Sant has just time enough for thinking *God above, that's deep. That must be to the heart*, when Paul, without another word, lifts the cloth away. The head is rolled sideways on the neck, the face still twisted, the good eye staring straight at Sant. There is an enormous wound above the eye, so bloodied and pulpy the damage can only be guessed at. All Sant's worst fears, laid before him.

'My lad did this?'

Still Paul says nothing.

'I want to see him,' says Sant.

'I am to take you to *myn heer* Silbergeld.'

'I WANT TO SEE MY LAD.'

Paul weighs sixteen stone, and he's used to seeing Yosha's orders carried through. But Sant is used to a crew of thirty, all of whom carry out his orders without question if they know what's good for them. There is only going to be one victor here.

Having conducted Sant to the door not of Yosha's room, but to that of the boy, Paul returns to the hall and sits there, waiting for whatever may befall the house next. And as he sits there, Beatrice comes up from the kitchen, weeping. All that bulk hides a very tender heart, and for Paul, all this in one household in one morning is simply more than he can bear. So he goes to her, a journey of a few short steps, but one that will lead to marriage, their own house, children – only that's another story.

Sant finds the boy sat on the bed in that attic room, face hidden, arms about his knees; the classic posture of the outcast in distress. 'Och, laddie,' Sant begins, and Jack looks up. One side of his face is purple, with a weeping gouge high on the cheek.

Sant sits himself down beside the boy. 'What happened here?' he asks, with all the gentleness he can muster.

His foundling raises a hand to his oozing cheekbone, examines the watery smear, then turns to Sant. 'He asked for it,' he says.

And, this, suddenly, is not what Sant had expected at all. Tears, he had been expecting – let the laddie have a weep, get the story from him, take it to Yosha, *sort this oot*. He'd already begun putting together the case for the defence: an accidental discovery, a fight, a fall, the spring on the blade of that knife – that had been the plan. Only the plan had not anticipated this – this hard-eyed, *dry*-eyed scorn.

'But why'd you take him on? Why not raise the house?'

'What,' says Jack, 'and have him tell them I was part of it? That I had let him in?'

'But no-one would have believed him! No-one would've believed him for a minute!'

'He'd still have said it. He'd have told everything,' Jack continues. And there, almost hidden in the bruises swelling round his eye, that glint of satisfaction. 'He ain't telling no-one nothing now.'

Sant stares at him. He rubs his brow. He doesn't need to know. He does. He has to ask.

'The boy at the docks. The lad who drowned.' Sant clears his throat. 'Was that you?'

'I kicked him, and he fell,' comes the reply. 'He bashed his head.'

'And did he fall intae the water? Or did you roll him in?'

No answer. Jack says nothing; his expression says it all. Withering contempt: *Of course I did. What d'you take me for?*

'You cannot *do* this,' Sant bursts out, raging now in earnest. 'You cannot kill a man to solve a problem—' You can. Sant has done so himself. His point is he did not do so when he was as young as this. His point is he would not have known how to begin to do so as young as this. His point is—

He looks at the boy's face – obdurate, knowing, victorious, unashamed – and his every point escapes him. Defeated, Sant goes to find Yosha.

There's a mighty argument in progress in Yosha's room. Pausing at the top of the stairs Jack listens, head cocked. The basis of the argument is no surprise; he'd guessed they'd send him on his way, worked that out from the first.

Wincing – his ribs are jarred, as well as the cut on his face – he lifts from the floor the bundle he's made, Whittington-style, of all his few possessions. A quick glance back at the room that had been his. It is indeed as if he'd never been in it – clean, empty, blanket folded at the bottom of the bed. Only if he's leaving, there's an unfinished something to sort out first.

Testing each step, he moves down the stairs. When he's outside Cornelius's room, he stows the bundle in the shadow on the landing. The raised voices are even louder now. But getting in and out of this house without anyone noticing, that's never been difficult.

The voices belong to Sant and Yosha, who are thick into what Sant would call a casting out. 'So now we see,' Yosha had begun, as soon as Sant entered the room. 'Now we see what it is you put under my roof. A crazy boy. An animal—'

For Sant this is the storm in the Baltic come again, the vessel going down beneath him, the boy overboard. 'Now you hold hard,' says Sant. 'The lad's done nothing—'

'Nothing?' thunders Yosha. 'You tell that to the *goniff* in my stable, kuck on him!' This is a situation fraught with such dangers Yosha would hardly know how to begin listing them, and his temper has not been improved by being kept waiting.

'He was defending *you*—'

'Paul saw him!' Yosha shrieks. 'He hears the noise, he looks from his window – there they are, fighting like bears. Your crazy boy knocks the man to the ground – did you see what he has done?'

'We have to get him out of here,' says Sant, grabbing at this as a desperate helmsman might the wheel.

'Who, your boy? I will take care of your boy. Your boy will be gone from here, you make no mistake.'

'Not Jack, the – the goniff,' says Sant, thinking *Jesus, what a word!*

'You,' says Yosha, pointing a rigid finger at Sant. 'You will deal with that.'

'Me?' Sant is dazed. 'What am I to do with him?'

'Bury him under the ballast in your hold,' Yosha replies. 'Put him in a sack and drop him overboard.' He accelerates in the burgermeister's chair across the room at Sant. '*Do I look as if I care?*'

Sant is backing toward the door. Bring the body of a homicide aboard? Why not ask him to set sail of a Friday, while you're at it; *eat* a bloody albatross. 'Not me. I'll not have a murdered corpse aboard my boat. Not on any part of her.'

'No?' says Yosha, eyes a-glint. 'And what part of *our* boat will you not have a corpse aboard? The part that still belongs to you? Or the half that now belongs to me?'

The stupefaction lasts a moment only. 'You son of a bitch,' says Sant. 'You whoreson, blasted, bloody—'

'I bloody what?' Yosha thunders once again, levering himself up against the strong arms of the burgermeister's chair. 'I bloody what? You think I don't know that God-damned name you got for me? You think I don't know about Lübeck, what you do there? I know everything! Say it! Say it! I bloody JEW!'

At the stable door Jack now pauses, briefly, looking at the body laid out on the floor. It would still give him considerable satisfaction to drop something heavy on its ugly face, but there's more important matters to attend to here. Prince Maurice has paused too, in his attempts to escape the smell of blood. Jack goes to the horse, pulls down Prince Maurice's head to rest against his shirt-front, and rubs him behind the ears. 'Quiet now,' Jack tells him. 'That's my good old boy.' The horse's eyes half-close, he lets one fore-hoof angle on its rim. 'There,' Jack says, satisfied. 'He's nothing to be scared of,' meaning the figure on the floor. 'He's just dead.'

He goes to the ladder, starts the climb into the loft. He has to do this slowly; those ribs of his are going to be a right fucken nuisance, he can see that now. A resolution, growing from his aching ribcage to the iron of his heart: *next time, don't come in from the front.*

Up in the hayloft, all is golden calm. Motes fall through the air; twittering swallows and their tender young just the other side of the eaves. He crawls across the straw to where the pitch of the roof meets the hayloft floor and digs down. Nothing there. She must've shifted. Moves along, digs down again.

Feels a fur-sheathed ribcage. Feels the flutter of a heart.

The sound of purring fills the air.

'Time's up, Catarina,' he says, and adds, 'you little whore.'

*

In Yosha's chamber, Sant is now the one seated. Yosha, with the assistance of two crutches, is on his feet, a thing Sant has never seen before. He holds a stoneware flask of brandy, and is pouring a measure for Sant. 'You are a strange man, Captain,' Yosha says. 'You risk your ship, you risk your crew, yet when God brings you safe through the tempest, do you thank Him for your deliverance? No. What makes you angry is that you must pay for a few extra carts. And you bring this boy to us, hurt and bleeding, but it is we who make a home for him, we who take him in. You think my heart doesn't weep at this, just as much as yours?'

Sant takes a breath. *The old man's calmer now*, he thinks. This is his chance. 'You are a rich man,' he begins. 'There are people you can go to. You tell them that squinny-faced bugger broke into your house, you tell them that—'

'I am a Jew,' Yosha says, leaning on his crutches. 'I am a Jew, and a law has been broken. A man is dead. That is all anyone will care about, believe you me. Listen, Sant. You know what differ-ence there is between these kind, well-ordered souls we see every day in this nice, well-ordered city, and the bastards who did this –' (a hand sweeps across the crutches) '– to me? One bad winter. A penny on the price of bread. And I got all my people here to think of. Everyone under this roof. Zoot, to think of; Cornelius. I can go to no-one. You and I are on our own.'

'No-one is going to take the part of some poxy little house-breaker against you,' says Sant, trying again.

'And no-one is going to take the part of a little dock-rat either,' Yosha counters. 'You think of that? You think what will happen to the boy? Flogged and branded, into prison till he's twenty. In with all the other little wretches. Right back at the bottom of the pile. You want that?'

Sant rubs a hand across his face. 'What do we do?'

'I have a friend,' Yosha says. 'Runs a school. He has a friend. Runs another. In Haarlem.'

A creak from the floor above his head, from his son's bedroom. Yosha pauses for a moment, then continues at a somewhat lower pitch: 'We send the boy there. He will be safe. No-one will know.'

'But he's just a lad!' cries Sant – one last, despairing, throw.

Yosha shakes his head. 'No. He is a little killer, Sant. And one day soon he will be big.'

It is not Zoot's responsibility to clean the windows in Yosha Silbergeld's fine house, but here she is, nonetheless, polishing the already spotless panes in the hallway with a handful of linen scrim. Not nine in the morning, yet she feels as if this day has already lasted weeks. Her son has taken refuge in her bed and is refusing to come out, and no-one has even had breakfast yet, a meal which by rights should have been cleared away hours ago. And Yosha and Captain Sant, still with the door closed, although their voices have been so loud the whole house must have heard them. *Chaos*, she thinks, *is come again*, and as one hand scrubs at an innocent flaw in the glass, the other dashes away an angry tear.

There's a creak from the stairs. She turns, and there's the boy, looking as surprised to find her here as she is herself. 'Jack?' she asks. 'What are you doing?'

'Heading for Haarlem,' he replies. 'Ain't that the plan?'

She sees the bundle in his hand. Oh, for goodness' sake! thinks Zoot. Surely he can't believe that they would turn him out upon the world alone. The remorse of children – one extreme to the other. 'But not like this! Not on your own!' She tries to take the bundle from him. 'Come with me, come downstairs. We will have breakfast, we will get you ready; we will find someone you can travel with, Paul, or – or the wine-man—'

Very gently, the boy removes the bundle from her grasp. 'Yosha's sorted it,' he says. 'The carrier's on his way, I'm to meet him at the corner.' And adds, as if to reassure her, 'Don't worry. I do best on my own.'

Zoot is nonplussed. She finds herself starting to argue: 'But how – but he' – could she have missed the arrival of a messenger? How has this been arranged? 'He will want to send money with you, clothes—'

'Yeah, it's all fixed,' says the boy. 'He's sending them on after. Stupid to travel with that stuff.' A smile of reassurance. His tone implies that really, this is very simple. What is it here she finds so hard to understand?

'But don't you –' Zoot begins, 'don't you want to say goodbye?'

He makes a face. 'Better not,' he says. Then his expression brightens. 'You tell them goodbye for me.'

'But Jack!' Her hand is on his arm.

'*What?*' he asks – fond, exasperated. 'Look,' he says, smiling, 'if I'm going, you've got to let me go.' And then he leans forward, puts his hand behind her, to her waist, and kisses her. Not on the cheek or the forehead, but properly, full on the lips.

Her first instinct is to put her hand across her mouth, as if protecting it. She finds herself staring at him, as if for explanation. 'Jack,' she says. And then, almost tearfully, 'What was it, happened to you? What has made you like this?'

It's as if what lives inside him is looking back at her for the very first time. 'Don't hate me,' he says. Then he hefts the bundle to his shoulder, twists the handle on the grand front door, opens it to the sunlight and is gone.

And she is still standing there, tears pouring down her face, when Sant comes down the stairs behind her. 'Ach, lassie,' Sant exclaims, seeing her distress. 'Ah, my puir wee dove!' *Never*, he thinks, *never has there been a woman as good, as kind as this.* 'It's no' the end of the world! We'll work it out, even if he has to go away—'

'He is gone,' says Zoot.

'Who is gone?' Sant asks, thinking *Paul? The goniff?* Now
that would be a turn-up for the books. 'Who is gone, eh?'

'Jack,' she says. 'He is gone.' Then she twists her head into
his shoulder and is weeping in his arms. Sant is too astounded
at this miracle for her words to have any meaning whatsoever.

'What d'you say?'

At that moment, from high above their heads, there comes a
wailing cry. Cornelius has returned to his room.

Sant is up the stairs a pair at a time, but Zoot, recognizing
her son's voice in that wail of disbelief, is faster, and first at the
door. Over her shoulder Sant sees Cornelius turn from the bed,
and hurl himself at his mother, shrieking, 'He found her! He
found her!'

Catarina lies upon the counterpane. Her claws knead the
quilt; the sound of her purring fills the room.

And at her belly, four blind kittens are lined up, pulling at
her teats: one grey and white, one white and grey, one every
colour that a cat can be, and one with an auburn tail.

At the point where the Prinsengracht meets the old river Amstel
there's a bridge, and at the bridge Jack pauses; drops his bundle
to the ground. *Haarlem*, he thinks. That little brown dot on the
map on the classroom wall. A backwater; a flea bite. Sod that.

So if not Haarlem, where?

He thinks of the map again, the flow of it, the spread of
lands, more of the world than anyone could need. Which way,
though? Left or right?

He takes Zoot's purse from his pocket, flips a coin in the air,
and catches it flat on the back of the other hand.

So that's that sorted.

By the foot of the bridge there's a beggar-woman sat upon
the ground. Her mouth is wrinkled as an old potato, and her
eyes sag at the tear-ducts and are garnet-red around the rims.
Nonetheless, she saw the coin. She holds a whining dog with

liver-spotted ears on a striped apron on her lap. Her hands are hooked and fused like the beaks of two birds of prey.

He throws the coin into the apron, where the dog goes snuffling after it as if it might be good to eat. 'It's a good day,' he tells her. Lifts the bundle back onto his shoulder, starts to walk.

CHAPTER FOUR

A Stranger, Unknown

Of Scouts, or Discoverers:

'They that shall be employed in this service must be choice men, valiant, vigilant and discreet: such as neither fear nor misconceit can easily distract.'

John Cruso, *Militarie Instructions for the Cavallrie*

JEAN FISKARDO'S HORSE. She'd been the subject of some merriment for Balthasar, back in the day, with her splashy markings and portly gait, more befitting a gypsy's pony than the mount for a cavalryman. In fact he'd never been sure that wasn't where Jean found her, grazing by some Roma camp. Now he comes down into the village, where it hides in its fold in the fields, and there she is. The half-timbered backs of the first of the houses, the skeleton of an ancient barn, and lying in its shade, surrounded by a flock of chickens all scratching dirt over themselves, that's her. He's so astonished that he speaks her name – 'Lucette!' – and at once she lifts her head and rises to her feet, scattering hens in all directions. Back in the day, Balthasar's eerie prowess as a scout had earned him the nickname of 'The Shadow Man'. Now, it seems, he can't even creep up on a horse.

He dismounts at the gate to her paddock, leans over the wall, wary of the flourishing crop of robust Picardy nettles, and Lucette comes up to him as friendly as a dog, just as she had always been. To see her; to pat her dusty hide; it's almost as if Jean himself might reappear, round the corner of that barn perhaps, grinning his mighty grin: *You thought me dead and gone?*

But no. The man is lost, of that there is no doubt. There had been a night, one amongst many in the Hôtel-Dieu in Beaune, greasy with fever, heaving every other moment with the cough in this new and jagged incarnation, his pen skipping and stuttering over the lines of the letter sent with such desperation to Sally –

> *…Please, ma belle, if he is with you, have him send me a word.*
> *I am bewildered that he has still not joined me here, and fearful*
> *there has been some rupture in our plans and that he might*
> *have come to harm.*

– until from one moment to the next Balthasar had understood with complete certainty that he would never lay eyes on Jean again, as immutable a difference in the world as if the other had appeared at the foot of his bed, declaring, 'Well, old friend, they've done for me.' This tiny village – this might be the last place Jean Fiskardo ever saw. He looks up, at some sound almost too small to register as such, and there in the haze of summer heat there is indeed a figure approaching around the corner of the barn, white and shimmering. He lowers his head, blinking, and when he raises it again the figure resolves itself – much too small for Jean, and the white only its apron, and a frilled and cowl-like

cap such as the women wear hereabouts. The girl holds a basket
on her arm, filled with cabbage leaves. Lucette gives a whinny of
welcome. The chickens gather, interrogative, round the girl's feet.
Balthasar is about to greet her – something passive, unalarming;
he is merely a weary traveller, here by simple chance – when he
sees her register him stood there with Lucette, and hesitating,
run her fingers round her face, against the frame of her cap, as if
clearing her hair. Then she walks straight up to him.

'I knew some'un 'ud come,' she says.

She unloops the rope from the top of the gate and has him
lead his horse into the barn, where she leaves him, wheezing
in the musty scent of a hundred old harvests, while outside
chickens fluff and cluck and Jean Fiskardo's horse crunches her
way through her breakfast. From somewhere close by comes
the sound of sawing, and a raucous whistled song. When she
returns, she's carrying a jug of cider and a beaker made of horn.
He's not drunk from such a thing since childhood. As he drinks,
the song breaks in on them again. 'Who's that?' he asks.

'Robert. My brother.'

The resignation in her voice prompts him to ask another
question. 'He wouldn't like my being here?'

'He wun't. He always said this was the worst kind of trouble,
for folk like us to find ourselves in. Said if anyone ever came
asking questions, we mustn't tell 'em nothing. I always said as
that was wrong. What if the man had friends, fretting for him?
What if he had family?'

She is holding something out to him, wrapped in a fold of
cloth and tied with a bow of tape.

'What's this?'

'It's all we have left of him. The man who died here.'

She watches as Balthasar unfolds it. His hands, he thinks,
move as if underwater, against some invisible force. Inside
the cloth, there is a scrap of paper. He unfolds it, attempts to

smooth it out. The ink is fading, the paper soft. In a little while it might be gone altogether. 'Did you read it?' he asks.

'I don't have reading.' She watches him, anxious and intent. Beneath her cap her shaded face is a white tulip, pale and perfect. 'Who was he?' she asks.

'He was my friend. And he did have family.' The paper trembles, the words shift and run. With an effort he stills himself to read them, but only the lines on either side the fold are still legible.

... St-Étienne-des-Champs, on the road from Laon, before the end of the month. And on the next line: *You will find there is great value to your silence.*

And no doubt to somebody there was. For the thousandth time he asks himself: Jean, what in God's name were you at? It makes no sense – Jean Fiskardo was never the plotter, never a man of guile; he had no need to be. You did what he wanted you to do, or you made your explanation to his fists. The memory of Jean, of his stride, that made candles rock in their sticks, of him a-roar with laughter, is suddenly so vivid, Balthasar feels his eyes begin to fill. The girl, watching him, breaks in gently with 'Was you to meet him here? With them other two?'

He clears his throat. 'We were to meet, yes, but our rendez-vous was meant to be at Beaune. Not here.'

He turns the letter over. The calligraphy outside and in, what little of it remains, is both expert and anonymous – a profes-sional scribe, no doubt; and then he sees, where the edge of the paper had been folded, a pinkish discolouration, like the kiss of a woman's carmined mouth. He rubs his thumb across it. The edge of the paper is torn. A tiny thread of silk, still adhering.

'There was a seal here.'

'There was.' She's nodding. 'Your friend, he held it to a candle. Melted it.'

He touches the mark again, as if touching it could make it give up its secrets. 'Did you see it? Did you see what it was?'

She nods again. 'It looked like a beehive.'

'A beehive?'

'A beehive with ribbons.' Gently still, she touches his arm. 'Do you want to see where he's laid?'

She leads him and his horse to the church via the field-side of the hedgerows. The notion that she is keeping him secret is unmistakable – even her walk is surreptitious, and there is much spying round corners before she lets them walk on. She'd make a good little scout herself, this one. But the hedges are so heavy with leaf no-one could see through them, and the sun, coming up to its zenith, has laid a spell of quiet over everything. The only thing moving is a skylark, which travels with them, tirelessly stitching earth to sky. At last he is standing with that steeple pointing up over his head, in a churchyard lush with summer green, the grass polka-dotted with clover and daisies, dizzy with bees. Balthasar's horse, feeling the grass around its hooves, lowers its muzzle with a groan.

Beside him the girl bobs a sudden little curtsey, from the path.

'My mum and dad,' she says, a trifle self-consciously, then, pointing, 'my grandmother, she's over there,' as if she were making introductions.

It's then he starts to wonder about her age. The cap hides her hair and shades her face, but she might almost be no older than Jean's lost and orphaned boy. God a'mighty, wonders Balthasar, how much guilt can one heart hold? But already she is directing him away from the sunlit open side of the churchyard to where the turf is rougher, darker, the sunlight not yet spilling down. The abode of strangers, the unloved and unclaimed. 'There,' she says, pointing.

A lozenge of green, raised above the grass around it. At the far end a board, roughly shaped (he thinks at once of the whistler, with his saw), sunk on end and lettered with the words

UN ÉTRANGER
INCONNU

So this is what it came down to. All that strength of arm; the ambition and the passion too; this. Here's the great mystery, as unreachable as ever – feeding worms and making nectar for the bees.

The girl is watching him. He feels her eyes upon him, his working mouth, the involuntary reaching out of his hands. If he were on his own here, he would be on his knees.

'It was done proper,' she assures him. 'He was wrapped in woollen and the priest was there. It was done right.'

'I know,' he says. 'I'm sure,' although of course he doesn't know, how could he? He wipes his cheek, presses his fingers to the bridge of his nose. He wants to describe Jean to her, to ask her in turn what she had made of him. Instead he asks, 'How did he die?'

'We don't know,' she says. She looks miserable.

'But you said there were two – two others. Did they ambush him?' If so, by God, they were lucky. Four, in an ambush with Jean, and you'd get your man, but for him to fall to only two—

'No,' she says. She looks amazed. 'No, there was nothing like that. Grand-mère, she laid him out, she said there was not a mark on him. It made her weep, she said, he was so fine a figure of a man.' She glances at him. 'We should have took more note. I know we should have done.' And then she kneels and starts to clear the weeds from round that lettered board. 'What was his name?' she asks.

'His name?'

'Your friend.'

'Jean,' he tells her. He wipes his cheek again. 'Jean Fiskardo.'

She lays her hand upon the board's top edge. 'We should put that here.'

He shakes his head, holds out his hand to help her to her feet. 'Keep it as our secret. Better you leave that as it is.'

She peers at him. That's not how it should be, she's thinking, he can tell. Her eyebrows have flown together in a frown. 'Tell me of those two men,' he says.

'They were here first,' she replies. 'They'd no good writ all over them. Sat about the place, like they was waiting, then right after your friend arrived, one of them was gone. I was glad to see the back of him. We'd a stable-boy that year, and our boy he said as he wouldn't stay under the same roof. And then my brother found the man heading for the attics.' Her face has hardened.

'The attics?'

'Our rooms is up there.' She gives a snort. 'Looking to steal.'

The attics. Maybe a thief, but equally, perhaps, the man had been looking for a vantage point, somewhere he could see but not be seen. So someone who knew Jean by sight...? 'Did he have a name?'

'Oh yes. Enric Maduna.' She pulls out the last syllable: *Madooona*. 'Like the Holy Virgin, he kept saying, then he'd laugh. He was a pig. He walked like this.' She stands and stomps away from him, swinging her legs one about the other, like a heavy chair being walked across the ground. A little mimic as well as a scout, this one: head rolled down into her shoulders and as she turns to face him, jaw thrust out. Who the hell was this? *And all while you should have been safe in Beaune with me. Jean, what were you doing here?*

'The devil knows where he come from, but I hope he's back there. The other, he was just – odd.'

'In what way, odd?'

'He was like a nothing,' she says. 'Not big, not loud, not swaggering. But there was something – and his clothes. His clothes were odd.' She considers a moment. 'He didn't have a proper collar to his shirt, just this bit of red cloth round his neck. And he kept his gloves on inside. I thought as maybe he'd been ill, and was a pilgrim – he'd a little token here, like pilgrims do, upon his coat –' and her hand touches above her left breast. 'He had a bottle with your friend – our best, I took it to him. They was just talking, that was all.' She moves her hand to her forehead, as if refreshing the memory. Beyond the churchyard a voice calls out, 'Mirelle? Mirelle?' and then the sound of a gate.

Her eyes dart behind him. The brother, undoubtedly. 'Mirelle!' the voice calls again. 'Where you got to, girl?'

Her words come faster. 'When he left, it looked like your friend had fallen asleep. He had his arm like this upon the table.' Up goes her forearm, pillowing her brow. 'And his head upon it. My brother said a fit, an apoplexy, but it was more than that, we knew.'

He asks, 'Will you be in trouble, for this?'

Her brave smile says *yes*. 'I'll say I came to talk with Grand-mère, I often do. But it ain't right, is it? Two men sit down together, and only one gets up – that shouldn't happen.'

No, he thinks. No, it should not. All as wrong as wrong could be. What they had done, he and Jean – what he had helped to plan, and Jean to execute – had seemed so simple, so straightforward: the excision of a cyst, a pustule, that was all, the removal from the world of one single human soul; but now he asks himself, *what were we part of?* 'This second man,' he asks quickly. 'Did he give a name too?'

'Not a proper one. He thought we was these stupid country-folk, so he gave us only this stupid name.'

'What was it?'

'A stupid nickname. Charles the Ghost.' She is pushing him toward his horse. 'You've got to go.'

... so as I write, here in Laon, that's what we have, and that's all that we have, aside from the grave where Jean lies in his long rest. Two men, and a beehive with ribbons.

As I read it, this Maduna was there to pick him out, but who the man might be is a mystery. How would he know Jean, yet I not know of him?

As for the other, the way the girl describes him – and she had sharp eyes and a good memory, that little one – with the red kerchief about his neck, he's a Croat. So hired for this, and if he was, I see his hand, may it rot, in what was done in Belle-Dame too.

Tilly has Croats in his army in Germany. I can't think of any better maelstrom for two such hagfish to swim in, so that's where I'll be too. Write to me at Forbach, should you hear anything more. The brothers there keep my letters for me.

This being a posting inn there is a taper and a stick of sealing wax upon the table where he writes. Balthasar folds his letter, tucking one edge under the rest, scribes upon the front

SIG. TINO RAVELLO
By hand to THE CARPENTER'S HAT
ABOVE ANNECY, SAVOY

He holds the wax into the flame, watches it drop onto the fold, then seals it with his thumbprint. Sits there some more, in contemplation. The letter will pass from hand to hand until it finds Ravello, back at the Carpenter's Hat, maybe, or some place even further off than that, if Ravello has left word where he'll be – a month, two months of travelling, maybe more. Ravello will have to pay to receive it, is how the posts work, so if it fails to find him, it will have no further life at all. Balthasar's thumbprint won't so much keep its contents safe as keep them mute.

Still he sits there, thinking. A beehive with ribbons... he can feel the answer waiting, an inch below the horizon of his memory. *I know I've seen that.* He tips his head forward, as if that will tumble the memory to the front. Whose crest was it? What name would have been enough to lure Jean to that tiny village, to lure him there in secrecy, to make him trust those promises of value in his silence?

You know, they had a priest to bury you. I'd love to have seen your face. Sometimes, even now, it's as if he still has Jean before him, face creased with laughter, roaring with delight at all the idiocies of the world.

He sighs, get to his feet, a hand against the place under his ribs where, ever since Beaune, his disease has smouldered within him.

Germany. Very well.

CHAPTER FIVE

Travellers

'My poor Heidelberg is gone!'

Frederick of Bohemia, the 'Winter King'

NOW, WE ARE going to make a map. In your imagination spread out a sheet of the best-quality paper you can come up with: watermarked across its width, thinning at the edges where the pulp ran out, and backed onto linen to make it last, because paper, don't forget, is expensive stuff. Our subject is Europa, and since we, and Time, and that troubled boy must all meet up again, we will set it forward: Year of our Lord 1622; and month of that year, September.

Firstly, such a map will need a frame. Scrolls and strapwork, fictive shading, flourishes and twirlicues. This is, after all, the age of the Baroque. Puff-cheeked zephyrs lean from the corners; there may even be the odd wafting cupid, fat as a little cloud. Hercules with club, perhaps, to stand for man's conquest of all the wonders of the world; Fortuna with her riches spilling from the cornucopia she carries in her arms. Out in the seas high-prowed galleons, the *Guid Marie* no doubt amongst them, share the waves with muscled mermen, spouting whales.

Time for some geography. This Europe is a little different to the one you know. Holland, for example, comes in two parts – the United Provinces on the top, home to Yosha Silbergeld; and the Spanish Netherlands hanging beneath them, home to many thousand Habsburg troops, which makes for challenging neighbourly relations, let us say. France is pretty much as you would know it now, but Germany, as Germany, simply doesn't exist. Germany is Mecklenburg, it's Brandenburg, it's Saxony. It's Bavaria. It's the Palatinates, Upper and Lower (ancestral homelands, remember, of handsome but unlucky Fred). It's Hesse, Brunswick, Westphalia; any number of separate duke-doms, fiefs and principalities, half of them Catholic, half of them not, all tied together in a network of mistrusts and rival-ries as delicately poised, as complex as an orrery, and every bit as prone to tilting out of balance. Over the Alps, Italy is another patchwork, just the same – Savoy, Venice, Genoa, Florence, the Papal States – a separate little kingdom each, changeable as chameleons. There are but two unaltering verities in Europe – Habsburg Austria and Habsburg Spain – and they have the rest of the continent pinned between them.

That's enough geography for now. Here's where the real work begins. You have to populate that map and make it live. Here we go: over those whispering forests – did you ever think Europe had so many trees? Over her lakes and rivers, thronged with craft – more like roads, the rivers are, thick with traffic; and did you ever think the roads could be so few, either? And how small they look, and how vulnerable, like threads! And each town a tiny nebula, marooned in space, and each, from up here, as pointy with spires as a pincushion is with pins. So many churches for just one God... although of course quite whose God he is, Catholic or Protestant, is a ticklish question and accounts for the trails of smoke blowing about up here. There's Bohemia, still smouldering away; there's the Palatinate, the army of General Tilly stomping through its valleys; there's Christian of Brunswick and his men, laying waste to all about them; in France there's those Huguenot heretics, embattled as ever; and way, way to the north there's beautiful Riga, Swedish soldiers in its streets – and who even knew the Swedish *had* an army, God above?

Time to get out of this. Come down to this unregarded little corner here. This is peaceful enough, is it not? What a wide road – how unlike most of them. How astonishingly deep in mud. And how empty – nothing on it but that solitary horse and cart. And what a sorry-looking horse. Skin draped over sticks. And what a comical expression on the carter's face, too.

This is the Bergstrasse, south-west Germany, the road from Darmstadt to Heidelberg, a trade route for centuries. And the carter, his name is Walther Kleber, and the dismay upon his face is because he'd taken one look at the state of that road, and known that here – *shit and God-damn* – here, he had a problem.

It started with that, really, one simple fact: a man can't push his cart and drive it all at once. *Shit and God-damn*, thought Kleber, glaring at the road – its broken banks and the puddles in the ruts, reflecting the grey of the sky. What did this? Were they driving elephants to market in Heidelberg now?

Never known an autumn like it. Day after day, the air as wet as in a wash-house. And cold... he'd stood there, had Kleber, blowing on his fingers, when to add to his woes his horse had begun its cat-like retching and drooling again. Here was another thing – horses. Nothing to 'em these days, didn't last a year. Which was what put the notion into his head – Hartmann's. Hartmann the horse-dealer. Hartmann could loan him a horse, and what with Hartmann's being just about the last stop on the road before the long stretch down to Heidelberg itself, there was often the odd lone traveller waiting there, anxious for a ride.

He'd clambered back aboard, lifted his whip. The horse shook its head; the strings of drool went flying. Hartmann's. A new beast; an extra pair of hands. Him to drive, the extra pair of hands to help push the cart through the mud. Two birds with one stone. Genius.

THE FIRST HINT he had that the day was going to take some unplanned course of its own came when he saw Hartmann's flag. Phoebus in his chariot was Hartmann's sign, flown from the pole atop his roof, but as it came in view, it seemed to Kleber that some joker had hung the flag at half-mast. Also, in the fields beyond Hartmann's, shouldn't there have been horses grazing? Instead, the fields were empty.

He brought the cart into Hartmann's yard, a flock of geese honking their outrage ahead of its wheels and a sour sense of foreboding already curdling his guts. His scabby old hound, waking at the noise, came up to the front of the cart, whining interest. Kleber cuffed it into silence, then stood on the seat with the reins in his hands.

'Hartmann!'

No answer. The bad feeling took the chance to improve its grip. The only things moving in the yard were the geese; the rest of the place – the barn, Hartmann's low, squat house, discoloured as a puffball – appeared to be deserted. What's more, there were a couple of window panes knocked in on the ground floor, and a dent in the wall by the door, missing a plate-sized chunk of yellowing plaster, like someone had hit it with a mallet.

Oleg, Hartmann's odd-job-man, crossing the yard before him. 'Hoi there! Oleg! Hey!'

Oleg came to his usual shambling halt, and glared at Kleber suspiciously. A gloomy, mournful soul, was Oleg. Everything about him drooped – hair, clothes, arms – and the man could be less help, for longer, than anyone Kleber knew. 'Where's Hartmann?' he demanded. You talk with the hurdy-gurdy man, not with his God-damned monkey.

'Hartmann's dead,' came the amazing reply.

Dead? Down came Kleber from the cart, at a scramble. '*Dead?* How?'

'They shot him,' said Oleg.

What? '*Shot* him? Who?'

'One o'them,' said Oleg, sagely, 'with a pistol. Came in here like they owned the place,' he continued, with a flourish of his arm; Oleg, Kleber realized, was miming the waving of just such a pistol as had apparently done for his employer. 'Told the old man they wanted his horses. Requisition, they said. Give him a receipt, they said. Old man wanted cash. Said without, they'd take his horses over his dead body. So they did,' Oleg concluded. 'Shot through the neck.' He pointed. There were dark splatters, dribbles, Kleber now saw, around the missing chunk of plaster. He felt some tube in his own neck contract in sympathy. *Ah, Christ...*

'When was this?'

Oleg scratched his head. 'Few days back. All over the place, they were. Up in the attics. Out in the barns. Helping themselves—'

'Who was it? Was it Brunswick's men?' Brunswick's army has a reputation foul as a Goth's, and, if you listened to the rumour-mongers, might be anywhere.

'No, no,' said Oleg. 'These was ours. Th'Emperor's troops.' And added, bitterly, 'Like there's a difference.'

Behind them, they heard the horse coughing.

'You're out of luck there too,' Oleg said. Describing Hartmann's death seemed to have perked him up. 'Not got but

one horse left, and it, even them locusts didn't want. But I'll
send the boy to fetch it, if you like.'

'The boy?'

'There,' said Oleg, pointing.

It was a trick of the low sun, the misty greyness of the air.
Kleber had spun about, and seen what looked for an instant like
a horseman – cloaked, be-hatted, straight in the saddle, and
the glint of a sword at his hip. He'd took a step back, startled,
shielding his eyes – and in a blink, the horseman was no more
than some boy riding Oleg's nag, bundle of palings clutched to
his side, gleaming in the wet.

A shout from Oleg. In answer, the boy turned the nag, and
slid from its back. Slouched toward them. His boots circled his
calves with every step, like the hoops of broken barrels, and his
wrists stuck out from his shirt-cuffs naked as drumsticks. Looked
like life had chewed him up and spat him out already. His first
words were 'Yeah, what?' Another Oleg in the making, clearly.

'Go fetch t'other 'orse,' said Oleg.

The boy glanced at Kleber. 'What for?' he demanded, Kleber
being clearly insufficient as a reason. He had an accent, something not quite Deutsch, and that adolescent harshness to his
voice – broken, but the pieces not yet come together in their
adult form.

'Go fetch t'other 'orse,' Oleg repeated, 'and do as told.' He
raised one heavy arm in cumbrous threat. 'You.'

They watched the boy slouch off. 'What's his story?' Kleber
asked.

'God knows, God cares,' Oleg replied, pushing open the
kitchen door. 'I'm sure I don't. You get 'em from all over,
scrapings like him. Blown on the winds. Come in the house.
Boy'll fetch t'other 'orse. Soldiers couldn't catch it, but it'll
come for him.'

*

Astounding. Here was Hartmann's kitchen, Hartmann's house... Kleber had sat here many a time, at this table, warmed by that fire. Yet no Hartmann, ever again. He didn't like to ask Oleg what had become of the body; you never knew with Oleg what might seem normal to him, left to his own devices. He could have brined Hartmann in a barrel as like as got him buried.

Oleg, at the fireplace, had lifted the lid from the pot hanging over the flames and was stirring its contents, releasing a smell of pumpkin. Last time Kleber had been here, Hartmann had a girl to cook. A washerwoman too.

'What happened to your women?'

'Run off,' Oleg replied. 'Soon as they heard the soldiers was coming. The old man, he told 'em not to be such fools. Said these was the Emperor's good Catholic soldiers, not Brunswick's Lutheran heretic bastards. Promised to buy 'em new gowns if they stayed. Said he'd make a killing, selling his horses.' Again, he brightened. 'Suppose you could say as he did.'

Kleber shook his head, slowly and sorrowfully. Inside that head, however, wheels were grinding against wheels. 'You any idea where they were headed? The soldiers?' He had an unpleas-ant suspicion he knew now what had turned the road south to Heidelberg into that morass: the passage of an army.

'Eastwards,' said Oleg. 'Sure of it, now you ask. Where you headed?'

'Heidelberg,' Kleber replied. He felt himself relax. 'Leastways, if I can find an extra pair of hands to help get me through the mud.'

Oleg looked up. 'Want to take the boy with you? He's working his way, he says.'

Kleber sat forward. 'Is he indeed?' He rubbed his chin. 'What's he work for?'

'Food,' Oleg replied, with a stir of the pot. 'Walked in here coupla days ago, said he'd work for a meal an' a bed. Mind, he's handier than most. Ask him,' said Oleg, spoon in hand, moving to the door. 'Here he is. Horse, too.'

A joke, had been Kleber's first reaction. It had to be a joke. '*This* is your other horse? This is it?'

'That's it.'

Kleber took a circuit round the thing. Hard to think what else to do. The horse just stood there. Once or twice it shook the bison-like mop of curls covering its face, snuffed at the boy's fingers, blew a single energetic snort. 'The fuck is it?' Kleber demanded. 'Half-bear?'

'It's got a bit of winter-wool, grant you,' Oleg had begun.

'A *bit*?'

'But it's strong, and it can shift. More'n I could say for yours,' said Oleg, pointing to where Kleber's horse sagged, drooling anew, between the poles of the cart. 'That and the boy, see you down to Heidelberg, easy.' He lifted his voice. 'Eh, *Junge*! Want a ride with Herr Kleber?'

The boy. Another unknown. His head had come up at Oleg's words; now he regarded Kleber as if measuring him up. 'Where to?'

'Heidelberg. You want a ride, I need a pair of hands to push. What d'you say?'

The boy looked over at the cart. 'What you carrying?' That accent again.

'Paper,' Kleber replied. And in case that might seem somehow paltry, added 'Homburg-made, one-hundred-eighty reams of it. Paper for all them learned souls a-studying away at the university in Heidelberg. Ten florins a ream that 'ud cost you. You want the ride or not?'

'I'll take it,' said the boy.

'And you'd best be handy, mark you.' He rolled up a shirt-sleeve, bared his bicep. 'Better have something here. There's mud on that road could suck the nails out your boots. Understand?'

'Understand.'

Kleber, eyeing the boy, felt his doubts hang in mid-air. He tapped his belt. 'And any funny business, you remember, I've a knife.'

The boy regarded him a moment. Eyes pale as the reflection in a puddle. A glint to them; ice on the road. Lifting aside the edge of his jacket, he displayed the knife at his own belt. 'So have I,' he said.

Not another Oleg. Not at all.

SO NOW HERE'S Walther Kleber in his cart, pulled gamely on by that ridiculous-looking horse, through mud as deep as earth turned by a plough. Stealthy as he can, he steals a glance behind him, out the corner of one eye. *If he moves up on me,* Kleber tells himself, *dog'll let me know.* But Kleber's scabby old hound, which doesn't have a name at all, and which had bared its teeth at the boy when first he climbed into the cart, now lies with its head upon the boy's mud-spattered legs, whuffing gently in its sleep.

Shit and God-damn...

How did he get himself into this? A glare at the horse, at the rug of hair across its back, a flick of the whip as it strains against the harness. A sucking sound and they jolt forward. And now the sun is lower, too. Will they make it to Heidelberg before dark? Kleber raises the flask to his lips again. The road is rounding a corner, and it seems to Kleber as he peers ahead that there's something in the way up there, something with human movement to it, irregularity. Suddenly the boy is right beside him. 'What is it?' he asks.

'Soldiers,' says Kleber. To his own amazement, he doesn't even sound surprised. 'Soldiers. Oleg, you fucker. Eastwards my arse.'

There down the road is the turnpike, volumes of smoke from its chimney, and a milling crowd, a whole day's worth of traffic, by the looks of it: drovers, farm-boys, travellers and wanderers; and barring the way to them all, a line of infantrymen across the road, stood there, arms folded. Up on the bank, a group of musketeers, taking turns lighting their pipes with a length of smoking match-cord. A gang of pikemen, sat upon the ground, hunched in their armour like snails, pikes laid beside them on the grass. Another group at the foot of a tree, deep in what looks like a game of cards, a further crowd of their brothers-in-arms stood round them, watching, because soldiers out the field will happily watch anything.

'Who are they?' asks the boy.

'How the hell should I know?' snarls Kleber, throwing down the reins. More soldiers have appeared from inside the turn-pike-keeper's house, staggering from the doorway, and seem to be celebrating, sloshing tankards. The crowd, more wary of these, moves back. 'Got armies crawling all over this country like maggots on a dead cat,' Kleber declares. 'Shit and God-damn.' Whistling up the dog, he starts off across the road. 'I'll find out what's doing. You stay there, you,' he orders, pointing at the boy – Walther Kleber, who, like all of us, believes his own life is the central drama of the world and who, like all of us, is wrong. 'And keep an eye on the horse, understand? Don't let none o'them misbegot thieving centurions near it.' A final shot: 'And keep yer muddy boots off the stock!'

The dog, shaking itself, jumps down and follows after. The boy watches them go. 'The name's Jack,' he says softly, under his breath.

THE ROAD HERE is so ancient that it's sunk between its banks; the trees meet overhead and throw a lattice-work of shadows underfoot, and as these shadows thicken, the crowd at the turnpike gives up all thought of getting any further on today, and begins staking claims to little portions of ground – laying down a cloak, perhaps; nursing a fractious child. Swaying through the crowd go the skirts of a pair of drabs, one wearing red and one wearing blue. There goes Red Skirt now, swinging her hips... and there's old Kleber, looping an arm about her waist, dipping his head to hers. Out comes the flask. In the moment before she takes the drink, Red Skirt shoots a glance at Blue, one of those unfathomable female looks, full of understanding and intent. But not one in that little trio seems to feel Jack's eyes upon them; he might not be there at all. The whole world feels closed off to him. What is he? He's this thing that sleeps under hedges, drinks from streams, takes shelter from winter storms in barns. Waits shivering at wooden jetties at dawn, ready to barter a day's labour for a day's food. Robs henhouses. Out-runs farmers' dogs. Zoot, he thinks, would turn her head if she should see him now. All these months of tramping, tramping, tramping, and all he's done, while his legs have pushed him further and further on, is make the same baffling circle in his thoughts: *What am I doing? What do I want?*

Don't fucken know!

The travellers, settling themselves for a night in the open, are being treated to a show. A squeal of dismay, and two figures emerge from the crowd; one very large, one small. The larger – bald, in fact entirely hairless-looking, and with a sort of doleful blankness to him – has his hands raised over his pate, as if to protect it, even though it is well out of reach of the smaller, who is now swatting him with its hat. 'What did I say?' the smaller figure demands, in its Rumpelstiltskin-size rage. 'I said hand it over gentle-like. And what do you do? You mash it in them damned great mitts of yours!'

The larger figure opens its hands. Egg and eggshell go sliding down its face. Laughter from the crowd. The smaller figure, spinning round, addresses its audience directly. 'Here it is, friends, here it is. I take this helpless soul under my wing –' more laughter as he attempts to reach an arm round his companion's shoulders '– and what do I get for my pains? An empty belly, friends. An empty belly.' The hat is proffered forward, as if its emptiness bears out the words. 'Now God knows, I don't ask much of life. I give, is what I do. Like to this poor goon here. But here I had an egg for my supper, and now I must go hungry. And without your charity, good souls, not only shall I famish, but so shall the poor goon. Look at him.'

The goon has a face as blank as a plate, and every bit as round. Overgrown, over-plump and over-pale, a vast Humpty-Dumpty of a man, who stands there while the hat performs its circle of the crowd. 'Can any of you spare aught for my poor goon? That's it, good souls, God sees, God blesses you. Anything at all. Thank you, *meine Dame*. No, no, bless *you* –'

And while this pantomime is acted out, two soldiers stagger up to the cart. "Ow much?' one asks, nodding toward the horse.

Jack tries to remember the German for *the horse ain't mine*, or *not for sale*, but the words won't come. He'd been building up a German dictionary in his head, going at it as a proper study, but now all the words seem to have fallen away, as if they are as weary as he. He's just too tired to care – too cold, too tired, too hungry. Even the sight of that egg had set his stomach groaning; so entirely empty that he can feel its sides pressing in on each other like an exhausted pair of bellows.

"Ow much?' the man demands again.

'Oh, piss off,' says Jack.

The pair survey him for a moment, blinking, holding each other up. Then one gives a shrug, and miraculously they veer away, back into the crowd.

He waits to be sure they're gone, then gets down, unhitches the horse and leads it in a good wide arc round the back of the turnpike, into the trees. Wiser to be off this road altogether. Somewhere inside the building, someone is playing a guitar.

Snatches of chorus boom out – something about someone getting roasted, or baked –

'Die Brunswieker, die Brunswieker, er sagt es ist zu heiß –'

The Brunswicker, the Brunswicker, he says it is too hot –

Brunswick baked ham. Hah hah hah. Jack finds he's smiling – muscles he hasn't used in weeks.

So Brunswick's the enemy, is it? So who are this lot, then?

He walks the horse until the noise from the turnpike is less than the silence of the woods and ties it to a tree. 'I'll come back,' he tells it, patting its felted flank. The horse shakes its ears the once, stoical as ever.

Working his way to the front of the building, he finds a place by its open door, and sits there, listening. In the riot of voices coming from inside he picks out the word 'Heidelberg', and then again and then again. Then a man rolls around the door and sits down almost on top of him.

A growl of warning. Jack mimes an apology, but the man has already lost interest. Slumping down, the man takes off his hat, revealing an impressive gash on his forehead, pulls off his gauntlets and starts arranging bread, sausage, cheese on a plate on his lap. Jack's stomach groans again. The man gives him an unfriendly glance. Jack moves away. The man gives one arm a good scratch, then the other, then his belly, as if limbering up all three, but as he makes to fall to, it seems his appetite deserts him. His face turns grey.

'Junge!' The man holds out the plate. 'Yeah, young'un, you. Here. Fill yer boots.'

Jack doesn't need asking twice. *'Danke. Dankeschön.'* It's as much as he can do not to lift the plate and tip everything on it into his mouth at once.

The bread is dry, the cheese like candle-wax, the sausage mostly gobs of fat. It's delicious. It's manna. Swallowing it down, it occurs to him that maybe there's a chance here for some information, too. Wording the question carefully in his head before he speaks, he asks, politely as he can, '*Entschuldigung* – we're near to Heidelberg?'

The man, who had slumped forward, comes to, with something of a start. He turns his face, now damp with sweat. 'That we are,' he says, slowly.

'There's fighting there?'

The man closes his eyes. 'Not no more there ain't.'

'So who won?' asks Jack.

'We did,' the man says, wearily, leaning back. 'The army of his Imperial Catholic Majesty Ferdinand the frigging Second.' Reaching for his hat, the man positions it over his eyes. 'Fuck off now, kid, eh?'

Stomach packed with sausage, bread and cheese, Jack sits with the wall of the house at his back and the setting sun warming his face. A fiddler – there's always a fiddler, any crowd – has struck up a tune and one of the soldiers, with the costive concentration of the truly drunk, has begun a laboured capering. The man has a three-legged cooking pot upon his head, and wound about him, like a toga, what appears to be a bedsheet. Squatting down at the side of the road, another group tips out the contents of a sack. Tumbling across the ground go candlesticks, a beaker enamelled green and blue, a silver bowl, a string of beads, a bag of coin. A scrabble over this, until the biggest man in the group brings his fist down on it, with an oath, at which his fellows lean away and start meekly drawing lots. Dividing up their loot, thinks Jack, realizing what he's seeing. In the time it took to hide the horse, the number of soldiers at the turnpike has doubled. It's strange, but being part of this (the noise, the crowd, the fiddler's music), it doesn't seem alarming. It makes him feel –

What? Happy? Safe? At home?

The blare of a cornet, and a body of horsemen breast the slope, their shapes detaching from the darkness of the road into the evening opal of the sky. Not just a cornet-player either, they've a standard-bearer with them too – the glossy shimmer of the standard like the first of the evening stars. The soldiers scattered across the road pull themselves into order, even the capering dolt with the pot on his head tries to stand straight and sober as the horsemen dismount, because there's one – and Jack finds he is himself scrambling to his feet as this one strides toward the open door – there's one with gold cord stitched down the sleeves of his coat and lace at his wrists as frothy as spindrift, and boots turned down below the knee that slap together like soft applause; and as the man enters the house the roar from inside could lift the roof off its walls.

And it comes to him, sharp and immediate as a burn: *I want that. I want that for me!*

For a little longer he sits there, because this feels like something should be sat with for a while. The answer to all those questions – surely it can't be as simple as this?

He realizes he's thirsty. He remembers there being a trough, round the back.

Finding his way to it, he stumbles across Walther Kleber, passed out snoring on the ground, and someone's turned out old Kleber's pockets too, by the looks of it. *I'll be damned*, thinks Jack. Maybe those girls weren't such sorry drabs after all; and that has him smiling anew, how even the most helpless-looking creature can surprise you, and that, of course, has him thinking *the horse*…

The wood is darker than the road, and the horse takes a little finding, a task not made easier by the fact that it's somehow contrived to tuck itself behind the tree. There are feathers scattered on the ground all round it, gleaming in the dark as pale as willow leaves, and white fluff in its matted mane. Must have been a bird's nest in the tree, thinks Jack, brushing the worst of it off, when he realizes the horse is trembling. 'Hey,' he asks it, surprised, 'what's up with you?'

In answer, the horse pushes its nose into his pocket, as if trying to hide. On the edge of Jack's vision something white-ish silently removes itself from view. An owl, he tells himself. But the back of his neck is prickling, and there, through the trees, is the yellow of a camp-fire, and the silhouettes of figures moving round it.

No-one makes camp that far back without some very good reason for hiding themselves.

'Come on,' he tells the horse, keeping his voice low. Obediently, it follows him, back to the turnpike. The camp-fire in the woods is invisible from here. He slakes his own thirst at the pump while the horse drinks from the trough. Stroking it as it drinks, the loose hairs in its coat come out in handfuls. Nice straight back, though. First time he's had a proper look at it. And good solid legs, if rather short.

The horse lifts its head. Its mane, where wet, curls up in ringlets.

'Didn't fancy helping 'emselves to you then, whoever they are?' he asks it, and even as he speaks there is again that flash of white across his vision, and a shape held trembling for a moment in the water of the trough. A face so bloodless that it gleams. Eyes so deep within the sockets you can't see if they're there at all. Something rising beside it, a bundle of twigs.

A hand.

He jumps back, holding his knife. He shouts, 'Who's there?'

No reply. Just the noise from the turnpike, just as before.

The face is still there in his head. Something had rolled in the sockets of the eyes, something as blind as a stone, and the skin had been marked in some way, all that gleaming pallor scrawled with lines of black, like it had been written on –

Something white and tiny floats down to the surface of the water in the trough.

Bird-fluff.

He gathers up the reins, grips them in tight under the horse's chin. 'You and me,' he tells it, 'are getting out of here.'

And out on the road, some new disturbance. Those travellers

dozing too close to the roadside are being kicked awake; Kleber's cart has a dozen men straining to push it against the bank. There is the sound of a bugle, thinned by distance. The horse throws up its head. Now there are men streaming from the turnpike's door, and torches being passed from hand to hand. The bugle again – clearer now, nearer now, and under its one note what sounds to Jack like nothing so much as an approaching storm. The horse is pulling at its reins. It puts up its head again, shrills a whinny into the night, and there, from the storm now thundering toward them, comes a shriek and whinny in return. There is a wind preceding this, whatever it is, leaves coming down. The wail of a child in the crowd. He can make out drumming – hooves –

– and there's a man standing in the centre of the road, reeling, weaving back and forth. It's the soldier with the gash on his forehead. His comrades, up on the bank, are yelling for him to come to them but still he stands there, arms out, like he's blind.

The noise has reached its height. It has to burst into something visible; then it does. Round the corner comes this mass of black, front edge rolling like a wave, flash of hooves, reach of leg, rolling eye, streaks of silver in the black, the jingle of harness, the harsh *Yar! Yar!* of the riders' voices, spurring their horses on. Jack looks for the injured soldier – no, he's off the road, dragged from it, two of his comrades have him in their arms – then all sight of the opposite bank is gone as this churning flood of man- and horse-flesh streams past – and more of them – and more –

Filling your ears, and the thunder of the hooves filling your breast, and your heart pounding with them –

The riders' faces, locked ahead. The horses tossing their manes. And more – and more –

And gone. Down the slope and gone. Nothing more of them than their thunder, and that, too, dying away.

In cautious ones and twos, travellers and soldiers alike step out onto the road. There's the odd sheet of paper, flapping about in the mud. Kleber's cart has lost a wheel and shed its load.

'Whew!' says a voice to his left. 'Now that was a sight to see.'

Jack turns, and there are the two from before, the blank-faced giant and his garrulous companion.

'That was a something, eh?'

Jack realizes he's spattered with mud from head to foot. 'What *were* they?' he asks.

'Croats,' the man replies. 'You can tell a'cause of the necker-chiefs. They all wear 'em.' He nods across the road, where the injured soldier's companions still hold him up. 'He was lucky,' the man continues. 'What I've heard, you do *not* want to get in their way.'

'Where were they going?' Jack asks. He feels breathless. 'Heidelberg?'

'Heidelberg?' The man smacks a knee. 'Nothing in Heidelberg now but tears and lamentations. No, Hertzberg is where they're headed.' He angles a thumb into his chest. 'Same as him and me.'

'Why? What's Hertzberg?'

'What's Hertzberg? The mustering place, that's what Hertzberg is.' More hilarity. 'You're green, ain't yer? You're so green we could feed you to a duck!'

On the other side of the road, his companions have sat the injured soldier on the ground, are fanning his face, opening his shirt.

'Eh, then,' the man says. He polishes a hand on his breeches, sticks it out. 'Peter,' he announces. 'Deaf Peter.' He makes a show of screwing a finger into one ear. 'Peter to my friends, deaf to my enemies.' He swings a leather satchel forward on his hip. 'Milit'ry courier. Third battalion, the Hohenzollern boys. That there,' Peter continues, indicating the giant, 'that's Jo-Jo. Don't mind him.' He circles the finger at his temple. 'Short of the full three minutes, if you get me. Bit soft boiled. So who are we addressing, eh?'

'Jack,' says Jack.

'Eh? Jag, did you say?'

Jack, Jacques, Jag, what's the difference? 'Jag, right.'

'Jag. Very good.' Peter casts an eye over the far side of the road where the injured man's companions have let the man fall flat and are backing away. 'So,' Peter continues, 'Jag. You do have the look of a wanderer to you, you do indeed. What can we do for you?'

Jack takes a breath. The thunder of those horses, he can feel them still.

Go on, my son.

'I'm looking to enlist.'

CHAPTER SIX

The Sentimental Lady

'First, the Emperor began a great war in Bohemia, which he overwhelmed and put under his religion, and thereafter in the following years, the lands of Brunswick, Mecklenburg, Brandenburg, Pomerania, Austria, Moravia, Silesia – yes, almost all of Germany…'

Diary of Hans Heberle, shoemaker

SHE ISN'T SENTIMENTAL, but she likes it when the same old faces come around. It's her boast that she's never forgotten a-one. A man comes through here as a raw recruit and for all the years after, if he behaved himself that first time round, is assured the same no-nonsense welcome: jug of beer, slice of salt-raised bread, chewy as the soles of his boots, and a plateful of whatever's on the spit.

This is Hertzberg. A town built on the passage of men, money, arms, which move through it all year long. Men, money, arms, and all that comes with them – freebooters and adventurers, tricksters and spies. You sit here long enough, she says, you'll see the whole world passing by. And like all such places, a lot gets lost along the way. Histories, loyalties... names, above all, which are a fluid and a changeable thing in Hertzberg, and not as they are elsewhere. Soldiers have their own brisk way with names; often the first and sometimes the only promotion to count will be when one of your fellows comes up with a nickname for you. In any case, as she's quick to point out, it ain't their names that signify, it's hers. Everyone knows hers. Fat Magda. Here they come, past Rauchmann's Brewery and over the bridge, past Hertzberg's famous mermaid clock, turn down the third street on the left and look for the door with the barrel swinging above it, painted with a woman's smiling face. "*Tag*, Frau Magda,' they call out, as they tramp in off the street: the great, the small, the new, the old, the few – the very few, these days – who remember Fat Magda's when it was a kitchen and a window; not half the length of the street, as it is now. In they come. "*Tag*, Frau Magda. How's life been treating you?'

None too badly, thank you.

Good fortune. It gives you something to lose.

So she goes to Mass, she says her prayers... clears her throat if she hears thunder, checks if the cat is sitting on its tail, never sleeps on her left (the Devil will come and sleep on your right), never goes to bed with the table uncleared (devils again – they come and feast), never mends clothes till they're off the wearer (or you'll stitch their shroud), turns knives to the door to keep bad luck outside, on its toes. In private, when troubled, even reads the cards.

And she is troubled tonight, is Magda. Her mouth, tiny and refined as that of a countess, is tight with unhappiness; her eyes, so appealing a blue, are empty of peace. Her hands, white as china and no bigger than a doll's, hesitate as they unwrap the cards and lay them on the table before her; at every sound she stops and waits and listens, half in hope and half in dread, but no, each time the stillness of her waiting ends in nothing. No-one's there. That's the problem.

A voice stirs in her head, a voice edged with the warning snarl of some big cat: *Maggie, you don't have to know where I am every livelong minute of the day.*

No, I don't, of course I don't. She bows her head and cuts the pack.

The Four of Cups. A card of the too-familiar, of routine, apathy; too much time spent in the past. Looking from it, her eye alights on her own drooping reflection held in the bulge of the mighty hourglass there on the coffer by the wall, a minia-ture Magda reflected against the whispering fall of sand. She's turned the glass three times, so that's an hour sat here waiting, on her own. *Oh, it's no use*, thinks Magda. *Where are you? Why are you so out of sorts? Is it my fault? Is it me? And you won't talk to me, so what can I do but ask the cards?*

Because the cards know. They always know. But the cards have two faces. For everything they reveal, there is always some-thing that they hide.

She bows her head again, lays the next.

Oh, this is worse and worse. The Five of Swords. A card of malice, violence; loss and leaving. Her shoulders sag. She's dreading now what the third card might be. The Hermit? The Falling Tower? She lifts her hand – and looks down in amaze-ment. Of all the cards, this one. He and his promises that all will mend: the Knight of Wands.

A sound from the doorway. Magda looks up, smiling, even as her guilty hands gather the cards away. A shape detaches itself, perhaps a little unsteadily, from where it had been leaning against the door-frame, looking in on her. The shape is tall, broad across the shoulder and narrow through the hips, and when it speaks, female.

'Passing the time?' it asks. The face is all in shadow, but if you were Magda you would see without seeing that sardonic tilt to one brow; and if you were Magda you would also be assaying that voice for any traces of what is by now no doubt a skinful of schnapps.

'I was waiting for you,' Magda replies.

A pause. 'I can't imagine why,' the figure says at last. 'It ain't like I've any other place to go, is it?'

THERE'S A SPECIAL gait men use, which comes with much experience of marching. You tilt your shoulders; hardly use your feet. You get it right it's like the world comes flowing toward you, rather than you going to meet it. Peter and Jo-Jo, they have it to a nicety. Jack, leading the horse, now burdened with Peter and Jo-Jo's kit, is doing the best he can.

'Now, my lad,' says Peter, dropping a friendly arm across Jack's shoulders, 'how it works is this. We don't call you a soldier till we've got you all sworn in. You take your oath to the Emperor, and it's the end of the old life and ho! for the new. But you need your friends like me and Jo-Jo here to show you how it's done.' He takes a bottle from his jerkin as he talks, and offers it to Jack, who shakes his head. There's a foul-enough taste coming up from the back of Jack's throat as it is; and now it's been joined by the most unmannerly headache, one that feels like it could press the eyes right out his skull.

'No?' Peter takes a swig. 'A'cause Hertzberg,' he continues, gesturing to the lights ahead, 'Hertzberg, it's got its rules, and you won't find scarce a soul in Hertzberg knows those rules as don't know me. You get my meaning.' He peers into Jack's face, seemingly to be sure Jack does. 'Ho, you'll like Hertzberg,' Peter assures him. 'Ho, a soldier's paradise, that is.' He grins. 'Jo-Jo – he's got his sister there.'

'That so?' says Jack, to be polite.

Deaf Peter drops his voice, his face acquires a conspiratorial grin. 'Oh, but she's a weaner. You wait till you see –'

Slowly, magnificently, Jo-Jo, ahead of them, turns his great blank face around. There's no sense that he's heard any of this, only that some word or other, dropping from cavity to cavity within the great space of his brain, has dropped into some place and made a splash. 'Peter –'

'Yes, my treasure?' A wink to Jack.

'We get to Hertzberg –' (the great blank face rotates to shine on Jack) '– we going to get paid for 'un?'

A moment's silence. Jack tells himself he isn't going to laugh.

'There is,' says Peter, at last, 'a certain sum as is occasionally paid to those who bring in proper lads to go for soldiers. But whether such will come our way or no is not for us to think on. We do this for our new friend Jag here.' He has his hand over where the bottle is stashed as he's speaking. This, it seems, is Peter's version of hand on heart. 'And not for any thought of gain.'

In through the town gate. The sentry, stamping his feet, waves them past with hardly a glance. The streets of Hertzberg are empty, the life of the place has all moved inside, away from the bone-cracking cold, and makes itself known only in the light laid across the street from the windows of Hertzberg's many taverns, the sound of song, or shouts of some erupting altercation.

'Step it up, Jag!' Peter calls out. He points to where the outline of a tower rears up ahead. 'There you go – mermaid clock, third on the left. Fat Magda's.'

EACH TABLE AT Fat Magda's seats ten men (or six pikemen), and every seat tonight is taken. Is any table restive? Any empty jugs being waved aloft? Miraculously, for the moment, it seems not. In the most ladylike manner possible, Magda takes the chance to let a little air in down the front of her gown. She feels the heat, does Magda. Well, she feels everything. Sometimes she wonders if that's why she's grown so plump: the body growing armour, protection from it all. Although to see her standing there, queen of her domain, you'd never know an unquiet thought had crossed her head, and certainly not as she greets you, as you walk in through the door: 'Gotz, my dear! A welcome to you, welcome back!'

Gotz and his crew are gunners. With Sergeant Gotz in the lead they take as they always do the table by the door. Gotz's crew has grown by one this season, and the new boy, Luckless, ends up perched on one buttock at the end of the bench, with the draught from the door blowing onto his back. In the short time since he was recruited Luckless has already lost his eyebrows to a length of spitting fuse and been knocked over by a powder wagon, and privately there isn't one amongst his fellows at the table doesn't have a wager on how soon his lights will be put out for good. Luckless makes to object to getting the worst seat yet again, but a glare from Gotz and he backs down. Gotz doesn't have a nickname. No-one would dare. According to Magda, he's a heart of gold. But according to Magda, everybody has.

And now here's Ilse, Magda's maid, pushing her way through the door from the kitchen. Mouth a little ajar as always, gallon jug gripped in one hand and her apron held before her with the other. What's in the apron? Salt-raised bread, with its tight shiny crust and the ooh-yes promise of its smell, and you too, if you'd just marched twenty miles in the rain in a day, you too would tear off your first bite and as you chewed it think *by Christ I could live off this alone, and be happy to, what's more.* And share that thought with your neighbour. The noise in the room, when you first come into it, is like being boxed round the ears. The smell is memorable too – waterlogged soldiery drying off: wet leather, black powder, the vinegar pong of sweat. The bread, the scent of roasting pork, the catch-your-throat caramel of Rauchmann's doppelbock beer. A soldier dreams of the long day ending in such a place as this.

Oh, but what's this? Someone is making the devil's own job of opening the door from the street. Back it scrapes, back and forth, finally coming open with such a bang that Luckless, already sat in the wash of icy cold, loses a mouthful of beer. Up he jumps – and he's a hefty lad, is Luckless, most gunners are – and shoves the newcomer (Magda, turning, stores an impression of some long dark shape, and of general raggedi- ness) – shoves the newcomer in the chest. Only the newcomer, rather than making his *Entschuldigung* and backing off, shoves back, at once, and in an unmistakable gesture claps a hand to his hip. And now here's Gotz, rising to his feet, Luckless's splutter of beer marking his jacket, and side on, as he is to Magda, with his bristling brows and broken nose and jutting chin coming together like the knuckles of a fist. *Oh-oh*, thinks Magda, *trouble*. Signing for Ilse to follow, she bustles across the room, calling as she goes, 'Gotz, my dear! It's for drinking, not washing yourself in!'

Laughter. Deftly, she slips herself between them. 'Here,' she says, as Ilse puts the jug on the table, 'here, my friends. On the house.'

Gotz, with a final narrow-eyed appraisal of the newcomer, subsides into his seat. Luckless takes his cue and does the same. The jug begins its journey round the table, tankard to tankard, man to man. There, thinks Magda. Peace restored. Keep a soldier warm and fed, he's docile as a calf. Only the new arrival, being so tall, masks who's there behind him, or perhaps in her peace-making she might not have been so swift.

'Magda!' comes the cry. 'Come tell me how you've missed me!'

Magda feels her heart give out a groan. Deaf Peter.

Soldiers don't give nicknames out of love. Deaf Peter's came from the fact that he was deaf to all suggestion that he wasn't wanted. 'Sticks to you,' declares that voice in Magda's head, as she has so often heard it do in life, 'like a *scab*.' And true, let Peter catch but the merest rustle of some poor soul that he might batten on to... some poor soul like Jo-Jo, for example. Here's the story, or at least, here's the story as Magda would tell it you: In this soldiers' paradise of Hertzberg there lived somehow a pair of utter innocents, brother (Jo-Jo) and little sister (Ilse). The army scooped the giant brother up before he was even shaving; Fat Magda made the little sister a home. And just as Ilse was Magda's charge, Peter made Jo-Jo his, and thus do the Peters of this world ensure they are endured.

'Well, Peter,' Magda says, resignedly, 'back with us again?' And nods to Jo-Jo, where he'd come creeping round the edge of the door, as if that way for all his bulk he'd somehow go unnoticed. And only then does she let her gaze fall on the new arrival. 'Who's this?' she asks.

'This,' says Peter, pushing the boy forward, 'is Jag.'

Jag. Tall, for sure, too thin, for sure; tide-marks of dirt mottling his clothes and, now he's not about to start a brawl, staring all about him, all amazed. *Poor lambkin*, Magda decides. *There's no proper harm in you*. Needs to grow into himself a bit maybe. All nose and teeth, the way they are that age. Retrieving her hand from Peter, she holds it out to him. The boy dips his head over it and brings his heels together. 'Good night,' he says, seriously, as if about to walk back out the door. Not a Deutscher, clearly. Then he sees Ilse, who having completed her usual, almost silent greeting of her brother, is staring at this newcomer, staring as she does at all new faces, till she has them fixed. You might look at Jo-Jo and think only what God had handed out in brawn, he'd took in brains; but look at Ilse and there's no way of pretending there's not some greater differ-ence here. Her eyes are slant and her nose and mouth are small and crushed together, and this staring of hers has in the past caused problems, cruel jibes. Yet the boy, feeling Ilse's eyes on him, neither stares back as so many do, trying to work out what this one's got wrong with her, nor seems embarrassed by her scrutiny. Instead he nods her a nod as well, arm across his waist, as polite in his greeting of her as he had been with Magda. *Well now*, Magda finds herself thinking, *someone loved you well enough to teach you manners, didn't they?*

And then comes the voice – the voice that clears a path for the speaker down the room, the room that falls quiet instantly, as on command. The boom, and then the snarl: 'Oh, will you look at that,' it says. 'Deaf Peter. All right – who didn't scrape their boots when they came in?'

A yelp of nervous laughter from Luckless, instantly hushed by his neighbour – *Are you mad? That's Paola, that is! Whatever you do, don't bring her down on you!*

Paola. Paola di Benedetta di Silvia, to be exact. Champion swordsman – and that would be swordswoman, if you please – in the army of the Marquis of Saluzzo. Champion, no less, to Carlo Emmanuel the Great, Duke of Savoy. Look at her as she strides down on the group there by the door. The great floating thunder-cloud of her hair. The line of buckles down her doublet, cinching her in, shoulder to hip. And that heathen tint to her skin, so a good Christian may hardly know *what* it is they're dealing with in her. Woman soldier. Hippolyte. Battle-bitch. Freak.

Ach, all that was long ago. She's domesticated, these days, is Paola. There's a lightning streak of white in that thundercloud of hair.

There's a black glove, where once was a strong and peerless hand.

She's also – and this is perhaps apparent only to Magda – once again right on the dangerous edge of drunk.

Here she comes, long legs striding, leather skirt snapping at her heels like a pack of hounds. And she halts before the boy – a slight exaggeration in her coming-to-a-halt, though again, no-one but Magda would notice it. The boy stares at her, wide-eyed, while Paola looks him up and down, from the wet mop of his hair to those boots hooped round his calves, then she sticks out her gloved hand and utters the one word:

'Give.'

The boy's eyes open even wider than before. 'Give,' Paola repeats. 'Can't you read?' The hand points up. There on the wall above the boy's head, Fat Magda's Four Commandments:

NO TALKING POLITICS

NO TALKING RELIGION

NO PISTOLS

and

NO KNIVES LONGER THAN A FINGER

And she raps with the glove at the clasp-knife on the boy's hip. The familiar wooden *tonk*. 'Too big,' she says. 'You understand? No knives longer than a finger. Nothing big enough to do mischief with.'

The boy's head goes back, in a way that reminds Magda of a suspicious young colt, and one ready to bite, perhaps, given the flash in his eye. He points at Gotz. One of Gotz's eyebrows lifts, as if to say *what's the little Scheisskopf about to start now?* 'So how come he gets to keep his?' the boy demands.

'*Him*, we know,' Paola replies. '*You*, we don't.' A jaunty step back. 'And you've the look of a hothead to me.'

'But it's mine,' says the boy – one hand over the knife, as if to protect it.

'Then you get it back when you leave. Now hand it over. Give.'

With as ill grace as he can, the boy gives up the knife. The noise in the room picks up by cautious degrees. 'What a welcome!' Peter exclaims, turning to Gotz's table. 'One day I swear, she'll turn my head!'

'And as for you, you human whitlow,' Paola tells him, 'pay your sodding bill.'

Peter falls back, hands upraised. 'Now, Paola—'

'Don't you *now Paola* me—' She stops. 'Where's he gone?'

What? Who? Magda, who'd had her wary eye on Gotz, sees to her amazement that the space where the boy had stood is empty. 'Your *boy*,' Paola is saying to Peter. 'Where'd he go?'

'Oh, him,' says Peter, sounding tetchy. 'He's put a horse in your yard; he'll be fussing about with that.'

'He's what? In our yard?'

Oh-oh, trouble. Magda can see where this is headed. 'Now, Paola,' she begins. 'The boy is a good boy, I'm sure. You hurt his feelings—'

'Oh, the best,' Peter puts in. He raises his voice, looks hopefully about the room. 'Worth a schilling of any company's money, him.'

Paola ignores him. She turns to Magda. 'So you've locked up?'

Too late. 'Ilse and I have been a little busy here—' Magda begins.

She hears Paola take in her breath. 'G-o-d help us.' The first word is drawn out like someone drawing back their arm to throw a rock. 'I swear,' says Paola, striding past, 'without me, this place would be in chaos in a day. And if I find that boy has helped himself to anything out there,' she adds, to Peter, 'you know whose bill that's going on, don't you, hey?'

Here's the yard. Neatly paved, lines of cobbles dividing it by four, and chill enough tonight that Paola, as the icy air hits the heat of alcohol inside her, must steady herself. A moment's muzz, no more. God help the poor soul dares suggest that Paola, these days, takes more than is good for her. Why would she? So what if there's another war? So what if this one she'll be watching from the wings?

This place is nothing to me, she tells herself. *I could be gone from here tomorrow. If I thought Magda could manage without me for even a day —*

Enough of this. She gives herself a shake. Christ, it is cold. Let the angels weep for those still marching. And one of those great-sized moons tonight that brings its face as close to the earth as a mother watching over her sleeping child, so the shadow of the mermaid clock is stretched across the yard like the finger of a sundial, as clear in the moonlight as if it were day. And there, across the yard, the storerooms, unlocked.

Paola unhooks the lantern from its place beside the kitchen door and strides toward them. An eye, as always at this time of year, out to the pasture, there at the back of the yard, for any day now the wagons of the Roma will be appearing there – 'Maggie, why?' she's asked, over and over again. 'There's not another place in Hertzberg would let those tricksters come within a mile of it.' She's like some demented mother-bird, is Magda, can't see an open mouth without wanting to fill it, and any outcast (such as the Roma), anything without a home –

Such as the boy. Here's the first storeroom. Paola has the lantern raised high as a challenge, the phrases seething in her head: *Out. Out, you thieving little sod, you get your ragged arse right out of here…*

No-one there. The cheeses in their coats of wax, the boxes of candles, sacks of flour. She eases the key from the lock, moves to storeroom number two. This, she's sure, is where she'll find him – there's wine in those straw-filled crates, hams dangling from the ceiling and, most tempting of all, schnapps in the bottles on the shelf – but no, again, all as it should be. There is, however, sound from the stable next along.

Quietly as a cat, she steps to the stable door. Throws it open. 'The devil! Help yourself, why don't you!'

The empty stable now has straw scattered underfoot, hay shaken into the manger, and this outlandish-looking little horse tethered in the corner. There's even a bucket of water, set under the animal's nose. The horse peers up at her, through the atrocious tangle of its mane, and gives a snort, like it's welcoming her in, and the boy, who had been wiping it down with a twist of straw, shakes the fringe from his eyes and glowers back at her. And the speech Paola had worked out in her head – the speech with which she'd been going to drive him from the yard altogether – it's like it put its foot down a rabbit-hole. She'd opened the door, the boy had lifted those glacial eyes of his, and it was like she took a punch to the head. She feels as if she's been sent sprawling.

So it's the boy speaks first. 'Excuses,' he says, 'is all faults mine.' Despite his words, he looks more than ready to defy her. *Trouble*, thinks Paola, regaining her balance. *Troubled*, suggests a voice in her head. Paola ignores it.

The boy speaks again. He points to the horse. 'Too cold for him outside.'

Now it's his accent throwing her off track. *Dammit*, thinks Paola. *Who is this raw-boned scruff, to lay down the law to me?* 'You can have all the stabling you want, my lad, if you can pay.'

He tightens his jaw, looks even surlier. 'I don't have money.'

She laughs. 'Oh, *there's* a surprise!'

The jaw tighter yet. 'I work it off.'

'You're right you will,' says Paola, coming closer. 'You can be sure of that.' The horse raises its head. There's water dripping from the long fur under its belly as from underneath a sill. The boy has gone back to those sweeping movements down its back with his twist of straw, and every swipe brings off a rain of drips and a mat of hair. A pair of discards – a matching pair. And him such a hard-eyed little villain, yet taking such tender care of this mongrel of a horse. She asks, 'How long have you been marching?'

'Since Heidelberg.' He folds the twist of straw and begins again. The horse shakes itself, like it's coming back to life. The boy pauses in his long, steady wiping and, close to, Paola sees he's shivering – quietly, persistently – with cold himself.

'That's a week's march from here,' she says. 'Where'd you sleep?'

'I bedded down with him.' He stands back, surveying his grooming. 'Otherwise I could just see me waking up and he'd be gone.'

'You mean you slept outside? But it's been raining without stop!'

'I know,' the boy replies. A grin, quick as a twitch. His hand strays to the horse's mane. 'Him and me – we're good and watered down by now.'

A week. Later she'll think how she'd known she'd do this, the moment before asking how long he'd been marching, but the words as they leave her mouth still open within her this *oh* of surprise. 'You want a place for you and your horse tonight?' she asks, and his face lights up with such sudden hope, it's as if she has a different boy in front of her entirely. 'You come with me,' she says.

She leads him back across the yard. 'There,' she says, pointing to the log-pile, furred with frost. 'You split them for us in the morning, that pays for tonight.'

He has his arms folded round him. His jacket is so damp that, pulled tight like that, the stuff of it shines. It gives Paola gooseflesh to look at him. 'Thank you,' he says.

'Don't thank me. I want them all done, understand?' She holds open the door. 'Now get in there. There's a place by the fire. You take it.'

WHICH IS WHY, much to her amazement, the next time Magda sees the boy he's threading his way to the seat by the fire with Paola following behind him much in the manner of a sheepdog with a stray. When she looks again, his head is resting on the warm, plastered flank of the chimney, his eyes are closed, and he seems to be asleep.

Oh, but he's pale. The wall beside his cheek looks like it has more blood in it than him.

'Peter,' says Magda, pausing, putting a jug down on his table, 'are you sure your boy is well?'

'*Ach,*' Peter says, filling his mug, 'he's gone off some on the journey for sure, but that's young'uns for you. No staying power. They was falling like nine-pins as we come here.' He glances over. 'Get our schilling for him off the nearest muster sergeant in the morning and we're done.' But as he peers across, Magda sees a sudden beady sharpness come into his eye. 'Here now, I'm forgetting,' he says, and drains the mug at a swallow. 'Jo-Jo and me, we still need to find a billet. We'll come back for the boy. You let him sleep a whiles, eh?'

'What's up with you, you sheep tick?' Paola asks, pushing past. 'Worried I'll put his supper on your tab?' Turning her back on him, she jerks a thumb. 'Boy's put his horse in the stable,' she declares to Magda. 'Just so's you know. I fixed with him he'd work it off tomorrow, fair enough?'

Later, upstairs, it's a different tale. 'You'd only have complained if I had thrown him out. *Oh, Paola, the poor lad.* Yes you would, I can hear you now.'

Magda sits quiet.

'It was the horse I took pity on,' Paola says next. 'You've never seen a beast in such a state.' She lowers her face, opening the buckles on her doublet one by one, pulling them back with the thumb of the glove. Time was, the stump inside the glove was still so raw and angry that was Magda's job, to undress her. Fold her clothes, brush out her hair. Time was, the woman inside the clothes was still so raw and angry too.

'Scourge of every regiment, the boys like him,' Paola goes on. 'Human jackdaws. Starlings. Thieves.' A sigh. 'All of them thieves, and I'm a bitch.'

'You are the dearest soul in all the world,' says Magda, patting the sheet beside her. 'Come to bed.'

CHAPTER SEVEN

A Visit from the Angel

Of the spotted fever:

'It is a continual malignant burning fever, the Sick
being affected with excessive Heat, Thirst, Watchings,
Pains in the Head and Faintings...'

William Salmon, *Compendium of the Theory and
Practice of Physick*

SALT-RAISED BREAD. You start with flour, milk and soda,
and a pile of something warm and steady that will hold its
heat (as, for example, a goodly heap of warmed rock-salt).
Set your bowl in that when all your house is gone to bed, and in
the morning, with baker's luck, the bowl will be full to the brim
with foam and your kitchen full of a tang as sharp as cheese.
Add water and more flour to make a batter, and let it rise again.

Magda times hers by the hourglass sat there on the coffer, but you may use what you please. It's a pleasant early morning task, bread-making, the kind of gentle thing that leaves your mind free to wander amongst the sounds of the new day doing their own waking-up about you: the crunch of wheels in the street outside, or birds, greeting the day, or the squeak of the kitchen door coming open, and the boy peering round it, staring like one of the Seven Sleepers and made even grubbier-looking by his sleep. Dirty as a cuttlefish, Paola would say.

'Come in, come in,' Magda invites him. Still he lingers by the door, although his eyes had darted straight to the table, laden with rewards from last night for the baker – cold pork, hot mustard, salt fingers of crackling. 'Are you hungry, Jag? Breakfast with me.' She is already piling a plate for him. 'There,' she says, pointing to the stool. 'Sit, sit.' Which he does, and picks a little at the plate when it's put before him, though not at all the appetite you'd expect in a boy that age, let alone one with that splay of shoulder and that stretch of leg.

'I don't have nothing to pay you with,' he says, as if in explanation.

His accent is so much a mix of other places, all you can say is that it's not of here. 'Where are you from, sweetling?' Magda asks. Magda prides herself on prising the conversational oyster from its shell. Most of the men who come through her door can't wait to tell their story, improved on fact as it may be.

But the boy replies only, 'North of here.'

Despite his reticence, she finds she's warming to him. It's the way he'd stood at the door, expecting nothing, how he didn't skirt the subject of his penniless state, the way he'd met her eyes. And watching him eat, good hands. It's Magda's belief you can tell a deal about a man from his hands. Wide means a warm heart; curved, a bad temper; long-fingered and he has a brain; short thumbs, he's a villain; and warts – didn't piss on enough toads when he was young.

'Paola says you work for your keep,' she tries next (if not by one route, then another). 'You should make a good breakfast for that.' She smiles. She has a pretty smile, has Magda, it curves her eyes into two little sickles, like one of those merry angels on the mermaid clock. And it's pleasant to have company, this early in the day. It's lonely down here sometimes. Most of the time, recently, in fact.

But the boy has pushed the plate away. 'I owe you enough as it is,' he says. 'I should get out there. Make a start.'

So spurned again and lonely still, Magda goes back to her bread-making. The dough has puffed up full as a milkmaid's bonnet. She scoops it from its bowl, lands it on the table (make sure you use plenty of flour) and starts to knead. Turn, fold. Push, pull. Warm work, this. She pauses to wipe a hand across her brow.

The kitchen door comes open, this time with a bang. 'Where's that boy?' Paola demands. Surveys the table, the two plates. 'Where is he, then?'

From the yard, there comes the clatter of logs being chopped. Paola goes to the window. Magda sees her shake her head. 'That boy is a good boy, Paola,' Magda says quietly, going to join her.

Through the window, there he is. They see him pause a moment, glance at the size of the woodpile, then he seems to shoulder this as just another thing to be got through, places the next log on the block, and swings again.

'He's got those pale eyes,' Paola says. An exasperated sigh. 'Them with those pale eyes, they're always trouble.'

That very moment, out there in the yard, him with those pale eyes hesitates, sways, and simply topples over, graceful as a tree.

The blast of dots came out of nowhere, swarming through his vision like a crowd of bees; the ground had flipped beneath him like a rug. Of a sudden he's wet with sweat from head to toe, and when he opens his eyes the yard seems to elongate before him.

The ache is back around his skull, tight as iron, and everything is coming at him very, very slow. The voice calling his name might be coming from some island out at sea. *Ja-a-a-g... J-a-a-a-a-g...*

Someone has their arm about him. A hand on his brow, and he groans in protest. It feels as if the winter sun is shining right through the top of his head.

'Holy Mother,' says the voice. 'You're hot as a brick.'

It's her. The tigress from last night. He tries to get up, tries to speak. Neither legs nor voice obey. The tigress scoops him up, like she was scooping up a kitten. 'Maggie,' she calls, and then the other woman is there, her own soft face all crumpled with concern.

They carry him inside – out of the cruel daylight, into the lovely dark. Now everything is coming at him in a flood of red. He hears the creak of stairs and realizes that he is being carried up them. A door dissolves in front of him, and there's a bed, a tester, with curtains, which shake like the bed is laughing. He feels himself being swung up onto it, and by now he's laughing too – the strangeness of everything, the ridiculous size of the pain in his head – and then they start to strip him, and he comes back to himself at once, batting their hands away. This is not like when he was bathed by Zoot. There's pinfeathers coming in down there now and everything. 'Jag, don't be a fool,' the tigress tells him, while the other one, the gentler one (who is already pulling off his broken old boots), assures him, 'Sweetheart, you won't have nothing we ain't seen before.' *Oh God*, he thinks, as the tigress shears him out his breeches as efficiently as if she were stripping a corpse, *I don't care any more, I can't, I haven't got the strength.* Off come the tatters of his shirt, and as they do, he feels the silver wolf against his collarbone. He closes his hand over it, as he used to do when first he was on his own, and feels its old ribbon finally give, and the wolf is safe and secret, closed in his hand.

And then the tigress is snarling, '*Ach!*' She bends across him. 'Jag, what the hell is this!'

The wolf is sharp within his palm. He grips it tight, waiting for the walls to stop their washing up-and-down. 'What is it?' he hears Magda ask.

'Maggie, get back,' the tigress orders her. 'Get away from him.'

One of the curtains of the bed is lifted high. The light falls on him and he groans again, covers his eyes with his arm. '*Ach!*' says the tigress, once more. 'Oh, son of a *bitch!*'

From under the arm he squints down at himself. Oh… his belly is covered in little red splatters, like wine stains. How did that happen? He lifts his free hand to his stomach, to investigate, but the marks are hard to aim at – there's the white shimmer of his thighs, and somewhere what he cannot help but mourn, even in these circumstances, as the pitiful curl of his parts, but it's as if he's moving away from himself all the time; and in any case, as she sees his hand hovering, the tigress smacks it back down by his side. 'Don't touch,' she orders him. 'You'll make them worse.' He stares from her to Magda, who has indeed retreated to the door, and hits some point within the wash of walls and floor of eerie certainty. Bad. Very bad indeed.

'Peter, you bastard,' the tigress is hissing under her breath. 'You misbegot cold-hearted little *shit.*'

It has many names, this. Jail fever. Ship fever. Spotted fever. Italian, French or Spanish fever, depending on which army brought it in its wake. That old Greek Galen knew it, set out the way it fogged its victims' minds.

Paola wouldn't know Galen from a pump handle, but she knows what this is. Typhus.

SOLDIERS HAVE THEIR own names for typhus. They call it the Fire, because it clears the ground. Or they call it the Angel, because either it seizes you, or it passes by.

'Let me but get my hands on him.'

Back, forth. Stride, turn. Snap, go the skirts at her heels. It's a good job the kitchen is wide as it is, is all Magda can think. 'Paola, who?'

'Peter, of course! He knew the lad was sickening, I'll lay good money that he did. Pestilent little –'

Stride, turn. On the coffer, the sands in the hourglass shiver. Magda is tempted to take it into her lap for protection.

'– pestilent little maggot. Christ, I could kill him.' Turn again. 'They'll close us up, you know. It once gets out as we've a case of typhus here, they'll nail the door shut.' She stops, skirts a-swirl. 'Here's what we do. We take the boy to Forbach.'

'*What?*'

'Put him in a wagon, I can have him there by sunset. Give him to the Franciscans. The hospice there—'

'I am not,' says Magda, with decision, 'loading that poor child into a wagon and sending him off to Forbach. Paola, shame on you!'

Paola has that look upon her face, as if Magda were some defiant enemy outpost. 'You don't know what this is,' she says. 'You don't know what it does. I do.'

It's not a thing you'd forget. Garrisoned under the flag of Carlo Emmanuel, in a sturdy little *castello* high in the passes of Montferrat, and expecting the French to fall upon them any minute. It's Paola's firm belief she saw the men who brought the fever with them, watched from the walls as this rag-bag company of reinforcements dragged themselves up to the gates. The first cases had been so sudden, so violent, they'd thought some traitor had poisoned the wells. It made men blind. It made them mad. It turned them into babies. While there remained enough of them with strength to do it, they threw the bodies into an open pit beyond the bastions. There's worse than Forbach, in Paola's view.

'I know this,' Magda is saying. 'I know that boy is staying right here. Where would you have been, if no-one had helped you?'

The last thing Paola saw, as the Angel closed its wings about her, was the flaking wall beside her bed, the last sound she heard the boom of cannon, over her labouring blood. When she'd opened her eyes again, the edge of that open pit was a mere arm's length away. There had been a man kneeling beside her, raising her head; a man with the palest eyes she'd ever seen. '*Voilà*,' he'd said. Plainly, the world had changed. '*Voilà*. I told you this one wasn't dead.'

And still is not, *dommage*. 'Fine, then,' says Paola, the steel back in her voice. 'He stays. But you don't go near him, understand? No fussing up and down the stairs, no little possets. I know you, *you stay clear*.'

'So who will nurse him?' Magda asks.

'Oh God help us,' Paola groans, throwing herself into a chair. 'It'll have to be me.'

So, typhus. There's rules.

The first of which is, if you've had it once, you're safe. *And don't we all hope that's the truth*, thinks Paola, shoving the corner of a fresh sheet under the boy's mattress. 'There,' she tells him. He's no doubt already busy sweating through these new linens just as he had the old. 'And shall we try to make these do a little longer, hmm?'

Rule two: it's a disease that likes propinquity. Give it some place packed tight – a dormitory, a dungeon – it'll hopscotch from one victim to the next until there's not one left. Some say the fever travels in the exhalations of the sick; some that it's passed by touch – of skin, clothes, hair. Most believe it hovers round the victim like a cloud. If you come near enough, the cloud adheres to you. You need to put a quarantine around it, moat it off.

'You've no call to be so rough with him,' says Magda, from the door.

'Rough?' Paola answers. 'Me? Why, I'm a saint toward him. I'm like a new Saint Catherine, by God.' Ignoring the boy (who flops like a puppet), she seizes the pillow behind his head and pulls the cover from it; having punched the pillow into its new case, she squares it behind the boy's head much as if its corners were his ears. The old pillow-case is hurled onto the pile of dirty linens on the floor. 'Not to mention my duties as a laundry maid. So that'll be me taking these to the wash-house, I suppose?'

The wash-house sits by the paddock; its sudsy waters drain into the grass. Magda is fussy with her linens, she likes them boiled white and sprinkled with rose-water, a scent that transfers to her skin; so inside the wash-house a mighty copper, big enough to tread grapes in, takes up the middle of the floor, with space beneath it for a charcoal fire. To blow up the fire to red-hot, to set the lye-and-water in the copper bubbling, there's a pair of bellows. To fish the linens out, a giant wooden paddle. To dry them, a cat's-cradle of washing-lines flaps and blows across the corner of the yard. These hide the wash-house from the kitchen; hence, when she first came here, when her life was at its worst, with her right arm, or what was left of it, still in a sling and the heart beneath the sling still roaring with agony too, the wash-house was where Paola went to drink. *A dire il vero*, truth be told, it still is.

Scowling, she dumps the basket of linens on the floor, starts sorting through them. She has the boy's dirty pillow-case draped across her arm, and as she makes to shake it out, something drops from it and lands beside her foot. Something that might have been hidden inside it, perhaps –

Holy God.

She's aware that if she were watching herself, she'd laugh. The puzzled way in which she'd bent toward the little silver token, down there on the floor, then sprung away from it as if it were a scorpion. She's tempted to poke at the thing with a stick. She knows what it is, of course she does. Never seen one before, however. Never heard of anyone who's seen one. Not and lived to speak of it, that is.

With the edge of her boot, and very gingerly, Paola nudges the silver wolf into the palm of the glove, and lifts it to the light.

'Jag,' she hears herself ask, 'how in God's name did you come by one of these?'

Day two. Looking down at the boy, Paola finds she can just about remember where he is now. The heat. The hollowness. The flood of sounds.

Some of the marks on his belly are turning black.

'Were you like this?' asks Magda, in a whisper, from the door.

'I think,' says Paola, slowly, unwillingly, 'I wasn't as bad as this, as fast as him.'

That old scar under the boy's ribs, Paola had noted it at once (don't tell her she doesn't know a stab wound when she sees one). Yesterday it had been flat and white, now it's red and raised and weeping. Even the boy's sweat is discoloured. Today, when she'd changed his sheets, his outline had been on them, ringed in a watery rose.

It's a disease with a memory. Finds all your old hurts; opens them again.

She has the silver wolf wrapped in her pocket. Who is he? What possible history, what memories might there be, in the boy's now scalding brain-pan, which could account for that?

'Paola,' says Magda, from the doorway, 'Paola, we're not going to lose him, are we?'

He hears the boom of voices, a roaring like the sea. The roar grows louder. The roar becomes a name. 'JACQUES!' The roar becomes his father's voice, enormous, thunderous: *JACQUES!*

He opens his eyes. Somewhere, a drum is beating. It takes many, many beats before he realizes this is his own heart, but then for one narrow wink of time he understands where he is exactly, where and why and how, everything as lucid as a mirror: this room, this bed, and he within it, entire and whole and as he used to be – *oh*, he thinks, lying there in the dark, in the unmistakable stillness of night, *oh, so I'm over this, it's done* – and then something bumps the bed.

Instantly, he knows what it is, just as it used to be in his childhood dreams. His pulse leaps like a fountain. *Le Garoul!* He feels it bump the bed, and then the walls. He has the image of it in his head – the bristled muzzle, lips peeling back from those mighty fangs, the clawed hands raised aloft. He hears its growl. This is no dream. He thinks in sudden panic, *I don't have my knife!* He grabs at a pillow. There is the scaly scrape of its tail against the wall, then as it leaps, a flock of birds bursts from the ceiling – birds that turn to single feathers as they fall, that fall upon his face, that melt like snow.

In that unhappy hour between night-end and daybreak, Paola wakes from a dream in which something had been stalking round the house, and to add to the unpleasantness of this, had got up on its hind legs to do so, and as she lies there, bothered and beset, at odds in every way a body can be, realizes that what had woken her was not the dream, nor the freshets of rain rattling the windows, but a thump from the room below. Leaving Magda and the cat both sound asleep, whiffling in duet, she pads down the half-flight of stairs to the room where they had put the boy and eases open the door.

A few feathers curl about her ankles. A pillow has been hurled across the room so hard it's split against the wall; and the boy is lying sideways, half in and half out the bed, one arm trailing to the floor. 'Oh, what *is* this—' she begins, but then as she goes to set him back against the pillows she sees the change in him, and bending closer, hears the change in his breathing too. That grind to it, like the lid being inched across a tomb.

'Oh, Jag,' she says. 'Don't you do this to us. Don't you dare.'

*

Dawn, and the rain redoubles. Dogs lie in their kennels, lifting a worried eyebrow to the sky, and even the most desperate drunk won't lurch abroad in this. The dining hall stays empty, its cartwheel chandeliers unlit. By noon it's almost dark as dusk; when the sun finally gives up, it goes down behind clouds as ragged as the flag from off a battlefield.

Magda has brought candles from the kitchen, set them round the boy's bed. 'There must be something we can do,' she says.

Paola sits with the boy's hand held in one of hers, peering into his face. She is mute; Magda might be invisible.

'Paola—'

The glove is raised, warning her off. Back she goes to the window. It's as close as she's allowed. Oh, the rasp of his breathing, like a file; like a prisoner working at his chains. If neither of them speaks it's the only sound in the room. 'Paola, please, there has to be something...'

She peeks over at the boy, but it's unbearable, to see him like this. This is what he'll look like in his winding sheet. She remembers when her father breathed his last, sitting watch with him like this, and the physician sat just as Paola is, holding her father's hand, until the thread of his pulse had frayed away to nothing and he was free. Her father too had made that groaning in his chest, as if all the hinges in his body were seizing up at once. 'Not long now,' the physician had said, as if this would be a comfort. *Oh*, she thinks, *I'm going to weep*. She turns her head, and there, out in the black and rainswept paddock there are lights, and not the reflection of her many candles, but lights that move, dancing from one pane of glass to the next.

'Paola!' she cries. 'It's the Roma! There is something we can do!'

The Roma. Magda doesn't recall how she came to understand that here were more folk for whom the world was not as it was to others, but it must have been around the time she realized that their headsman, Rufus, had been deprived of an ear; and that her father let the Roma set up camp not because they brought such potions with them that could unknot the tree-root gnarls in his hands; he let them stay because he was afraid of them.

The world since then has changed for the Roma as it has for so many, which is to say, for the worse, which accounts (thinks Magda, as she stands by the rail of the paddock in the dark, rain pelting her face and the wind ripping at her skirts) for the number of young men there are now in Rufus's camp, with their shuttered eyes and the size of the knives they carry. With Rufus and his brother Benedicte she knows where she is, but with those younger men of his – well, you trust the farmer, not his dogs.

'Rufus! Rufus, are you with us? Are you there?'

She has to grip the rail to keep her feet. What a storm this has become, good God! And pitch black before her, for at the sound of her voice, every single one of those lights had been extinguished at once. Nonetheless, she senses movement before her in the blackness, nervy crossings and re-crossings of what would have been her path. 'Rufus! Are you there? It's Magda!'

And there is his voice. 'Frau Magda!' it calls, out of the storm of wind and rain; then there is the man himself, flaming red hair plastered to his brow, a hand across his eyes to shield them from the rain, and then to her astonishment –

'Frau Magda! Do you have him? Do you have the boy?'

All the years she's known him, and Rufus has never so much as taken her hand before. Now he's hustling her back into the house at such speed she can barely get the words out: 'But how—?'

'Frau Magda, we must *hurry*.' He is pulling her across the kitchen to the stairs.

'But how could you know about the boy? How could you know he was here?'

'Benedicte,' Rufus says. 'Benedicte saw him.'

'How did Benedicte see him?'

'Frau Magda, Benedicte saw this boy before he was even born.' They are at the bedroom door. 'And you have no idea, the *katastrof* that it would be if he were to leave us now.'

She opens the door. Paola looks up. '*Gute Frau*, please,' says Rufus, stepping in, cautious as ever where Paola is concerned, but all his attention on the boy. 'I am here only to help, I promise you. Let me do what I can.

'Oh, do your worst,' says Paola with her big-cat snarl, relinquishing her place.

Rufus places a hand on the boy's forehead. 'Ay-yi-yi,' he says, feeling its heat. Lifts the boy's hands, squeezing them as if testing for resistance, exploring fingers, forearm, pulse. 'This runs much too fast,' he declares, holding the arm out to them. He lays his hand to the boy's forehead again. 'And this is made much too hot. We must slow the one, and cool the other. Good lady Paola, if you will assist – if you will hold his arm so, like this, with the hand raised –'

He's lifting the knife from his belt even as he speaks. 'You're going to bleed him?' Paola asks. 'That's the best you can come up with?'

'I could wait to boil milk, or to warm honey,' Rufus replies, 'but Frau Paola, *we have no time*, so yes, it must be his blood, do you see? We need a liquid and it must be thick and warm. And Frau Magda, a bowl, but small, to drink from, like a gallipot, and a little spoon, and a cloth to save your bed if you would be so good – and please, we must *hurry*.'

Downstairs again. 'Frau Magda?' There's Ilse, peering down from the landing above. 'Frau Magda, there's a dog. I heard 'un.'

'It's nothing but the storm, Ilse. Go to your bed now, there's a good soul.'

Back in the boy's room, Rufus takes the cloth from her, lays it on the bed, centres the bowl upon it. He's a man of precision, is Rufus, as red-headed men so often are. Takes a cord from his pocket. Knots it at the boy's elbow.

'And so, Frau Paola, if you will hold his arm steady –'

The blood comes up as thick and dark as tar. Rufus lets it drip into the bowl, then places the bloodied arm carefully back onto the boy's chest. He draws from his pocket a box like a tobacco-box, black with age. Opens it with care, and with his head drawn back.

Inside, the box is divided into compartments; each protected by a tiny lid.

With the tip of his knife, Rufus lifts one lid, then another, and begins extracting minute amounts of some dried matter – speckles and dust – which he taps into the bowl. As he works, he talks.

'You know this?' he asks. 'Wolf's-bane. It has a pretty flower. Children must not touch it. Even the touch will kill a child. And this, this is hemlock. Also most potent. Very strong.' A speck into the glass. A glance at the boy, a hand laid to his cheek. 'Ah, my friend,' Rufus says. 'Death is reaching out for you. And he is hard, and he is cruel, but this time he must go away empty-handed.'

Another speck added to the first. In goes the spoon into the bowl, round and round. The sound it makes might almost be an echo of that awful rasping from the bed.

'Most important,' Rufus is saying, 'not to mix these dry, do you see? The powder. Most dangerous, if it is breathed. They say the Croats use it so. A vicious, secret poison. It must be mixed with something thick and warm, so that the powder will be held and soothed within it.' He lays the spoon upon the cloth. 'You have Croats here, you know that? In camp by the river. Many soldiers there. So we must come the long way round.' A glance at the boy. 'And so nearly too late,' he adds. He lays his hand once more to the boy's cheek. 'Ah, *moosh*,' he says, 'you are so close to gone as almost makes no difference. Where do we hide you, eh? Where do we hide you, to fool him, so he passes by? Where is the last place he would look for you?'

He takes the boy's chin in his hand, thumb and forefinger either side of the jaw.

'I think we have to hide you with the dead.'

And he pulls the boy's mouth open, and tips the bloody mix inside.

Magda has covered her eyes. Squeezing them shut behind her palms, she hears Paola exclaim, 'Rufus, he's not breathing.'

'Wait,' Rufus replies.

A roll of thunder up above, so vast that Paola has to shout.

'Rufus, he's *not breathing.*'

'*Wait.*'

And then a moment with no sound at all. '*Rufus,*' she hears Paola say again, and then from the bed the suck of breath – impossibly long, pulled in and let out in three great gasps, like something surfacing – and when she looks the boy's eyes are open, wide and wondering, dark as a newborn's, and Rufus is peering into them, saying, 'Hello, *moosh.* Hello, my friend. It's good to meet you.' He puts his hand to the boy's forehead, passes it down over the boy's face.

'And now,' says Rufus, 'he will sleep.'

CHAPTER EIGHT

The Knight of Wands

... Now, news of your Enric Maduna. This clown leaves a wake like a whale. He's found himself a warm place to shit in a cavalry regiment out of Styria; in fact the regiment may even be his – by all accounts, it has Our Lady on its flag.

But of this Charles the Ghost, all I have are whispers of a Croat in the household of the Prince-Bishop of Prague, who undertook some piece of black work out in France before the war. I have no other name for him, nor anything beyond the fact that those few who'll speak of him all look over their shoulders first.

And by repute, he wears the token of the hard men on his coat. I need not say this, but I will – go very carefully, my friend. Tread light as air about this business, if you please.

Tino Ravello to Captain Balthasar

THE SCENT OF rose-water and a voice calling Jag, Jag…

'Jag? Open your eyes, sweetling. Open your eyes.'

A horizon, shockingly bright, after nothing but dark for so long. Something moves across it. The voice again, warm with relief.

'There now. That's the way.'

A woman's face. Magda. He remembers. 'There you are,' she says. She sounds delighted. She sits back, fanning herself. 'Oh, but you gave us such a fright!'

The room is moving in and out, as if the walls are breathing. Gradually the movement ceases. The window locks itself in place against the wall, the end of the bed settles down.

'I was dreaming,' he says, slow as a sleepwalker. It's very strange to feel his mouth move, his lips and tongue have to keep conferring with each other – *how is it that we used to do this? Oh yes, we remember now.*

'Were you, sweetheart? What were you dreaming?'

'There was a man,' he says. 'He could fight anything.'

'Did he have red hair? If he did, that was Rufus.' She nods her head, looking pleased. 'He saved your life.'

The man had peered in at him, as if peering down a well. He had seemed very tall. The man had smiled, then laid a finger to his lips. And walked away, as down a hall of mirrors, seeming to leave one little bit of his reflection always a stride behind.

THE FIRST TIME he tries to get out of bed, his legs collapse beneath him like straws. The tigress finds him folded onto the floor. She waits as, sweating with effort, he turns himself about to face her. There are feathers sticking to his palms. 'Looking for something?' she asks.

The silver wolf, on a new cord, twirls between her forefinger and thumb.

She comes closer. He considers making a grab for it, but something tells him she'd be quicker. 'How'd you come by this, Jag?' she asks next.

It fell –

It fell from my mother's hand –

No you don't. That door is locked, you keep it so.

'I found it,' he says. He thinks, *Don't let her see how much you want it back.*

'You found it,' the tigress repeats. 'And was the finding of it anything to do with your getting yourself stabbed?'

His face is warming. He pushes himself upright, using the bed. 'I wasn't stabbed because of that lells her.

'Sure of that?' She peers at him. 'Good God, you don't even know what it is, do you?'

Of course he knows what it is. It's all he has of everything there was before. It's all that is left. 'It's mine,' he says.

'Yours.' She watches him as if expecting more, then laughs and shakes her head. 'You're a strange one, you are, Jag. You're just about the strangest one I've ever met.' She drops the wolf into his palm. 'You keep that hid,' she says. 'You keep it hid as good as you've ever hid anything, hear me?'

Out she goes, that thundercloud of hair swaying across her back. As well as her leather doublet, she'd been wearing great swinging breeches, rough as sacking and full as a skirt. *And she says* I'm *strange?* he thinks.

He waits till the door is closed, then hangs the silver wolf back about his neck.

THE MERMAID CLOCK makes a noise before it strikes, as if it were clearing its throat. Up in his room, he listens to it chime its way around the hours and watches the comings and goings in the world. A barrow from the butcher with piglet carcasses done up in muslin like so many little brides; a brewer's wagon and the echo of barrels rolled across the yard. And then this tribe who seem to have set up home in the paddock. Big, commodious-looking tents; cooking fires, ponies cropping the turf. The men do little more than smoke their pipes, but the women visit with each other, make small private female gatherings. There's also a child. He watches it cross the yard at a fast and guilty-looking trot. And once or twice in the early morning there's a figure dressed in a long pale robe, who seems familiar, in some most puzzling way. And most mornings there is Magda too. You'd almost think she was lonely.

'Who are they?' he asks. She's brought him new clothes – boots, a shirt, an old, old doublet, dagged and slashed ('My father's,' she says, 'but you must have them now'). She's fussing round the room, tidying this, folding that. To his horror her hand hovers over the cloth shielding his chamber-pot, as if she would inspect its contents too. 'And who's that one who wears the nightgown?' he asks her, hurriedly.

'They are the Roma.' She settles herself on the end of the bed, feet high off the floor. *She's so* little, he thinks. 'And the one in the nightgown, as you put it, his name is Benedicte.'

'Is he –' He wants to say a zany, lost his wits, but he's wary of giving offence. 'Is he as he should be?'

'No, he is not.' A shake of the head, a sigh. 'Not any more.'

'What happened to him?'

'He ran most horribly afoul the Prince-Bishop of Prague,' she says, as if that should explain everything.

It does not. 'Who is the Prince-Bishop of Prague?'

'He is a horror,' says Magda. 'He is greedier than Midas and crueller than Tarquin. All those who raise a voice against him suffer for it – they, their families, down to the babes in their cradles. Benedicte, he cast into an oubliette beneath his castle and he kept him there in darkness ten years and more. Benedicte was a young man when he was imprisoned, hardly older than you. When he was released, he was as you see him now. It was the most evil of punishments.'

He thinks of the darkness in which he had lain so recently himself, the way it still lurks in his head. 'What did this Benedicte do?'

A bellow from downstairs. 'Maggie? MAGGIE! There's maybe twenty loaves down here, all begging me to take them from the fire! I can't save them on my own!'

'He foretold the Prince-Bishop's death,' says Magda, swinging her feet to the floor. 'In the midst of the Prince-Bishop's great Twelfth Night feast, and to his face, what's more. He held the Prince-Bishop by the hand, and he told him, the Dead Man is coming. He will sweep you from the earth. He will send you down to hell. In the midst of all that company, Benedicte tells the man that he and his are damned. I wish I had been there to see it.'

'And who is the Dead Man?'

'Oh, that.' She sighs. 'The only one who has ever known that is Benedicte, and I doubt even he could tell you now, poor soul.' She picks up the chamber-pot and gives its contents an appreciative sniff. Pats his arm. 'You're doing *very* well.'

A few days more, and his legs can carry him downstairs. Magda sets a chair for him outside the kitchen door, and a blanket to wrap himself in, and he sits there, eyes closed against the brightness of the winter sun, being careful not to breathe too deep, and the child from the gypsy camp creeps up as close as it dares, and throws clods of earth at him. When he tries to give chase – pulling up, gasping, after a few short yards – it pushes its head through the fence that apparently marks the division between their territories, and hisses at him.

'What's *wrong* with it?' he asks, coming back into the kitchen, shaking the earth from his hair.

Paola is at the table, surrounded by books of accounts. 'That is Emilian,' she tells him. 'Rufus is his father. So it may be that

Emilian resents the time his father spent on you. Or, it may be that in some other way you have offended him. *Or*, it may be that they are the Roma, and consequently everything about them is as mad as it can be. Your guess is good as mine.'

'Move aside there, sweetling,' says Magda. She has a bowl of batter in her hands, a good quart of rising liquor. She puts it on the table, pats his cheek. 'Getting some weight back, then? That's good to see.' She smooths her apron. 'Oh, we're behind ourselves today.'

On his own, then.

Back he goes to the chair outside the door. Settles himself, one eye opened to a slit. Blanket carefully arranged.

After a moment, sure enough, here it comes (the little wart), creeping along the fence. Behind him, in the kitchen he hears Magda asking, 'Now what did I do with my bowl?'

The child is in the yard. Through the one eye, he sees it start its run-up. That eldritch cry of rage –

– changed to a sudden wail. The women, coming to the door, arrive as the bowl is circling on the ground with the child, coated head to foot in batter, on its arse. Jack rises to his feet, and flicks the blanket at it. The child scrambles up. He flicks the blanket out again, and the child is gone – wailing, hands above its head – back across the yard, skidding in its batter-filled shoes, through the fence and away. Its wail precedes it, down the paddock.

Jack folds the blanket over his arm and drops the women a bow. 'I think I'm pretty much mended,' he says.

Paola is the first to recover herself. 'In that case, you can make yourself useful round here. You can tell us what to do with that horse of yours for a start.'

His horse?

'Here,' says Paola, opening the stable door.

His first thought is *that's not my horse*, though clearly it has to be; how many other horses can there be with a mane in shining ringlets, like a wig? And a neat little head like that? And his horse's five-note whicker of greeting?

'Cleans up pretty good,' comments Paola. 'Don't he?'

As if to confirm its identity, the horse trots over to him and does that trick again, of putting its nose in his pocket.

He strokes its neck – sheeny as satin, stuffed tight as a sleeve. When he turns to her again, his face is one single grin from ear to ear. 'You made him better,' he says, as simple as a child.

She's never seen a smile like that on him before. It's there again, that moment of confusion; like a bar or two of music drifting in from some forgotten song; no sooner heard than gone.

'No reason to let a good horse spoil, just because you weren't around to care for it,' she replies. Comes closer, knuckles the horse with the glove. 'Where'd you find him?'

'It's more we found each other,' says he, 'to be honest.'

'That so? You helped yourself, did you?' Now it's her turn to smile. 'You don't get 'em so often hereabouts, these little mountain horses. I used to see them in Milan from time to time. They were bastards to rope, and worse to break, but once you'd got one, it was a friend for life. What's his name?'

'He don't have one.'

'No? Then that's what you should call him. Milano.'

'Milano,' he repeats, and the horse turns its head.

She feels in her pocket, brings out the knife. 'And I suppose we should trust you with this again, as well.'

He takes it from her, but his face has clouded. 'I must owe you a fortune,' he says.

'You're right there, my lad.'

'I could work it off.'

'You could and you will. Ready to turn your hand to the log-pile again?'

She sees him blench. There are still blotches from the fever on his neck; when he pales they flare like burns. 'Don't you fret,' says Paola. 'I've something gentler in mind for you.'

*

Which is how he comes to be standing in the wash-house, wearing a waxed canvas apron long as a skirt and stirring, in the giant copper with the giant paddle, sheets, pillows, aprons, tablecloths. Hoiks out a sheet and wraps it, still almost too hot to touch, round the smooth-worn pole there at the back of the room, and twists and twists and twists it, till the water streams from the cloth and fills the gutter cut across the wash-house floor. And the same with the next, and the next after that, till his fingerprints are soggy, and the air behind the wash-house misty as a Roman bath; and between the wash-house and the kitchen there are seven lanes of washing, steaming in the bright cold air.

Which is how he comes to be stood in the cat's-cradle of lines, pegging up the last of the sheets.

Which is where Emilian finds him. Which is where Emilian, with wooden sword held rigidly before him, sneaks up on him from behind and stabs him in the calf.

Jack, grabbing his calf, gives a yell. Emilian hisses his goose-hiss of defiance – *Heesh!* – and disappears into the lanes of billowing sheets.

Jack looks down at his calf, and then at his hand, which now has blood upon it. Who the hell (*who the hell!*) would arm that fingerling maniac with a weapon? He turns around, on the lop, and from somewhere behind the rows of washing comes a *shee-hee-heesh* of triumph.

Right.

He grabs the sapling supporting the nearest line (to hell with the clean sheets). Finds a grip at the fork of the pole; tries a flourish or two. Then, with a sense of experiment, a proper thrust and parry. At once his body responds as if the last time he did this was only yesterday. It feels odd to be in that sideways stance again, but it feels good, too, and just as used to happen in the class with Master Nicholas he has at once that perfect inner image of himself – spine flexed, hands and feet as compass points – and a perfect image of his surroundings too, from the fence there behind him to the rest of the yard ahead, and all the lanes of washing, bellying in and out in the breeze.

All save one. The one sheet, as the breeze presses it back, that presses over a suggestion of a rounded forehead and a pointed nose.

Emilian charges from behind the sheet, sword held before him like a battering ram. This time Jack evades him easily; as Emilian runs, Jack simply steps over his head. Emilian disappears amongst the lines of laundry. Cautiously, Jack pokes the end of the pole through into the next lane. It is attacked at once. He can hear Emilian hissing curses as he batters at it with his wooden sword – *ferocious*, thinks Jack, *ferocious, but not that bright*. He withdraws the pole – a final screech of fury – waits a moment, then, going to the other end of the sheet, pulls it aside. There is Emilian, or there is his patched and ragged rump, as he peers around the sheet in turn to see where Jack might be. 'Boo,' says Jack, poking Emilian's arse.

Emilian spins about, and falls over.

'Get up,' says Jack. He pokes Emilian lightly in the chest. Emilian scrambles up and whacks at the pole anew. Jack pokes him in the shoulder. Emilian gives a roar of disbelief, as if asking how can this thing keep on evading him? Jack drops down low and pokes him in the ribs. Emilian goes back a step. Then another. They're coming out of the lanes of laundry now. And fair enough, his opponent is half his size, and he has to be careful none of those taps and pokes are hard enough to raise a bruise; but it does feel good, this, it feels damned good, just to be moving in this way again, so as he dances Emilian backward, and sees the tigress stood outside the kitchen door, he lifts his free arm in a swift, exuberant wave.

And Paola? What does she see?

That outflung arm, to begin with, loose and lazy as a tendril. Only it's not. Paola knows it's not, Paola can see every tiny change of balance the arm makes. Even the fingers move, like a musician, stopping the strings of a lute. But then it is like music, this, or should be, winding its way from feet to hips to shoulders, down the sword-arm, down the blade; and every time Emilian comes at him, the boy has some new variation ready. Emilian makes a wild slash at the boy's legs; the boy side-steps, drops down, and pokes Emilian under the arm. Emilian (arms clamped to his sides) comes at him front-on with a yell; the boy tilts backward, the balancing arm curves up, and Emilian is tipped over whatever-it-is the boy has as a sword and tumbles to his knees. The boy puts what Paola now sees is a pole from the washing-line against Emilian's neck. 'Got you,' she hears the boy say. 'Beg for mercy.'

Emilian is inflating like an angry cat. His mouth comes open in a shriek of fury.

'Emilian!'

The shriek is stilled. Emilian, crestfallen, watches as she strides toward him. 'Get out of here. You heard me. Scat!'

Emilian snatches up his sword. One last hiss of defiance and he's gone. She and the boy are left facing each other.

He's leaning on the pole. His expression says he knows what he just did was foolish, but there's a little spark of triumph to him, all the same.

'So, Jag,' she says. 'Very neat. Where'd you learn?'

Recognition. The spark of triumph grows. 'Amsterdam.'

'Who with?'

'Master Nicholas.'

'Never heard of him.' She taps the pole with the side of her foot. 'Ever wondered how you'd do in a real fight?'

He catches the tone in her voice, and the spark is gone. 'I thought I was good,' he says.

'Oh, you are, Jag, you are. I'll bet you ran rings round 'em, back in Amsterdam. I'll bet you were the best in school by far. Want to know how long it takes, to make a proper swordsman?'

She waits for the shrug, which she knows will come.

'How long, then?' he asks at last.

'All your life.' She points a finger at him. 'You stay here.'

And yes, he's puzzled, as she goes into the house; but he's still there, if even more puzzled, when she comes back out to him again, with the two objects shrouded in their wrappings held before her.

'That'll do for you,' says Paola, unwrapping the first.

There's no scabbard, and wire is coming adrift from the grip. As swords go, it's a pensioner, this one, fit for practice only. Even so, as she hands it to him, she hears him take in his breath.

She turns her attention to the second package. Unswaddles it as gently as if it were a babe. 'But this,' says Paola, lovingly, 'this one is something special.' She holds the sword up to the sun, sniffs the oil on its blade. 'Athene,' she says, holding it so he can see the letters of the name engraved along the blade. She angles it to the light. 'You see that blue? Only one place in the world can make a blade as fine as this, and that's Solingen. I was there when this one was forged. I watched her being born. And then I named her. This one was mine.'

The splutter of his laughter. 'Yours?'

'Yes, mine,' Paola answers. 'Tell me, how is that any stranger than you in a washerwoman's apron, hmm?' She holds up her hands. 'Of course, I was more adroit with her when I still had both of these.'

Which does at least give her the satisfaction of seeing him blush. 'Oh, there's a deal more to the world than you've seen of it, my lad,' Paola continues. 'Take that apron off.'

He does.

'And step out there. Let's have some room.'

He follows her to the centre of the yard. It seems to Paola that he still doesn't quite believe what she intends, but he gets the message fast enough when she lashes Athene left-right through the air. The blade hums. 'Oh, listen to that,' Paola says. 'Listen to her sing.' She drops her right leg forward. The boy falls into the same pose, mirroring her. The tips of the two swords circle each other, then, as if of their own volition, meet, sliding one around the other like a tentative caress; and there's that sound, that skirl, edge to edge, steel to steel.

She sees his head go back; the flitter of excitement cross his face.

'Well now, my lad,' says Paola. 'Let's see what you've got.'

THE RAUCHMANN BREWERY in Hertzberg is set close by the river, whose waters Eberhardt Rauchmann uses to steep his precious malted barley. The barley comes from Munich almost three hundred miles to the south-east, and it ain't cheap, Rauchmann's doppelbock, but with the armies heavy with a summer's pay or a summer's loot, Hertzberg provides an insatiable market for all. This year the town is so full Eberhardt can barely force his wagon through the streets.

Behind him the mermaid clock clears its throat and starts its carillon. Noon – just about the time that a hard-working brewer might think of sitting down with a stein of his best. That's something else he likes about Magda, she understands a man should have a chance to draw breath. The thought puts a smile behind his eyes, and lends portly, balding Eberhardt some glimmer of the ardency of youth. He raps upon the kitchen door. 'Ah, there you are, my dear,' Magda says, standing back to welcome him in. 'I was thinking it was time we saw you.'

They have to manhandle the barrels into the kitchen, rolling them onto the trestles by the kitchen's coolest wall. 'You lost your strongman this year?' asks Eberhardt, mopping his brow. 'I saw Jo-Jo, in the camp down by the river. Peter too.' He watches as Magda completes the delicate operation of tapping a barrel. Out comes the bung, in at once goes the tap, with no more lost than fine arterial spray, to show the beer in there is living. A man – a brewer – could make a proud husband to any woman can tap a barrel neat as that.

'Jo-Jo is always welcome here,' says Magda. 'You see him again, you tell him so.' She takes two tankards from the sideboard, and bends to the tap.

They're like the foam on two flagons of beer, thinks Eberhardt, watching her. They're like two boiled white piglets curled up on a tray. They're like two chalices laid side-by-side. They're like two sacks of barley –

Out comes the beer in a rippled stream, smooth and full and dark as rubies. 'Eberhardt, your health.'

A moment's reverential silence. 'Oh by the saints,' says Magda, raising a hand to wipe her lip. 'Oh, that's good. Eberhardt, you've excelled yourself.'

What a woman. Eberhardt gives Magda a genial smile. 'So,' he says. 'If you've no Jo-Jo, what are you going to do if you need a little muscle around here? Or an escort into town? Fact of the matter,' continues Eberhardt, settling into his seat, 'next sitting of the council, there'll be questions asked about that camp. Time to clear the streets. We'll be voting for a cordon and a curfew, and to double the watch, to boot. You'll be there?'

'I daresay, I daresay.' Her dimpled smile. 'What one woman's vote can do, it will.'

'Glad to hear it. Because there's some right rough-looking villains about this year, I tell you. Bad as the Roma. I see you've let them back again and all.'

'The Roma come or go as they please,' says Magda, firmly. 'Always have and always will. As for us, we're not on our own. We've a new lad helping us this year. A hard worker, too.'

Is that a fact? Eberhardt is none so sure he likes the sound of this. He removes his attention from Magda's bosom. 'Oh yes? Where is he then? Could have done with his help, getting those barrels in here.'

And Magda tilts her head. 'Listen,' she says.

From the far end of the yard comes the unmistakable percussion of a swordfight, punctuated by Paola's husky laughter. Eberhardt is amazed. 'Is he any good?'

'He must be,' Magda replies. 'They've been out there an hour, and he's still coming back at her.'

Sunrise. Here's an owl, drifting back to its roost in the roof of the wash-house. Here's that figure in the long pale robe, arms upraised, turning his marbled eyes toward its silent flight. And here's Jack, waking in that room on the dog-leg of the stairs, and trying to move and giving a groan.

It feels like someone stuck a skewer through his calves, wound up two inches of muscle and tied it off. It feels like his shoulders have been worked over with a mallet. Even his fingers ache.

He hears the door open. Someone grabs his big toe under the blanket and waggles it side to side. He sits up with a yelp.

'Come on, sleepyhead,' says Paola. She's dressed, and is holding both swords. 'Time for a half-hour before breakfast.'

A WEEK LATER, Eberhardt is there again, pulling his horse to a *whoa* in the yard, and the foundry-like racket of a swordfight is the first thing he hears. 'What, still?' he asks, as he follows Magda inside.

'Practice,' Magda tells him. Her cap is awry, and she sounds a little – well, for Magda, as if she's a little short on patience with this situation. Mentally, Eberhardt rubs his hands together. Sooner or later she's got to see it, how a man – the right man – could make a difference here.

'So, the news,' he says, once he and Magda are sat at the kitchen table, tankard of doppelbock apiece. He raises his voice a little, to cover the noise from the yard. 'Christian of

Brunswick, his goose is cooked. They say General Tilly is putting together an army to wipe that heretic dog from the map for once and all.'

'They do, do they?' Magda asks. Another of those dimpled smiles. 'And who's they?'

'Ah, you may smile,' Eberhardt tells her. 'But I had this off the man who knows. I had this off Ravello. He's up at the Golden Oak.'

'The scouts?' Her face lifts. 'And was the Shadow Man—'

'Not with 'em, no. Not as I saw.'

The smile is gone. In the silence that follows, the racket from the yard shoulders its way into the room.

'She,' says Eberhardt, and jerks his head toward the noise, 'she still got the knives out for him, eh?'

'Always has and always will,' says Magda, sadly.

Eberhardt takes a last pull at his beer. 'Sitting of the council, a week today,' he tells her. 'Cordon and a curfew, that's what we need. And Tilly to take the whole boiling lot of 'em with 'im, soon as can be.'

With Eberhardt gone, Magda sits at the kitchen table once more on her own. The puffs and pants of effort and the clash of steel on steel are louder than ever. They must be fighting right up against the house.

But Paola is happy, she tells herself. *She's drinking almost nothing and she's happy.*

Then from outside there comes a sudden exclamation. 'Oh, you cunning little bastard!'

Magda pulls the door open. Paola has Jag pinned against the wall. The two of them are face to face, and Paola's eyes are shining and her cheeks a-bloom. She has the boy's right arm, his sword-arm, gripped in her good hand, stretched so high the boy is almost on his toes. Her forearm, with the glove, is pressed across his throat. But at Paola's waist, the tip of the boy's knife is nuzzling her waistband.

'That's a neat trick,' Paola is saying. 'I thought I had you. That's a damned neat trick.' She glances down. 'And that's your left hand, too. How the devil did you do that?'

'Got you,' says the boy. His chest is heaving. There is a sheen of sweat on his throat. Magda has the same unpleasant sense of being both voyeur and interloper as she would have had if she had broken in upon a kiss. She clears her throat. Loudly.

'*If* you two are quite done trying to kill each other, I have an errand in town. And I wish Jag to come with me. As my escort.'

Hertzberg. The wandering squads of soldiers, shouldering each other aside; the preening horsemen; the carts, spattering one and all alike. Go past the street where the armourers work, you have to shout to be heard; down that of the farriers and horse-dealers, and the air is threaded through-and-through with neighs and whinnies. The boy likes that one. She sees his head whip round.

'Where are we going?' he asks.

'The Golden Oak,' Magda says. She hears herself; the short temper in her tone. In her head she still sees the two of them, pressed against that wall, and Paola's shining eyes. That moment of deep looking. *Oh, you old cat*, she tells herself. *You're being ridiculous.* Rather more gently, she adds, 'We're looking for one man, for news of another.'

The only thing that business slows for in Hertzberg is to watch the mermaid clock strike noon, and sure enough the crowd around them has come to a halt. Here comes the carillon, and then below the clock face, two doors open, and out from one comes a troop of angels, raising trumpets to their lips.

'And who's the man we're looking for?' Jag asks, bending his head to hers.

'Ravello,' Magda replies. 'He's a scout.'

The angels have been replaced by the Three Wise Men, leading their camels. The carillon sounds again, and since we are so clearly in the Holy Land, the Three Wise Men give way to a Saracen and a helmeted knight, woodenly jerking their swords up and down.

'And who's it we want news of?'

'Another scout. The best of all. They call him the Shadow Man.'

The knight is pursued by a wooden lion, with gilded mane rotating like a sunflower. The crowd below the clock gives the lion a friendly cheer.

'And why do we want news of him?' the boy asks.

'Because he's a friend. An old, old friend. He and me, we go back – oh so far. And when a woman is first in business on her own, she needs her friends.'

The cheering rises to a lusty roar. The mermaid is making her appearance, shamelessly bare-breasted, turning her torso this way and that as she admires herself in her mirror and combs her yellow hair. A second troop of angels, with harps and dulcimers, as the carillon sings out its last few notes and the mechanism of the clock begins to work in earnest.

'You didn't have Paola with you then?'

She laughs. 'Bless you, Jag, this was years afore Paola came to Hertzberg. In a way it was down to the Shadow Man that she came here at all, in fact.'

The crowd lurches forward. 'Oh,' he says. 'So Paola and this Shadow Man, they were—'

'Oh dear Lord no,' says Magda, laughing. 'They are about as far from such as any two could be.' She has to raise her voice again: now the mermaid clock has led the way, every clock in Herzberg is chiming noon together. 'So when we are back home, Jag, if we have news of the Shadow Man, we keep it to ourselves, you follow me?' She points upward, to the sign swinging over their heads. 'We're here.'

*

The Golden Oak. A step up from the enlisted man's favourite, the dining hall; this is a place for the professional traveller.
Stone-built, a gallery running round its courtyard at the height
of the rooms, and at the centre of everything, the venerable
oak itself. A mighty tree; when Ravello has stayed here in the
summer its leaves have brushed his windows, cast a summer's
greenness like the light through stained-glass windows on his
floor. This being winter though, for now that floor is strewn
with cosy rush. He's not expecting visitors. The scratch upon
his door occasions swift preparations on his part: in particular, a
speedy inventory of the room – any papers in sight? Any black
work (so-called)? 'Who's out there?' he demands.

But he knows who it is at once: the sweetness of the answering voice, albeit slightly breathless-sounding, after hauling
herself up the stairs. 'May we come in?'

'Frau Magda!' Ravello exclaims with pleasure, pulling the
door open, and then 'Good God!' as Jean Fiskardo enters the
room behind her.

It takes only a moment to realize his mistake – not Jean, no,
not the bulk, nor the cheery air of hearty violence that Ravello
remembers as following the man about like a ripple in the air.
Only a moment, and less than half of one to cover it: not Jean,
although the similarity is startling. Those chilly eyes – is this
some military type they're breeding now? He elaborates his
greeting to hide his amazement, taking Magda by the one hand
and touching the other to brow, lips, heart. Then he puts his
best smile on his face, and cocks an eyebrow. 'And who is this?'

'This is Jag,' says Magda, fanning herself with her hand. 'He's
been staying with us a while.'

Indeed? Ravello transfers the smile from Magda to her escort.
The escort summons up a nod. Extraordinary. *Extraordinary.*
'And where might Jag be from?'

'Heidelberg,' the boy says, promptly. Ravello has the impression the boy had subjected the room to a survey every bit as

thorough as Ravello's own before answering. Sharp, for such a young'un.

'And what might bring young master Jag to Hertzberg?'

'I was looking to enlist,' the boy replies.

Magda is moving round the room, inspecting, running a fingertip along the mantelpiece. 'Looking to enlist and came down with a touch of fever,' she puts in. 'So he's been staying with us awhile till he finds himself again.' She refuses Ravello's offer of the chair ('That looks too bony for me!') and settles herself, like a hen settling her feathers, on the bed. 'Now,' she says. 'I'm hoping you have some news.'

'News?' Ravello has any amount of it, some worth many thalers if whispered at the right time into the right ear. With an effort, he takes his eyes off the boy. 'What news would that be?'

'The Shadow Man,' says Magda, pointing her gaze at him. 'You're here, so where is he?'

'The Shadow Man. Ah yes. *Mi dispiace*, Frau Magda, he is at Forbach – ah, now –' for Magda has her hand to her mouth and her eyes have widened with distress. 'I won't pretend our friend is at his best.' (An understatement. Not since those dreadful days in Beaune has Ravello known the Shadow Man to look so frail.) 'But he rises late, he sits in the sun, the monks make him sirrops and tinctures – no smoky rooms, no carousing… I was writing to him,' he adds, gesturing to the table at the window, where lies paper, quill-pen, ink; and a tray with a bottle of raisiny vin santo, perfuming the air. A happy inspiration. 'Soon we will drink to his health restored in person, I am sure. For now, however –' He fills a glass, and passes it to Magda. 'And a little of this, to go with it?' The kitchen at the Golden Oak, which prizes Ravello's custom and knows enough of his business to wish to keep him happy, sent up the bottle accompanied by a thick golden waffle, gleaming with melted butter and dusted with cinnamon. But now he looks, they did not send up anything to cut it with. 'Ah – a moment—'

'Let me,' says the boy, and taking the plate, produces a clasp-knife from his pocket. He springs the blade, and slices the waffle into four. 'Here,' he says, handing it back.

Ravello looks from the knife to the boy and then, to be certain, to be completely and entirely sure, to the knife once more. He is aware of the eerie calm of his own breathing, over the gallop of his heart. He passes the plate to Magda, and watches as she takes a piece. 'Thank you, my dear,' she says. No, she is oblivious, clearly wholly oblivious, not a clue. 'And thank you, Jag,' he says, only a shade more fervidly than he intends. He pours another glass of wine, holding it out to the boy, but the boy wrinkles his nose and shakes his head. No taste for sweet wines, clearly, any more than did his father. Ravello transfers the glass to his own lips, and drains it at a swallow. 'Another?' he asks.

Magda shakes her head. 'My kitchen calls me.' She levers herself from the bed, the boy extending a hand to help her up. 'When you finish your letter, tell the Shadow Man I will have a bottle of weinbrand sent here, to welcome him. The best we have.' She casts a glance toward the mantelpiece. 'And tell the girl to dust his room more carefully than she does yours.'

Ravello knows exactly why his room is in need of dusting; when she would otherwise have been taking care of it, the maid at the Golden Oak was retreating before him, giggling, as he followed her across the floor on his knees, begging for a kiss. This, however, seems rather less the *punto alto* of the day than it did. 'Madame,' he says, reverently, touching his fingers to her, but in reverse this time – heart, lips, and head. 'And to you, Jag.' Recklessly he adds, 'May we meet again.'

When they are gone, Ravello sits down at his letter anew. Sits, and waits for the right words to come, running the sentences back and forth within his head, because a man has the pleasure of writing something like this the once only. He takes up his quill, dips it, and begins:

And if you can drag yourself away from those Franciscans of yours, you might care to meet the new lad they have lodging at Magda's. He has his father's eyes. And, it would appear, your old knife.

They reach the street. Jag is pointedly silent. They reach the marketplace. He is silent still. 'Cat got your tongue?' Magda enquires.

'Him,' says Jag. 'Don't think I cared for him.'

'Ravello? Why not?'

'He looked like he was thinking something as he wasn't going to share.'

'He did?' She gives a sigh. 'It could be. It's the scouts, Jag, it's how they are. They lead complicated lives.' She walks on. 'They live with secrets. They're who you go to if you've black work to be done.'

'Black work?'

'You know. Matters out of sight. So they learn to watch themselves. But if they give their word, they never break it. Even the Roma will work for the scouts, and the Roma don't trust anyone.'

They pass the clock. 'So who is he, this other one, this Shadow Man? Why's he called that?'

'It's a joke.' On impulse she tucks her hand under his arm. 'So fine a scout, he never cast one. That good at it, d'you see?'

On they go. 'So that's your friend. This Shadow Man.'

'Yes. My good friend. My best, after Paola, you might say.'

'So, if he comes here, why ain't he staying with you?'

'Because of Paola.' Another sigh. 'Paola and he – they have a history, and it's not a happy one. They both loved the same man, and he was lost, and Paola held the Shadow Man to blame.'

Here they are, almost home. 'So this Shadow Man,' says the boy. Very thoughtful. 'He's a molly, is he?'

'No, he is *not* a molly.' She should be exasperated, but she finds that she's smiling. 'His friend – the man Paola loved – he was a soldier. The Shadow Man scouted for his company. They served together. Fought alongside. It makes a bond. In any case –'

Here they are, at the gate to the yard.

'– what do you know of mollies? If I might ask.'

One of those great rare smiles of his. He bends his head. 'I ain't quite so green as that, y'know.'

And it's there on the tip of her tongue, the question she's longed to ask so many times – 'What *is* your story, Jag?' – when Paola's voice chops through the air between them.

'Don't you come sniffing back round here, you little *SHIT*!'

She's at the gate, driving Peter before her. She's waving Athene about his ears. She's loud enough for passers-by to turn and look. 'Now, Paola—' Peter tries, scrambling out of the way. He don't look good. One cuff flapping at the wrist, and the yellowed bruises of some recent altercation on his face. Life without Fat Magda's as a refuge has clearly run him hard.

'And don't you *now Paola* me, neither. You brought that boy here, you knew damn well he was sick, and you threw him on our hands without a thought. You've ate your last here, Peter. I see you here again I'll take a horsewhip to you.' And she shoves him in the shoulder with the glove.

Beneath the glove is solid oak. It packs a punch. Peter is on his arse in the middle of the road. Those passers-by who'd turned to look are pointing, tittering behind their hands.

And then as Magda watches, as the boy stands laughing with the rest, his and Paola's eyes meet once again, and first Paola throws him a smile of beaming complicity and then she sweeps him a bow – leg out, arm swept, and she comes up beaming still. A private joke.

And just as it had been in the courtyard, in that moment any soul watching them could not count for less.

It's maybe then –

No.

Don't think of it. You'll make it real.

That prick of suspicion. Like a tare caught in her clothes, hooked into her skin.

No. Ignore it.

Those bursts of laughter out there in the yard. The two bodies, dipping, turning, mirroring each other.

It's not happening. It can't.

Their passing, in the hall, or through a doorway. 'After you, *signora.*' 'No, no. After you, *mein Kapitan.*' Ilse passes between them and they bow her through together.

No. I'm seeing something when there's nothing there.

That moment in the courtyard with them stood against each other, their mouths so close they might have been breathing the same breath. What would have happened next had she, Magda, not opened the door?

She asks the cards.

The Nine of Cups. Reunion.

She walks in on them, at the kitchen table, one dark head, with that streak of white, bent in toward the other, which is the blond of old rope. At Magda's entrance, the two heads move gently but perceptibly apart.

She hears Paola with him, laughing, fond. Paola has a nickname for him now. Magda hears her sing it out, twenty times a day: '*Oh, Giacomo —*'

The Two of Pentacles. Great change.

She lays the next, but feels she knows already what it must be.

The Lovers.

Magda sets her face, and gets up from her reading.

As she stands, a card falls from her lap. Unseen, it drifts to the floor. The cat sniffs at it, hisses, and retreats.

There he sits, armoured, crowned, enthroned. The King of Swords.

CHAPTER NINE

The Spring and the Cup

'Only mountains never meet.'

Old French proverb

A T ITS MIDPOINT, the bridge at Hertzberg has a copper spike driven into the road, marking where the writ of the city-fathers ends and reminding you that, beyond this point, the law is what you will.

On the far bank of the river, scattered along it like the detritus of a flood, is the soldiers' camp.

If he could, Peter would have set up camp on the bridge itself, but that's forbidden. So he'd taken the next safest spot, at the bridge's far end, spreading out his and Jo-Jo's blankets under the protection of a new-sprung group of alders. Give it a while, he'd thought, a decent interval, the boy dead, buried, let 'em get over it, and back he'd go, full of sympathies.

For the first few weeks they'd done fine. The weather had cleared, the ground dried out, the river rippled past him in his sleep, bearing pleasant dreams. True, Jo-Jo complained he was cold, he was hungered; true, they had to dispute the foreshore with a gang of washerwomen, beating out their linens on the bridge's fat stone feet, and accusing him and Jo-Jo of making the water smutty with the ashes of their fire, but what of that? To show the women what for, he took to shitting on the smooth rocks where the women laid their laundry out to dry. Behind them the camp was growing; soon enough everyone would be using the shore as a latrine. The women 'ud better get used to the idea, and move along theirselves.

The women did not get used to the idea. The harpies came back in the middle of the night with sticks, and beat him like a carpet.

It took two days before he was limber enough to walk, by which time the rest of his regiment had come in. The Hohenzollern boys. Not that any of them thought to seek him out to tell him so, oh no, Peter found out only when he saw one of his brothers-in-arms, gloriously mazy, tip right over the side of the bridge.

Peter didn't hesitate a moment. 'By God, he's drunk,' he roared, springing to his feet. 'Jo-Jo! They must'a been paid!'

The queue for wages, when he found it, reached down the street. At the far end a lieutenant sat at a table with a coffer to his side, guarded by a half-dozen halberdiers. Mutterings and grumblings passed up and down the queue:

'That lot, they're up to something…'

'They're working some cheat on us…'

'They ain't got enough to pay us all, that's what it is…'

He reached the front. The lieutenant peered up at him. 'Name?'

'Peter Taube. Milit'ry courier. Third battalion.'

The man turned the page. The cloth on the table fluttered in the wind. 'Paid you,' he announced, laconically.

Peter spluttered, 'No you ain't!'

'See here?' The man jammed a thumbnail beside a name on his list. 'Paid you.'

There was his name, a cross in the margin beside it. 'That ain't my mark!' Peter exclaimed, and then pushing his face forward, demanded, 'You think I don't know what you're at?'

The man, lowering his voice, replied, 'Then you'll know to keep your mouth shut and come back next week, won't you?'

'But I need me pay now!'

The man leaned back, regarded Peter a moment, then lifted his quill, laid his rule along Peter's name, and slowly and deliberately drew a line through it. 'So now you're paid,' he said. 'So off you fuck. Next!'

The man behind Peter was already jostling him aside. 'You bastards!' Peter exclaimed, retreating, shaking his fists. 'I'll get what's mine, you see if I don't!'

It was the day after that he'd tried returning to Fat Magda's. Look where that got him.

Where he and Jo-Jo have ended up, the bridge is now a far-off shimmer. Everyone is indeed using the shore as a latrine, and here is where the worst of it washes up. Along with busted boots and shoes, lost hats, strayed laundry, and bits of clay pipe which make the shoreline crunchy as walking on shells. It's sunset; music drifts toward him from further along the bank, but does nothing to sweeten his mood.

That damned boy.

That's where it started, he sees that now. Why, that boy (that viper he has nourished in his bosom) wouldn't even have known Fat Magda's existed, were it not for him!

Could've left him anywhere along the road, but no. He'd seen the young'un was sickening, so he'd carried him where he'd be cared for, safe –

(He feels the fat warmth of the lie begin its growth.)

– because that's what he is, is Peter, he's one who takes care of others whatever the cost to himself –

And you'd think they'd take care of him. He can't last a winter, not out here. This morning he'd woke with his hair frosted to the earth. Fat Magda's – why, the years he's known those women. His sisters-in-arms, was how he'd thought of them, a second home, and now –

(A blubbery self-pity overcomes him.)

It's him. That damned boy. He's turned 'em against me, my oldest friends –

A cry from along the shore. Jo-Jo is there, fishing, with a bent wire and a gob of chicken fat. Now he's making his way back up the bank with something catching the light off the end of his hook. 'Peter, look! Lookit this!' He arrives before Peter, beaming. 'Supper!' he announces.

A fish squirms on the end of the hook. A fish so small the hook has all but disembowelled it.

Peter grabs at the fish, pulls it off the hook, throws it to the ground and for good measure stamps upon it too. He seizes a pinch of Jo-Jo's upper arm and twists. 'You call that supper? You want to starve us? You want to leave me to waste away?' He hauls Jo-Jo about to face the camp, the shifting multi-coloured mass. 'D'y'see that? Look at this place. There's Spanish and Italianos, there's Austrians and Polacks, there's Bulgars and Ongrians, and them – do you see them? Them with the wolf upon their flag? Crow-ats. Crow-ats,' he continues. 'Homeland a whole year's march away. That's like halfway to hell. And any of 'em, from *anywhere*, can walk into Magda's and they'll get a welcome. But that bastard fucken boy, he's fixed it so as I cain't show my face there no more!'

Astonishment. 'No he ain't, Peter, Paola's angry a'cause we left 'un—'

'Oh yes he *has!*'

Another pinch of flesh. Jo-Jo is whimpering, tears squeezing down his cheeks. 'Peter, that's hurting!'

'And what've I got? What've I got, eh? He gets the warm bed

and the full belly, and me, *me –*' Peter is in a rage, but ain't that what Jo-Jo's for? 'I get you, you great loon – you, what eats us bare and is too fucken soft to keep a guard at night! You, what lets me get beat up by women! That's what I got, for all my pains and trouble!' He pulls Jo-Jo's face down to his. 'But I'll be even, you'll see. You needn't think as I'm done yet. I'll be even with him if it's the last thing I do!'

In the middle of the night he wakes, face stinging with cold.
    Jo-Jo is gone.

HERE WE ARE: a fine, bright morning, the sort that comes with winter sun to nip your cheeks and puts a sparkle in the eye of all creation, and here is Jack, surrounded by cheeses, barrels, sacks of flour; the storerooms open and his wits on high alert. Strangers do wander in; and it wouldn't be the first time the sound of a barrel being rolled across the yard has uncurled from some forgotten corner a sleeping drunk, sore-headed as a hibernating bear.

What he's hearing now, though, is only the Roma girl cross-ing the yard. The sound she makes comes both from the rustle of the enormous number of layers to her skirts, and the tinkle of her belt. He's never seen her face and is intrigued to do so – there's a darkness about her that reminds him of Paola (it is a source of great inner turmoil to Jack how much reminds him of Paola, just at present) – but whenever she crosses the yard she ducks her head and pulls her shawl in tight, hiding almost all of her face but her nose. Jack has a sense they don't like strangers' eyes on them, the Roma women, and he's noticed that they don't let men come near 'em either, keeping a kind of cordon round themselves with the vast bell of their skirts. *There's a lot of rules to being a Roma*, thinks Jack, half-listening for the girl's tinkling music, as she walks toward the field. Lot of rules to being a Roma woman, that's for sure.

The tinkling music stops. He hears her voice. 'Step aside, please.'

Turning, he sees her standing back from the gap in the fence, and the reason she's doing so is that there's a man standing there. Who must have come into the yard without a sound – which annoys Jack, to begin with – and who in response to this request steps forward, to block her way into the field completely.

From the Roma camp, nothing stirs.

'Hey,' calls Jack. He's aware of a rough edge to his voice, which seems to arrive on its own and that, as he crosses the yard, he's striding.

As Jack comes nearer, the man by the fence tilts his head to one side, sizing him up. Jack feels his own head tilt, realizes he is doing the same. The man is not so tall, not so well built either, in fact running a little to fat, but he's very well dressed, with a thick dark cloak slung over his jacket and a hat of sheeny felt. And he's very, very pale. Almost a sick-bed pallor, thinks Jack, remembering his own, were it not for the weight in the man's jowls.

Just visible at his throat, a strip of red cloth, knotted under the chin.

'You lost, friend? Looking for something?' Jack asks. He's an obscure idea it would be wise to sound both older than he is and more proprietorial.

The man lifts a hand, to scratch at the edge of one nostril. 'A wooman,' he says, matter-of-fact.

'No women here,' says Jack. 'Not what you're looking for.' He feels he should offer some apology to the girl as he says it – stood right there, for God's sake – but she has her shawl pulled tight about her face again.

The finger, abandoning the nostril, points back toward the girl. 'What is that?'

'Not. What. You're. Looking. For,' Jack repeats, leaving a space between each word. 'This ain't no bordel.' The silver wolf, on its cord against his chest, feels almost as if it's getting hot. 'Down by the river, that's the house you want. The one with the empty scabbard over the door.'

The man waits; as if he's running through some catalogue of possibilities of which neither Jack nor the girl (still stood there, silent, motionless) could even dream. And then the sound of another body blundering its way through the gate.

"Lo, Jag,' Jo-Jo calls, then for the first time notices the girl, the man, and halts.

The man sizes Jo-Jo up much as he had done Jack. He smiles. He has very small white teeth, like pips within his gums. '*U redu*,' he says, pleasantly. He nods to the girl, turns, saunters past Jo-Jo, and is gone.

Freak. Jack has a faint hope the girl would have found most of that incomprehensible, but it's impossible to tell; her face is as hidden as ever. He moves away from her, so there can be no doubt that she's free to pass and that the episode is over. As she walks into the field he casts a last glance over his shoulder at the gate to the street. There's a bar to be dropped across last thing at night, but the gate in Amsterdam was not so different, and that was breach-able, too. *A bar AND a bolt*, thinks Jack, and then again, *freak*.

It's the minute or more of the wait that stays with him. The effort of keeping his face still, as the other's eyes went over it. Like being crawled on by a fly.

'Jag, 'oo was that?' asks Jo-Jo, coming up.

'Don't know,' he replies. 'Don't want to know.' Enough with freaks finding their way into the yard. Paola might be out here with one of her inspections any minute. (There, you see? Her again.)

Jo-Jo is viewing the stores. 'You got any spare?' he asks, sounding hopeful.

'What, you hungry? Peter not feeding you no more?'

Jo-Jo shifts from one foot to the other. 'No more Peter,' he says at last.

Jack eyes him. 'You and Peter had a falling-out?'

'No more Peter,' Jo-Jo repeats.

'No?'

'No.' More shifting of feet.

Ah, the hell I care, thinks Jack. 'Jo-Jo, you help me put this stuff away, and you can take your pick.'

The encounter with the stranger has dropped to the bottom of his mind within the hour.

The mermaid clock has sung its way past noon; the smiling angels come and gone and Jo-Jo waddled off to the kitchen when Jack hears the sound of something a good deal bigger than the cat skittering up behind him. When he turns about, there's Emilian. 'What do you want?' Jack asks.

Emilian holds out his hand.

'What?'

The hand is shaken in a peremptory manner. Take it!

'You bite me, you little arseworm,' says Jack, 'and I'll flatten you.'

Emilian gives him a look that suggests such a sentiment pains him even as it dishonours the speaker. He takes Jack's hand in his, and starts pulling him into the field.

There seems to be a watch now, on the camp. As Emilian pulls him toward the tents, two men start up the field toward him: one to the left and one to the right. And these two don't look at all like that other oddity, the one in the long pale robe. These wear thick boots and heavy jackets, and sport knives with which you could gut a bull, tucked in the scarves round their waists. Jack is suddenly aware that there's a devil of a lot of field opening up between him and Fat Magda's, and has a distinct suspicion that here he may have overstepped more boundaries than one. He makes to pull Emilian to a stop, and as he does, a female voice shouts something out, and there is the girl, and striding up the field beside her, a third man, arm raised aloft as if in greeting.

Jack, eyeing the two men flanking him, points to Emilian and calls, 'He brought me.'

'Yes,' comes the reply, then, with a gesture to the girl, 'His mother told him to.'

The girl is this little tyke's *mother*?

The man arrives before him. He has flaming red hair – the reddest hair Jack has ever seen, even more outrageous a colour than you'd find amongst the Dutch – and close to, something uneven about one side of his head, hidden beneath the tassel of his cap. The man holds out a hand. '*Sastimos*,' he says. 'Welcome. I am Rufus.'

'Rufus,' Jack repeats, and then, 'Emilian's father.'

'Yes,' says the man. He gestures to the girl, who now holds Emilian by the hand. 'And this is Yuna. My wife.' He sounds amused; most likely, thinks Jack, at the amazement Jack feels gathering unstoppably on his own face. But then you look at the girl, now she's dropped that shawl, her forearms heavy with silver, her breast and neck the same, and the self-possession in the way she stands, and it's obvious whose wife she'd be. The man moves his own hand, as if to recall it to Jack's attention. As Jack takes it he thinks first, *This is me shaking hands with a Roma, this is turning out a most strange day and no mistaking*, and then from the way the hand sits inert in his own, and the extra width to the man's smile, that shaking hands is something the Roma don't do amongst themselves, and that they find it comic.

'They call me Jag, here,' Jack says.

'Yes,' says Rufus. 'We know that name for you. But you will not remember. You were busy dying,' he continues, smiling broadly. 'We are so glad you did not. My brother especially. It would be his pleasure if you and he could meet.'

They walk him into the camp, Yuna and Emilian in the lead and the two guards at the rear. There's a scamper of movement from around the fires as they approach, two more women and half-a-dozen children too, all tucking themselves out of sight. And the men, watching with expressionless faces as Yuna leads them to a tent set up outside the circle of the rest. There's an odd detritus on the ground around it, a dander of fluff and small feathers. Rufus, lifting aside the flap that serves as a door, calls softly into its interior, then beckons Jack to follow.

Inside it is dark as a cave. Jack enters, and as he enters, something touches him lightly on the forehead, seems to wheel across his brow then spin away. There is movement in the darkness – a figure clad in something long and pale, rising to its feet. It holds out one hand, fingers splayed, as the blind will do. Out of the darkness, a long and gentle 'Aaaah –'

'This is my brother Benedicte,' Rufus says. 'Benedicte, here he is. This is Jag.'

Benedicte sits at one side of the tent, cross-legged on a leather cushion; Jack sits opposite him, on another. There is a little velvet-covered table between them, which Jack had discovered by striking it with his knees. Hanging above his head are innumerable tiny spiralling somethings, one of which must have been what struck him on the forehead as he came in. They look like some child's modelling of the forms of birds – walnut-shell bodies, acorn heads, a drift of fluff for a crest and single feathers as wings. Rufus has lit a lamp, but dropped the canvas over the entrance, so the darkness inside is almost as deep as before. But some details, caught in the light, have stayed – Benedicte's face, the blank eggs of his eyes, the skin of his forearms, striated with lines of ink.

'It was you at the turnpike. On the road to Heidelberg.'

The blank-eyed face tilts slightly, as if in modest acknowledgement. *So he can hear*, thinks Jack, *even if he don't speak.*

'Forgive me,' Rufus is saying. 'It was my doing, that you did not meet then.' He has sat down beside his brother. 'Better like this, I told him. Yes?'

There is a quill and a blank sheet of paper on the table. Benedicte turns his face, puts his mouth against Rufus's ear. There is a sound like a breeze through dry grass. This, Jack realizes, is Benedicte speaking. Rufus says, 'My brother wishes to see you. You do not object?'

See me how? Object to what?

That long-fingered hand is raised once more. Even the palm is written on – not words, that Jack can see, but endless scribbled lines, some dark and new, some old and faded, all of them in some language that seems to have neither beginning nor end. The delicate fingers, in mid-air, have begun to lift and fall, like a spider, testing to see where its legs will go next. Benedicte's mouth is still at his brother's ear. Rufus is saying, 'My brother sees – stories. He has seen yours. He thinks you should see it too. If you permit.'

'If he wishes, for sure,' Jack replies. This is some masquerade, he's thinking, done to keep this poor soul happy. It would be churlish not to play along.

'Give me your hand,' Rufus says. He lays Jack's hand upon the sheet of paper, then covers it with his own.

Benedicte leans forward. There is movement in those blank white eyes; the eyelids quiver, the eyeballs roll. That almost-not-there whispering is ceaseless. And then Jack senses movement, above his head. One by one, as if caught in a breeze, all those tiny models have begun to spin.

Rufus's voice comes out of the dark. It says, 'Close your eyes.'

At once there is a flash of light as bright as through a crystal. It burns through Jack's eyelids, comes with him even as he jerks his head away. It's sun on a snowfield – it is a snowfield, and something moving from its horizon toward him, very fast but very far away. The way it moves makes him think it is an animal, bounding at full stretch. There is a voice in his ear or in his head, he can't tell which, saying with great emphasis, 'You must be *mindful* when it snows.' The sky on the horizon darkens. Stars appear, in their dozens. The animal is still bounding toward him. The voice, saying softly, 'This is what follows you,' and now there is some other sound as well, swallowing the whispered words, and he sees the snowfield dip at its centre, dip and start to fall, and realizes he's listening to the whispering fall of sand. *I'm in the hourglass*, he thinks, but without panic, almost without surprise.

The snow is funnelling down. The animal has gone, but in its place the funnel has a spot of darkness at its centre. He sees his feet go sliding toward it, holds up his arms and lets himself go, rolling left-wise, right-wise in the snow, down through the funnel of the hourglass, down, down, down. He falls through lines of scribble that catch and hold him like a net, and when he looks down he is looking into a refulgent golden glow, as bright as if he were sitting in the trumpet of a daffodil. There is a rough wall in front of him, the sense of some low entrance-way behind, and slowly on the wall in front there appear the shadows of objects, in great profusion, and then their forms – dishes, piled one atop the other, tazzas, candlesticks as tall as in a church, bowls, chalices, goblets, the proud statue of a deer, and all of it shimmering, glimmering, glittering gold. He hears himself exclaim at it, and then the darkness above starts spreading down into it, as if the wall were no more than wet paper, and when he looks up, those many stars above are all being joined one to the other by lines of fire, until there is an enormous face looking down at him from the darkness, a skull outlined in flame, and as he watches, one of its eyes closes, in a wink. There is laughter, deep male laughter, many voices, all at once, and then the mouth opens, and everything is gone, consumed in blinding, unbearable white.

And then his father's voice. It says, quite unmistakably, 'We Poitou men.'

And then the voice is a woman's, singing. *No*, he thinks, at once. *No* – and in his thoughts he is pushing himself away from it, or it away from him, an effort so huge it feels as if he is tearing the heart out of his own breast to do it.

'Petit Jacques,' her voice persists, 'come here, come here.'

The scent of lavender.

His eyes are open. He is in darkness still. He can make out the legs of the little table, and feel beneath him a woollen rug. Benedicte is leaning down toward him, that thin hand hovering above his head, almost as if to pat him, to console. A tingling sensation on his forehead, and then he hears Rufus saying, 'I have him.'

Slowly, he is set back on his feet. He asks, 'Did I faint?' and the answer comes back, 'In a manner of speaking.'

His eyes adjust. Benedicte is sat opposite, unmoving, eyes closed, hands folded in his sleeves. That sheet of paper on the table now covered in line after line after line of scrawled dark text.

'Some air,' Rufus is saying.

With help, he makes it outside. 'Catch your breath,' Rufus urges, sitting him down.

He shakes his head. His ears are ringing. Beyond him, the scrub of the paddock, at its end the brush of trees against the sky – all, shockingly, just as it was before. He rubs a hand across his face. 'I heard my father's voice,' he says.

'Yes,' Rufus answers, 'so did we.' He takes a pipe from one pocket, a tobacco pouch from the other. A glance to his side, as if waiting for Jack to say more. 'You don't like to speak of your family?'

'I am my family,' says Jack. 'What else is there to say?'

A puff at the pipe. Then Rufus says, 'Your story will not stay in this place much longer, Jag. You are going to live with the hunters, not with the prey.'

'How does he *do* that?' If he closes his eyes he can still see that thing bounding at him across the snow, then the gold, the fiery skull... 'How does he put those pictures in your head?'

'I cannot tell you,' Rufus answers. 'We have no idea. It has been like this with my brother ever since he was a little child. He looks, he sees. He touches, he foretells.' He leans forward, and presses one finger into Jack's forehead. 'Everything waits in there, you know. More space than in the sky.' A puff of the pipe, a little smoke sent up to join whatever else is waiting. 'With the old Emperor, under Rudolf, we were men of science. My brother dreamed of discovering how it was he could do what he does, as an explorer dreams of discovering a new world. Then the old Emperor died, and we were nothing. We were put amongst the jugglers and clowns.'

The sound of movement from within the tent. Jack says, 'Magda told me what was done to him.'

'No,' says Rufus, calmly as before. 'She did not. She did not tell you, because she does not know. My brother did not lose his eyes because of the darkness of his cell. The Prince-Bishop had molten wax dripped into them. It does not kill, you see, but it will blind, if it is done enough. And there was a boy, some scion of the Prince-Bishop's family, of the Maduna, a bud of that cankered tree. Very young to be so vile. He would come down to my brother's cell and have the jailers let him in, and when my brother was helpless, he would hunt him in the dark. My brother was an innocent. This piece of poison, he amused himself upon him. Took him for his sport.' A pause. 'My brother lost his voice, screaming for me to come and rescue him. And when at last he was released, he had left his wits in the darkness too. Everything was gone from him. Everything but the sight within.' A longer pause. 'You know what it is, I think, to be unable to protect someone you love. Nothing hurts more.'

There is a bursting sensation about Jack's heart, a swelling like a wave between rocks. 'No,' he says, at last. 'No, nothing does.' There is a long beat of silence. Then Jack says, 'I hope as he comes through for you, this Dead Man. I hope as he does what your brother saw him do.'

'Oh, there is no doubt,' Rufus replies. 'Nothing can change that. He is already on his way.' The pipe is knocked out against the ground; Rufus gets to his feet. 'Come,' he says. 'There are wolves out there. I will take you back.'

WHAT'S BETTER THAN a good warm kitchen, against all that wintry darkness gathering outside? Surely anyone with any sense would have settled themselves in here long ago. 'Where's Giacomo?' Paola demands, striding in, rubbing her arms. 'Where's he got to?' Everyone else is there, Jo-Jo, Magda, Ilse – she looks again. Magda inexplicably arrayed in her best Bruges velvet, and Ilse tending to her hair. 'And what's all this?'

'Ilse dear,' Magda answers, 'do you know where Jag might be?'

Ilse is transforming Magda's usual modest bun of hair into one of those confections of back-combed froth now so ridiculously fashionable, tweaking every last strand to radiate round Magda's face like a halo. 'He'm with the Roma,' she replies. 'Emilian fetched him.' Back and forth her fingers go, flourishing the comb. On the table beside her, Paola now sees, lies Magda's jewellery case, open to show her gold earrings and her onyx necklace, and Magda's finest cloak, carefully folded to keep its silken lining uppermost, is laid across the bench.

'The devil is he doing with them? And what's all this titivating for?'

'The meeting of the council,' says Magda, as the necklace is fastened round her neck.

'That's today?' Paola peers more closely. Magda, she sees, is not only haloed but powdered – face and shoulders shimmering, lips rubbed red. 'Making a *festa* of it, are you?'

'If you like,' says Magda. 'And there is a supper after, so I'll be gone for that too.' She pats at the rear of the halo, the combs holding it in place. 'Very good, Ilse.' Her feet are visible beneath the hem of her gown. She wears her highest heels, with the squirrel fur at the ankles.

'For heaven's sake, Maggie, don't tell me you're walking there in those? It's set to snow!'

'I am aware of what the weather holds,' Magda replies. 'I will be travelling with Eberhardt.' She's peering in her looking-glass, tilting her head. 'He is bringing his carriage. I did explain all this to you, Paola, days ago. You grow forgetful.' A glance into the mirror, catching Ilse's eye. 'I don't know, Ilse dear, truly. I told her, *and* I told her cub.'

A snort of laughter from Ilse, instantly silenced behind her hand. Paola regards them sourly. 'So what do I do this evening?' she demands. 'Run the place on my own?'

'I thought you did that anyway,' Magda replies, still with that maddening calm. 'But you've Ilse to help you, should you need. And Jag as well. In fact, I doubt the two of you will even notice I am gone.'

The sound of a heavy-wheeled carriage in the street outside. 'There,' Magda says, sweeping up her cloak. 'That is Eberhardt. I must be gone.'

They hear her opening the door, and Eberhardt's hearty greeting. Paola feels Ilse's eyes upon her, waiting.

The sound of the carriage, departing.

'*Well*,' Paolo pronounces, seating herself at the table. 'If she reckons as we're opening without her she can think again. Ilse, pass me the bottle there.'

'This 'un's empty, all but, Frau Paola,' Ilse answers promptly, holding the bottle to the light.

'Then you can just get yourself outside and fetch me another, can't you?' Paola says.

Five minutes into their journey, Eberhard Rauchmann (who

still cannot believe his luck) reaches across to offer his pas-
senger a nip of something warming from his flask, and is both
astounded and dismayed to see she has tears in her eyes.

THEY REACH THE FENCE, do Rufus and Jack, the fence that does
indeed now mark the boundary between this world and something else, and casting an eye back into that other, Jack hears
himself asking, 'Did you see everything I did?'

'Everything. This is how we do it, now my brother has no
eyes or voice. Think of him as the spring, and me as the cup.'
A broad grin. 'And you as the thirsty traveller. What did you
think to the room?'

'What room?'

'The room full of gold, of course. The one that is waiting for
you.'

He shakes his head. 'Rufus, there ain't no room full of gold
waiting for me.' But it has reminded him of something. 'When
I was sick,' he says, 'I had this dream there was a man, come to
look in at me. Magda said it must have been you. It looked like
he was stood in a hall of mirrors. Was it you? Could it have been?'

'A hall of mirrors?' Rufus repeats. He sounds surprised then
amused, is chuckling. 'No, *moosh*, that was not me.' He raises a
hand in farewell, then pointing one finger from it, says, 'Look
at those stars. I believe that it will snow.'

And when Jack looks up, he sees that every star above his
head is sporting a warning halo of powdered crystal, and when
he looks back, Rufus is gone.

There across the courtyard is the window of the kitchen;
there inside is Jo-Jo, at the table. He looks for Magda, then
thinks *No, of course, the meeting of the council.* Instead there's
Paola, with her back to him – the tight shape of her waist, the
soft blur of her hair. Ah, God, as if life weren't baffling enough

already. *And here's me, just as ever, on the outside, looking in.*

And then –

That prickle at the back of his neck. He turns, slowly, pivoting on one foot – *All right, what is it, what little thing's awry* – and then through the window of the wash-house, a wink of light, and that's not some little thing. That's of a different nature altogether.

The light is wavering. *Someone in there with a lantern.* His knife is in his fist almost before he knows it. He eases himself closer.

And now from the wash-house he hears laughter. The light lifted higher. The doorway fills with it, just long enough for him to mark one man, holding the lantern, and another with his back to the door, and both of them looking at something in the corner of the wash-house, down on the floor. And both with those God-damn strips of cloth around their necks, just like that fucken freak this morning, and the minute he sees them, he understands: the man this morning went away irked, and these two are his revenge.

He lets out his breath. He moves up to the door.

Two, yes. One holding the lantern, and in his other hand a pistol, and the second man standing over Ilse, who is down on the floor, dress ripped, cap pulled awry, blood in her hair, and an expression on her face of complete incomprehension. The man standing over her has his feet planted apart, and isn't moving at all.

Other than one elbow at waist-height, moving back and forth like a piston.

And again, the other laughs.

Jack knows what the man is doing, knows exactly what the man is doing, has done it enough times himself; and the notion that this makes him somehow like these adds a Goliath-sized punch of some most complicated anger of its own. He grabs the wooden paddle from beside the door and belts the man over the head with it so hard he hears the paddle split. The man drops straight down, like a nail being hammered. And the other, with the lantern, turns at once, and fires.

It may be the damp in the air, but there's a wet-sounding *fzzzzt* of ignition – soon as he hears it, Jack knows no bullet is going to follow that – and sure enough, no crack of firing.

He uses the paddle again, to jab the second man in the throat. The man falls backward into the copper. A tidal wave lifts out the copper and pours across the floor. He's pulling Ilse to her feet while the water floods about them, pushing her through the door, hauling the door shut behind her.

No fucken lock…

He braces one foot against the wall, both hands through the handle of the door. Noises already from within, the sound of someone splashing their way out the copper, and a bellow, and something in reply.

Ilse, beside him, like she's frozen to the spot. 'Ilse, get Paola!'

Still she stands there. An awful suspicion – he was too late. 'Ilse – did they hurt you?'

'They'm hurt my dress,' Ilse replies. She's lifting the torn edges, as if all she has to do is bring sleeve and bodice together again and everything will be mended. Her slow delivery gives the words great dignity.

There is scrabbling at the door from inside, then a hefty tug. His fingers, knitted round the handle, are burning with effort. He braces his leg anew. 'Ilse, get Paola! Get Jo-Jo! Run inside! Go!'

He hears her go, the scamper of her feet. The door is bowing from its frame. He gives one final pull from his side, violent as he can, then lets the door go, dancing backward as it bangs open. He hears one of the bastards inside fall over, at least. Then for a moment nothing but the black square of the doorway, just as before, and then they come nosing out of it, like jackals.

This had to happen, he tells himself. He backs up, knife out, guarding the space before him. *Sooner or later, your first proper fight.*

They keep on moving, left and right. One has the pistol, now held by the barrel like a club, and a knife of his own; the other, a sword. He knows at once, *that's the officer.*

The officer has blood trickling down his forehead. He moves a little unsteadily, pacing to his right. Jack understands what they're trying to do: get enough ground between them so he can't watch both at once. He drops his shoulders, moves back again, but in a walled yard you can't keep on doing that –

The man pauses, raises an arm. Blood must've trickled into his eye. Puts up his sleeve to wipe it –

Jack runs at him and kicks him in the balls. He puts all the viciousness he can into the kick, and the man drops his sword and hinges over, with a long *aaaaah* of disbelief. Jack grabs the man's head by the hair and brings his knee up into the man's face; he feels the explosion of blood right through his breeches. The man falls backward. His nose is not so much bust as butterflied across his face. Jack hears the second man running up; seizes the sword from where it fell and, leaping back, starts circling. The man is snarling something under his breath. Where he moves, he leaves a trail of drips.

'Yeah, what?' Jack yells at him. 'Look at your slime-trail, you fucken snake. You think you can come in here as you please? I'll fucken skin you. I'll wear *you* for a neckerchief, you piece of shit.'

Their circling has put the man close by his officer, who's trying to rise, reaching out an arm. The man bends, puts his own arm under the other, lifts him to his feet. They're like a pair in a three-legged race. Can't fight like that. *I've won*, thinks Jack, almost in disbelief, *fight's over*. The man says something more, indistinct, then from behind the officer's back, from under the buff-coat, produces another pistol, primed and ready. He raises it, grinning. Cocks the hammer. Possibilities explode within Jack's head – *might not kill me. Might be another mis-fire. I might dodge it.* Then: *This is really going to hurt.*

The pistol levels with his face.

And stays there.

The man's own expression changes, to one of vast dismay.

And from behind both men comes Paola's voice, saying, 'I wouldn't. Not if I was you.'

The men turn, the officer going down on one leg, the other hauling him up again, and all the while with that look on his face like someone just gave him the worst news of his life. Paola, coming into view, has the glove hooked in the back of the man's collar, and a pistol jammed right up between the cheeks of his arse. The minute he sees it, Jack starts laughing. And Jo-Jo is behind her, armed with Magda's cleaver from the kitchen.

Paola says, 'Get his pistol.'

He sheathes the sword in his belt and takes the pistol. The hand releasing it is nerveless. The officer, still just about held on his feet by the other, gives a groan. The amount of blood coming from his nose is extraordinary. Paola watches till Jack has the pistol turned on the two men, then she says, 'And now you're leaving.'

Between them, they escort the men to the gate. At the gate, Paola steps back, covering them both. Jack holds the gate open for the two to pass through. As the one passes by him, holding the other up, Jacks lowers his voice and says (but just as pleas-ant-toned as Paola), 'You tell 'em, where you come from. No women here.' The man glares at him. Jack closes the gate. He turns to Paola, grinning, victorious.

There's no smile in return. 'Drop the bar across it,' is all she says, and turning her back on him, heads for the house. Jo-Jo follows.

As he watches her walk away, he realizes that it's begun to snow.

*

She walks into the house, does Paola, not a single stride that isn't firm and purposeful, though her whole body is beating with a rage so cold and so implacable, it's a wonder the snow-flakes, as they fall on her, don't stick. *Those bastard sons of dogs... Nothing's safe from them, not women, children...*

Ilse is by the kitchen fire, as silent and unmoving as when Paola left her, save for that one hand held to her shoulder, trying over and over again to put her torn sleeve back into place, but on her face not bewilderment, not incomprehension any more; instead this dreadful sorrow. After all the years of safety, the world has turned on her again.

'Stay with her,' Paola tells Jo-Jo. Time to get her other cub indoors. She goes out into the yard to fetch him, and there he is, out in the gently falling snow.

And he's dancing. Sword in his hand and dancing, every step he'd taken in that fight, fitting his feet to the marks left before – this boy, this lonely-hearted, uncomplaining madcap boy, dancing his dance of solitary victory, dancing in triumph, like he'd scattered every demon on God's earth, and she knows, does Paola, how many more and how much worse there are out there, and she's not going to be able to protect him from any of them. All she can do is keep him safe this minute, in her arms.

So she does.

Snow in his hair, on his shoulders, on his lashes, and there must have been a snowflake on his mouth as well; so her first taste of him is ice.

It's a long kiss; it's a long, long kiss. It has all the days and hours in it that it took to bring it into being. Drawing back from him, Paola says, 'You ever breathe a word of this to Magda, I will kill you,' and he replies, 'I know it,' but he is already coming in

to kiss her again, his mouth returning to hers like the sealing
of a pact.

*

At the landing, at the door to his room, she whispers, 'You
know how to do this?' In the hollow between her belly and her
hip there's his cock-stand, brave and urgent as a calf butting its
dam. 'Yes,' he says, then 'No,' he says, then 'What?' which has
her laughing, silent laughter, a finger to her lips. Above their
heads, they can hear Jo-Jo singing his sister a lullaby.

At the bed, she strips him; naked as Adam. He's trembling as
much as when she first set eyes on him, and the fur on his belly
looks like it's standing as taut as his cock. It seems to Paola that
if she put her finger into the air between them, it would spark.
'Oh, Jag,' she says. She gives a nod, downwards. 'That's going
to go off if I so much as touch it, ain't it?'

'No,' he says. He sounds both proud and mildly affronted.
'No, it ain't.'

Kneeling on the bed, she undresses herself, in turn. She does this
telling herself it doesn't matter and she doesn't care, that for the
times she is no longer young as she was or beautiful, either, but
when she lifts her shift above her head, when to his Adam, she
is Eve, and no, there is no other world but this, when he reaches
up and puts his fingertips against her breast and says with such
tenderness and such amazement, 'They're so soft. Paola, they're
so *soft*,' then she thinks, then, I am Helen of Troy. She takes his
hand, and puts it between her thighs, into her sex, and he makes
this sound that is both sigh and groan and uncontrollable and
stifled all at once. 'There,' she tells him, in a whisper. 'That's
what you want to feel. That's when a woman is ready for you.'

*

When they get to it, she straddles him, of course she does; helps him find the way into her, slick and wet and warm. 'Jag,' she says, looking down at him. 'Sweetheart. Breathe.'

When he comes, it's like riding a horse. 'Oh *Christ*, Paola!' And then, 'Oh, *oh*,' with this dying fall to it, as if this were simultaneously the most wonderful and the saddest thing ever to have befallen him. Paola puts her hand across his mouth, head back, rocking in silent triumph.

AND THEN –

Then they lie there, in this too-small bed, turned one to the other, nose to nose, grinning like guilty children. '*Well*,' she says. 'That was – merry.'

His eyes are shining. 'How did you –' he begins, 'how did you come to be –' then gives up the search for the words entirely. 'How did you just come to be?' he asks.

Because of course when you are first abed, you can ask each other anything.

'You mean my colour, or my being a champion?' She smiles. 'My father was a swordsmith; there were always men at our door; very few of them knew their manners; he thought it wise that I should learn to fight.' She holds up her good arm, as if admiring its modelling. 'And my mother, I think, was his slave. All he ever told me of her was that she came from the desert, and poor soul, she was in the ground before I'd even cut my teeth.' A sigh. 'I tell you, Jag, it's no life for a woman, being a woman; not with the world as it is. All she could give me was her colour. But it's served me well, all in all. No-one ever forgot meeting me. And those men I bested, they could say they were beaten by a heathen savage, rather than a woman.' She props herself up, on the good arm. 'Sweetheart, promise me. Don't be a soldier.'

He pulls his head back, as if to bring such an oddball notion into better focus. 'Why not?'

'Because it would be such a waste of you. You might be anything. Think of all you might be.'

'You were a soldier,' he points out.

She has the glove tucked like a nestling under her chin. 'And look what happened to me.'

He puts his hand around her wrist, or where, under the glove, her wrist would be. 'How did it happen?' he asks.

'I met the one.'

'What one?'

'The one we all meet, sooner or later. In my case, an old greybeard of a peasant, pissing himself with terror, only he was armed with an axe.' She lifts the glove, turning it so he can see: the leather sleeve to her elbow, buckled and strapped to her shoulder. 'I lost everything, when I gained this. My speed, my edge, my place in the world – even the man I loved.'

'He left you?' He sounds outraged, that way that only the young ever do.

'No, I left him.' She tucks the glove back out of sight, under the pillow. 'I saw the pity in his eyes when the sawbones was done with me, I saw right away how I had changed for him, and I knew we were finished, that very minute. He and I – we'd matched each other, it was what made us a pair. I was so good, Jag. I was a thing of grace with a sword in my hand. I was the best you're ever like to see.'

'But you still are,' he says.

'Well, thankee. You didn't do so bad tonight yourself.'

'That was *well* worth it,' he assures her, and now that light in his eye has the spark of something else to it, too. *Oh-ho*, she thinks. *Adam has tasted of the apple, and it was good.*

'Jag,' she begins, 'this can never happen again. You know that, don't you? You know it cannot?'

'Yes,' he says, after a moment, shouldering it, but now his voice sounds thick. *Oh, you old bitch*, she thinks. She nudges him, nodding toward his cock, lying plump and happy against his thigh. 'Bald King Henry,' she says.

'What?'

'Bald King Henry. The man I loved, he was a Frenchman. That's what he called his.'

A gust of laughter, and the deepest blush. He says, as if in explanation, 'My father was a Frenchman. And a soldier, too.'

'Was he? And you lost him?' And when he nods his head, 'It's always the good ones you lose. It's never the Peters of this world go early, mark me on that. Poor Jag.' She settles herself again. 'I was three years serving with the French. Maybe I heard of him.'

And then she says, 'What was his name?'

SHE'D TRIED THE gate into the yard, had Magda, but someone had dropped the bar across it, so she'd had to go to the street door, and beat and bellow upon that, and then when Jo-Jo opens it, he has her kitchen cleaver in his hand.

'Jo-Jo?' she asks, stepping in, stamping the snow off her feet. 'What's that for?'

'Keeping 'em safe,' Jo-Jo replies.

'Keeping who safe?'

'All of 'em. Like what Jag did.'

She gapes at him. 'Jo-Jo, has something happened here?'

'There was men,' says Jo-Jo.

There could hardly be three words less expected, or better guaranteed to provoke instant dismay. 'What men? Where's Paola?'

'She'm Jag, they gone upstairs.'

She finds Paola on their bed – their bed, at least, because she had found herself wondering in this cold, abstracted way; because she had paused, going past the door to the room on the dog-leg of the stairs; but no. Here she is. Their bed. Albeit plainly naked. Swaddled in the covers like an infant; hiding her face. Magda sits down beside this muffled form. 'I hear we had an invasion,' she begins.

No response.

'And Jag saved us,' Magda continues.

This time, something mumbled in reply.

'And then you bedded him.'

A sigh or shudder, some reaction too physical to hide. Magda composes herself.

'I knew this was going to happen,' she says. 'I didn't need the cards to tell me that.' A pause; she finds she must compose herself again. 'You know I love you,' she begins. 'I loved you from the first moment you rode in here. I loved you even then, when you were with Jean. And when you came back here, with your poor arm in its sling, I felt so guilty, I was so overjoyed.' She lets out her breath. 'So perhaps I'm being punished for that.'

Another strange movement beside her, like a spasm.

'Because I'm sure you're sorry,' Magda continues, 'but still, the thing is done.'

And now Paola at last lifts herself from the bed, the glove covering her face, her face as if seeking refuge in it, her hand gathering the bedclothes to her breast. And she says, 'Magda, he's theirs.'

What? 'Who is theirs? Who is *they*?'

'Jean and that English mouse he wed. Jag is their boy.'

HE WAKES AND knows he is without her. He wakes, and it's late, the sun full on the bed, and the kitchen noise seems oddly muted too, and both of those might be a warning, now he thinks of it, to watch himself, to take heed as he steps into the day. He swings his feet to the floor and stands there, naked, taking the measure of the silence. He knows this, this sense of time suspended, knows what it means. It means there'll be a price to pay, that it's out there, waiting. Have a care…

He looks down at himself. Squares his shoulders. *But*, he thinks, smiling, *but, that was me then.*

He's something different now.

In the kitchen there's no-one but Jo-Jo, the usual brimming bowl before him. A dip of the head in greeting. Jack nods his own head in reply. 'Magda still abed?' he asks, as lightly as he can.

'Both,' Jo-Jo answers. He dips a hunk of bread into the bowl, and sucks it dry. A light comes into his eye. 'Like what you were,' he adds. A sound comes from him, like the noise a dog makes in its sleep. *Unf-unf-unf.* Jo-Jo, it seems, is laughing.

Horrified, he makes to respond, although respond with what he can't think, beyond *Jo-Jo, you ain't to say a word of that, not ever, understand?* when he hears the stairs squeak behind him. He spins around, and there's Ilse – a little swollen round the eyes, a tad lopsided in the face, and the minute she sees him, she goes to him, wraps her arms about his waist and puts her head upon his breast. There is the usual surge as Jo-Jo gets to his feet (the room instantly seeming half the size it had before), then Jo-Jo is there as well, arm laid across his shoulders, and Jo-Jo is saying, 'You're all right, you are, Jag.'

He'd been ready for anything but praise. 'I'm not, Jo-Jo,' he hears himself begin. For some ridiculous reason his eyes are filling. 'Truly, I'm not.' He tries to think of a reason why. There's any number of them: I've took life (twice. *Twice*). I've thieved (Zoot's purse, untended laundry, henhouse eggs). I bedded Paola.

I was a bad son. And so my mother –

I was a bad son, and so –

The pressure from the arm increases. Jo-Jo, it seems, is adding his embrace to his sister's. 'You are, Jag. I sez you're all right.'

And there he is, caught in their hug, the orphan, the outcast and the oddity, when there is another tread upon the stairs and there is Magda. Magda arrayed like an empress in velvet and gold. Magda with jewels in her ears; and then coming down the stairs behind her and walking as if she's being led to the scaffold, there is Paola too. He dares to shoot a glance at her. Her eyes come up. Every meaning hid behind them.

'Jo-Jo, Ilse,' says Magda, magisterially, 'find some other place to be.' She flaps her hands, like she was shooing birds. 'Paola and I, we need to talk with Jag.'

'Right you are,' says Jo-Jo, without rancour. He takes Ilse by the arm. 'Come along, little sis.'

The door from the kitchen to the dining hall is chiselled round its border with a pattern of stars. Against one of these, on the dining-hall side of the door, Jo-Jo has placed an ear. 'Can you hear, little sis?' he whispers, and crouched below him, sees Ilse nod her head.

On the other side of the door a great, young, strong male shout of disbelief.

'He's angered,' Ilse whispers.

'No, he ain't angered, little sis. Not for real. He's just took by surprise. There's a deal about himself as Jag don't know, but that he should.'

'How'd you know there is?' Ilse asks.

'Rufus told me,' Jo-Jo says, grandly. It's wrong to be prideful, he knows, but hang that. There was old Peter and his tricks, but Jo-Jo has never been a part of a secret like this before. 'There's been folk looking for Jag for I don't know how long. But they all got it arsewise, Rufus says. It's not who Jag is as matters, it's who he's going to be.' He listens for a moment more with great attention, then eases the door closed that last half-inch. 'Come along, little sis,' he tells her. There's no point Ilse hearing more, it'll only fright her. 'Let's you and me go get some air.'

He looks from one woman to the other. The echo of his shout is still in the room. 'You *knew* him?' he asks. 'You knew my *father*?'

'*I* knew him,' says Magda, firmly. A little glance at Paola, to her side, sat so her very stillness pulls your eye. 'He was here in his recruiting days,' Magda goes on. 'He told me of your mother, and of you…' She reaches for his hand. 'We are so very sorry, lad.'

His face is working, he can feel it. Still nothing from Paola. He drops his eyes. 'He just never came home,' he says.

'I know, sweetling, I know.' Another glance at Paola, and a sigh. '*We* know. But we can help you, Jag, and there are others too. We weren't your father's only friends. You're not on your own in the world, not at all.'

And then Paola at last lifts her head. She lifts, with the glove, the curtain of hair that had fallen across her face, and she looks directly at him, and she says, 'So was it your father, gave your silver wolf to you?'

'What silver wolf?' Magda asks.

'Show her,' Paola commands.

So he lifts it from around his neck, and places it on the table, and Magda, with a little gasp, takes her hand away. 'Is that–?'

'Did it come from him?' Paola is asking. 'This matters, Jag. Did it come from him?'

'No,' he tells her, baffled, unprepared. But no, *no*, it did not.

'Are you certain?' Paola persists, and then, 'Good God,' she says. 'You don't even know what it is, do you?'

Not so. He knows what it is to him; it's all he has. It's all he has left of anyone. But he thinks none of this is what Paola means, so once again he shakes his head.

She reaches out, and with the glove, nudges it. 'It's a badge,' she says. 'It's what the hard men wear.'

'The hard men?' he repeats.

'The ones who say they're proof against anything. Any weapon made of lead, or iron or steel. They make a pact with the Devil, a covenant, and after that they're hard, they can't be killed. That's what it is. It's the badge of a hard man. And that's why you have to keep it hid. Because whosever it was, he sold his soul for it, and whoever he is, he will *kill* to get it back.'

She stops, and looks into his face. 'And you're still not about to tell us how you came by it, are you?'

CHAPTER TEN

The King of Swords

'… let them remember that War follows Peace, as naturally as Night does follow Day; and that after a sweet calm, a dreadful storm is to be looked for…'

Sir James Turner, *Pallas Armata*

BETRAYED, that's what he is. Betrayed and deserted. Jo-Jo's not coming back.

Now even the town is closed to him. Last time he'd limped his way over the bridge, two watchmen had marched him back across it, thrown him down. 'You stay there!' one had said, grinding the toe of his boot upon the copper spike to make the point. 'You stay that side of it, y'ragged arse.'

The skin of his hands is cracking open with the cold. There used to be Jo-Jo, to warm himself upon, Jo-Jo to help him beg – they were a team, they were as one. Now what is he?

Abandoned. Helpless. And betrayed. Even the men of his own regiment won't let him scrounge off them no more, drive him away with kicks and blows, like a dog. He's got to find some allies in this camp. He'll wake (or rather won't) froze, like them little birds he gleans from the foreshore. Little toe-claws all curled up, little eyes all sunk – and once you've sizzled 'em on a stick, by God there ain't no more'n a bite on each.

Even his fellow outcasts don't want to know him. There they are, all gathered about that flag with the upreared wolf, and all of 'em seemingly shunned, out on the edge of the camp, just like he, but these, these don't seem to care. Don't have to. They have those fine warm tents to sleep in. They got provisions. Will they take pity? Not a chance.

He spies upon them as the afternoons grow dark. Listens to them talking, their odd accents, listens to their music-making, too. Fife and a drum they got, and a fat-bellied guitar. A musical people, clearly. Misjudged, like as not. Just as he.

With his courage in his hands, he singles one out – one who must've took a sad battering not so long ago, for his nose looks like someone flattened it with a spade. He starts by coming up beside the man to pee, it being Peter's experience that a man with his cock out will hesitate before thumping you, and that the making of water together is in any case a comradely act.

'I'd 'ate to see the other fellow,' he begins.

The man does nothing more than grunt.

'I mean, I bet he's in worse shape than you.'

The man shakes himself off, and walks away, without a word. Still, it's a start.

What he needs now is some little gift. Can't teach Peter much about the etiquette of making friends, dear me no.

He watches and waits. As it gets darker, he creeps deeper into the camp. He has a good big stone in his satchel, stuffed down inside a sock. It makes a decent weapon.

A little later and he's creeping back; a bottle of schnapps where the stone had been.

Works like a charm. Here he is, sat round the fire with 'em, all friends together. Bit of music going on behind them and the bottle coming his way again. Peter is drunk; when he moves his head it seems to him the stars are moving too. 'Tilly!' he cries, raising the bottle high. 'Gen'ral Tilly, bless his name! Who's with me?' Now if only one of 'em 'ud offer him a little food, to go with the schnapps... he turns to the man on his right. 'What this needs,' he begins, 'is a little bit of meat to go with it. Meat and a little bit of bread.'

The man smiles. His pale jowls crease. He says, over Peter's shoulder, to the man with the broken nose, 'He was watching us?', and when the answer comes back, smiles again. He pats the satchel at Peter's side. 'You haf secrets here?' he enquires.

Peter had stuffed the satchel with leaves. 'Secrets?' Peter gives a laugh. 'Don't ask, for you wouldn't want to know.' He taps his nose. 'It's why I pick my company, my friend. Why you find me out here. Now, as I was saying – if there was summat here to eat, wun't that round the day off well?'

Now that's a shame, the guitar has stopped. Sounds like the player is shuffling closer. After the bottle, no doubt. And here's his neighbour again, leaning forward, them little fingers at the satchel's straps. 'I said *leave* –' Peter begins, and then, 'Here! Look at that!' He sits back in astonishment. 'Why, I've seen one of those afore! I've seen one of those and none too long ago, neither.'

The man has put his hand across it now, almost protectively, but no mistaking what Peter saw, there on the fellow's jacket, the firelight caught it plain as day. The warmth now running through him, it's not schnapps, it's the glow of revenge.

'You lost one then?' he asks, grinning into the man's pale face. 'You got a runaway? For if you have, then I know where he is. And he's a thing like that, just like to that, upon a cord about his neck. A silver wolf!'

A REMARKABLE SKY. Rufus tilts his head back to admire it. Each star as sharp as if it had been drilled, the moon so clear you can count the silver freckles on her face. The cry of an owl, the sift of its wings, and look! – one single star goes streaking to her end across the firmament. A remarkable sky, full of portent, so what might it bring?

Ah.

Turning his head, Rufus sees Benedicte, surer in the dark than in the light of day, making his way toward him. 'Are they coming?'

Benedicte, in that husk of a voice of his, answers, 'Are we ready?'

'Always,' Rufus replies. He rises, stretches his back, claps his hands three times above his head. Without hurry, from around the camp-fires, figures also making ready, rising up. As Rufus walks through the camp, his foot-soldiers fall silently into line behind him.

Yuna, with Emilian on her lap, watches from the doorway of her tent as they pass. *Well*, she thinks. *They will not be expecting us, at least.*

A cough, delicately stifled. Emilian twists his head around, peering behind his mother into the tent's interior. Yuna's tent is bigger than the rest; there is plenty of room for the man sat there behind them, leaning his chin on the knop of his stick. *And he?* Emilian asks.

I don't like him and I don't trust him, his mother replies. The soft churr of their own tongue, its unexpected changes of direction (to keep the gadjo mystified). *And he is polluted with sickness too. When he is gone, we burn his seat. But Jag is at least as important to him as he is to your father, and tonight Jag is all that matters.*

She kisses her son on his forehead. A little music from her necklaces, slipping across each other. 'Go now,' she says. 'You know what you are to do. And be sure they bring the horse as well. Jag will never be happy without it.'

'Ilse? Little sis?' He has his instructions, Jo-Jo does, and they are most particular as to timing. 'Ilse?'

She looks up. She'd been on her knees before the fireplace in the kitchen, drawing out the ashes. 'Leave that now,' he tells her. 'You got to come along with me. Here's your cloak.'

He holds it out for her. 'Put it on now, sis. You're a-going down to the camp with Emilian, you are. We got bad souls coming here.'

She clutches the cloak to her breast. 'Like before?'

'Aye, them,' Jo-Jo replies.

'Are they coming for me?'

'No, baby girl. They're coming for Jag.'

TWELVE OF THE CLOCK, or almost. The mermaid clock has just begun its carillon. Jack sits in his room on the dog-leg of the stairs, in such confusion that it feels as if his thoughts are playing tug-o-war. In one hand he holds the silver wolf. Can Paola be right? Can that be what this is?

But that would make no sense –

You know, he thinks, looking down at it, there in his palm. Those hard red eyes, they know it all.

Give me something. Tell me something.

His mother had held this in her hand, too. She had it with her as she closed her eyes. As she stepped forward. As she plummeted away from everything –

Maman has a secret, Petit Jacques.

Downstairs, he might have spoken. He might have said –

No, he might not. Because speaking of it would mean speaking of his mother, and that he cannot do.

He lifts the silver wolf back over his head. *Whatever you are*, he thinks.

And then from out there on the stairs, there's movement. A shift in the air. He feels it, he looks up. He says, 'Paola?' He moves forward.

And walks into darkness made solid. Darkness that both envelops and smothers him. He feels himself being pinioned, lifted off his feet; something thick and stifling pressed against his face. It's cloth, it's fustian – it's a blanket. He's trapped in a blanket. He fights with his elbows, scissors his legs; as he struggles his boots bang into someone's legs. Someone is carrying him across the room. Then a squeak of metal, and through the frozen air the sound of the mermaid clock; the ending of its carillon and then the clearing of its throat. The window has been opened. A grunt, some repositioning taking place, and he struggles anew, kicking, jerking his head left to right, and a voice through the blanket, a mouth by his ear, muffled but unmistakable:

'I don'wanna hurt'oo, Jag.'

'Jo-Jo!' They're tilting backwards. 'Jo-Jo! The hell are you doing? What are you at?'

Coldness, all about him. The angle of the tilt is now extreme, and with it, a terrifying sense of weight within weightlessness, of complete disorientation. *We're going through the window!*

'JO-JO!'

Clutched in Jo-Jo's embrace, he is tipped backward through the window to the sound of midnight, falling across the town.

Oh, but it's late. The mermaid clock has finished its carillon, the last notes dying away, the last few souls been chivvied from the dining hall; and here is Magda, on her knees before the kitchen fireplace, raking the ashes to the front of the hearth, a task that Ilse, for some mysterious reason, seems to have abandoned halfway through. *But then let's face it*, Magda thinks, *we've all been somewhat distracted in our doings here today.*

She hears the door from the dining hall open, then Paola's step. Outside the mermaid clock begins to sound. *One –*

An arm comes round her. Paola is helping her to her feet.

'It's I should be wearing the ashes,' Paola says, 'not you.'

'Well, yes,' Magda answers. 'Yes. You should.' She takes a breath, pauses, tilts her head. Some noise upstairs. No, it was nothing. Magda knows the sounds of her house as well as she knows the syllables of her own name. *Two –*

She steels herself. 'Paola,' she begins, 'you're going to have to decide.'

'I know,' Paola answers, oddly humble. *Three –*

'You have to decide if you're part of this place or no. If you're part of us, or no. One way or the other. Because the way things are –'

Now that wasn't the clock. But was it upstairs, or outside?

'– people will be hurt. You not least of all.'

Four. She stops again. Is there something going on out there? She pushes on. 'And I can't tell you. You have to sort this for yourself.'

Five, goes the mermaid clock. Scuffle-scuffle, go the sounds outside. It *is* outside. 'Did you—' she begins again, and then, 'Oh, *Paola!*' because now with no warning the kitchen door is open; now with no warning there are armed men in her kitchen, shouldering their way in from the yard.

There is that little pause, as there so often is when opposing forces meet. Ridiculous, but Magda's impulse (finest woman landlord, and all that) is to urge the men toward the empty dining hall. What stops her is the voice exclaiming, 'I *said*, a'right, *a'right*, I'm getting in there, ain't I?' and then there is Peter, being shoved into the room by a man whose face is spectacled with bruises. Then she understands. Them. This is them.

'Peter!' Paola is roaring. 'You shit-stain! You dare to bring these here?'

'Oh, hold your tongue, you sooty bitch,' Peter snarls at her. He looks panicky, disordered. 'If you 'adn't made a nest for that boy here, none o'this 'ud be happening! None of it!'

The man holding him cuffs him round the head. Peter staggers forward, collides with the table, drops to his knees. Now the man approaches Paola. There is recognition in his face. He makes to snatch at her. Paola uses her good arm to push Magda behind her, and in the same moment smacks the man in the mouth with the glove. Were Magda not so scared she thinks she might applaud; years since Paola was in a fight yet there is not a moment's hesitation, nothing. The man is reeling, he has blood on his lip. He spins about. He spies the sword they had hung above the fireplace, bellows an oath and snatches it down. He is advancing on them, sword in hand, when a voice interrupts him: 'Gentlemen, gentlemen! Is this how we behave?'

There is another man, pushing his way to the front. He smiles, holds up his hand. He has the most curiously tiny teeth. The eyes above the smile alter not at all. 'We do not, after all, wish to alarm the watch.' He throws back his fine dark cloak, removes his glossy hat and, as he stands there, Magda spies that little glint of silver at the front of his coat.

'Now,' the man is saying. 'Ladies –' A small, stiff bow. 'Forgive me, but for this little while, your house is mine.' Another dead-eyed smile. 'Bring Herr Peter to me.'

Peter is dragged forward. 'Herr Peter,' the man says. 'Where is this boy?'

'I dunno, do I?' Peter wails in reply. 'You could'a let me do it quiet like. I said, I'd bring him out to you, but oh no, you got to come a-slamming in here – aaah! *Aaarghh!*' The man holding him is leaning his whole weight on Peter's shoulders; he is once more on his knees.

'Oh, Peter,' Magda hears herself exclaim, 'how could you!'

The man with the silver wolf holds up his hand. 'I know you do not know,' he says. 'You know nothing. You *are* nothing. You are shit from the street.' He nods toward Magda and Paola. 'But they do. Ask them. If you matter, they will speak.'

Peter, voice a-tremble, begins. 'Now look,' he says. 'That boy – I could'a told you he was a wrong'un, right from the start.' He tries to rise up on one knee. His captor presses him down again. 'They want him, that's all. They just want him.'

'You want the boy?' Paola asks. She's looking the man straight in the eye. 'We ran him out of here days back. He was a thief. As for Peter, you're right. A nothing who knows nothing. He's no use to you. You might as well throw him back in the street right now.'

The man gives a sigh. 'Peter,' he says, 'you told me you were as a brother here. You lie to me?'

'No, no!' Peter wails. 'It's she who's lying! I'm the – I'm the heart here! I'm the soul!'

The man looks back and forth between them. Outside, above the sleeping town, oblivious, the last strokes of midnight die away. *We are on our own*, Magda thinks.

'One of you will tell me where this boy is, I can promise that,' the man says. Another scrutiny, back and forth, and then he shakes from his sleeve a stiletto. He says to the man restraining Peter, 'Put his head to the table.' The stiletto poised over Peter's face, over his ear. 'Deaf Peter,' the man says. 'How if I make you deaf for real?'

Peter's eyes, trying to see the stiletto, are almost turning over in his head. In his desperation, he has nearly broken free. He shrieks, 'It's them two who know where he is, not me! Do what you want with them! Lemme go!'

'*You spill blood in OUR KITCHEN, you bastard sons of dogs –*' Paola is bellowing, extraordinarily loud. Her hand, reaching behind her, tugs at Magda's skirts. '*HERE IN OUR KITCHEN, I'll have you fuckers clear it up yourselves.*' Jag's room is right above them. Now Magda understands. She girds herself. 'You heard her! IN OUR KITCHEN! *How dare you?*'

The man with the silver wolf is staring at them, all amazed. Then his expression clears. 'Ah,' he says. 'The boy is upstairs. They think to warn him.' He turns to the man with the bruises on his face. 'Go fetch.'

The man grins, tilts his sword in readiness and tromps up the stairs. They hear him above their heads. They hear him cross the floor of the room one way, then come back the other. Magda hears her own breath – a mouse, working a bellows. The footsteps cease. Then a shout. 'Here is no-one!'

And then unmistakably, the sound of a shot. A shot, and the weight of a body hitting the floor.

And the body of the man comes sliding down the stairs, and Rufus, pistol in each hand, comes striding down the stairs behind it. The man with the silver wolf turns sideways, lifts an arm; his fine dark cloak hiding him like a curtain. Rufus fires.

On the coffer, the hourglass explodes.

Magda thinks first of all that Rufus missed his aim (although *how*, at that range?), then that the one shot must have ricocheted, because in the second after, the entire window detonates, exploding inward, showering them all. Her kitchen is filled with blue smoke. Only then does she understand: that there was not one shot, there were dozens, and that there is not simply this creature and his men in her kitchen, Rufus and his Roma are there too; but by then Paola has thrown her to the floor and rolled the both of them under the table. From down here all she can see are everybody's feet dancing this insane gavotte, sweeping left, right, back one way, back the other. The table is being knocked from side to side above her. She feels glass against her cheek – glass and the sand from her hourglass – and tries to turn her head but Paola is holding her so flat to the floor she can't move. The glove is pressed to her skull. There is a hiss in her ear: 'Maggie, stay *down!*' Then a man lands on the floor beyond them, on his tailbone, looking astonished, and someone shoots him in the head. Little dots of liquid spatter over her. Paola, above her, is swearing oath after oath, as steadily as if she was reading from a list. Magda squeezes her eyes tight shut, forces her hands over her ears. She hears things falling – earthenware, which shatters; copper, which rings like a bell; bodies, which drop heaviest of all. The table is knocked sideways again, oaken foot-pads screeching over the floor. Rufus's voice – furious, violent, louder than anyone else. An answer. Another shot. A pause. And then one more.

And then Paola's weight is lifted off her, and she is pulled to sit up, in the wreckage of her kitchen.

The queasy seesaw of understanding. What has happened comes swimming up to her in wave after wave, one bloody detail succeeding the last. One of the Roma is slumped on the coffer, very, very dead, while Rufus and the rest of his men are turning over body after body on the floor. Rufus is raging, incomprehensible. Something is batting at her – she tries to catch it, stop it, whatever it is, and realizes only then that it is Paola: 'Are you hurt, Maggie? Are you whole?'

'Yes,' she says, 'yes.' She sounds astonished. 'I am, yes,' she says again, as if she must convince herself, then hears her own voice exclaiming, 'Oh, Paola! Your hand!'

The leather skin of the glove is flapping, the fingers broken, loose. The wooden hand beneath has been cracked in two, the dull grey slug of a bullet now sunk within it, glowering back at them. 'Oh, for fuck's *sake*!' Paola exclaims, lifting her arm, and then, 'Oh, Maggie, Maggie! That would have been your head!' Magda feels herself pulled forward, she feels Paola's arm about her. She feels Paola's kisses on her forehead. 'What would I have done, what would I have done,' Paola is saying, 'if anything had happened to you?'

Her head is being pulled to Paola's breast. Now she hears Paola calling out above her head, 'Rufus, do you have him?'

and Rufus exclaiming, 'No, damn him, damn him, he has escaped!' *Oh*, Magda thinks, *I am going to swoon.* The balm of peril passed and done is flooding her, relief of every sort, deep and warm as a bath. She thinks, *I must close my eyes.* She hears Paola's reply: 'Not the fucken hard man, Rufus, Jag! Do you have *him?*' And now Rufus answers, 'Yes, we have him. He is safe.'

She lets her eyes close. They close upon some after-image of a figure on its belly, creeping across the floor. She opens them again. There is a man, with glossy hat upon his head, pulling himself toward the door. 'There,' she says, or tries to, but the word dries in her mouth. The man is reaching upward, reaching for the latch, weakly, fumbling, as if ashamed. She grabs at Paola. 'There,' she manages, 'there!'

And now they do see, all at once. Rufus goes plunging across the room, but two of his Roma are there first, hauling the crouching figure upright. The hat has been rammed right down over its face. It droops between them. Rufus yells, 'Take off the hat!' and they do –

And it is Peter. Peter, already sagging to the floor. Something has punched out his eyes.

THEY'D HIT THE GROUND, he and Jo-Jo, and the air was smacked out of him with such force it seemed impossible his lungs would ever manage to fill again. Stunned in every particle, but somehow still alive, he hears a wheeze from beneath him. He opens his mouth and the air finds its way. He manages to gasp out 'Jo-Jo!' and there's a groan.

'Jo-Jo!'

Another groan. 'Get 'im *orffffff* me.' The arms holding him have loosened. There's something under them. Feels like straw. Did they land on a pile of straw? Who put that there?

And as if in answer, now there are more hands, pulling him upright. He is caught again, held round chest and knees. He's being carried like a carpet. Urgent, muted voices over him, and not a word of it comprehensible, but it comes to him for the first time that there is something meant going on here, that all this has planning, reason. Then, unmistakably, he hears Milano, his horse's snort of irritation when he's being hurried.

'Don't you hurt him! Don't you hurt him, you hear?'

All he gets for that is a hand pressing the blanket over his mouth. His progress has become bumpier, has a crunch underfoot, as of frozen grass. Are they in the paddock? Is this the Roma? He feels himself being lifted up –

– and thrown onto what feel like cushions. They move beneath him – he moves – everything is moving. He sits up, tears the blanket from his head. He hears Yuna's voice, shrilling out, up ahead.

He'd been pitched into a wagon. The voice up front is urging faster, faster. It comes to him that Yuna is their coachman. Then Milano's snort again, behind him. His horse is tied to the back of the wagon; and beyond, at the top of the field, the kitchen windows of Fat Magda's, once more a blaze of light. Figures outlined against it. Dimly heard – Christ, are they *shots*?

'Very clever,' comes the voice. 'To take a name so near your own.' The speaker coughs, as if to clear its throat. 'Makes it easier to remember. Swift.'

He struggles to his knees, has to reach out both arms to steady himself. Yuna's voice again, urging her ponies on. He can make out nothing. 'The fuck are you?' he shouts, into the dark. 'The *fuck* is going on?'

Something shifts at the wagon's far end. 'Don't you worry on their account,' says the voice. 'Those women, they will be far, far safer with you gone.'

Whatever it is, it's coming closer. He braces himself, tries to find some stance solid enough from which to throw a punch.

The speaker leans forward. 'Show me,' it says. 'That thing you wear about your neck. Show me.'

Eyes like two coals. Cheekbones that jut like elbows. A death's head.

'You don't remember me, do you?' says Balthasar.

PART II

August 1610–October 1617

CHAPTER ONE

The Death of Kings

'I am very much afraid that the states of the Empire, quarrelling so fiercely among themselves, may start a fatal conflagration embracing not only each other, but all those other countries that are connected with Germany...'

Maurice 'the Learned', Landgrave of Hesse-Kassel

EVERY STORY NEEDS a hero: here he is. Not much to write about as yet, perhaps – small, fractious, dressed in a dingy linen vest and bouncing on his father's knee. A breeze blowing about them; flapping canvas, dry-baked earth. Looking back, he knows this to have been an army camp, a leaguer, or the remains of one. Looking back, he knows too that the voice booming like God Almighty's from the sky was in fact his father's.

He's four years old. He starts here. In a way, everything does.

'Let's face it, Balthasar, there's nothing here for me. I'm dead as he is, God save his precious sovereign soul. Swept from the stables like old straw.'

He's a big man, the speaker. A big man, with a big voice, who never learned to whisper, and thoroughly despises those who do. Not exactly at home with the role of nursemaid, either, judging by the strength of that bounce. A good job the child takes after its father, and is as robust-looking as he is.

'Those with the reins in Paris now,' the speaker continues, 'those round the Queen, God rot her, they wouldn't touch me with a pike-staff.'

Ah, the death of kings. The rest of us may leave this planet with as little ceremony as blowing out a candle, but a king? Nothing is left unchanged. Especially if that death came in the form of an assassination. Three months later and the shock of it is still there in the eyes of every man you might encounter here in this camp, here on the plain of Paris, this hot, tired August day. An entire regiment of lost souls, all of them wondering: what will become of us now?

'I've a mind to go into Italy,' the speaker continues. 'I've a name there still, I hope. Or Poland. Ain't they at war? Or Muscovy. Who's Muscovy fighting this year?'

'Poland?' his listener replies. 'Muscovy? You can't find some conflict further off than that?'

Jean Fiskardo, captain of cavalry, father of one, throws wide an arm. 'The hell then, take your pick! You find the fight, I'll join it. But I tell you, here, I'm dead. Or I am as long as that Habsburg sow is in charge, damn her and her blood and her eyes.'

Three months ago France had an army, ready to go to war, and a king ready to lead that army into battle. Three months ago Jean had a commission in that army, a command. Now the King sleeps in his tomb in St Denis, in spite of the stone-cutters, busy above:

HENRI IV ✝ ROI DE FRANCE

DUC DE NAVARRE

MORT À PARIS 1610

and Jean is out of a job.

Which is where Balthasar comes in. 'What's Sally say to Italy?' Balthasar asks, preparing the ground. 'Or Muscovy, come to that?'

Ah, Sally. With her buttery curls and dimpled smile and her enchanting guesswork French, and oh, that accent when she speaks – may *le bon Dieu* grant a man strength – could have a priest forget his vows just watching her mouth move.

'Oh, *Sally*,' says Jean, with the heavy emphasis of dog in dog-house, dropping its muzzle down onto its paws. 'She's over there with the leaguer bitches –' (by which Jean means the regiment's many whores, as opposed to its few legally married wives) '– telling them her woes. She's like a siphon, Balthasar. I can't touch her without there being tears. I spoke of my going away and she called me a gargoyle.'

Sure enough, there at the fire-pit, a clutch of women in that reared-up pyramidal grouping they always adopt when one of their sisters has been hard-done-by, and there at the base of the pyramid, being consoled, one small bright head. Bright as a blossom, is how Balthasar thinks of Sally. 'A gargoyle?' he repeats.

Jean Fiskardo, who can have an entire company of horse, in line, wheel round a spot no bigger than a handprint, looks sheepish and drops his gaze. 'Because they're made of stone. I'm at my wit's end, I tell you.'

Balthasar leans forward. Together he and Jean helped fight the way for Good King Henry to the throne, applauded his choice of mistresses, bewailed his choice of wife, and got drunk together at the birth of his heir; and as Balthasar knows full well, the only way to guide Jean to anything is to let him take the lead. 'Ah, if only,' Balthasar begins. He checks over one shoulder. 'If only there were some opposition, close to home. A means to restore balance—'

'We're Little Austria,' says Jean, with venom, 'and may as well get used to the fact.'

'Oh, I don't know so much,' says Balthasar, which, to any man who knows him, means he does, and a great deal more besides. He coughs, to break the ropes in his chest. Every autumn Balthasar is driven to his bed, shuddering with coughs and sneezes; now, to his annoyance, the summer's dust has begun to trouble him as well. 'There is already a faction at court,' he begins.

'It's a court,' Jean says, testily. 'What else is it good for?'

'This is something more than the usual grudge-holders. Something... more determined.' Balthasar lets his gaze come back to Jean. He waits.

Jean sits back, narrowing his eyes. Jean's eyes are pale as sea-glass (his son has inherited the same), and narrowed, they take on a look as hard as nail-heads. You never know, with the scouts, who's talking to them, and who they're talking to, either. 'And?' Jean asks.

With the toe of his boot, Balthasar inscribes a C in the dusty earth. Jean looks down at it, and lifting his son from his lap sits Petit Jacques's little rump entirely on top of the C, obliterating it. 'Condé,' Jean says, in a carefully neutral tone. 'The Duc de Condé. How did you hear this, Balthasar?'

'Eyes and ears. I'm a scout,' says Balthasar. 'It's what I'm paid to do.'

'You're still being paid?'

'Handsomely,' says Balthasar.

Another pause. The nail-heads glitter. 'Condé is no warrior. All he has in his guardroom are dishes of candies to sweeten your breath.'

'He doesn't need to be. He's no intention of going to war; all he needs is a show of force. Reine Marie has no friends but her lapdogs and her uncle. And her uncle won't go to war for her, he's got troubles enough of his own. All those festering heretics, God love them, rebellion's become their second catechism.' He grins at his friend, who is not only his opposite in every way physically, but in his religion too. 'Well, you would know. So, yes, an opposition – and with just such a show of force behind it as the right man, with the right name, might help recruit.'

Jean Fiskardo reaches down toward his son, who is now scaling his leg, grabbing handfuls of his father's beribboned breeches and bellowing at the top of his voice, 'Moi! *Moi!*' He sets the boy once more astride his knee. 'These folk so generous they pay you for your efforts as a scout,' he begins (bounce, bounce, *bounce*), 'even though France has no war. Their name wouldn't also begin with a C, would it?'

'Coincidence,' says Balthasar, with an even broader grin. 'It can be the oddest thing.'

'Recruit an army,' says Jean.

'And be paid for it.'

'Checkmate the Queen.'

'Exactly. Where'd you start?'

Jean rubs his chin, crooks a finger round his mouth, thinking. 'Savoy,' he says. 'If a man has a reputation he should use it. Tell me – did you give my name to Condé, or did he give mine to you?'

'I was told what was required,' says Balthasar. 'I described you. I said you were one of those Condé should have inside the tent pissing out, not outside the tent pissing in. There's one thing, though, Jean. This would be no sort of business for a wife and child. Somewhere would still have to be found for them.'

Jean Fiskardo, thinking hard, chin resting on his thumb, index finger curled over his upper lip. Balthasar waits.

'In that case,' says Jean, 'Sally and Jacques are going where I know they will be safe no matter what. Sally and Jacques are going back to Poitou, where nothing happens, ever. Sally and Jacques are going to Belle-Dame.'

THIS IS BELLE-DAME. The fields, the river and the sea. The village windmill on one flank; the balding headland on the other. The strange world of the salt-flats with their precious *fleur de sel*; and the sheep that live upon the salt-flats, eating seaweed, and deliver a mutton more finely flavoured than any other in France. Jean Fiskardo, that noted warrior, Poitou-born and Poitou-bred, he knows it well. Wind-nipped and starving, Jean spent his first year in the army on those salt-flats, training and drilling (*To horse! To the right hand! To the left, double! Uncap your pistols! Guard your cock! Order your hammer! Present and give fire!*), and at the end of it, swore to himself that never again would his life take place on any stage so insignificant or with so many blasted, half-wit sheep. The only good thing about the year had been this bantam of a boy (compared to Jean's own bullock-like physique), who'd introduced himself as Balthasar and proffered a hand even more chilblained than Jean's own. They'd drilled, they'd trained, against all the odds they grew, they lusted with pitiful intensity after the miller's wife, who had a jaunty walk, and a habit of going about unlaced. Her husband was supposed to keep a musket, permanently loaded, above his door. Guard your cock? 'Chance,' as Balthasar put it, 'would be a fine thing.'

Now the miller's wife is the miller's widow, and spends her time bullying her daughter-in-law, and here amongst the sheep, here Jean is again. Jean used to play a game with Sally, when they were first wed. It always began with Jean tucking Sally's head against his shoulder and saying, 'When we are in my château…' It might go anywhere after that. When I am made colonel. When you are dressed in silks from top to toe. Never once did it include this: when I leave you and our son here in this two-room cottage on the lane up to the headland, forgotten by the rest of the world, almost forgotten by the rest of Belle-Dame, too. *Fate*, thinks Jean, as he lies abed in that same cottage, *has played the rogue with me.* Meditatively, he scratches at the hair on his stomach, fish-hooked with sweat. This is meant to be his last day here. Which fact, Jean feels, is somehow sat upon the bed, monitoring his progress.

He lifts himself up on one elbow, causing the mattress beneath him, newly stuffed with hay, to release a smell as soft as cow-breath. As Jean moves, the muscles of his back reconfigure into a whole other landscape: quarries and sinkholes, scars old and new; and as he looks at his wife, inwardly, he sighs. Sally faces away from him; one of those invisible barriers that fall from time to time between husband and wife marches like a border down the middle of the bed. Tentatively, a man testing the strength of a possibly hostile force, Jean places a hand on the saddle of her hip.

The hip is warm, white, soft. Surprisingly, Jean senses some will within the hip to turn toward him. He puts his arm about his wife, and lowers his face into the fat curls of her hair. He says, 'Have I told you why it's called Belle-Dame, this place?'

And at that she does turn to him. This, then, is Sally, Jean's English wife. Apple blossom and wheat fields, is Sally. Pink and white and gold. Chubby-cheeked, chubby-arsed (that hip has the swell of a pumpkin); breasts white as syllabub, heavy as bells since she nursed their son, and a cunny thatched with gold. And eyes as rich and dark a brown as agates, that look up at Jean unblinkingly as she suggests, 'Because it's where soldiers leave their wives?'

'Sall-ee!' Jean is taken aback. It's most unlike his *jolie blonde* to be as vinegary as that. You'd be uneasy if you met Jean on your own (his size, those eyes, that growl to his voice), and fifteen years of soldiering have battered his features into a striking asymmetry, but when he looks at Sally, the transformation of his face is such that he can almost feel the features shift about.

'Sall-ee,' he begins, as he has done a hundred times already. 'It would not be safe for you to be with me. This is not what it was before –'

No, wash off its face, remove the fancy clothes, and this is rebellion, plain and simple.

'But I can think of you here, and know that you are safe –'

He looks down at her. Her eyes, at mention of his *thinking* of her, have once more grown horribly bright. She rolls against him, wailing, 'But I want you here too!' speaking English now, as if somehow in English this admission isn't going to count. 'Why can't we be here together?'

Because I want more, thinks Jean. With a commission he had command of his life, the world no longer had command of him – as it had done that year upon the salt-flats, for example. He lies back, stretches his arm to be a pillow under her head. '*Ma blonde*,' he murmurs. '*Ma blonde*.' She'll have to be stronger than this. She'll have to be stronger than him. 'You want to know why it is called Belle-Dame?'

'I don't, and I don't care.'

'Try to guess.'

He feels her struggle to pull the sobs back down. 'Because it's beautiful?'

'*Non*. It is because of the hills, the shape of them. It's like a woman. *Couchée*. On her back. Opening her legs to the sea.'

After a moment, he feels her unwilling laughter. 'Ah, Jean –'

He tightens his arms about her. There's a little prompting coming from his cock, a nudge of enquiry – might there be time? Just once more, to remember her –

And then a cry of wild excitement from outside. 'Dada! Dada!'

Jean Fiskardo lies back, groaning. Pulling his breeches to him, he buttons himself up and calls, 'What is it, Petit Jacques?'

'Dada, the boats!'

He goes to the window, throws the shutters wide, admitting a scent of lavender so strong you'd almost expect it to have stained the air. Behind him, he hears Sally picking her petticoats from the floor. *I will be damned*, he thinks, *if I will let this be the end of me.* And there's his son, stood atop the garden wall, and pointing with both hands at once, over the village rooftops and out to the river beyond. 'What about the boats?' Jean calls.

His son turns to him a face glowing with delight. 'They're moving!'

So they are. The fishing boats, heading out on the evening tide, leaving Belle-Dame behind.

Time to go.

THIS IS BELLE-DAME. The fields, the river and the sea. All of it new and all of it amazing. The fields, the river –

The boats.

The boats upon the river, yes. And the quay where the fishermen land their catch (the crabs still ready to make a run for it, out of the basket and back to the sea, the fish so fresh they're stiff as if they're still alive, just holding their breath to fool you). The market, with the stalls selling butter and honey and goats' cheese tarts, and the old women who stare at Maman and mutter with their hands across their mouths, but feed him (some of them) with crusts of sharp burnt pastry, and little hard sweets that taste the way lavender smells.

And the church where (strangely) no-one seems to go, and the enormous shaggy donkey in the field beside the church, and the lane up to their house, and the woods behind, and the path through the woods to the headland, and the place you can see from the headland which manages to be both huge and far away all at once, and which looks like a giant's sandcastle, and which Maman says is called La Rochelle. And the scatter of the village below them, and the rippling, living muscle of the river beyond that, drifting unconcerned past all alike, out to that answer to all things, the sea.

And the boats.

I would like a little boat.

Would you indeed? It's been a landlocked childhood thus far, but that can change.

So this is Belle-Dame. The fields, the river and the sea. And the fishermen and farmers, and the wives and children of the fishermen and farmers, and the old women of the village, *les veuves*, who have seen everything before.

And now the English woman, and her child.

Just one more thing. When is it Dada's coming back?

'Soon, Jack. Soon.'

Courage, ma blonde.

⸺ ❦ ⸺

WINTER ROARS INTO Belle-Dame straight off the north Atlantic; spits rain down the chimneys, blows sheep off their feet. In the field beside the lane Hector, the enormous shaggy donkey (one of that splendid breed, the *baudet du Poitou*), stands nose-on to the blast, rills of silver streaming down his sides; while up at the cottage the wind knocks over the rain-butt, and the rain soaks through the wall. Black stars of mould break out across the limewash. To Jack, it looks as if they're trying to make a map.

He sits on his stool in the kitchen, elbows on the tiles of his favourite windowsill, watching the rain come at the glass as if hurled at it in handfuls. This window is his favourite because the tiles here show a horseman, galloping along. Worryingly, the tiles on the other windowsill don't show him galloping back. They show four little children, playing leapfrog. Bowling a hoop. One on its own, blindfolded, arms outstretched.

It's a game, says Maman, wearily. Blind Man's Buff. Only in France it's called Colin-Maillard. The other children run away and try not to be caught.

He feels extremely sorry for poor Colin, whose Dada has galloped away.

Somewhere in here there's a span of days – he isn't sure how many, but it could even be as long a time as *soon* – when Maman doesn't get out of bed at all.

Here comes Christmas. The fields are pale with frost, the hedges bare as combs. All across France there's many a kitchen where Mother Goose lies lifeless in the housewife's lap and the air is thick with down; many a barn where some poor porker, stuffed full of autumn acorns, is stretched trotter to trotter across the beams, dripping its last into a pail.

And out on France's borders, many an empty lane that echoes at night to the passing of horses and men.

Come home. I will go mad with loneliness. Jean, please come home.

CHAPTER TWO

Here Before

'Fortune is unconstant in all things, and in nothing more than in matters of War...'

Sir James Turner, *Pallas Armata*

R EINHOLD MEIER, Tabitha's father: old, but not as old as he will be, fat, but not as fat as he'll become, and with the kind of prodigious memory stands a man in his profession in good stead. It tells him now, for example, that these two shouldering their way in through his door, into the Carpenter's Hat, these two he's seen before and, almost at once, shakes loose a name for each: Jean Fiskardo (the big bastard; do not mess with him), and the smaller one, his brother-in-arms, one Captain Balthasar. Jean has had time enough, since we saw him last, to grow a beard; Balthasar, in the sharp and unforgiving air, is coughing. Here they come, into the merry noise of his hostelry; and Reinhold, rotating his gaze slowly, magnificently, sees them heading to the table now being occupied by one –

Now this is interesting, because the table the two men are heading toward (the crowd separating before them like the sea before Moses, as any crowd finding itself in Jean's way tends to do) is occupied by that broker of the clandestine, Ravello.

As they make their way across the room the two men pass a game of dice, another of backgammon, a dinner-party of Venetian merchants crooning madrigals *a cappella*, a pedlar attempting to sell the dinner-party a tiny trembling monkey in a tasselled bolero, and Reinhold's daughter, Tabby, face bright with fiery rouge, breasts bared almost to the nipple. What they do not pass, as Jean Fiskardo had already begun to fear would be the case, are any signs of men for hire. Jean can remember when, to make your way up through its paddock to the Carpenter's Hat, you were hunting for a space to tread between the tents.

As they come up to him, Ravello rises to his feet, greets Balthasar and, eyeing his companion, says, 'Jean Fiskardo. It's been a time.'

'Jean,' says Balthasar, 'Ravello. You recall?'

'The fair at Lyons. You won't recall,' Ravello answers, sounding wholly un-put-out by this. 'You had that little English rose upon your arm.' He kisses his fingers. '*Ravissante*. And now, I hear, she is your wife! And children? Are you blessed?'

'One,' says Jean. 'A boy.' He points at Balthasar. 'His godson.' He squints at Ravello, as if trying to place him. Ravello is smiling his usual innocent smile, but those eyes of his are busy as ever: jumping between Jean (now eyeing the mighty platter, glossy with melted cheese, that Ravello has before him) and Balthasar, and noting in particular the colour that the cough has raised in the other's face. Then they hop back to Jean.

'Help yourself,' says Ravello, pushing the platter across. Beneath the melted cheese are boiled potatoes, cornichons, fried sausage. 'There's mustard too.' He raises an arm, clicks his fingers. 'Bottle of Rousette,' he says. 'Good with everything. If you don't know it, you should. Now. How many men are you looking for?'

'Five hundred,' says Jean, as casually as he can. 'Close as we can get.'

Ravello's eyebrows lift. 'Plough-boys? Or are they meant to know their way about?'

'They're meant to look as if they do, at least,' Balthasar puts in. His cough has left him watery-eyed. Ravello's gaze comes back to him – and pauses.

'How long have you been travelling to find me?'

'A month,' comes the reply. 'La Rochelle to Annecy? A month.'

'How long have you had the cough?'

Balthasar waves the question away. 'Clears the pipes,' he says. 'You know me. Simply clearing the pipes.'

Cupid waits round every corner, the dinner-party informs the room, tunefully. *Man must ever be on guard.* The bottle arrives, with the girl, who makes as if to put herself in Ravello's lap. Jean, watching, thinks first of Petit Jacques, demanding they play horse, then, achingly, of Sally. 'Later, treasure,' Ravello tells the girl, moustache brushing her naked shoulder. 'This is business. Off you go.' The girl makes a pout of displeasure, but takes herself off nonetheless. Jean watches her go. It has been many things, the Carpenter's Hat. Refuge, last stand, whore-house, command post; and when Jean was here before, the place was thick with men for hire, soldiers of fortune every one. Not, it would seem, no more. The Carpenter's Hat has grown civil. *Civilianized*, thinks Jean, with contempt. Look at those damn Venetians for a start. They'd not have lasted two minutes here, before.

The Venetians sing on, oblivious: *Or with his tricks and wiles and fancies, he will have on end your yard.*

'Your health,' Ravello is saying. 'And may Reine Marie rot.'

He waits for their verdict. He waits for Balthasar to cease, once more, to cough. 'Good, yes? Starts like strawberries, ends like gravel. Now. Five hundred men. You're not going to find them down here in Savoy.'

'So I see,' says Jean, morosely, looking round. 'The devil happened to the place?'

'Business,' says Ravello. 'Where the men of war lead, the men of business follow. You want five hundred fighting men, the trade's moved north'ards. Germany, the Dutch… All those furious heretics, don't y'know.' Of a sudden he glances at Jean, who has lifted his gaze. 'Forgive me,' Ravello says, hurriedly. 'I spoke without thinking. No offence meant.'

'None taken.' *A month*, Jean is thinking. *A month wasted.* He takes a mouthful of sausage and potato, and with difficulty hangs on to it as Ravello continues. 'Only one place to set about recruiting a number such as that is up in the borderlands. Where you need to be is Hertzberg.'

'Hertzberg?' This is Jean. 'You can't mean it. *Hertzberg?*'

'The very place. You know it?'

'I did. But the Hertzberg I knew was a scuff-mark. There was a brewery—'

'Rauchmann's,' says Ravello, nodding his head.

'There was the Golden Oak—'

'Still there, but grown too. Like the oak.' With a grin, he lowers his head. 'Makes this place look like a rabbit-hutch.'

'And there was Magda's,' Jean concludes. 'And that was it. Blink and you'd missed it.'

'Times change,' Ravello tells him, leaning back. 'Hertzberg has an inn on every corner now. Swordsmiths. Armourers. Horse-dealers. Everything you'd need. And every freebooter you could lay a name to, all of 'em spoiling for a fee and a fight. When were you there last?'

He has to lift his voice. A final mighty note resounds from the dinner-party. The monkey, chittering with terror, runs up the pedlar's arm; Tabby, as if sucked toward the noise, places a hand upon one brocade-clad Venetian shoulder, and looks down at the wearer with a smile.

'Years ago,' answers Jean. 'Hertzberg. I'll be damned.'

The dinner-party has begun a drumming on the table with their fingertips. *Lirum, lirum, lirum,* they sing. The *lirums* are meant to imitate the strumming of a lute. The song, this year, is everywhere. Jean rolls his eyes and rises to his feet. Ravello looks up at him, enquiringly. *Lirum, lirum, lirum.*

'Shit-house,' says Jean, by way of explanation.

'Where it was,' Ravello advises, cheerily. 'Follow the stink.'

More *lirums* from other corners of the room. Tabby lifts her chin, la-la-ing the melody. She has a pretty voice, and her deep breaths as she sings push her breasts up against the edge of her bodice like cream about to spill from a jug. *Lirum, lirum.* The owner of that fine brocade coat is entranced.

A man, apron round his waist, has come to lean against their table. He has a fleshy, fallen-looking face, topped with a few strands of hair. As if announcing himself, he produces a loud sniff. 'Reinhold!' exclaims Ravello, sounding delighted, and adds, admiringly, 'That girl of yours has done some growing, ain't she?'

'*Oh,*' Tabby is singing, '*let the silent lute resound. You hear my song, my love.*'

Reinhold Meier wipes his sleeve under his nose. 'That one,' he says. 'That one slipped her lead with me a good few years ago. Like her fucken mother. Women,' he continues, catching Balthasar's eye. 'So your friend ain't brung his whore with him this time?' He turns again to Ravello. 'Proper hell-cat,' he adds, with a wink.

'*You come to me, and not from duuuu-uuuty,*' sings Tabby, eyes closed. '*Though time has marched across my brow, and faded is my beau-uuuu-ty.*'

'His whore?' Ravello enquires. 'What whore was this?'

'Came riding up here, legs wrapped round 'er 'orse like a man.

Woman soldier. You know 'er, come *on*,' and Reinhold biffs Ravello in the shoulder as an aid to memory. 'Come a cropper,' he continues, with relish, waggling a hand in the air. 'Lost one of these.'

'Good God, you mean *Paola*,' Ravello exclaims. He winks at Balthasar. 'Whey-hoo! That so? Paola and Jean?'

'Long ago,' Balthasar replies. 'Years ago. There was a moment, yes. But years ago.' He takes a swig of Rousette, winces. 'A name from the past.'

'*My lute shall siii-iii-ing once moooooore!*' sings Tabby, ringing that top note like a bell. 'Bravo!' cries Ravello, with the rest. 'Bravo!' He turns back to Balthasar. 'Well, hardly,' he says. 'If we're talking about the same Paola, she's just up the road. She's in Hertzberg.'

'Anyhow,' Reinhold says, in the silence that follows. He turns to Ravello. 'Come to tell you, that fellow you was waiting for. He's hanging around out the back.'

'Is he?' Ravello replies, eyes on Balthasar the while.

'Yeah, and I'll take it kindly if you and he 'ud find some other place to rendezvous.'

'But Reinhold,' Ravello exclaims, with a beaming smile, 'compared to you, where else is there?'

Reinhold departs. Ravello waits.

'Paola and *Jean*?' he says, at last.

'Long ago,' Balthasar repeats. 'Long before Sally. *Long* before.'

'You sure? That's not what your face is telling me.'

'Never mind my face. What's this that she's in Hertzberg?'

'She and Magda,' Ravello says. 'Magda cooks, Paola keeps the books. They're doing well.'

'I imagine Paola could make any place as served a drink a profit,' says Balthasar, sourly.

Ravello grins like a dog. 'Not your type, eh? You don't care for your women wearing britches?'

'No, I don't. Nor do I like 'em drunk, nor profane, nor leading

Jean a dance.' Nor crushing his heart like a grape, so that the very next woman he sees, he must make his, irretrievably – no matter how unsuited (in the very private opinion of his very closest friend) he and the woman in question may be. 'She walked out on him, you know that? An hour after the surgeon was finished with her, she was gone. Left a note on her pillow, saying how he'd never see her again. The woman's mad,' Balthasar spits out, 'crazy as a cut snake. I'd hoped she'd disappeared for good.'

'Then you've a problem, my friend,' says Ravello. 'Because you want men in the numbers you're looking for, Hertzberg is the only place you'll find 'em. And while you're headed that way,' he continues, 'you might make a stop at Forbach. The Franciscans have an infirmary there. Let them have them a listen to that cough of yours.'

Balthasar folds his arms. 'I'll be sure to give them the pleasure. So who's the fellow you've been waiting for? Anyone we'd know?'

'I doubt it,' Ravello replies.

'Anyone we'd want to know?'

'Doubt that even more. He's a Roma.'

Balthasar shakes his head. 'By God, Ravello, you've strange tastes in friends.'

'Do you think?' Ravello asks. 'My Roma, they go every-where. And everywhere they go, the world pretends they don't exist. You'd be amazed how much you get to see when that's the case. My friend Rufus, for example – he's a petitioner at the court of the Prince-Bishop of Prague, suing for a pardon for his brother. Thanks to him, I know more of the working of the Prince-Bishop's household than the Bishop does himself.' He nods toward the door, when Jean has reappeared. 'Hertzberg,' Ravello says. 'Paola or no. Now, are you going to tell him, or am I?'

⌁⊙⌁

HERE'S HOW IT'S DONE, this business, the buying and selling of men.

You sell the horse you've ridden from Poitou, spending the last of your ready cash on something a tad less travel-stained – no flashy snorter, but a beast that at least makes you look less like you've just come in from the fields – and on it, you ride into Hertzberg, which is indeed scuff-mark no more; and then you ride a whiles about it; enough to see, and to be seen. You are not, of course, the only contractor, so-called, in town, but you are the only one named Jean Fiskardo, and you announce this name loudly, as you book yourself and your companion a room at the Golden Oak. And as you lug your and your companion's kit up the stairs (and why don't he lug his own? The bloody cough, that's why), you are aware that heads lift behind you, and that your name is being passed like some winning ticket hand to hand.

You spend the next day or so walking about the town. (Or most of it. It might be noted that your steps never take you down a particular street near to the mermaid clock.) You fall into conversation, here and there. You let it be known you're looking only for the best.

You get drunk with an Estonian captain of horse, who's been earning his pay in the Duchy of Cleves, but the conflict there is a mess, he says, is done with, nothing further to be had. He's about to take himself and his squad of freebooters off to Vienna, to fight the Turk. 'Estonia's a friend to the Emperor, is it?' you ask, and the man gawps at you in horror. You lower your head. You murmur, 'Grace alone, faith alone,' and the man's face clears, as if by magic. 'I know how it is,' you say, 'especially with men dependent on you. You feel you have to take the first sure thing. You don't. You don't have to take the Habsburg thaler, either.'

Debauching, this is called; taking another army's recruits. It's a subtle art, a little like seduction. Takes the same cool nerve.

You go back to the Golden Oak. You can hear Balthasar coughing even before you reach the top of the stairs. You empty the bowl beside his bed. Glittering with sweat, he asks you how the day went. You tell him, 'Easy. Everyone hates the Habsburgs. Even the Habsburgs hate the Habsburgs.'

He says he should be out there with you.

Listen, you tell him. If it weren't for you, I would be out there, a freebooter, myself.

He's restive still; glassy-eyed. You gave them too much, he says.

Gave who too much?

The Franciscans. Another splutter of coughing. There's nothing wrong with me.

You sit yourself down on the bed. You pitched off your horse, you tell him. You spat blood. You may be worth nothing to the rest of the world, but you're worth ten francs to the good brothers to me. Now shut up and sleep.

Next morning, you take yourself for a stroll along the river. The sky is a glowing winter-white, the water crisped into ice around the reed-beds. Frozen puddles snap beneath your boots. There's smoke up ahead. A camp. Huddled round it, a litter of infantrymen – deserters, probably, and they'll need new boots and not a few of them re-arming, too; but this is how, when those others ask, you can tell them you've fifty men already under seal. You stroll back to the Golden Oak, and the first thing you see is a nonchalant queue arranged around the court-yard. The Estonian captain is at its head. You want only the best, you'd said. Well of course, and what man thinks himself any less than that?

The Estonian captain has thirty men, each of them with horses, arms, experience to spare. He brings you them all.

You bring Balthasar down to the courtyard, swaddle him in a blanket, and spend the afternoon listening as he explains with a deal more patience than you could command that no, just as always, each man gets a *douceur* here, you'll be paid the rest when you arrive at the mustering place near Aisne – the Duc de Condé's home ground. And we want you there by the first day of Lent, boys. Any later is too late. Now make your mark.

Which is also when you will be paid yourself. Which means perhaps if you can find a way to get it to her, more for Sally – when? Easter?

Any later is too late.

'You want more, enlist with the Franciscans,' Balthasar is telling one complainer. 'He *gives* money away to them.'

By the end of the first week you have three hundred signed and sealed, and Balthasar is walking about the Golden Oak growling orders, with a muffler round his throat.

By the end of the second week, eight-score more. That'll do.

So this will be your final night in Hertzberg after all these years, and you find yourself wandering the town in a sort of farewell. And your steps take you to bid adieu to its famous mermaid clock. You watch it strike. You watch the show of figures, parading under its face. And then something has you turn about, and you go first to the end of that particular street, just to look, but then wouldn't you know it, it's unclear what you're looking at – scaffolding, canvas, something roped off – so you go a yard or two or ten down the street, and there it is, the swinging barrel, painted with a woman's smiling face, just as you remember it, and there's the door.

You knock. You are aware of a sensation like excited footsteps running up and down your gut. You hear someone on the other side of the door. The sensation in your gut starts jumping up and down with glee. The door comes open. You stand before it, supplicant as a pilgrim.

Magda. Just as you remember her, plump as ever, not aged by as much as a line. She takes a breath when she sees you and puts a bejewelled hand to her breast, but you have the feeling she's not so surprised you're here.

'We heard you were in town,' she says, stepping back to let you enter. Even the smell of the room is the same – deep-soaked in beer, although overlaid with the bitter smell of fresh mortar. The wall to the street is down to waist-height, and set upon it there's a framework, this side of that billowing canvas, for three mighty windows. Balanced across two tables there's a cartwheel chandelier so new the iron it's made of shines like tin. 'What's all this?' you ask, and Magda, raising her hands, says, 'We've had a few good years. We thought it was time to invest.'

We. Ever since she opened the door, you have been waiting to hear steps behind her, or upstairs. You turn back to Magda, but before the question is out of your mouth, she's answered it.

'She's in Saarbrücken, Jean,' Magda says, leading you to the kitchen. 'She isn't here.'

'Saarbrücken?' And you laugh, as you follow her, to show how little this matters. 'The devil is she doing there?'

'The glassmakers are there.' She's bustling about, drawing a jug of beer from the barrel in the corner. 'For our windows. Paola –'

Oh, to hear her name spoken, here where she lives. It drops through you like a spike.

'Paola sees to such matters. I do the food, and the beer.' She places the jug and a tankard on the table before him.

You look about the kitchen, this place behind the scenes. Nothing is changed here, either. There's the coffer, there's Magda's giant hourglass still in pride of place – nothing is changed, but everything is. You feel, of a sudden, as if everything in your life had lost the path it should be taking long before. 'So life is good? What do the cards say?'

A sharp look. 'Oh, you mock, but they told me you were coming.' She sits herself down, opposite. 'So now you're here, how is the world with you?'

Well. I am wed, I have a child, yet still I find myself sitting here all hollowed out because a woman I last saw more than five long years ago is not here also. 'I'm wed,' you begin.

'We heard.'

'We have a son.'

'We heard that too.'

You stare at the tabletop. 'How is she, Magda?'

'She's well.' She composes herself as she answers, folding her neat ringed hands – that characteristic settling of herself in place, a hen upon her nest.

'Does she look the same?'

Magda laughs. 'It's been five years, Jean. We all change.'

'You haven't.' You wait. 'Has she?'

'You mean is she still at odds with you? I don't know. You made her angry. But it was five years ago.'

'*I* made *her* angry? What did I do?'

'You pitied her,' says Magda. 'You pitied her, and you let her see that you did. How could she endure that? You of all people should know her better than that.'

Briefly, you close your eyes. You will be damned if they will get the chance to give you away again. 'But she's well?' you ask. 'Her arm healed?'

'It did. Have you?'

If there is an answer to that, it's not one you're going to give here. 'Tell her I asked after her,' you say, and get to your feet.

Magda the good hostess follows. At the door you turn. 'Will she *ever* forgive me? Do the cards tell you that?'

'The cards tell us what will come to us, Jean. Not how we might deal with it, when it does. But when they spoke of you, they told me you should watch yourself.'

'That's damned good of 'em, Maggie,' you hear yourself reply. 'I'll be sure to bear that in mind.'

'And they told me you should watch your temper, too,' says Magda.

The door is closed.

*

She waits until she hears the footsteps reach the street, until she can be sure there'll be no second thoughts. Then she picks up the jug and swills it onto the ashes in the fire; she locks the door to the yard; she blows out one candle and picks up the other, and, holding up her skirts, toils up the stairs. Taps upon the bedroom door, which opens under the tap.

The candle plays across a curtained bed, from which one booted foot emerges, and one hand hangs down, as if their owner had first sat upon the bed, then let herself fall backwards across it. There is an empty bottle, on its side, on the floor beneath the hand.

'He's gone,' says Magda.

The boot gives a twitch. 'Good,' comes Paola's reply.

SO HERE IS JEAN FISKARDO, making his way back to the Golden Oak, while beneath his breastbone the wraith of an old love subsides fretfully and painfully back into its grave. In its place there rises something very different. He had but one more evening here – how could he have been such a fool as to go seeking her like that? What sort of lovesick simpleton is he? And now he is not only angry at himself but filled with chagrin too. *I need a drink*, thinks Jean.

You want a drink at this hour in a place the size of the Golden Oak, what you need is a potboy.

There's a choice of potboys at the Golden Oak: Bruno or Oskar. Its patrons are divided as to which of them is the more likely to be hung first. An unholy duo of peerers-in at windows, scavengers of small change, losers of the boots you left outside your door for them to clean, and forgetters of orders for new candles and more bread. He finds them at the door to the Golden Oak's own dining room, one either side, peering in. 'Bottle of the best,' he tells them.

Neither boy moves. Jean raises a hand; Oskar moves his head out of its range – a friendly acknowledgement. 'I said a bottle, maggot.' Then Jean, too, peers into the room, which is deserted save for one lone diner, a newcomer, jug of beer on the table beside him.

'What are we looking at?' Jean asks.

'Oh, he's a bugger,' Oskar replies.

'He's a fucking bugger,' Bruno puts in. 'Been after me arse, Capting,' he adds, in his adenoidal way.

Jean looks from one boy to the other: Oskar with his chin of unreaped bum-fluff, and his cheeks with their crop of adolescent pustules; Bruno with his pug nose, breathing through his mouth. 'Trust me, no-one on God's green earth is after either of you, let alone your arse.'

'He is, Capting, oh he is,' Bruno insists. 'Been sidling up on me all day. Well, if 'e wanted me arse, he's got it.' Both boys are sniggering now. 'You tell 'im, I stuck me fingers up me ring and I then stuck 'em in 'is beer!' And Bruno flourishes the fingers beneath Jean's nose as if offering him a nosegay. Jean recoils, the man looks up, and at once gets to his feet. The boys are gone like smoke.

'Kapitan Fiskardo!' the newcomer says, advancing. He sounds aggrieved. 'I wait for you all day!'

The newcomer has a gold hoop slotted through the rim of his right ear. The newcomer has a roll of fat at the back of his neck thick as a weisswurst. There is an air to him of something fattened, bletted; despite his unlined cheeks, of being already run to seed.

The newcomer introduces himself. 'Enric Maduna,' he says, sticking out a hand. He offers Jean a glass of beer, which to the man's amazement Jean turns down. 'But this is doppelbock,' the man insists. 'Rauchmann's. The finest!'

'I've a bottle coming,' Jean assures him.

The man squints at him. Jean has an idea he is in none too sharp a focus. 'To business,' Maduna announces. 'Kapitan. I am 'ere –' (he wags a forefinger) '– I am 'ere about the business of the Prince-Bishop of Prague.' He leans forward. 'I am – I am of the family,' he declares, modestly.

'That so?' says Jean.

'The Prince-Bishop of Prague.' Maduna leans back. 'You hear of him, *jah?*'

'Some,' says Jean. It's not exactly a lie. In his present mood he need only hear the man's title to be thinking *Habsburg lackey. Papist ape.*

Maduna settles himself more comfortably. 'An' the Bishop of Prague, what he wants is men. An' you got men, *jah?*'

At last Jean understands what's being proposed here. He narrows his eyes, leans forward, chin propped on his thumb, finger curled around his mouth. 'You're asking me to debauch my own troops? You want to sign them to the Bishop of Prague?'

'Exactly so!' says Maduna, enthusiastically.

'And why would the Bishop of Prague want men?'

Maduna starts a frantic blinking; eyes disappearing like a frog's. It seems not to have occurred to him that he might be questioned. *A fool*, thinks Jean. *A drunkard and a fool.* He has a long fuse, does Jean, but tonight he feels that fuse is short enough to be within those last few, final, spitting inches of its life.

'Eh,' says Maduna, at last. 'The Old Emperor *ist* ailing, there will be a new – is wise, now, in Prague, to have men.'

'I'll take your word for it. But why would I be willing to pass mine over to him?'

Maduna looks sly. He says, 'I pay you for them, Kapitan.'

'And what if I'm promised a fee for them already?'

More blinking. 'I pay you more.'

'Do you so?' says Jean. One half of his mind is still working over Paola: *she knew that I was here. She knew I was here and didn't care.* He leans across the table with a suddenness the other man, startled, clearly interprets as a lunge. *Amateur*, thinks Jean. Is there any type he despises more? 'How much?'

The crafty expression returns, mantling over the man's face. Beneath it, the frantic calculations swim back and forth. *Been sent here with his orders and a purse*, thinks Jean, *and now the sot is trying to work out how much he can keep for himself.*

'Need some help?' Jean offers, grinning, showing his teeth.

Maduna, plainly discomfited, rushing his words. 'I pay you five florin.'

'Florins? You might still have your florins down south, but we use thalers here, my friend.'

The other takes a breath. 'I am confuse. Thaler, I mean. Thaler.'

'The price for a man is ten,' Jean tells him. It's nothing like, but why not?

'Ten thaler, yes.'

'Well now,' says Jean, as if considering. 'Ten times four hundred thalers. You've deep pockets, I see.'

'No – no,' the other begins. 'For twenty. We want twenty.' Sweat, now, on the man's forehead. 'Twenty of your best.'

'Of my best? What, like apples? I'm a grocer now, am I?'

In walks Bruno, cradling a bottle, puts it on the table before Jean. After much show of breathing and polishing, he places a glass daintily beside it. 'There you go, Capting,' says Bruno. 'Bottle of Tirol.'

'On his tab,' says Jean, indicating Maduna.

Maduna manages an uneasy laugh. 'Ah, Kapitan, you play with me, *jah*?'

Don't I just. 'So,' says Jean, sitting back. 'Two hundred thalers for twenty men. You drive a bargain, you do. Your Prince-Bishop should be proud.'

The compliment is obviously unexpected, and you'd think rare for this one, any case – but the man is still fool enough to puff himself up at it. 'So how much for me?' Jean asks.

Maduna has the look of one nonplussed as to how his foot-hold in this conversation keeps slipping. That frog-like blinking has started up again. 'For you?'

'For sure. You want me to sign over my recruits to some Habsburg kiss-arse, got to be something in it for me.' And when the other answers not at all, Jean goes on, 'You're fuckwit enough to pay four times the rate for them, I reckon I'm worth another hundred of my own, don't you? To have me *not* noise abroad what a useless tyro the Prince-Bishop sends to run his errands. Sound fair?'

There is a silence. The other man's face now looks not so much stilled as stiffened. 'I think you do not sell your men to me, Kapitan,' he says, at last.

'Hand over twenty of my recruits to some bastard in Prague with an altar-candle for a prick, who's already fool enough to send you about his business? You think right.'

The man is getting to his feet. 'Very good, Kapitan, very good,' he says. 'You make sport with me, very good. I find other men.'

'You do that,' says Jean. 'Good luck with it. You find any men worth having in Hertzberg, they're yours. But my sugges-tion –' (and he too rises to his feet, and he has a knack of doing this, does Jean, in a manner designed to remind any other of the advantage of his height) '– my suggestion is you find yourself some other line of business, while you're at it. Because contrac-tor, you ain't.'

If this other were any kind of man at all, his next move would be to lay his hand to his sword. He does not. His face is swollen with fury. Jean raises his glass, tipping it to indicate the door. 'G'night!'

A decent pause later, and somewhat mellowed by having most of the bottle of Trollinger inside him, Jean gets up from the table, and makes his own way to the door. He stands for a moment admiring the oak in the moonlight, and, as he does so, spots Maduna's pale scalp, the man crouched down, waiting in stealthy ambush behind the oak. Well now. What to do here?

He can move with surprising quietness, can Jean, when he has to.

The kitchen door comes open – Oskar throwing a bucketful of slops vaguely in the direction of the drain. Maduna's head turns toward the noise. Jean, now less than a yard away, shoots out a hand and bangs Maduna's head into the trunk of the oak, then wraps an arm about his neck, lifting his feet from the ground. Maduna may be being throttled, but there's more fight in him than Jean had reckoned on; he kicks against the trunk of the tree and Jean staggers back, Maduna coming with him. Their noise has brought Bruno and Oskar running from the kitchen. With Maduna as a human breastplate, Jean runs not at the tree, but at the little window where the stairs begin. Maduna's head goes through the glass, violently enough to bend the leads; he gives a groan, and slides from Jean's grasp. Jean, Oskar and Bruno stare at each other over the man's prone body. The first outraged bellow from upstairs: 'Who's raising hell down there this time of the night?'

'Eh, it's the potboys!' Jean calls back. 'Dropped a barrel down the stairs!'

'Oh, *those* little fuckers,' the voice comments, knowledge-ably. One by one, the lights that had appeared upstairs are extinguished.

'What do we do now, Capting?' Bruno asks, in a whisper.

Good question. But the pieces of a plan, a jape, and a great jape it will be, are already drawing together in Jean's head. 'This place still got a boat?'

They carry Maduna down to the riverbank, Jean at the shoulders, the boys carrying the legs. The Golden Oak's flat-bottomed punt is pulled up on the mud. The river slinks past – to Jean's mind, as if it might enjoy its role in such a bit of sport as this. 'There you go, you bugger,' Bruno comments cheerily, as they lay Maduna in the punt. 'Nice bit of river-air for you.' And then, sharp with excitement, ''Ere! Capting! Look at this!'

A purse has fallen from Maduna's pocket. Bruno holds it up like a trophy: 'It's heavy, Capting!'

Lord, so it is. Jean opens the purse and a handful of gold falls into his palm: fresh-minted, bright as little suns. And just to make them even more appealing, no doubt fresh from the coffers of the Prince-Bishop himself. 'Christ!' says Oskar, and punches Bruno on the arm. 'He could'a *had* your arse, for one o'them!' He peers up into Jean's face. 'We gonna keep 'em?'

Jean, straddling the punt, lifts Maduna's head. This one won't wake for hours. And Maduna had lain in ambush for him. And Maduna is a Habsburg louse. And today has failed to please Jean, but this plan does.

When we are rich. 'Well,' says Jean, 'it ain't as if we're tipping him *in* the river, is it?' *The gods*, he tells himself, *owe me one.* He picks out two of the coins, holds them up to the boys. 'One apiece,' he says, 'to keep your little gobs shut. Agreed?'

Agreed. 'What about the rest of it, Capting?' Oskar asks.

'Don't you worry about that,' says Jean, merrily. Isn't Dame Fortune obliged to favour the bold? 'I know *just* where that can find a home.'

He puts his boot against the punt's nib-like stern, and gives a shove. The punt glides out, Maduna still visible within it. It turns end to end once, twice, then as if finding its place in the run of the river it's gone, shooting into the darkness, and the thing is done; irrevocable.

CHAPTER THREE

An Alliance

'Little by little, the bird builds its nest.'

Old French proverb

S PRINGTIME AT LAST. The river seems wider, the curve
of the fields more vast; it's as if la Belle-Dame felt the
warmth in the air, breathed in and opened her chest.
Hector begins an optimistic braying for a mate; lambs wobble
and twitch across the bottom of the fields, and down in the
village, the market reopens for business.

It's female territory, the market at Belle-Dame. The fishermen may land the catch, the farmers pull the crops from the
fields, but it's the wives and daughters cry their wares behind
each stall: 'Fresh lobsters! Fresh as day!' 'The finest cream, the
finest cheese!' 'Try this, try this! Honey so soft, you'd swear the
bees must sup on silk!'

Beneath their seagull hullabaloo, the real business of debate is under way.

'And have you heard what that Habsburg sow has done now? She has made that Concini –' (a sniff – you can imagine the man being crushed underfoot, like a snail) '– that Concini, a marquis, no less! The Marquis d'Ancre he is to be now. Think of it! The husband of her waiting-woman! I despair, I do, truly. What are we come to?'

'Oh, so no doubt yet more riches for him, her precious Concini, while my husband must find forty francs a year to work the marsh. Forty francs!'

The husband in question is a harvester of that same famous *fleur de sel*. He's known across the village as Salty Pierre. This is Madame Salty Pierre, leaning behind her stall to that of her neighbour, Madame Didier-France.

'Forty francs? Simply to work the marsh?' Madame Didier-France echoes. 'Oh the day!'

Monsieur Didier-France is a fisherman. His wife's stall is briny with odours, and fascinating to the flies. Madame Didier-France's hands pass back and forth across it, an endless shuttle on an invisible loom. 'Didier-France says he expects to be all but taxed on the holes in his nets,' she declares, mournfully. (Back and forth go the hands, buzz-buzz-buzz go the flies.)

'And,' confides Madame Pierre, 'there are those who say Concini now enjoys *all* the Queen's favours *and more*.' A nod of the head for emphasis. 'But then what do you expect of a woman such as our Queen, with her yellow hair? You know what they say about blondes.' She bends forward again. 'A lustful constitution!'

'Take care, my dear! Mind who might hear you!'

Madame Pierre and Madame Didier-France watch as Sally makes her uncertain way down the lane of stalls, blonde curls escaping from her cap. Madame Didier-France leans in closer to her neighbour. 'Do you think she heard you?'

Madame Pierre shakes her head. 'Even if she did, it would have meant nothing to her. Have you ever tried to speak with her? I don't think she understands more than one word in three.'

'I've never heard her speak at all,' Madame Didier-France confesses. 'All she has ever done with me is make those little smiles.'

'My dear, they are a strange people altogether, the English. Seal themselves up like oysters. It comes of living on an island, if you ask me.'

'Still,' says Madame Didier-France, watching, as Sally, curls like rosebuds bobbing on the breeze, makes her way around the market with her son. 'Still, she is very pretty, is she not?' says Madame Didier-France, wistfully.

'Madame!'

Instantly, Madame Didier-France sits up as straight as if she had been challenged by a sentry. Both she and Madame Pierre pivot on their stools. In all her sour and thin-lipped inky blackness, they thus face Madame Marthe.

'Madame Didier-France,' snaps Madame Marthe, 'you send your flies to bother me!'

Madame Didier-France bows her head in shame. 'Indeed, Madame Marthe, I do assure you that I never did,' she replies, from between her cantilevered shoulder-blades.

'I think it is a little difficult,' suggests Madame Pierre, 'to control a fly.'

'Not,' says Madame Marthe, 'not if you do not *waft them about*. If you do not *waft them about*, it is not difficult at all.' And to prove the point her hand snaps out, seizes a fly that has paused to strop its legs upon her tablecloth and squishes it flat between finger and thumb. 'There, do you see, Madame? Then it is not difficult *at all.*'

Sally, meanwhile, has come to a stop at the one stall in the market not devoted to the serious business of food, one instead fluttery with news-sheets and gaudy with haberdashery. The stall-holder here sometimes has her little boy with her, a spindly-looking child whose grave face sits behind a pair of blue-tinted spectacles. It is Sally's hope that she might induce Jack and this child to become friends but there seems little chance of that so far: all Jack does is circle the other child from a scornful distance, and the mother is correspondingly unfriendly in return. And now her son is tugging at his leading reins again, so violently he tugs his mother backwards, and now his lusty treble pipes out, '*BON-jour*, Monsieur Gustave!'

Monsieur Gustave, scion of Belle-Dame's oldest family, owner of its largest farm and, incidentally, of that two-room cottage on the path up to the headland, removes his hat. '*Ah! Bonjour*, Petit Jacques,' he replies. Like many of those without children of their own, Monsieur Gustave is unfailingly polite to the children of others. 'Are you well?'

'Very well,' Jack replies. 'And how is it with you?' he asks, eyes fixed on Monsieur Gustave's moustache, which is so enormous it covers his mouth completely. Sometimes the only way you can tell it's Monsieur Gustave speaking is if his moustache is going up and down.

What a strange little thing it is, thinks Monsieur Gustave. It's as if it's been forced somehow. Like endive. He turns to the mother. 'And you, madame – do you flourish?' The invisibility of the English woman over the winter months had troubled Monsieur Gustave, who knows another lonely soul when he sees one.

'I am most extreme,' Sally assures him, bravely.

'And your house,' Monsieur Gustave continues. 'You are comfortable there? There is firewood enough to keep you warm?'

There is not. But nor is there money to spare to buy more. Nor any sign of such. Nor any word from Jean. Sally, flustered, is about to concoct a reply when the noise of the market is interrupted by the racket of something coming down the road. There are horses, there are wheels – there is a carriage. How unexpected. The entire market pauses in its doings and stops to watch as the carriage comes in sight. It's quite a thing to see. Its roof is spiky as a sea-urchin with the legs of upturned bits of furniture, all lashed into place; there are pots and pans, strung together like onions, hanging down over its front. The coachman, standing, pulls his horses to a stop, the pots and pans clatter and bang. He calls out, 'Is this Belle-Dame?'

A murmur assures him that it is. The driver sits. 'We're 'ere, madame,' he yelps.

'Yes, thank you,' comes a woman's voice from the carriage's interior. 'I am aware of that.'

The door to the carriage is swung open – with difficulty, there is what appears to be a torchére wedged through the open window – and a cache of cushions tumbles out, carrying with it a little girl. The child picks herself up without complaint and waits while the woman emerges, backwards, shielding her head. The woman stands. Unhooks the necklace that has become caught in her hair – hair that is grey as wool, and stands out round her head like a bush; arms long as broom-sticks, mannishly undimpled.

The woman shakes out her skirts. 'Ye Gods,' she says, loudly. 'This place ain't changed much, has it? *What* a miracle.'

Les veuves have started a hissing, like geese. Madame Marthe, at their front, has her head projected forward like an old heron, sighting fish. 'Well, *Anne*,' she says.

'Yes, it's me,' the woman answers. 'Aren't you delighted? Home sweet home!'

And Jack may be the only one to notice it, but Monsieur Gustave has dropped his hat, and looks as stunned as one of those freshly landed fish.

―eᴏOᴏᴐ―

THE TALL UGLY woman with the very loud voice has moved into
the house at the bottom of the lane. They hear her, out in her
garden, directing all the people who have to help her move her
furniture into her house; only some of it doesn't get into the
house at all. The big torchére is left outside for days. When Jack
spies on her from the field above the cottage, he sees it in her
garden, holding up a washing-line.

The tall ugly woman shouts at people over her hedge. When
les veuves go up the street together, driving their goats, she
jumps out at them so suddenly that the goats scatter all over the
place, and when she comes back into her garden she's hooting
with laughter and slapping her knees. The tall ugly woman is
mad, there's no other explanation possible.

Then one morning she's not in her garden, she's in theirs.
'It's too much,' she says, walking in. (Into their kitchen!
Didn't even ask!) 'What pitiful sticks of furniture I managed
to bring with me, now I have a house they hardly fit into.
Do you need anything? Another table? Chairs? I had a set of
hangings –'

'Hangings?' Maman repeats faintly, as the woman – what
was she called? Anne, that was it – walks around the room. She
hardly seems to notice they're at breakfast; in fact she hardly
seems to notice this isn't her house at all. Meanwhile her little
girl waits at the door, but when Jack points his stare at her to
see what she intends doing about her mother's behaviour, all
she does is roll her eyes to heaven.

'Hangings. From my house in Paris. Tapestry pieces. Dido
and Aeneas.' The woman is talking much too fast; he can tell,
looking at Maman's face, that Maman can hardly understand
her. 'How is Aeneas, by the way?'

'Aeneas?' Maman says.

'Your husband,' the woman replies, coming to a stop. 'He
and our brave rebels. I wondered if perhaps as Madame Jean
Fiskardo you might have some news.'

'Jack,' says Maman, hurriedly, 'you've finished your breakfast, go outside and play.'

The little girl peels herself away from the wall of the house when she sees him. She's wearing shoes with red heels. These are so striking that for a moment 'shoes with red heels' almost join the list beginning 'Dada coming home' and 'a boat'.

'*Bonjour,*' the little girl says, pleasantly, and smiles. Jack's throat feels like it does when he takes too big a bite of bread. The little girl regards him through her lashes. 'My name is Marguerite,' she says. 'I'm six. How old are you?'

'Five.' There had been a birthday, in the new year.

She frowns at him. 'Why aren't you in breeches yet?'

Jack is pierced to the quick. 'Why are you in skirts?' he demands.

Marguerite hinges forward, giggling. It makes you see who her maman is, when she does that. 'Because I'm a girl,' she replies. Her face grows serious. 'Don't you know any girls?' She takes his arm and pulls him round to face the gate. There are other children clustered there – another little girl, and three small boys; the one with the blue spectacles amongst them. How has she managed to collect all these?

'This is Adèle,' she begins, pointing them out, 'this is Sebastien, this is Didier-Marie and this is Claude. His eyes don't work,' she confides, sorrowfully. Then, 'We've come to say hello,' she announces, as if this invasion of his garden was the most logical thing in the world. 'Only we're so-o-o bo-o-o-red.' Then she does a sudden jump, like a rabbit, so she's standing right up close to him again. 'Do you know any games?'

'Lots,' he declares, hotly. 'I know lots.' Climbing trees, skimming stones, making dens, folding paper boats... are any of these things you can do with girls?

She tugs his arm. 'Then will you come and play? Will you come play with us, Petit Jacques?'

*

'So,' says Anne, sitting down. She puffs a little air into her skirts. 'Good God, it's hard to believe. After all I've been through, here I am again.'

'Again?' asks Sally, dazed. Something about her visitor makes her feel out of breath. 'You know Belle-Dame?'

Anne does a great harsh bark of laughter. 'I was born here,' she replies. 'The very house I'm back in now. Only it was bigger then,' she adds with a sigh, 'I'm sure it was. *Zut*, it's true, no-one does talk to you, do they?' And then, before the gap where there should be an answer to this can get any bigger, Anne continues smoothly, 'Of course, none of them have any time for me, either. Unless it is to gloat.' Her visitor bends forward. 'I committed a sin.'

'You did?'

'The worst.' Her hands are raised in horror. 'I dared to leave the village. Even worse, I left it for a man. Paris, he said. The world, he said. Oh, I was such a fool. Don't you get lonely, by the way, up here on your own?'

Sally draws back, but hears herself saying, 'Oh, but I'm used to it – to this – I have Jack –'

Anne tilts her head, as if Sally will make more sense at an angle. She smiles, and her smile lifts her whole face, even her ears. 'And I have Marguerite. The only worthwhile thing my husband managed to achieve in twelve years of marriage. But she's six. And a six-year-old's idea of conversation?' Anne pulls a face. 'Maman, I've counted all my shoes. Maman, which flower is the best? Maman, where do the stars go?' It's a startlingly good impersonation, and to her amazement, Sally hears herself burst out laughing.

'There,' says Anne, sounding pleased. 'You understand me. So, my late-lamented husband is – lamented, and yours is how and where we do not speak. The two of us might join forces. Don't you think?'

—᧳◉᧳—

BELLE-DAME'S GEOGRAPHY may be strikingly symbolic, but it's also very simple. There is the single road into the village, as it hunkers in its cleft between the hills, which comes to a stop before the church. You too, if you so wish, may stop before the church – its path untrodden and the roof sprouting weeds – and if you're a good Catholic, breathe a sigh. Looking beyond the church (if you have the knack of reading a landscape, that is), you might spot the path leading uphill to the fields above the church, and if you are very sharp-eyed indeed, the lane leading up to the headland. But you would not think, looking at it from the village, that there could be another house up there at all. No lights are visible, nor any smoke from any chimney, and the road itself seems to decide the point, petering out to a flinty trickle, with the last few houses in the village pressing so tightly upon it that their roofs almost overlap. A rider would have to dismount, lead his horse between the houses, the noisy flints cracking beneath its hooves. Which makes the achievement of the man standing outside Sally's cottage in this early light all the more remarkable, as not a single soul in Belle-Dame is aware he's there at all. The man gives a delicate cough, and knocks upon the door.

Sally, sitting up in bed, calls out in English, 'Who's there?' before remembering who she is and where she is these days. Untucking herself from around the inert little comma of her son, she slips from the bed and pulls her shawl about her. There is another knock. '*Qui est-ce?*' she calls. Behind her, she hears Jack sit up, his querulous 'Maman?' She turns to him and holds a finger to her lips. Like all soldiers' children, he is silent at once. From outside another cough, discreet as a Lord Chamberlain's. '*Sall-ee?*' a voice calls. '*C'est toi?*' It's not Jean, she knows it's not, but there's only one other person it could be and any number of awful reasons why he might be at her door. Fumbling the key in the lock, she pulls the door open.

And the man enters, Sally retreating before him, holding her hands over her heart. 'Oh God,' she says. 'What's happened? Where is Jean?'

'He is strong, he is well, he sends his love, he sends me here,' says the man. He looks pleased with himself. He gives that little cough again.

Still she retreats. 'But he's not – he isn't hurt? Where is he?'

'Sall-ee,' says the man, with fond reproof. He takes off his hat. 'No, Jean is thriving. Full of plans. He sends me with this for you.' The man opens his arms.

'Oh!' says Sally, dropping her hands. 'Oh, thank heaven!' and rushes into the hug with hardly less gusto than if it had been Jean himself standing there.

'And he sends this as well,' the man adds, after a moment's gentlemanly contact (no more). He pulls from his pocket a little leather bag, and upends it over the table. There is at once a twinkling spill of light into every corner of the room.

'*Oh!*' Sally exclaims again, and throws her shawl over it.

'Maman!' comes a plaintive voice. Both of them turn, to see the small figure standing at the bedroom door bemused, still half-asleep.

'*Ah, mon Dieu,*' the man says, softly. 'Look at those eyes. Why, that could be Jean, standing there.'

'Jack,' says Sally, sounding proud. 'Come here and meet your Dada's friend. This is Captain Balthasar.'

She sits Balthasar down at the table, it being understood that as soon as a soldier stops moving, the first thing he wants is food. Darting from cupboard to fireplace to table she sets before him pickled choucroute, ham and bread. There's always bread. This loaf has something fungoid to its shape, and when Balthasar bites into it, a dense sour centre, which strongly suggests it wasn't given time to rise. 'I baked it,' says Sally, modestly, sitting down to watch him chew. Balthasar, who had sustained himself those last few hours in the saddle with dreams of roast goose, a sauce of cherries slipping down its breast, swallows, sits back, and says, 'Ah!'

He looks around the room. Not large, not grand, far from Jean's dreams for her, he knows. He's a little embarrassed, now, to have made such an entrance. And here is Jean's startling-looking child, come edging up to him. The boy's gaze keeps sneaking to the sword, hung over the chair-back.

I wonder if he remembers?

Balthasar lifts the sword over his head, and holds it out to the boy, presenting it hilt first. The boy, wary, narrows his eyes and retreats.

'This little one does not remember me,' Balthasar says, sadly.

Sally pulls the boy into her lap. 'Last time you saw him,' she says, softly, 'we were still in camp.' She leans forward, putting her hand over Balthasar's. The touch of her fingers is like petals falling on his skin. 'Balthasar, where is Jean?'

'Thinking of you every day,' says Balthasar, stoutly. 'And dreaming of you every night, I dare say.'

'But he's safe? He's well?'

'Sally, trust me,' Balthasar tells her. 'He is in his element.'

A sigh of relief. 'And how has it been with you, Balthasar?' she asks. 'With the –' and her hand, at her throat, makes small opening and closing gestures, like a gasping fish. It's all anyone remembers of him: Balthasar and his cough. 'Monsieur Tissu', Jean used to call him, mocking, albeit affectionately, what seemed a high-strung manner for a soldier, as well as a fragile set of pipes.

'Never better,' Balthasar declares, dauntless. 'Strong as a lion.' And even as he says it, he feels that scratch at his throat and his lungs start to squeeze. The scratch becomes a claw. The blood is rushing to his face. The boy, startled, jumping off Sally's lap, swims across his flooded vision, and then there's Sally, holding a cup to his lips. 'Here. Drink. Just a little. Just a sip.' He sits back, eyes streaming. Wipes his mouth. There was a time, a good few years back now, when his cough was a mere stripling itself, that he and Sally – she hopelessly young and adrift in the ways of army life – sat up together many a dawn like this.

'How far have you come?' she asks.

'Too far.' He blinks to clear his vision. 'The roads are falling apart. Towns close their gates. We are an unhappy country.' He wants to cough again, but fights it down. 'I see the church here has been left to rot.'

A sorrowful nodding of her head. 'They journey to their services in La Rochelle. Or you hear them in the summer, all together, singing their psalms in the fields. I'm not supposed to know, of course, but they all think I'm beyond salvation in any case. I'm not like Jean, I'm not a Huguenot, and then I'm English, too.' She lifts her eyes to his. 'I can't remember when I last knelt down to pray in church. Jean says it doesn't matter. He says all that matters is that God still knows your name.'

'Well, he would, wouldn't he?' says Balthasar. 'The miserable heretic.'

And at that she throws back her head so the golden curls bounce. 'Oh, Balthasar, it is so *good* to see you again.' He remembers Jean swaggering into the guardroom, producing the girl from under his cloak. 'Look what I have here,' he'd said. And then that golden head, her tiny and uncertain smile. 'A little runaway,' Jean had announced. 'She says she's from Dunkirk, that English rat-hole. And it was raining. God's name, what's a man of honour to do?' And then a week later, in his cups: 'She is driving me insane. Nothing, I tell you, Balthasar, nothing. Is it because she's English? Are they born for the nunnery?'

'She is too good for you,' Balthasar had said, looking him in the eye.

'Shit then, I'll marry her,' Jean had declared. 'If that's the only way I can get up her skirts.'

And now here she is, laying her hand on his and smiling up into his face, and Balthasar understands – oh, he understands only too well – and no wonder it drove Jean crazy. With caution, he clears his throat. 'And can I tell Jean that you are thriving too?'

She pulls her boy back against her. 'Things are better now. We have our friends here, Jack and I. But that winter was hard. Please God, Jean will be home before the next.'

There's scant chance of that, Balthasar knows it. A diversion, that's what's called for here. There's her son. 'Jacques,' says Balthasar, leaning across. 'You are a good boy, yes?'

A nod.

'You take good care of your maman?'

Another nod.

'Then you must have this. Hold out your hand.' He reaches into his pocket, and lays in the boy's hand his clasp-knife. It's almost too heavy for the child to hold. 'For when you are older,' says Balthasar, closing the boy's fingers round it. 'Maman will keep it safe for you for now.' There through the window there's the sun, as bright as silver, and as pale. 'Sally,' he says, 'I must be on my way.'

'Where does that way take you?' she asks.

'I?' Balthasar answers, bravely. 'Paris. I'm going back to school.'

A trembling smile. 'Not back to Jean?'

'One last campaign? With this chest?' He makes a fist, knocks himself over the breastbone. 'Listen to that,' he says. 'Full as a coffin. No, no. Let Jean wield the cudgels, set the world to rights. I'll see out my days teaching beardless youths to find their way across a map. A little room, my name upon the door. The Street of the Old Soldiers, that's where you should look for me.' As he straightens up, his lungs creak like wet leather. '*Au'voir, ma belle*,' he announces, in a loud and cheery tone. 'And *à bientôt*, Petit Jacques. Next time you remember me, *hein*?'

*

They stand in the doorway, he and Maman, and watch the man go. The knife in Jack's hand feels heavy as a stone. There's a smooth silver button at one end, and at the other a sharp point hiding, like a tooth.

He won't remember Balthasar, when they meet again. What he will remember is this: the wet in the air, the weight of the knife, the sun coming up from the sea. And the sharp point, hiding.

Horse and rider reach the first stand of trees – and disappear. Like magic.

That is what grown-ups do. Appear and disappear. The fact that Maman doesn't disappear is just another sign she's not really a grown-up at all.

He hears Maman sigh, then her hand lifts from his shoulder, and she turns to go inside. When she reaches the table it's as if she's simply drifted to a stop. She holds up a coin, turning it this way and that. A titmouse of yellow flits across the walls.

'Oh, Jack,' she says. 'What are we going to do with all of this?'

CHAPTER FOUR

Coming Home

'The childe is now out of hand, as we say, and quickly
out of sight, and as busie as an Ant in the Summer.'

Ezekias Woodward, *A Childe's Patrimony*

MARKET DAY ONCE MORE – almost as it was, but not
exactly so. The roofs of the stalls are paler by another
summer's worth of sun, another winter's dole of rain;
and those trees that merely overhung the river wash their fingers
in it now. Let's do this (because we can): move time back by a
quarter of an hour or so, and take yourself up to the cottage. Put
in your head its fireplace – the smell of ash, the tremble of soot
(the chimney could do with sweeping), and a hand – not yours,
but Sally's, breaking the frame of this picture to push against the
loose brick down there in the hearth, and extract from its hidey-
hole the leather bag of thin gold coins. Remember Balthasar
spilling them across the kitchen table? Then the bag was plump

as an owl, with its two ties sitting up so perkily, like ears; now it
has room within itself to turn its head over, as if it was having
a doze. But no need to start fretting quite yet, there's plenty
of coin to go, and the first day of every month, like this, Sally
removes just one, holds it to her lips to bless its sender with a kiss
and to safeguard him with a prayer, then knots the coin in her
handkerchief. And arm in arm with Anne, goes down to market.
And her chin is up and her step is proud and her gaze, as she
walks between the lanes of stalls, almost as unabashed as Anne's.

Almost.

'Look at her. The old witch. Look at her mouth. All drawn
up like her old cat's arsehole,' hisses Anne.

'Oh, Anne!'

'I'd like to take her to the headland and hurl her out to sea.'
Aloud, as they pass, Anne sings out, 'Good day, Madame
Marthe.'

Madame Marthe is chasing flies from the cheeses on her
stall. Flick, flick goes the fly-whisk. Her expression suggests
she'd like to flick Anne away with the same facility.

'Now what was I saying?' Anne goes on. 'Oh, I remember.
That droop-nosed idiot Condé – what is the man playing at?
We know he has this army, what's he doing with it? Nothing, is
the answer. Runs it up and down like a hound on a leash. What
difference will that make? Is Reine Marie losing sleep? Does
Concini – oh pardon *me*, the Marquis d'Ancre – does he have
grey hairs? No, he's too busy counting his honours and estates.
I lose all patience, I do truly. Ah, *bonjour*, Didier-France!'

Didier-France, rolling a dripping barrel. '*Bonjour*, Madame
Anne!' A finger to his sunburned pate. '*Bonjour*, Madame Fiskardo.'

'*Bonjour*, Monsieur Didier-France,' answers Sally, to whom
the language of her neighbours holds no terrors now. '*Ça va?*'

The barrel makes a shelly crunching as it rolls. 'Oysters,'
comments Anne. 'Wasted on me, of course. I shall die as dried
up as a crust. I might get a cat, what do you think? I can train it to

fight Madame Marthe's. Ah, good morning to you, Séraphine. What's new, what's news?'

'Good day to you, Madame Anne,' replies Séraphine, from behind her stall.

'And where is Claude today?' asks Anne.

'With your daughter, I believe,' Claude's mother replies, stony-faced. 'And with Madame Fiskardo's son. And last time there were torn breeches. And wet feet.'

'Ah well. Boys will be boys,' says Anne, airily, lifting a pamphlet closer to her nose. 'Perhaps young Claude *likes* getting his feet wet.'

Séraphine regards her coolly. 'I hear Monsieur Gustave plans to call upon you, Madame Anne.'

'Do you?' Anne exclaims. The pamphlet is pressed into unexpected service as a fan. 'Goodness, why ever would he do that?'

THE GANG OF children roam the woods, the fields. The hills of Belle-Dame have been mined with passages and dens. Trees have been climbed and swings hung from their branches; lessons have gone unlearned and chores been left undone; they have hidden behind walls and been chased out of orchards; brought frogspawn home in their shoes and hurled themselves through piles of autumn leaves. Today, however, their leader has decided on an expedition to the headland. The sky is blue, the winds are soft. No chance of a sudden gust carrying some little one off the headland altogether. Being in command, as Jack will tell you, means you have to think of things like that.

It takes an age to get them all up through the woods. There are falls and grazed knees, tears. It amazes Jack how quickly other children grow tired, how hard you have to work to keep their spirits up. And what a good idea it is to have a few lieutenants too. Sebastien (whose father is the miller) and Didier-Marie (son of Didier-France) are his usual choices, but Jack's most trusted second-in-command is a girl.

'La Charente,' Jack declares, waving a hand to indicate the river, as Marguerite encourages the laggards at the back. He presses on, to where the trees grow out at crazy angles, battered by the wind. Wild rabbits by the dozen live up here, scattering across the turf as the children approach.

If you look back, you can see Hector in his paddock. And there's Madame Hector – Perdita. This year two enormous shaggy donkeys share the field beside the church.

There's the boatshed, and there outside it is the boat-builder, Pastou. Even from this distance you can tell it's him, because of his hat. And there's a new boat taking shape down there, by the looks of it. A moment while Jack completes the building of the boat and, in his imagination, sends it scudding across the Charente.

Enough. The goal of the expedition is now in sight. High on the headland, right on its brow, is a mighty boulder, eight tons of blue granite, once as upright as a pointing finger, now half-buried in the turf. What is it doing here? No-one seems to know. But it's been a friend to every village child for centuries, and it's a rule with Jack as it has been for generations before him – if you climb the headland, then you have to climb the stone.

Practised, Jack scales the stone with ease. Marguerite scrambles up after him. The other children haul each other up; if they huddle together there is just room enough for all. Once everyone's in place, Jack strikes his customary pose: knee bent, sword (in his imagination at least) at his hip. He scans the river, shielding his eyes. The other children jostle and squeak behind him. 'Quiet!' he tells them. Something he's never seen before is moving up the river on the tide – wallowing, rounded, sitting very low. Jack can just make out the men leaning over its sides, poling this strange thing over the shallows. It has one sail, a lazy square of deep, dark green, flat in the still air. 'What is it?' whispers Marguerite.

He racks his brains. He ought to know, he knows he ought to know. He wants to say something impressive. He can feel Claude watching him. He's puny, is Claude, always having to be helped through hedges, over stiles; it's wrong there should be so superior a manner on top of so stupid a body – one that can't even climb a tree without getting stuck.

It's immense, this craft, the length of Pastou's shed. Anything as big as that has to have a name.

The word comes up through his memory like a trout rising to a fly. 'Perhaps it is a *rebel*,' says Jack, inspired.

The children stare at him. 'You are the rebels,' Claude says, at last. 'You and your papa.' He blinks and pushes his spectacles up his nose. The strange craft has almost disappeared around the curve of the Charente. Claude points after it. 'That is a barge from Amsterdam. It is coming here for wine.'

'Maman!' No more sidling up to her these days; her son announces his return with such a racket that he makes her jump.

'Maman, are we the *rebels*?'

Sally is at the table, mending in her lap. 'No,' she answers. 'Why, who says that we are?'

'*Claude*,' says her son, with odium.

'Then he's wrong,' says Sally, firmly, before adding as a back-up, 'and he's talking of things he can't possibly know.'

'And he said Dada was a rebel too.'

Ah. Now this one is a little harder to dismiss. Her son stares at her. Comprehension floods his face. She sees it happen. She sees his whole world change.

Later. Dark now, the velvet of a summer's night, and the barking of the miller's dog resounding out across the river sharp as pistol shots.

'But *Dada* is a rebel?'

Sally turns about, holding her son's nightshirt in her hands. 'Jack, you have to understand,' she says. 'Dada and the rebels, it's not a thing to talk about.' She strokes his hair, pats at his head. 'Do you understand, baby? It's important. Keep Dada safe in there. Now say your prayers.'

Fingertip to fingertip: God bless Maman, God bless Anne and Marguerite, God bless me. And don't make me like Claude, Jack thinks to himself.

She holds the candle over him. Her hair, in the candlelight, shines like the petals of a buttercup. She's not like other mothers, never will be. Finally she says, 'Did you ask God to keep Dada safe and well?'

Oh. PleaseGodkeepDadasafeandwell. The candle is pinched out; he snuggles down, but he can tell she's there. 'Maman?'

'What is it, baby?'

'I'll be a rebel when I'm big.'

You will not, Sally resolves. 'Oh, there are many things that you might be. You could be a farmer, like Monsieur Gustave. Or a fisherman, like Didier-Marie's papa.'

'I can't.' He's doing that small frown of his, she can tell.

'Why not?'

'Because we haven't got a boat.'

In the dark, Jack feels his mother sit down on the bed. Out of the dark there comes an enormous sigh.

'If we took some of Dada's gold and had Pastou build you a boat,' says Sally, '*if*, Jack, mind? Only if – but *if* we did, you would have to learn to sail it properly, you understand? And you would have to promise me that you will learn to swim.'

THE PUSH AND pull of tides in the Charente sweeps in the white sand from the grey Atlantic and piles it up in sculpted drifts and shoals, and here on one such drift, as close to the excitements going on mid-stream as she can get herself, stands Marguerite. Behind her on the riverbank stand her maman, Anne, and Jack's maman, Sally, and before her, with Pastou holding its prow, there lies *Le Petit Jacques*. It's painted blue, its sail is red, and everyone keeps telling Marguerite *it's not an it, it's a she*. Sitting inside the boat, her owner, shivering with excitement; grouped off to the side and naked as fish, Sebastien, Didier-Marie and Claude. The boys are almost out of their depth, and are paddling to stay in line, all save poor bespectacled Claude, who wouldn't be able to see to swim out of the river again if his glasses should fall off, so has had to promise that he won't go deeper than his waist. But even he has been allowed to shed his clothes, and Marguerite has just worked out a most important thing: that with the world as it is, and the times as they are, it might have been a far better idea to have been born into it *male*.

Standing before the boat, hip-deep, is Monsieur Gustave. '*Attention!*' Monsieur Gustave calls, and Pastou starts paying out the line. The boat drifts from him by a yard. The boys begin to cheer. '*Eh bien,*' Monsieur Gustave is saying. He raises a finger to the wind. 'Jacques!'

Her owner's face, tight with concentration, comes peering round the sail.

'When you feel the wind hit the sail, push the rudder against it.'

The sail, all of a sudden, fills like someone pushing their tongue into their cheek. A scramble of activity within the boat. *Le Petit Jacques* curves away from them, tilting with her side so low to the river that it looks to Marguerite as if the water will get in. The line from the boat to Pastou snaps taut, spraying diamonds. 'Away! Against!' calls Monsieur Gustave, as Pastou pays out more rope. The mast comes upright, then teeters over the other way. 'Gently, Jack, gently,' Jack's maman calls out, surprising them all. 'Like Dada with a horse, remember?'

By slow degrees, the mast comes up, like the hand of a clock finding noon.

'Now back to me!' calls Monsieur Gustave. The red sail loses the wind and ripples, slack. Pastou has covered his eyes. Jack's face comes round the sail again, scowling, calculating furiously – and the sail curves out once more. *Le Petit Jacques* struggles forward by a yard, the wind patting both sides of the sail just as the fancy takes it.

'Almost! Almost! Feel for the wind!' The boat has stuttered to a stop. Monsieur Gustave will have to wade out to rescue it – no, *her*. Marguerite sees Jack scramble from one side of the boat to the other. His elbows appear, hooked over the side, then his shoulders, then his head, tilted back, looking up at the sail. A cautious foot pushes against it. As the sail slowly fills, Jack's hand darts for the tiller, and with her mast at a gentle one o'clock, *Le Petit Jacques* begins to move back toward them, this time travelling as smoothly across the water as an iron chasing wrinkles. Behind her, Marguerite hears her mother start to applaud.

'Oh, bravo!' Anne declares. 'Bravo, Petit Jacques! There,' she says, turning to Sally. 'There, my dear. He has the trick of it already. Why, it could be in his blood.'

In Sally's head there is at once the image of her father's ship, its prow reared up over the harbour wall at Dunkirk, as if without the ropes holding it down it would clamber over the wall and be off, hunting new prey. With an effort she murmurs, 'No, it is Monsieur Gustave. None of this would be happening without him. He has always been so kind.'

Le Petit Jacques has come to rest against a sandbank. Monsieur Gustave is splashing toward her.

Anne clears her throat. 'Yes,' she says. 'Yes. But then he always was. So kind, I mean.' A careful pause. 'I think he has forgiven even me.'

And feeling Sally's eyes upon her, she continues, 'Oh, didn't you know? I was sure one of those old witches would

have told you. Before I ran away to Paris, he and I were meant
to marry.'

THE FINEST OF Jack's dens is on the slope above the cottage.
You enter by crawling under an enormous blackberry bush, but
once inside there's room and to spare. Here they are, the chosen
few: Marguerite, of course; Adèle, whose father is Salty Pierre,
and who (after Jack) is Marguerite's best friend; Sebastien and
Didier-Marie. Through the den's leafy walls, you can keep
watch on the river (*Le Petit Jacques* tilted on the mud – the tide
is as low as it gets, and the Charente has shrunk to a ribbon of
mercury), and spy on the lane up to the cottage, and even down
into the garden of the cottage itself – or at least you would be
able to if Jacques's maman ever cut her hedge. As it is, all you
can see is a tangle of green – impenetrable, seemingly, as the
walls of the den itself. The whole world humming with heat,
the whole of Belle-Dame torpid beneath it – all save the children, gathered here. A new game is afoot.

The game is called Rebellion! and it explains the appearance
of the children in the den. Each wears a scarf crosswise about
their torsos (save for Didier-Marie, who sports a strip of fishing
net), and hanging from it either an actual wooden sword, or a
favourably shaped stick. The boys are bare-chested, the girls'
hair tumbling loose. Adèle, shockingly, has pulled her skirts
between her legs and tucked them in her belt, so now appears
to be wearing short padded hose of the type favoured by that
old sea-dog Monsieur François Drake; while Marguerite wears
Jack's nightshirt. A startling splash of home-made blood disfig-
ures a bandage knotted round her head. Jack himself wears his
mother's velvet waistcoat and has his clasp-knife slotted into his
belt. A length of threadbare tapestry, in which, still just discern-
ible, Dido collapses on her pyre, is pinned to his shoulders as a

cloak. As the finishing touch (and as the rebel-in-chief) a sooty but unsteady adult finger has traced a fashionable goatee and moustache across his chin and upper lip. Whose was the finger? Anne's. Who had come striding up the lane, Marguerite in one hand, and a bottle clutched in the other, while the boys were chasing a rat along the ditch. 'Come along, come along, haven't you heard?' she'd demanded, bursting in on Sally. 'Those two equal idiots, Condé and Reine Marie – they've made peace!'

She'd put the bottle on the table with a bang. 'It's got bubbles in it,' Jack pointed out.

'I know, I know. It happens to some of them. In Paris we used to throw them out, but it doesn't spoil the flavour, and beggars can't be choosers, hey?'

From the den the children can hear the women now – abrupt bursts of laughter, the occasional loud-voiced declamation. But here in the den Marguerite has scratched her bare leg on a prickle, Adèle been frightened by a wasp. 'What do we do now, Jacques?' asks Sebastien, when Didier-Marie, peering downhill through the leaves, announces, 'There's someone at your house, Jacques.'

The children scramble forward.

'Who?'

'Where?'

'Down there,' Didier-Marie replies. 'I think he's lost.'

The man standing outside Jacques's house certainly acts as if he's lost – going up to the windows, peering in, coming back to look at the house from the path, then going up to the windows again.

'What should we do, Jacques?' asks Marguerite, crowding in beside him.

Jack pulls the clasp-knife from his belt and flourishes it in the air. Surely it's obvious what they should do. 'We circle his flank, and attack from the rear!'

*

The man stands back from the house. He has shed jacket and hat, and looks rather less the stranger than he did. But he seems thoroughly at a loss. He'd thought, a moment ago, that he could hear laughter, but before he could work out where the sound was coming from, it had ceased. Nothing now but birdsong and the movement of the leaves. He's almost beginning to wonder if he isn't hearing ghosts. It's been known – men returning home to find the nest cold and empty, left to rot. *Impossible*, he tells himself. *She must be here, where else could she go?*

But if she is here, then how – *how* – all this? The garden – it was the sight of the garden first brought his heart into his throat, the hedge bellying over the road, the gate almost obscured with whiplash growths that seemed to fight to keep him out. The moss where once a neat brick path, the rain-butt split, moss up the wall there too; the windows so obscured he can't see if that is movement inside, or merely the glint of the sun. *But I sent her gold, enough for everything!* He gives a groan. At that moment, something sharp is shoved into his back. '*Haut les mains!*' comes the command.

The man stands stock-still, then he raises both hands, slowly. Clearly he's had this happen to him before. At the same time there's a questioning expression on his face, as if he's asking himself why is the fierce command coming from so low down, and why is it delivered in a voice so very high? Slowly, he turns his head.

He is surrounded.

He is surrounded by goblins. A horde. They are pushing him back against the house. They are giggling with glee. The goblin at the front is pushing a clasp-knife into his gut – not a toy, mark you, but a knife such as the man might use himself. This goblin has a piece of sacking trailing down its back and its hair is past its shoulders. It wears – it seems to be wearing – a waistcoat very like one he remembers as being worn by his own wife. Beside it, hiding its giggles behind its hand, is another, who seems to have suffered a head-wound. The goblin at the front – good God, what is that black on its face? – is waving the knife at his gut. It glares at him. Its eyes are pale as sea-glass.

'*Je suis le commandant de ces rebelles!*' it declares, while the other goblins back this up by striking attitudes of menace and growling through clenched teeth. '*Donne-moi ton argent*,' the captain continues, very fierce, '*ou t'es foutu!*'

Foutu. A soldier's word. There are many ways a man might react to being told to hand over his money or he's fucked, but the stranger's reaction is to drop to his knees, seize the goblin by the shoulders and exclaim, '*Jacques? Mon Dieu, mon fils!*' The rebel-captain's reaction is to reach out and touch the man's bearded face. Which is when the door of the house finally opens. The man stands up. The woman in the doorway utters a cry – not of welcome or delight but of simple astonishment, a cry whose import is so frank that the man takes a step backward. 'Sall-ee?' he says.

This is his wife – horribly thinner than he remembers her, hair loose as a girl's, stumbling toward him. This is his house – filthy, neglected. This is his son – as filthy, as neglected, running wild. There is another woman too, who barely registers, other than some impression of height, inelegance, a most ill-favoured face. The challenge in her tone, though, that goes in.

'Ah,' this other woman says. She's swaying, rather, on her feet. 'You must be Jean.'

CHAPTER FIVE

Not Enough

'Like as the weather under the heavens altereth, so that we now feel a faire warm sunshine, anon lightning and thunder, and also presently after, rain: even so do the thoughts of man change and alter.'

Abraham Scultetus, *A Sermon Preached at Heidelberg*

S O. THIS ENTITY, Papa, not Dada, has come home, and there are changes.

One: he will no longer sleep in the bedroom with Maman –

'Why not?'

– He will no longer sleep in the bedroom with Maman because that is Papa's place.

'But you can sleep out here, on the floor.' This stranger is the newcomer; why is it Petit Jacques who must be incommoded?

– Papa does not sleep on the floor. Sall-ee!

Maman appears. She looks wary.

'Sall-ee, explain. Tell your son why he no longer sleeps in the bed with you.'

'Because,' says Maman, 'now you are a big boy we are going to have a proper bed built here for you.' She indicates the space beneath the kitchen window. 'Right here.'

The new bed feels enormous. He wakes to find he's drifted, in his sleep, from the head of the bed to its foot. Disoriented, he flops to the floor and staggers into the bedroom, searching for Maman. And finds Papa lying on top of her, with his naked bottom in the air. 'What are you doing?' he asks, intrigued.

Two: he will no longer go running in to Maman as soon as he wakes. Instead he will knock at the door and wait.

'Why?'

To show respect. To show he is a little gentleman, a man of honour. In fact a gentleman would bow to his parents when he first sees them in the morning. *Comme ça*, with an arm across the waist. That is what a man of honour would do. Does Jacques not wish to be a man of honour?

'Jean, don't be ridiculous,' says Maman, laughing. 'We are not in your château yet.'

Three: he will stop following Pastou about. Pastou is here to work.

Pastou fixes new slats to the shutters, and prunes the lavender bushes by the door with such savagery that they look dead. His soft grey hat, floppy as one of Maman's bits of mending, bobs around the garden as he and Jean dig it over, front to back. Pastou never takes his hat off, no matter how hot the sun. The children of the village believe this is because under Pastou's hat he has a hole, which is why Pastou has to do things so steadily and carefully, in order that nothing important falls out.

And why his speech is so fascinatingly slow. Whole days can pass between the beginning of one of Pastou's sentences and its end; while he talks, his gaze cartwheels all the way round the horizon and all the way back.

'But we wait for Pastou to find a toad, Papa.'

– It is most important, does he understand? The garden must be put to use, Papa's gold, it will not last forever… *Why* do they wait for Pastou to find a toad?

'Because then we piss on it.'

– He will *absolutely* stop pissing on toads. It is the behaviour of an *urchin* –

'But Pastou says it's good luck.'

– It signifies nothing what Pastou says. It will cease at once, does he hear?

But it does signify what Pastou says. Pastou knows things about things Jack didn't even know had things to know things about. Why trees all face the same way. How rabbits hear through their feet. And the name of the monster imprisoned on the headland, buried beneath the stone.

When Jack thinks of the monster buried on the headland, and the number of times he has stood upon the stone, the soles of his feet seem to pucker, like when he's been swimming.

'What is its name, Pastou?'

Pastou leans his slow weight on his patient spade. There is a potager taking shape now in the garden. They will sow beans, onions, chervil, artichokes. 'It is a ghost,' he says.

'But what's its name?'

The beans are pink, and freckled as a thrush. They come out of Pastou's pocket two days later, once the potager is dug. Jack makes a hole, Pastou drops in a bean. Jack makes a hole, Pastou drops in a bean. They reach the end of the row, and Pastou, his gaze looping hedgerow, field, horizon all at the same unhurried pace, says, 'Its name is Le Garoul.'

Le Garoul has the face of a wolf, the body of a man and the tail of a dragon. It holds the heads of its enemies, dripping, beneath its claws.

Some nights, in his dreams, when the wind comes off the sea, it sounds as if it's circling the cottage. How can it be outside *and* on the headland, trapped beneath the stone?

Because it is a ghost. And ghosts have powers.

Ah –

He tells the other children about Le Garoul. He lays it on particularly thick with Claude.

Four: he will stop – Jacques, are you listening to your Papa? He will stop tormenting Claude.

'But Claude is an idiot, Papa. He can't even climb a tree –'

– It signifies nothing whether Claude can climb a tree or not, Jacques will stop tormenting him, does he hear? In point of fact, Claude is a very clever little boy, who already knows his letters and his sums, which is more than Jacques does, *non*? In fact now Papa thinks of it, it is high time Jacques was made to learn his letters too, so from now on there will be lessons every morning – name of God, *Sall-ee*, catch him, quick!

Five: when his Papa is addressing him, he will stand still and listen. He will not run to hide in his den in the woods. If he does so again, Papa will find his den, and burn it –

Six: he will not call Papa a *crapule*, and he will never, ever, put a toad in Papa and Maman's bed. Papa is most angry with him. Yes, Maman is angry with him too. It may look as if she is laughing, but that is because she is English, and the English are mad.

Seven: he, and all the other children, will stop playing that horrible game.

'What game, Papa?'

'You know *exactement* the game I mean.'

This game is called The King is Dead, and is only ever played out of sight, so how Papa should come to know of it is shocking. It consists of Jack lying down, hands folded on his chest, and the other children burying him with grass and flowers. Then Marguerite kneels at his head (the climax of the game) and brings him back to life with a kiss. He shrugs. He had begun to think the game was childish, anyway. But he had grown rather fond of the kisses...

Where on the mantelpiece Maman's mirror-glass used to sit, a framed engraving has appeared, courtesy of Séraphine's stall. It shows a very grand carriage, obstructed in its passage by a wagon-load of hay. Outside the carriage, there is a man with a knife, climbing up on the wheel. Inside the carriage, a man in a hat has his hands raised in astonishment.

'Is that the King?'

'That is the King. That is how he died,' Papa replies.

'How did the man with the knife know the carriage would have to stop?'

'That,' says Papa, 'is what we all wanted to know.'

And eight –

Eight: a horse appears in the field above the church. 'Oh good God,' says Maman, when she sees it.

'You teach him how to sail a boat; I teach him how to ride,' says Jean, imperturbable.

The horse has white splashes on her legs, and another on her nose. Otherwise she's dark as earth. In horse-years she's a matron, and like many a matron, has grown rather solidly plump, but also like many a matron, has kept impressively strong and shapely legs. She raises her head when she hears Jacques and Papa approach, then comes thudding down the field toward them. '*Voilà*,' says Papa. 'Now you make friends. Rub your hands together. Make them warm.' And he takes his son's hands, and rubs them together as briskly as if he were rubbing two sticks to make a flame.

'Now hold your fingers flat. Let her get the taste of you. We will see if she likes you.'

The horse snuffs over Jack's palms. A long pale tongue curls from her mouth, and licks the sweat from his skin. Jack is giggling with delight. 'What's her name?' he asks, entranced.

'Lucette,' replies Papa. 'You want to try her?'

'Oh, yes!' says Jack, before Maman can intervene.

Papa has to adjust the stirrups, then he swings Jack up. The hills, the village, the river, whirl away beneath him – and stay there. He can see everything, out to the far horizon of the sea. He feels Lucette's breathing, the steady push of her ribs against his legs, and he can sense – it's almost as if he can measure – what her strength, her turn of speed will be. 'Jean, she's too big!' Sally calls. Horsemen moving through the camps sent chickens, cooking pots, toddling children bowling before them; it was her constant terror one would take it into its head to short-cut right across their tent and squash her precious baby flat.

'Is she too big?' asks Papa. 'Are you afraid?'

Too big? She's perfect. His smile is as huge as the sun.

'*Eh bien*,' says Papa. '*Allons-y!*' and smacks Lucette across her rump.

She moves. This giant beast, she moves. Her feet come up, her feet go down. She's walking in a circle round Papa, with Jack on her back feeling as if he's going to burst with wonder. 'Now be sure you don't grip her too tight,' says Papa. 'Let her carry you.' The circle widens. 'Remember,' says Papa. 'With horses, you can tell them only once what you want them to do, so you must tell them clearly. Now make your back straight. Sit forward, Jacques. A horseman sits on this,' and Papa uses his hand to demonstrate what a horseman sits on, exactly.

Ah, so that's why no soldier are girls...

'And your feet, not your knees. Press in with your heels.'

He does. The smooth round-and-round suddenly feels as if Lucette is going up a flight of stairs. One bump lifts him out of the saddle altogether. It's like being in his boat, riding a swell. He braces for the next, and as Lucette lifts, he lifts with her.

Papa claps his hands together. '*Ah! Parfait! Voilà, Sally, regarde ton fiston!*'

Up down. Up down. Papa is still exclaiming *Ah! Parfait! Mon fils! Superbe!* when there's a sudden wail from Maman. He glances back – and Maman and Papa are yards away. The leading rein trails in the grass; Lucette is his, and heading for the hedge. For one wild moment Jack thinks perhaps he's meant to let her go through it, then he remembers, *gently, gently, Petit Jacques, like Dada with a horse*, and pulls on the reins like he'd push on a rudder –

And Lucette turns in her own length, slows from her trot to a walk, and walks the few yards back. And Papa lifts him off – breathless, speechless, praises ringing in his ears – and puts him on his shoulders, and walks him back down through the village calling out to everyone they see, '*Voilà! Mon fils! Jacques le chevalier!*'

THE FIELD ABOVE the cottage is one of the best places in Belle-Dame to enjoy a sunset, and here, this particular evening, doing just that, are Jean Fiskardo and his son. Birds twitter in the hedges all around them as the day comes to its end, while down in the field, Hector and Perdita nuzzle a tiny foal. There go the last of the fishing boats; here come the first of the stars. Every detail, in this soft light, is clear as if it had been etched on glass.

Nothing ever changes here, thinks Jean. Nothing changes, nothing happens. Men age (his hand strays to the little extra roll of Jean that there is now above his belt), their wives poke fun at them, their children grow. Everything else goes on exactly as before. He glances at his son, sat there beside him.

Yes. Their children grow. The ladder of lines marking his son's height now shows, in Jean's untutored hand, 'Anniversaire Sept', 'Anniversaire Huit', 'Anniversaire Neuf', and is right past the latch on the kitchen door. Sally's *petit fiston* is strong enough to be allowed to sail his boat out to the rocks below the headland, where the blue lobsters back into their crevices and wave their claws to tell the rare intruder *go away*; gallant enough to know to present the lobsters to Anne; and when Anne cooks the lobsters with butter and *pineau*, well mannered enough these days to be allowed to sit up with the adults, with Marguerite flopped against him when she falls asleep. He can stack the woodpile on his own; he's helped Monsieur Gustave kill a pig; and on the days when Jean goes into La Rochelle, it's Jack who carries Lucette's saddle up to the field, and when Jean rides back of an evening Jack is there to greet him, and to brush Lucette down and make her comfortable. 'A good horse,' Jean tells him, 'is the most important thing a man can own.'

They often find themselves up here like this. Sometimes they simply sit, looking down on the village, sometimes they sit and talk as well.

'Why, Papa?'

It's the longest they will spend together in their lives.

'Because they know their way home,' Jean replies, and is congratulating himself on so pat an answer, when his son, who's done some growing in his head over the last little while as well, says quietly, 'Well. In the end, they do.'

A silence. Black as a spider, Madame Marthe's cat stalks across the bottom of the field.

'I was away a long time, wasn't I?' says Jean, at last. And when his son says nothing, he continues, 'Jacques, listen. The thing about life as a soldier is – it is very simple. You know who you are, you know what you're to do; if you are a good soldier, you know how to do it well. And sometimes when you think of your life not as a soldier, that – well, that can seem not so simple a thing at all. You want to come back, but you want to come back a hero, do you see? And that can take a little while. And if it does, well, maybe then – maybe then you are not quite so prompt about coming home as you should be.' He glances at his son. 'We had much to do,' he adds.

That unwavering gaze; it's like trying to lie to his own reflection.

Jean gives a sigh. He loops an arm about his son.

'Jacques, this world, it is not perfect, and neither is your Papa. But we Poitou men, we are like Hector down there. Strong,' says Jean, making a fist. 'Stubborn, our enemies say. And we are born like you, with our wits about us.' He taps his son's forehead. 'Swift, we call it, in the cavalry. You understand what that means? It means you turn fast. It means whatever happens, you know what to do.' He turns his son's head left to right, as if he were working the stopper from a bottle. Jack begins to laugh. 'And in the end, trust me, we know where we belong.' And now Jean rubs at his stomach. 'And when we come back from La Rochelle, we are very, very hungry. Up now, or we will be late, and I will be in trouble with Maman.'

They walk together down the field. 'Anne says Reine Marie has a Poitou man as her new councillor,' says Jack.

Jean gives a grunt. There has been much talk of Reine Marie's new councillor within the taverns of La Rochelle – at least there has been in those (dark with discontents) that Jean frequents with Salty Pierre. 'She does,' he replies. 'Armand du Plessis. His father was a soldier, a brave man. The son, though, is another sort. A churchman. Ink in his veins. Not as we.'

'Strong,' says Jack. 'Stubborn. Swift.'

'That's us. Now quick march, Jacques, Maman will have supper waiting.'

'But we eat with Anne tonight.'

His father groans. 'Anne, Sally, Marguerite… they will outnumber us.'

'Monsieur Gustave will be there too, Anne says.'

Jean, who might once have made a certain amount of sport with this information, says nothing. He knows, and knows that Monsieur Gustave knows he knows, that lately Jean Fiskardo has become a little tardy with his rent.

*

Of course, there are any number of ways a man such as Jean Fiskardo might provide for his family. He might go into business with Salty Pierre –

One whole summer riding out to the salt-flats on the marsh; a winter of kicking his heels in ante-room after ante-room in La Rochelle, while Salty Pierre does battle with the government *officier* within. Passed on from one to the next – *putain de merde*, says Jean, there's more of them than we had soldiers in the army. And at the end of it –

At the end of it, what? What he gets back is hardly more than he put in.

'Taxes, Monsieur Jean. Reine Marie takes everything. These days I barely make what I need to feed my own.'

Not enough.

But still. Any number of ways, and plenty of time to decide the best. He might buy some land. The miller has some land to sell, Jean could pay some local man to plant a crop, and share the profits –

'Profits?' says Monsieur Gustave, pulling at his moustache. 'You are no farmer, Monsieur Jean. Profits in two, three years perhaps, when the land has been broken. Not before.'

Not enough.

No reason why he should take some snap decision. If not farming (and in all honesty, he never truly felt that was for him), what, then? What does he know?

Well... horses?

He will breed horses, that's the thing –

'Horses?' says Didier-France, sounding mystified. 'I'm sure you'd breed the very best, Monsieur Jean, but what would we want with them? Here we are fishermen!'

And now perhaps there is not so much time. And now sometimes, in the cottage when the day is done, with his wife darning her inexpert way through her never-ending pile of mending; and his son cross-legged on his bed, whittling some tiny refinement to the rigging of his boat and lost in a world of his own; and Jean himself, listening to the bag of coin under the loose brick in the fireplace sighing as it subsides, as the coins are extracted need by need and day by day; or later, lying sleepless, when he gets up from the bed and goes to the window and looks down on the sleeping village, all those tiny houses, and the silver river, leaving them all behind, sometimes then too, then too he seems to hear that same voice whisper –

Not enough.

CHAPTER SIX

Joy and Thanksgiving

'Honest and well-affected Reader, for thy greater con-
tentment, I am bold to present thee with this Iubilee of
the whole French Nation upon the death of the Marquise de'Ancre...'

'The Joy and Thanksgiving of all France...
for the death of the Marquise d'Ancre'

HERE IS JACK, on one of those drifts of white sand. The
dry grains coat his feet like slippers, the early spring
sun strokes his neck, the sparkles on the river are as
bright as sequins, and Marguerite is with him; and life, to be
honest, will not hold many days as good as this, not for a long,
long time to come.

Marguerite holds a length of driftwood in her hand, long as
one of Pharaoh's serpents. Marguerite is teaching Jack to read.
'Emmmm,' she says, and draws on the sand what looks to Jack
a little like a seagull, stooping to its prey.

'Ah.' Long-ago memories of tripods, the sort used in camp over a fire.

'E-*rrrrrrr*.' A musket-rest?

G. U. E. R. I. T. E.

He watches, fascinated. Their bare feet embroider round her name.

'Now you,' she says, and hands the stick to him.

M.

A.

G.

'That's wrong!'

'Claude, be quiet!' Marguerite commands, with awful majesty. Oh yes, Claude is there as well. But Claude, as usual, doesn't figure. All Jack has eyes for is –

MARGUERITE.

'There!' says Marguerite. 'You did it! There!'

MARGUERITE. Why, this is easy, but they're running out of space. Through the water to the next sandbank, Marguerite holding up her skirts, Claude splashing along behind, calling, 'It gets deep there!'

MARGUERITE. She's smiling at him through her lashes, and something flips in his head like a coin, bright as those sequinned sparkles. Heads, tails… this'll make her smile. All the sailing and riding have revealed to Jack a most interesting fact, that once his right hand has learned something, the left hand seems to know it too. Across the face of the sandbank, under the last right-handed MARGUERITE he writes another with his left.

Marguerite, though, does not smile. She comes round behind him, as if she must prove to herself what she saw. 'How'd you do that?' she asks. 'I can't do that, how can you?'

Easy, is the answer; without a thought. Left-handed, he holds the stick out to her. 'You try.'

She backs away. 'No. You do it. Do it again.'

Right. MARGUERITE. Left. MARGUERITE. She's smiling now. She's giggling, in fact. 'Jacques,' she says, her own hands gripped together in excitement, 'Jacques, that's magic.'

'Have him write his own name,' says Claude, from the sand-bank's edge.

His own name? He looks for its shape in his head, but there's nothing there.

'Try, Jacques,' says Marguerite, hopefully.

'He can't!' Claude shouts in triumph.

Jack turns around. He feels his temper rising, burning hotter than the sun. It is as if the fact of Claude has come to the end of all the space Jack is going to allow it to have.

Claude is capering about him. 'Jacques can't write his na-ame, Jacques can't write his na-ame –'

Maybe not. He does, however, know how to punch you on the nose.

'We understand,' Claude's father says, as he stands beside Jean in the garden of the cottage. 'Not every child can govern them-selves as well as Claude.'

It feels rather good, this. To stand with Jean Fiskardo in his garden, and take the man to task for the behaviour of his son. 'And this is not the first time, nor the only thing,' Claude's father continues. 'Madame Marthe will tell you. Trying to ride her billy-goat – when he fell from it, he broke her fence.'

'I have paid Madame Marthe for her fence,' says Jean.

'He leads the other children on. He and Didier-Marie – seeing who could swim the river. Didier-France will tell you, it is a miracle that neither boy was drowned. Your son—'

'—will be whipped,' says Jean, tightening the belt wrapped around his fist, and directing his voice in a monstrous roar at the woods above the cottage, 'JACQUES! COME HERE THIS MINUTE, DO YOU HEAR?'

Rooks rise above them, circling the trees, but otherwise,

nothing. Any more than there was the previous twenty times. Jean has been roaring at the wood so long he is growing hoarse.

'My wife,' Claude's father begins, 'my wife says –'

Look at our child, Séraphine had shrieked. *Look at his face, look at his nose, look at his tooth!* as Claude bawled into her apron. *The whole family – the father with his grand ideas, the mother an English whore, and the boy is a tyrant! An Attila in the making!*

On taking thought, perhaps best not to quote his wife. 'If he could be brought to see the consequences of his temper—' Claude's father begins.

'He'll see the consequences, trust me on that,' Jean tells him, and roars again, 'JACQUES! I WILL GIVE YOU ONE MORE CHANCE! IF I HAVE TO COME UP THERE TO FIND YOU—'

A voice behind them, drily amused. 'I wouldn't rate your chances very high,' it says.

Jean turns. Claude's father turns, and takes a step back. There is a horseman at the gate, and two more waiting behind him. 'Your boy has the higher ground,' the horseman says. 'And you never were the least of use, in any wooded country. He'd hear you yards away. I could hear you, right down in the village. That, said I, to our friends here,' says Balthasar, indicating the matching pair behind him, 'that is our man.' He swings a leg over his saddle and dismounts. 'Condé is imprisoned, Jean,' he says, coming forward. 'Reine Marie had him arrested. And – if your friend there will excuse us – I'm here to offer you a job.'

On the one side of the road, the mounted horsemen wait, their horses pulling at the grass. Their swords poke out behind them like beansticks. On the other, from behind the wall, the children watch.

'Who are they? Are they servants?'

'No, they're *guards*. That's why they stay out there.'

'Why are they here?' whispers Didier-Marie.

'Perhaps it's because of Jack,' suggests Claude, who has two black eyes, a cut on his nose and the bridge of his spectacles bound up with wire. His voice has a whistle to it, thanks to the broken tooth. 'Perhaps they've come to take him to prison.'

Silently, Adèle begins to cry.

'Claude, don't be *stupid*,' Marguerite hisses, ferociously. 'They've come because of Condé and the Queen.'

The door of the cottage opens.

'There,' says Marguerite. 'Monsieur Jean.'

Jean, emerging from his own front door ('I need a breath of air,' he'd told Balthasar), finds he must resist the urge to duck his head. But it is extraordinary how much taller, stronger, younger he feels. Vision sharper, hearing more acute. An ear cocked to the bedroom –

No. No sounds of lamentation from the bedroom now. Sally has had her outburst of tears mopped up by Anne – Anne, who had come puffing up the lane in the horsemen's wake ('Visitors, Jean?'). Both women now sit hushed and waiting. *A first in Anne's case*, thinks Jean, smiling.

He sits himself down on the bench by the door. He feels like something emerging from a hibernation. A lion, perhaps. Do lions hibernate? 'Who's truly behind this, Balthasar?'

'Ah, that,' says Balthasar, easing himself down in turn. 'No-one speaks the name, but my guess? My guess is, little boy Louis.'

'Little boy Louis?' whispers Jean, incredulous. 'That – that *infant*?'

'Little boy Louis – excuse me, Jean, Monsieur le Roi – he's grown. It's as if no-one has noticed. There's a moral to this story. Don't keep a king in waiting short of pocket money. Even if all he does is spend it on canary birds.'

Jean scrubs at his forehead. 'But Vitry asked for me? There must be a hundred other men would be game for this. Why me?'

'Because this must be quick, and it will be dirty. And you've a reputation, Jean. Apologies, but there it is.'

'And after,' Jean asks. 'Once the thing is done?'

'After? Well, you all run about the Louvre yelling your heads off, as no doubt everyone will be doing by then, and once the place is well and truly in a ferment, then you quietly slip away. We'll fix a rendezvous. Vitry takes the plaudits of a nation, Reine Marie takes her chances wherever she can find them; Concini – well, Concini will be very, very dead, and little boy Louis, he and his canary birds – he will be king.'

'Louis,' says Jean, and shakes his head.

'He is the son of Henry of Navarre,' says Balthasar, quietly. 'He cannot be entirely foolish, nor entirely bad.' A sigh. 'There are not so many of us left, you know. Those who go back to the days of the white plume.'

'*My arse in the saddle and a gun in my fist,*' says Jean, and Balthasar permits himself a twist of a smile. 'Remember that? Now that, Balthasar, that was a king.'

'Those days are gone. I tell you, how it is in Paris now – you can feel the lines being drawn. We are becoming little Austria, you were right. Our France, a Habsburg puppet. Concini will have us at war against the Dutch inside the year.'

'But kill him—'

'And you kill his plans.'

'His council—'

'Place-holders. Men of straw.'

'That reptile du Plessis—'

'Ah, he's another matter. Don't judge him too swiftly, Jean, he has the reputation of a long thinker, that one. He sees where Concini would take us, clearly as anyone. All that, or one man. A bullet in the head. So what do you say? One time more?'

Jean lifts his own head, looks Balthasar in the eye. 'Balthasar, this business of assassination – when it goes wrong, then it goes very wrong indeed. So if it does – no, hear me out, old friend.

If it does – would you take Sally and Jacques? Because Sally doesn't do well on her own. And my boy – he needs a father. Would you do this? Will you give me your word?'

'My word and my bond,' says Balthasar. 'How can you ask? My word and my bond.'

And now Jean puts his hands on his knees, ready to rise, ready for action. And now there is the same light in his eye as there is in Balthasar's. 'Good enough. So. What's the plan?'

Across the road, the children watch. They see the two men get up from the bench and go inside. Then Sebastien elbows Marguerite in the ribs. 'Look,' he says. 'Jacques.'

Stepping down between the trees, wary as a deer. There'll be the beating to end all beatings at the end of this, he's well aware of that. But Papa's roaring has stopped, and there's no sign of Claude's father either, *putain de salaud de merde.* Now's the moment to make his escape, if ever.

A halt at the corner of the house. If he can get past the house, he can get down to the river. Launch his boat. Let Papa come looking for him then.

He keeps himself flat to the wall.

'Jacques!'

He stops, amazed. Surely whatever he did, it can't have been bad enough to warrant bringing Anne into it?

But here she is, at the bedroom window. 'In,' she tells him. 'Enough of this. Come in.' And there is Maman, sitting on the bed. He takes in her face – that same old lost white look she sometimes had during their first winter here, and he has the odd sensation, as he swings his feet over the windowsill and down onto the bedroom floor, of standing on one of those sandbanks again, one out in the current, where you can feel the edge crumbling away beneath you.

There are voices coming from the kitchen. 'Who is it?' he asks, and realizes he too is whispering. 'What's happened?'

Then the bedroom door opens, and Papa is standing there.

'Come here,' Papa says.

He goes. Beyond the darkness of the kitchen, through the brightness of its door, he sees a man, waiting. He looks at his father, for an explanation, and then he sees Jean is wearing his sword.

And then he knows. Whoever these men may be, his father is going away with them. He looks at the man waiting outside, in silhouette; he looks at the horsemen in the lane. *I hate you*, thinks Jack, but of who?

Behind him, the sound of Maman sobbing anew, and of Anne soothing her.

'Jacques, look at me.' His father turns his head about. 'No long farewells,' he says.

'No,' Jack replies. At least he opens his mouth, but the *no* emerges mute.

A glance from Papa to the bedroom. 'You will take care of Maman while I'm gone.'

Yes.

'You keep the woodpile good and high, yes? And an eye to the old tiles on the roof.' The voice grows careless-sounding, rough. 'I meant to have the old ones put to rights this spring.'

'Yes sir,' Jack manages, at last. He feels a tear slide past his nose.

His father, low-voiced, says, 'You are in charge now, Jacques, understand? You are the man here until I come home.' Then he lifts a hand, and Jack feels his father wipe the tear away with the edge of his thumb.

'And when I do,' says Jean, 'everything will be changed.'

NEW WEEDS INVADE the drills of the potager; Jack roots them up. When the storms of March batter the boats moored on the river, he drags *Le Petit Jacques* high up the beach, where she'll be safe.

He keeps the woodpile up to the level of the window.

He keeps a narrow scrutiny on the old tiles of the roof.

Every night he says his prayers: *Bring Papa home.*

Bring him home SAFE.

And whenever his hands are in his pockets, he keeps his fingers crossed.

Just to be certain.

March blows itself in, and out. April comes dancing forward, flowers in her hands.

SPRING-CLEANING. In Belle-Dame the beach is curtained with fishing nets, being inspected for snags and tears, and every hedgerow is bright with linens, losing their winter frowziness in the sun.

In Paris, Concino Concini, Marquis d'Ancre, walks from his house on the Quai de l'École. There is a garden behind his house, at its finest in the spring; it makes by far the prettiest way to enter the palais du Louvre, and by far the most discreet, as well.

Idling on the Pont Neuf, Balthasar and Jean watch.

'You see? Every morning,' says Balthasar. 'Likes the sneaking about, that one.'

Above them the statue of Henry IV looks down with fatherly mien. The statue – so newly set up that its bronze still glitters in the sun – has made this midpoint on the Pont Neuf a popular place for loiterers. In Jean's opinion the sculptor made a particularly handy job of Good King Henry's horse, who is roundly muscled and reminds him of Lucette.

'Up you get,' says Balthasar. 'Now watch.'

From his new vantage point atop King Henry's plinth, and with an arm wrapped round his horse's front leg, Jean watches as the bobbing hats of Concini and his retinue come to the end of their stroll across the garden, pass briefly out of sight, and then emerge into the small lane at its rear. Confronting them is the wall of the Louvre, a ditch and a door. And a little bridge to the door – part stone, part timber, so half of it can be lifted like a drawbridge. Beyond that, the Louvre proper, south wing, where it so happens one also finds the *appartements* of Reine Marie. Vulgar gossips have dubbed the little bridge the *pont d'amour*, obviously.

'Attendants,' Jean points out. 'A herd.' Looking down at Balthasar, he frowns. Balthasar has that glassy look again, prelude to another bout of fever. When Jean looks back, Concini and his retinue have disappeared.

'Half of us inside the courtyard,' Balthasar had explained, as they'd sat hugger-mugger in the cadets' refectory. The cadets rampaged around them, the occasional pellet of bread or chicken-bone flew over their heads. *While we*, thought Jean, *sit curled about our cups of wine. We could not look more like a conspiracy if we tried.*

'Once he's within the courtyard too, we raise that little bridge. Cut him off, and as many of his retinue as we can. And then we – you – act. Because he must resist, do you see? We make a legitimate request, on the order of the King, and he resists.'

This is the plan.

He's a little fellow, is Concini, for all the trouble he's caused, and while everyone at court wears heels, men and women alike, Concini's are that little higher than the rest. They tap the stones of the path through the garden like bird's claws, then out into the lane. Paris has been rinsed by spring showers this morning but Concini's high-heeled shoes drive through mud and puddles, all alike. His attendants take note: His Excellency is intent. There is a letter in his hand.

This – this *thing*, thinks Jean, listening to the little bridge being lowered, this fleck of spittle playing at being a man, couldn't they simply run up behind it and go *BOO?* This creature is unworthy of a bullet. He looks up at the slice of Parisian sky, above the courtyard where he now waits. A chalk-smudge of cloud, a fluttering pigeon. With him, holding their breath, the Baron de Vitry, plus a select few of the royal guard. Vitry holds a handsome pistol, cocked, across his chest. 'It will be the work of a moment,' the Baron had explained. 'But it's on your cue, Fiskardo, do you see? It is the King's command, yet he refuses it. Only if he resists do we have the King's permission…' His voice faded away. 'Do we have the King's permission…'

'To shoot,' Jean had said. 'Becoming rather the French way this, don't you think? Assassination?'

Back in the refectory the Baron, wrists a-froth with reticella lace, moustache like an upturned trident, had caught Balthasar's eye. 'This one is as blunt as you said he was, ain't he?' he'd commented. 'You've set your rendezvous?'

'The hospice at Beaune,' Jean replied.

'Beaune?'

'It's nearer than Forbach.'

And Balthasar, eyes bright and hectic with what he hoped to God was no more than the excitement of it all, had pulled himself back to the moment long enough to shrug his shoulders and smile.

'The King is dead,' said Jean, raising his glass. 'Long live the King.'

As Concini walks, the seal of the letter flaps against his knuckles. He's brisk, is Concini, impatient, and part of the function of his many attendants is to add to the air of speed and busy-ness surrounding him. And now he is crossing the little wooden bridge, head down, still reading his letter.

That small group of the royal guard marches across the court-yard, Jean at its head.

Concini neither pauses nor looks up. The letter bears the seal of the Bishop of Luçon, Armand du Plessis, that Poitou man from the muddy estates round the tiny town of Richelieu.

The Bishop is a man Concini considers his own creature, a diligent servant of wearisome gravitas – or did so consider, right up until the moment when he broke the seal and started reading. Nothing wearisome here. The letter describes a plot, a conspiracy (damn the noise of those men, crossing the court-yard behind him!), a web of lies and seeming that might have come from Concini himself; a scheme of swift intent, whose aim and mark is unmistakably –

– is unmistakably –

– It is borne in upon Concini that the only noise in the court-yard is his.

He turns.

The guards are between him and his entourage. The little bridge he had just crossed has been raised. Those few who followed him over stand caught behind the royal guard, nonplussed.

A hand comes down upon his shoulder. Concini executes an ungainly turn. Two men confront him. One, the Baron de Vitry, he knows; the other he does not. This second man, thumb and fingers clamped into the meat of Concini's shoulder, asks, 'You are Concini?' There is an accent – something rough and countrified.

He hears some innocent amongst his own attendants call out, 'It is he! He who is reading!'

The vicious pressure of the grip increases. Its owner announces, 'Monsieur le Marquis, the King has commanded your arrest. There is a warrant raised against you.'

The King? thinks Concini, *but there is no such creature!* 'Against me?' he stammers. 'Against *me?*' Absurd, the whole thing, clearly the gravest error is – is –

The King. The first glimmer of comprehension. His hand goes scuffling for his sword. The brute – the ogre – holding him closes his own hand over Concini's, all but melding it into the metal of the sword-hilt, and all but bending Concini in two.

He shrieks for his attendants: '*À moi! À moi!*' He hears the brute holding him down comment, 'Monsieur le Baron, he resists.' Concini, with preternatural terror, senses the approach of death like some great symphonic chord. He shrieks, '*Non! Non!*' He hears an oath, in that same rough voice as before – 'Christ's blood and balls!' And then he is on his knees, on the flagstones. His head is being angled. His hat lies there before him on the flagstones. He feels the kiss of the pistol behind his ear, and goes rigid at once.

Quick and dirty.

The loudest noise in all the world.

In amongst everything else (the squealing starting up amongst Concini's retinue, the shouts of the *corps de garde*), Jean, turning his head from the blast of powder and of course the muck of Concini's brains, finds he is gazing up at one of the courtyard's many empty windows, and no, it isn't empty, not at all. There is a figure there – a thin pale face, tipped with a beard, and a sleeve, in bishop's white and black, gently drawing the curtain closed. For a moment what he is seeing makes no sense to him at all – and then it makes sense of everything.

We Poitou men.

Jean's laugh is so great, so explosive, it almost drowns out the sound of the shot.

CHAPTER SEVEN

Black Work

'States need war at certain times to purge themselves
of evil humours...'

Armand du Plessis, Cardinal Richelieu

R AIN. The roof of the château shining, as if newly
brushed with silver paint. Rain, weighing down the
branches of the trees within the park, dislodging the
filth from the gutters and pattering down the chimneys into
fireplaces that have been cold all year and need a deal more coal
on them than they have at present to take the chill from the
rooms. Rain, depressing the spirits, beading the hair, darkening
the hems of the women's skirts and splashing the ankles of the
serving girl, lopsided under the weight of a copper of coals, as
she clacks her way across the courtyard in her wooden clogs.
This is Boue. There she goes, hauling open the door to the great
hall, dragging the copper of coals inside, closing the door with
a bang and using her shawl to mop her head and neck. She's a
hefty lass, is Boue, and quite the lowest of the low within the

household, and, as of now, with a trio of ugly scratches glaring from her neck.

There is a narrow slit of window by the door, from the days when life was even more unpredictable than it is now. Putting her eye to it, Boue sees a man on the far side of the courtyard, a man who, as he peers about, is careful to keep a hand protectively over one ear. Boue's expression flickers into one of those few tiny moments of satisfaction that the world allows her, then she picks up the copper and, lopsided once again, starts walking through the hall. Here are more of the fancy-pants the Bishop brought with him from Paris, pulling the dust-sheets off the furniture and exclaiming in horror at its lack of style; here, even more curiously, are two men on ladders on either side of a painting that has hung in the hall for as long as Boue can remember, but which is clearly now destined for one of the château's attics. Why, is a mystery. The painting shows a boy of about ten, with an uneven-looking mouth, and behind him, much larger, and her hand tight on his shoulder, a woman dressed in deep mourning, with a frizz of blonde hair. The expression on the woman's face might be described as challenging, but other than that there's nothing so unobjectionable in it that Boue can see – what's one more painting of a fancy-pants, amongst so many? – although the men up the ladders and a third, directing operations from the floor and waving a testy arm for Boue to make her way around them, seem hardly able to get it down off its chains fast enough.

The doleful jangling of a bell from deeper in the house. The Bishop of Luçon, poor soul, has the constitution of a sickly child, and cannot abide the cold.

'Thus,' says the Bishop of Luçon, 'we take my geographical location, and from it, measure the degree of my exile.'

The Bishop moves left to right as he talks; movement, he finds, helps with the winnowing of his thoughts. Also it is so very cold within the room; were he to remain motionless, he fears his toes will numb. Worse, such an affliction might reanimate his gout. But no matter how afflicted the body, nothing stops the mind. On and on it goes, in perpetual calculation.

'And we may conclude that it is not so much.' Between his pouched and mournful eyes, his thin nose quivers. Late May, almost June and the room is cold enough for the tip of that nose to bear a dewdrop. 'A messenger might ride from Paris to Luçon in a week. So in seven days, I might be restored to the court. At any time, I might be, if one were to look at it like that. A simple knock upon the door.'

He glances down at his desk hopefully, but the linden tea prepared so carefully by his cook, from such a meagre harvesting of buds, sits in its bowl fragrance-less and cold. 'My exile in turn gives me the measure of His Majesty's mistrust. And it is entirely understandable he should mistrust me, at first. When he has need of me – and he will have need of me – then he will change his mind.' He looks at his visitor, noting that the glass of *pineau* he had himself placed at the man's right hand is still untouched. Does the fellow not feel the draught in here, scything across the floorboards? Is he not chilled from his long journey in the rain? Why, the fellow's horse had been wet as a seal. But then (thinks the Bishop), Croatia, if that is indeed the birthplace of his silent guest, Croatia – does the name not strike the ear as a place bound to be full of nothing but bears and snow?

'*But*,' he begins again, raising a forefinger, '*but*, if at this delicate time His Majesty's suspicions are increased by so much as a tittle – by even the smallest part – then, I fear my exile would extend beyond all measuring. So this must not happen. This, we must prevent.'

Still no reaction from his listener. The fellow's utter blankness is astonishing. It's almost insolent, in the Bishop's view, who also thinks his visitor most ill-presented, in an unmatched suit of clothes and over them a buff-coat like a common soldier. No collar to his shirt at all, only a strip of cloth tied round his neck. Some outlandish Croat fashion, without doubt. As is presumably the little silver token the man wears pinned to that coat – something like an old-fashioned badge of pilgrimage, yet not.

The Bishop pushes his hands into the deep sleeves of his gown. 'Your recommendations,' he continues, 'are most interesting. I see you have served as a cavalryman, yes?' When there is again no reply he continues, 'The fellow who will assist you in this – this – present matter, Enric, is the same. His skills, such as they are – all learned at the cannon's mouth.' A pause. 'And my brother in Christ, the Prince-Bishop of Prague – he writes that you have performed this service several times for him. All requirements met, and no loose ends.' He looks up. 'It is especially desirable that we should have no loose ends here. Monsieur, uh—' He looks at his desk again. 'There seems to be some confusion. I see at least two names. Which do you go by?'

His visitor regards him, coldly.

'Come, man, all you gentlemen of business go under more than one name, I know it. But there needs to be something I can call you.'

'Carlo,' his visitor offers up, at last.

'Monsieur Carlo. Very good. As I was saying, there must be nothing to raise suspicion that this man met his end by anything other than God's will. The Prince-Bishop assures me this again is your special skill.' He waits. 'Acquit yourself well in this, and you will find me at least as generous an employer as him.'

At the mention of money, at last his guest reacts. 'This man—' his guest begins.

A scratching at the door. Enter Boue, with her copper of coals, just as the Bishop answers, 'This man Fiskardo, yes?' He ignores Boue entirely – what's she to him? – but he winces exaggeratedly as she pours the coals from her scuttle onto the reviving flames. The Bishop of Luçon cannot abide such rude domestic racket, either.

'This man,' says his visitor, 'he is where?' His face is as expressionless as before, but his head is tilted slightly, taking note of Boue, or taking note to be exact of those livid scratches on her neck.

'Laon. Or the road thereto.' The Bishop rubs his hands; heat is at last beginning to creep across the room. 'He has been lured to an inn there with the promise of payment for his silence.' Boue, straightening, bobs a curtsey. 'Yes, yes, you, go,' says the Bishop, flapping a hand at her.

'And this man,' his guest continues, as the door closes behind her, 'what is it that he does to you?' His delivery is peculiarly precise, like a man picking flesh from the bones of a fish.

A sigh. 'Jean Fiskardo was witness to a certain event. And he has grown alert, let us say, to the – to the machinery behind it. Do you see? A man who has answers, that man has fed, he is full, he will keep his mouth *shut*. But a man with suspicions is dangerous. He hungers. He asks questions—'

'No, he was not a witness,' his guest interrupts. 'He *was* the act. He takes this man – this man, what is the name?'

The energetic movement back and forth behind the desk has ceased. Carlo Fantom allows himself an inward smile: the moment when they cease to lie to him always contains some tiny part of the great release, the mighty calm, of when they cease to breathe. 'Concini,' the Bishop of Luçon says, quietly.

'Concini, yes. He takes this man, Concini, and he holds him tight while that other shoots Concini in the head. This Concini, he was the Queen's man too, *korrekt*? You, she makes her almoner, but him, she makes her *Maréchal*.'

'Concini was a man raised high. But even Solomon—'

'And now this man Fiskardo, now he guesses that you were perhaps behind this all along. *Korrekt?*' his guest enquires.

The Bishop of Luçon subsides into his chair. 'By report, he had no brains at all. He has *greatly* disappointed me.' The Bishop sighs. 'But that is the problem with puppets. Sometimes they will look up.'

The door reopens. 'Ah, Enric,' the Bishop says. 'This is Monsieur Carlo. He will be acting in my service, in this matter.'

The two men view each other. Carlo lets his gaze rest on the other's ear, which is both red and swollen, as if recently on the receiving end of a blow.

'Enric,' says the Bishop, 'will you see to providing our friend here with a horse? One in good order, and comfortable. You both have a ride ahead of you. My Andalusian, perhaps.'

'Andalusian's thrown a shoe,' Enric offers. His fingers wander past his collar to his ear.

'The Dane, then.'

'Galled,' comes the reply.

'Then line up what we have,' says the Bishop, 'and our guest shall choose his own.' As the door closes again, he holds up his hands. 'Ah, Enric. A satellite to the Prince-Bishop's own family; a young man with every advantage, and the brains to make use of none of them. Hopelessly miscarried the very first commission with which the Prince-Bishop had entrusted him. But at least he will be the means to identify this Fiskardo for you. Come. I will walk you out.'

Down the corridor they go, the Bishop with his hand raised to his guest's shoulder. The servants scatter at their approach, hiding themselves in doorways, under furniture. The two men pass the painting, off its chains and lying against the wall. The Bishop glances at the painted figure of the boy. A slobberer, they say, bad as the King of England. But that's what you get if you marry a Habsburg, a son with a slobbering mouth. Some other work will need to be found to replace it, something costly, with the boy in all his pomp, full-grown. Without his mother, the Queen.

Oh, you will need me again. You will all come to need me. 'You are a man of questions yourself, Monsieur Carlo,' the Bishop begins, pleasantly. 'Are you, now, fed?'

His guest smiles. The man has curiously tiny teeth, like a lizard's, as if not properly erupted from the gums. 'Only one more.'

They are at the door. 'Ask, please.'

'This man Concini,' Carlo begins. 'He was your patron, was he not? Raises you up, makes you great in favour with your Reine Marie – when he dies, you fall. All the way back here. Cold rooms, lame horses – why do you kill this man? Is it because he was made rich? Is it because you want the favour of the King?'

Armand du Plessis, Bishop of Luçon, whom the world will come to know by a far grander name, leans forward. He is on eye-level with the silver token on the other's coat. No, it is not a pilgrim's badge, not at all.

'Concini would have taken us to war,' he replies. '*But* to the wrong one.'

His guest looks down at him, he in his churchman's deep-sleeved gown. 'There is such a thing?' the man asks. Again, that row of little teeth.

'Oh, assuredly,' the Bishop replies. 'The wrong war is the one you have to fight yourself. The *right* war is the one your enemies fight amongst themselves.' He peers out into the dismal courtyard. 'War with the Dutch would have been nothing but a sideshow. Wasteful and pointless. But the right war is coming, mark my words. And when it comes, it will be in Germany.' There is Enric, a string of horses plodding behind him. 'Oh.' The Bishop lays a hand upon the other's arm. 'One thing more. 'It is the greatest shame, but there is a wife. An Englishwoman. He keeps her in the country, on the coast. I cannot tell how much he may have shared with her, and so –'

'Women are trouble,' says Carlo, slowly.

'Indeed they are,' the Bishop agrees, the complaints of whose own mistress, plucked so rudely from her Parisian apartment, are yet another burden he must bear. 'But in this case, I think not so much. Where she lives, there is no-one. A tiny place. Hardly to be spoken of, but you will find it easily. Belle-Dame. You might do it almost as a – as a full-stop to the other.'

'The wife,' says Carlo, 'will be a thousand. As much as the man.'

'As much as the man?' the Bishop repeats, incredulous. 'Jean Fiskardo is a captain of cavalry, a veteran. His trade is slaughter. If he thinks he is under attack, he will defend himself with ferocity. *How* can a *woman* be as much as he?'

'They take longer,' his visitor replies. 'You would be surprised how hard some of them will fight.'

'I see.' The Bishop rocks back and forth once more upon his toes. 'And in this market, I suppose, I have no other option.'

'Try your hand at it again on your own,' suggests his visitor. 'Why not?'

For a moment he sees the anger there, and then it is gone, sealed, like a pot of caustic under its lid. The Bishop of Luçon proffers his hand, warm from the sleeve of his gown. 'As you wish, Monsieur Carlo. Do my business. Do not fail. Tie off that last loose end.'

The rain has been replaced by wind. And there is Boue, once more crossing the courtyard, carrying her copper to fill again with coals. As he walks to the line of horses Carlo watches her. He estimates she is about fourteen. He cocks an eye at this Enric. The cold wind on that ear must be tormenting. He thinks, perhaps, he has a brother here.

'You try her?'

The other follows his gaze. For one clearly so limited in intellect, you'd think he'd do a better job of looking stupid than that. As if taken by surprise, he answers, 'Only to see her jump.' A glance at Carlo. He looks down. 'Her meat ain't to my taste,' he mutters.

Indeed? Carlo assesses him anew. Boue is now beyond the
courtyard, out of sight. Carlo continues, 'She is of the Bishop's
household? From Paris?'

'Her?' A snarl of contempt. 'She's nothing. Comes from
Luçon. A woodlouse.'

Carlo puts his arm across the other's shoulders. 'Let's try
together,' he says.

AT THE HOTEL Vaso d'Oro in Rome, the beds are hung with silk.
At the sign of the Four Winds in Frankfurt, the host sends up hot
water, fragrant with herbs, to restore his guests. Unfortunately
this is Picardy, where the inns are the foulest in Europe.

The Écu de France. Dismounting, Jean stands for a moment,
contemplating the sign; from its condition one would think
it had been dragged from a pond. This is the place, though.
St-Étienne-des-Champs. This must be the place.

He leads Lucette round the back of the building, knowing
exactly what he can expect – a yard with a pump, a trough and a
run of ramshackle stables. Not a soul appears to ask if they can
be of service, so he fills the trough, and lets Lucette drink her
fill. For a moment he has the strongest, strangest sense of being
overwatched, but it's for a moment only – gone before he even
has Lucette tethered to the pump.

Opening the door to the inn he smells the damp at once, the
damp and the smoke – the place smells like a rained-on fire-pit.
He steps down, onto a floor of pressed earth. A wooden partition funnels him forward into a long, low room, ribbed with
beams, so long and dark in fact that the end of it is almost lost
to view. Smoke hangs in the air; his eyes are smarting. There is
straw under his boots and every step releases the odour of slops.
As his eyes get used to the dark he sees two men hunched over
a game of dominoes, a serving girl, stood with her hands tucked

beneath her apron, blinkered by her cap, and another man, with a sack tied round his waist, lumbering toward him as if to throw him out.

And it doesn't matter. The foulness, meanness, lowness of the place, nothing of this sort matters any more. He has done everything a man need do.

'I'll want a bed,' says Jean, as the man lumbers up. 'One night, maybe two. I am – I have to meet here, with a friend.'

The man leads him back past the door. 'I've left my horse,' says Jean. 'Out there.'

A grunt. 'Mirelle will see to that.'

Along the partition, up a creaking flight of stairs ('Mind,' says the man, with satisfaction, as he hears Jean trip), and a door, on a wooden latch basic as a clothes-peg. By the light of the candle in his landlord's fist, Jean sees a room just about long enough to lie down in, divided by a curtain. A mattress of plaited straw laid on the floor. No sheets, no pillows, no blanket even – lousy, flea-thick as they might well be. And the walls so dark, so soaked with secrets you half-expect to hear them whispering. Jean looks up, and is looking up at rafters. 'You've nothing more than this?'

'This, or out with your horse,' the man replies.

Stepping over the mattress, Jean draws back the curtain to reveal another, and then a third beyond that. On the nearest, laid out with military neatness, a man's cloak and hat. The other has an empty bottle abandoned at its foot. 'Whose are those?' Jean demands.

'Come up a coupla days ago,' his host answers, turning to go out. 'One's kicking his heels about the place somewheres. T'other's minding his business by the fire. Is it one of them you're meeting?'

'I doubt it,' says Jean.

A grunt. 'You want feeding, pot-luck is all you get. And it'll be an hour.'

An hour. He goes to check upon the girl's idea of seeing to Lucette (a place too mean to stretch even to a stable-boy?), but to his surprise finds his horse tied up securely in the nearest of the stables, provided with a mangerful of hay, and the girl brushing her down. The girl jumps like the child she is when she sees him, as if taking such kind care is something to be hidden. 'She looks like a cow,' the girl says, backing away. 'That brown and white.'

He flips her a half-franc piece in thanks, and is crossing the yard, smiling to himself at her accent, when he has that unmistakable sensation of being overwatched again. He's glancing up and all around when he hears the stiff whinny of a horse, the thud of hoof on door. A good big hoof, at that; then its head, in profile, peering out. He goes back to the girl.

'Whose is the other horse?' he asks.

'Gentleman inside,' she tells him. 'By the fire.'

'Ain't there another here, as well?' Jean asks.

'There was. *He's* took unself off,' the girl answers. She sounds pleased. And indeed, from the front of the building, the noise of a rider departing.

He goes back inside, smiling. *Jaunty-om. Toyk unsel oyfff. I can tell Sally*, he thinks. *Tell her I found an accent to rival hers.*

Inside, joining the taints of old damp and old soot is now that of tallow. The landlord is lighting more candles, going round the walls, and the domino-players have left their game and are clustered under one such spot of light, examining a handbill. 'Ah,' says one, turning the paper over. 'So she's gone to earth at Blois, has she? The bitch.'

Marie, Queen-Regent no longer. Jean has the impulse (and must remind himself, it will be with him all his life) to go to them and tell them, *Me. I had my hand in that. It was me.*

'Strange days we live in. Strange, strange days.'

'And strange fish it throws up, too.' Both men peer down the room toward the fire. There is a settle down there, but it's been pulled round to face the fire, and its back, curved as a barrel, is high enough to hide its occupant. Jean rather fancies somewhere closed in like that for himself.

Halfway along the room there's another low partition and a pair of timbers, probably holding the ceiling up. And another high-backed settle, and a table too. *Perfect*, thinks Jean, with a soldier's eye for terrain, and, threading between the timbers as through a turnstile, sits himself down. He has the door in full view – the girl, too, as she comes back in. As Jean watches, the girl stops by the first set of candles and, using their back-plate as a mirror, adjusts the sit of her cap. Tucks in a strand of hair. Examines one cheek.

A man comes in, and then a pair. The girl greets them all. The landlord reappears from the cellar, carrying a jug, then creaks his way back down the cellar steps. Jean, tucked away behind the timbers, has the pleasant sense that he's become invisible. He arches his back and stretches out his legs. A warm fatigue spreads up him from his toes. He feels the letter in his pocket, takes it and smooths it out; then remembering how he is amongst folk once again, amongst eyes, he tears the seal from its ribbon, and holds it to the nearest candle till it's gone.

The girl is approaching his table. A lovely smile, he thinks, for such a trod-on looking little thing, and the cheek is blemish-less.

'Do you eat with us?'

'It's what, tonight?' Jean asks, folding the letter back out of sight.

'Potage.'

Which could be anything. 'Are you the cook?' And when the girl answers, shyly, 'Me and Grand-mère,' Jean replies, 'Then I'm sure it will be a feast.'

The girl departs. As she passes the domino-players one calls out after her, 'Mirelle! Tell your brother, come join us for a game!' Ah, how good it is, to watch life going on like this. To sit here, having played one's part, and watch. *I never took the proper time for this before*, thinks Jean. Now that must change. Mankind, humanity, the common herd, he could embrace them all.

Christ, I am tired.

'My fellow – sufferer. Traveller, I mean.'

Jean knows at once (it's that old soldier's trick, the eyes in the back of the head) that the settle by the fire will have moved, the space there opened, this has come out of it. And he is not in the mood for company. He looks up.

The first thing to strike him is the sorriness of the clothes. The man standing before him wears doublet and breeches of a melancholy russet; the breeches droop like bell-flowers, the russets do not match. Nor does the man have any collar to his shirt, merely a strip of red cloth in a fat knot under his chin. The face atop the knot of red is flattish, fattish, young-ish, pale-ish, and with a fussy little beard. There's stubble on the lard-white chops, and a combative light in the eye, as if daring Jean to mock, and knowing, sadly, that he will. That's how Jean reads it, anyhow.

Strange fish indeed.

'Yours,' says Jean, pointing to the ceiling. 'Your hat and cloak. The room upstairs. Your horse outside.'

The younger man nods. He holds a bottle and two thick-stemmed glasses. 'I thought, perhaps –' He waves the bottle up and down. Oddly, indoors, he still wears riding gloves.

Humanity, mankind, the common herd, thinks Jean, reminding himself. 'Join me,' he says, relenting.

The stranger pulls up a stool and sits. Pulls off one of those heavy gloves, extends his hand. His fingers are pudgy but pointed-looking; they put Jean in mind of some delicate instrument, tweezers perhaps. 'Carlo,' the young man says. 'Carlo Fantom.' Up close, one eyelid jumps, as if with nerves.

'Guillaume Pastou,' says Jean. It's the name he's been using since Paris, and the way Jean sees it, Pastou should be honoured. He takes the hand and shakes it, but the hand, which had looked fat and warm, is shockingly chill, like evaporating spirit. The stranger draws his glove back on. 'I feel the cold,' he says, by way of explanation. He fills a glass for Jean, then lifts his own, delicately, by its foot. That eyelid, dancing. *What a lily*, thinks Jean.

'Your health.'

There's an accent there, but not one that Jean recognizes. 'Your horse,' he begins, looking for clues. 'That is the horse of a man who does a deal of travelling.'

The stranger rolls his eyes. 'Where I come from, we say a journey is a fragment of hell.'

'A wise people, where you come from,' says Jean, smiling.

'No, not so much. Those of us who are, we leave.'

A strange way for a man to talk about his motherland. 'And home is…?'

'Croatia.' One of those gloved hands strokes at the knot below his chin. 'I am – how you say? Crabat.'

Ah, indeed? 'So what brings you here?' Jean asks, intrigued.

The stranger regards him coolly. That eyelid, Jean notes, has stopped jumping. 'I am not here,' the man replies. 'I am *en route* to anywhere else.'

A wit, thinks Jean. He's almost warming to the man. A mordant wit, indeed. For the first time he notices the badge, pinned to the man's shoulder. What is it? That bony ribcage, and the upcurled tail. Some kind of hound, perhaps?

'A city,' the man continues. 'Any city. A place with proper rooms. A bed with curtains, mattress. I long for a proper mattress.'

The traveller's lament. *This*, thinks Jean, *may go on for some time.* He props his chin on his hand, lets his middle finger curl over his mouth. His listening face, Sally calls it, knowing it means he's doing no such thing.

I'll shift us out the cottage for a start. Jean has no clear idea of what he'll walk away with from this, but his boy is going to finish his growing somewhere with a staircase at the least. And a paddock. Stabling. Put Lucette, bless her, out to grass. Himself, upstairs, in his study (book-lined), in a robe (fur-lined), watching from his window. His boy with a fine colt out in the paddock, schooling; Sally running up – no, no, Sally gracefully ascending – the staircase, to knock upon his door. There suddenly appears behind her in his daydream not a lady's maid but a nurse, holding a chubby baby in her arms, wrapped in white lace. Another boy?

A baby daughter. And they'll call her – Cécile.

And a garden, and a chair out in the garden, in the sun. Somewhere for Balthasar.

He sits there, almost laughing at himself. He feels ridiculous, light-headed. But then again, why not? A man can take his future in his hands, grasp it, and change the world.

'And a woman,' his new companion is saying. 'I long for women.'

And at that he does laugh, the young man is so frank. 'There are women here,' he says, as a joke, nodding toward the girl, now clearing the domino-players' table. Carlo Fantom swings his head. It seems to Jean that as she feels the gaze, the girl grows still.

'She is no good,' says the other, apparently in all seriousness. 'She will know where to hide.'

Another odd remark, odd and unpleasing. And something else as well: the speed in the swinging round, the bulk in the man's upper body. And the horse, outside. 'You're a soldier,' says Jean.

Again that cool regard. 'For now I am. I was recruited.'

'I've done my share of recruiting, in my time,' says Jean, meaning *you lie to me, I'll find you out*.

The stranger smiles. 'But not of me, however.'

A show of strength. Jean keeps his own voice as cool-toned as he can. 'You'd have refused me?'

And again, a smile. The motion of rubbing gloved thumb over fingertips. 'I fight for silver thalers, not beliefs.'

It's blunt, give the man that. Jean has the oddest conviction that what he is looking at in this fellow is something wholly new. And the most unpleasant sensation too, his hands and feet are prickling, and there seems to be a chill wrapped round his spine. He sits up, and, to make this as off-hand as he can, reaches for the bottle. 'So you're a freebooter. A mercenary.'

'I fight where there is fighting to be done,' the young man continues. 'And I was promised –' (and here he leans forward, so his eyes stare directly into Jean's) '– I was promised a fine fat war in France. Now I am told that war will never be, and if I want one, I must travel into Germany. All over, in a twinkling. Reine Marie is run away; little boy Louis, he sits on the throne; the man Concini, someone shoots him in the head. So you tell me what I am doing here. Jean Fiskardo.'

Jean's hand, on the bottle, jumps away. He sees the bottle roll along the table, chugging out its contents as it rolls. No room to stand, no room to draw his sword. That chill grips tighter on his spine. The bottle tilts at the table's edge. Carlo Fantom drops a shoulder and catches it with ease.

'Calm, calm,' he says, reprovingly. 'You jump so, and the turnips there will look. Now –' (lowering his voice again) '– you and I have business. Sit forward, as you were.' He reaches in his jacket, brings out a paper. 'Open it,' he says, placing it on the table before Jean. 'Don't you want to know?'

'Know what?' Jean hisses back.

'How much you get.'

Jean stares at him. 'It's you? The one I was to wait for? You?'

'Open it,' says Carlo Fantom, folding his arms.

Jean takes the paper, snaps the seal. The paper crackles as he flattens it.

'Good God!'

The sum is huge. It's greater than any computation he has ever made. The house, in his mind's eye, is sprouting turrets, pinnacles, a gravel drive, a carriage at the door. He can't believe it. Everything. Everything, at last.

His companion is saying, 'You know, they drag Concini's wife from her bed. Now she is in prison. I do not rate her chances very high.'

Jean's thoughts are racing. He has sweat – good God! – running inside his shirt. 'That is nothing to do with me.'

'Oh, but it is, Jean Fiskardo, it is. You have a wife, not so?'

Who will wear silk to the end of her days. Who will want for nothing, ever. 'Yes,' says Jean. His mouth is dry. His tongue feels thick. He seizes his glass and drains it. 'Yes, I have.'

'An Englishwoman, so I hear.' Carlo Fantom sits back. 'I never try an Englishwoman. Which is a shame. They tell me Englishwomen – fight.' He smiles.

And it's not a good smile. It's not the smile a man would wish thoughts of his wife to place on anyone's face, no matter what service they have done him. 'You should watchet – should watch yourself, hereabouts,' says Jean. Christ, is he drunk? 'Freebooters. Not popular.'

'Oh, I will not be here long. I need a war. I will go into Germany.'

'No wuh – no war in Germany,' says Jean, and shakes his head.

'There will be,' comes the complacent reply.

'No. You have it wrong. In Hungary, there is a war. In Russia, too. Poland – yes. Sweden, yes. Italy, always. Germany, no.' He makes to wave his arm –

And the arm drops, nerveless, from the table to his lap. His flesh, his clothes, they have the weight of armour.

'You were strong,' says Carlo Fantom, quietly. 'It takes a while with you.'

Jean stares at him. In disbelief, his eyes flick from the bottle to his glass.

Carlo Fantom follows his gaze. 'No, no, no,' he says. Takes off his glove again, and holds the hand in front of Jean's face.

There is a light, pearlescent powder in the creases of the palm.

Carlo Fantom replaces the glove. 'You do this,' he tells Jean, and, putting his elbow on the table, mimics Jean's pose, with middle finger curled across his mouth. 'Enric tells me.'

There is a scraping sound. Jean is trying to lift himself out of the settle. Carlo Fantom waits until the effort ceases, then he says, 'It is ironical, this one. The harder you fight it, the quicker it works.'

I have to move, thinks Jean. *I have to make some noise.* His hard, fixed stare elides past Carlo Fantom to the group around the landlord. He can hear their conversation. *God help me* –

And sees the girl. Stood at the edge of the group.

All his force, bent upon willing her to turn her head.

'Jean Fiskardo,' his companion says. The words are distorted, they go past, then come back. 'You work it out, don't you? The little boy with the canary birds, to plan all that? You work it out, and then you let him see that you do. You think the man is fool enough to let you live?'

He has to breathe. As he breathes, the chill moves higher. Every time he breathes.

'Now,' says Carlo. 'Our landlord there – not good for business, this. He'll plant you in the churchyard fast as he can.'

The girl must turn her head, she has to see. If he could only move –

A blur of movement at the corner of his eye. A tapping on his cheek. 'Hey. Hey. Listen to me, my friend. You're in there still, you hear me, I know that you do.'

She saw the movement. Her head, it's turning –

'And if your friends come asking questions, they find nothing. Just the sad tale – a sudden illness, taken by death so fast. In all his fame and fortune. *Quelle dommage.*'

– she turns her head, she's looking straight at him, but she won't move, he knows she won't, she won't come near them, not while this man is here.

'Hey. Hey. You still in there?'

He sees Carlo rising from his seat, an effect like watching a reflection in a mirror, not real, not real at all. Sees him lean in close. Sees his own face in Carlo's eyes.

He can move. He must.

'You're still there, I can tell.'

He can get up, he can go to her. He can feel himself rising.

There's a voice. 'You truly think you were worth this?' The flourish of the paper. Jean bats it away. He's making for that pair of timbers.

'You're not worth this. This is what he pays me, for getting rid of you.'

He's at the timbers, squeezing through. But they're swelling, sprouting leaves. He's in the lane, walking up to the cottage. The uncut hedges whip toward him in a squall of leaves. There is a thundercloud above him, and around his head a storm of flies.

He can hear a child's voice, singing.

'And for your wife, they pay me as much again.'

Carlo Fantom sits back in his seat. When the man opposite tilts to the side, Carlo reaches across and props him upright. And when at last the chin falls to the chest, he takes the man's arms, guides them out across the table and lets the head come down to rest on them.

He gets to his feet, and gives the head a pat.

Takes a candle, finds his way upstairs, collects his cloak and hat.

When he comes down again, the room is quiet and dark, save for the glow of the fire. Just as he turns to leave, however, he sees a kite-shaped blur of white, waiting by the door. The girl.

'My friend,' he begins. 'At the table there.'

The white shape disappears at once, back into the shadow.

'He takes too much to drink,' says Carlo, making his voice ringingly clear. 'I'd leave him sleep, *mon ange*, if I were you.'

And puts on his hat, and goes out.

CHAPTER EIGHT

No Loose Ends

Ma belle, is Jean with you? We had a rendezvous set here at Beaune, but here there is no sign of him, and for far too long. I know he dreamed of coming back to you the hero – do you have him? Please, ma belle, if he is with you, have him send me a word. I am bewildered that he has still not joined me here, and fearful there has been some rupture in our plans and that he might have come to harm.

They tell me all of France is still a-boil. It is not a good time to have a friend unaccounted for. Call me an old woman, but I am unquiet. Sally, I need to know. Where is he?

Captain Balthasar to Mme Jean Fiskardo, s.v.p, of
Belle-Dame, of La Rochelle

THE WORLD TURNS. The bull becomes the twins; the
twins, the crab; the crab gives way to the lion. The gates
of Paris reopen. Life goes hurrying on.

All this time, Balthasar's letter has been working its way from
Beaune to Poitou. It crossed the Loire, it heard the bells of
Bourges cathedral, then those of Châteauroux. It reached the
Marais, which it traversed, as one must, by boat, then sat for a
week in one of Salty Pierre's favourite taverns in La Rochelle,
before someone there remembered his connection to Belle-
Dame, and thought to show it to him. Salty Pierre had folded
the letter into his pocket, and delivered it to his neighbour
Monsieur Gustave. Now its journey is almost over, and its
arrival will be witnessed by Jean Fiskardo's son, who sits this
morning at his old vantage point, the field above the cottage.

He's spent a deal of his time up here, these last weeks. Not
down in the village, where conversations halt when he goes by
and stir again uneasily behind his back; and not with his mother,
with her least of all. What's wrong with her? The sudden tears
she won't explain, the causeless panics, and worst of all, her
silences, as if she'd shut herself behind a door. This morning
she had wandered off into the garden without a word, and she's
there still, with her shawl pulled round her shoulders, staring
down the lane. Where is his father? What is he meant to do?

She says he moves her things. He asks her, why would he, and
she turns the question back on him – 'Yes, why, Jacques, why?'

She keeps looking about, as if they share the cottage with a
thing that he can't see. He wakes one night, and finds her at
the cottage's open door, in her nightgown, in the moonlight,
having a conversation, through clenched teeth, with something
that isn't there.

After that, he'd begun organizing his days so he could come
up here, keep watch.

And watching, now, he sees Monsieur Gustave at the door
to Anne's house, holding a letter in his hands. A wood pigeon

calls behind him: coo-*coo*-coo, like a notification. A shiver runs through the trees, over the grass, up his arms. Now Anne and Monsieur Gustave are looking at the letter, talking. Anne goes back into the house, and returns with her shawl, and then the pair of them set off together, up the lane.

He'll think, later, how strange it was: the dread increasing, from that moment on, the closer the letter came to his own door. He'll wonder why he didn't go down to meet them, and the only answer he will ever find within himself is that he already knew.

They try to bring Sally in from the garden, but the disquiet on her face is such that they give up. Unspoken between them, the understanding that whatever they are dealing with here, great caution is needed in its handling. 'I'm waiting for Jean,' she says, by way of explanation, as if encouraging them to agree: *Yes, you are. Not long now.*

'Sally, we have news,' Anne tells her.

'You do?' She looks at the letter in Monsieur Gustave's hand. 'He wrote to you?' She looks at Anne, accusingly. 'Why didn't he write to me?'

'The letter is from Captain Balthasar,' says Anne, and puts her arm round Sally's shoulders. 'Sally, let us take you inside.'

'No – no.' She pulls her shawl tighter. 'Read it to me.'

So Monsieur Gustave reads the letter and, looking helplessly at Anne, folds it when he has done, and Sally asks, 'When is it dated?'

'It was written in May,' Monsieur Gustave answers. He consults the letter. 'The tenth of May.'

'But this is August,' Sally says. There is a wandering quality to her voice. 'This is August. Where is he? Where is my Jean?' And then with no warning she folds against Anne, folding and falling to her knees, and when her head at last comes up again, she is a different thing.

*

Up in the field the wood pigeon is silent now. There's nothing but the wind and far, far off, the sea.

And Anne and Monsieur Gustave, standing over what looks like a heap of clothes on the grass, the same muddled heap you get when the clothes-line snaps.

They try to lift her up; she slips between them. He can make out the sudden disorder of her hair. Her hands come up; he sees that she is tearing at it. The wind brings him sound now, high and thin.

He starts to run. Down the field, leaping the dips and dents, his heart like it's being shook to pieces, his legs like a giant's, seven league strides. He reaches the track. Its stones roll beneath his feet –

– and there's a dog.

He knows this dog, it bites. It's stood there, mid-path, hackles up and growling. It turns its head in his direction, and its lips ripple back from its teeth. It's bonier than when he saw it last, and there's a sore on its side. It weaves its head about, lets off a cannonade of furious barks. Then it stands there, chops agape.

And still that sound from ahead, at the rhythm of breathing: let in, screamed out.

This dog is old. It's blind. No-one seems to own it, no-one is going to care if it lives or dies. He picks up a stone from the path. He starts to walk toward it. It feels as if there is a giant holding him upright, working his legs. The dog, hearing his step, backs up, whimpering.

He walks to the headland through the woods. The dog finds its way behind him by keeping its nose in his hand. When they come out of the woods, he leads it to the stone, and there they sit. The dog smacks its tongue around its chops, as if tasting the wind. Maybe it's never been up here before. It looks comical when it sits down: its back legs splay out so its paws come off the ground, and its teats line up like the buttons on a waistcoat. He puts his arm round its shoulders. When the wind blows you can still hear Sally screaming, but the screams are fewer now, further apart.

He leans his head against the dog's neck. He doesn't even know he's crying till he feels that the fur on its neck is wet. He lifts his head, and the dog whines and licks his face. 'My father,' he says. 'He's never coming home.'

THAT AUTUMN IN Belle-Dame it rains. Streams of earth wash down from the headland, staining the sea; mould reappears on the wall in the kitchen; the roof leaks over his bed.

Maman sits beside the fireplace, seeing nothing, talking to no-one.

And on the headland the eight-ton finger of blue granite, which has been wreathed with blossoms, lit with torches, round which once huddled Roman legionnaires (bedraggled, rainswept, far from home), which has seen Viking longships turning on the tide, finally lifts its root from the waterlogged earth and kisses the turf along its entire length.

Rain washes into the hole, its edges crumble. Come spring new grass will blur the socket, brambles creep across the stone. If there is anything trapped under there, it had better get out while it can.

Are there ghosts? Perhaps.

Are there monsters?

For sure.

THIS DAY, this last of days, a fog has crept into Belle-Dame from the sea. It fills the valley of the river, edges between the houses, makes each garden one foot long. It lets itself in down the chimneys – Anne, walking into her kitchen, finds the room made blurry with it and stood at the table her daughter, already dressed in cape and hood. 'Oh, look at this,' says Anne. 'Didn't you even think to stir the fire?' She rattles the poker into the embers. 'Now you must let me make you something before you go out. What shall it be – a tartine? Hot milk, with an egg?'

Her daughter shakes her head. 'When I come back.'

'But you must take something –' Her daughter already has the door open. 'Margot, please!' And then more softly, 'Don't you want to wait for him?'

Marguerite gives a sad shake of her head. 'He won't come if I'm here, Maman. You know that.'

Down on the river the fog is so thick that if you put your hand out into it, your hand disappears. Every boat out there has a man at the bow, leaning out far as he dare and shouting, '*Ga-a-a-rdez! Ga-a-a-rdez!*'

Not this boat, though. This one, for all the patches on its sail, comes in over the shallows as sure as a homing bird. Its helmsman turns it in a swift smooth curve that brings it to rest on the shingle, then, bare-legged, out he gets. Takes from inside the boat a pair of boots, and throws them up the beach, then with both hands lifts out a dripping, heavy-bellied sack and carries it up to them. Even at this short distance the fog swallows the outline of his boat, and those bigger craft you hear moving down the river are moving down it as unseen as ghosts.

The boy pulls on the boots.

The sack begins to move across the sand. Lumpen convulsions, rolling it back to the water.

The boy watches the sack for a moment or two, then goes to it, opens it, and comes out with a good-sized eel, which wraps its body in a living knot round the boy's forearm, looping and writhing.

The boy takes a clasp-knife from his pocket, springs the blade, and as he does so, turns the eel's head over, so it lies on its back. One by one, the coils loosen and fall away. The eel lies quiet, slack.

The boy puts the knife to the pale throat and presses down. Nothing in his face alters. He puts the body of the eel into the sack, wipes the knife on his breeches and sets off, up the beach.

This is not the same boy as before. This one spends so much of every day with his face in a scowl that there are frown lines digging in between his eyebrows. None of the other children will go near him – these days fight with Jack Fiskardo and it's not the hair-tugging, shirt-pulling scuffles of the other boys; Jack uses his fists and he punches to hurt.

As he reaches the street the dog slips in behind him. Where he hesitates, it waits. And when he makes up his mind, it follows him to Anne's.

It's taught Anne patience, this. She's learned not to try to pull him inside. She's learned not to speak her mind, either. Instead she makes chit-chat: 'Now wouldn't you know it, a day as raw as this, and the fire won't draw. If you could just – there, Jack, see if you can get some warmth out of it, I don't know what's wrong with it, truly.' Then once he's in, she can shut the door, and turning to the table cluck her tongue and say, 'And look at this. Marguerite made herself a tartine and now she's left it. What a waste of good butter. You couldn't eat it, could you?'

It's his hands that grieve her the most. His hands could break your heart. Red with the cold, and the dirt on them, and the wounds – it's as if all the hurt comes out there, nowhere else. They're the hands of a labourer, not of a child. She has to remind herself, this is better than it was. One of the first times he'd appeared on her doorstep, it was with a full set of nail-marks clawed down his face. Like a fool she'd taken his chin, twisted his face to the light, demanding, 'Who did this? Jack, did Sally do this to you?' There's been no sign of him after that for days. That was when they'd realized he was sleeping away from the cottage, in one of his old dens.

'Take some hot milk and nutmeg. I'll make myself one too.' Anne can hear how she is gabbling. 'Marguerite will be back soon. She's gone with – she went out mushrooming. When she's back I'll make omelette. Won't you eat with us, Jacques? A tartine's not a breakfast. You could take some for Sally... It's a bitter morning,' Anne says, with a glance at the fog, pressing its face to her window. If only she can keep him here a moment longer, in the warm.

He won't take charity, not even the suggestion of it. 'Brought you this,' he says, holding out the sack.

'What's this, an eel? Oh, it's a fine one. Where do you find these? Sit down a moment, tell me.'

That wretched dog, outside, is scratching at the door.

He shakes his head. 'I can't,' he says. It's all so simple when you're young as he. 'I can't leave her any longer on her own.'

Strange stuff, this fog. Toiling up to the windmill behind Marguerite, Claude had found himself standing in a channel of clear air, the fog parting in front of him like the waters before Moses. The sun was coming up, the curling edges of the fog above his head were lined with gold, and stood where the gilded edges met, at the far end of the channel, the unexpected profile of a horseman. 'Look at that!' he'd exclaimed.

'Oh, Claude, shut up,' said Marguerite – skirts held in one hand, basket in the other. 'Why do you always have to be so stupid?'

Marguerite is of uncertain temper these days. 'Her age,' Claude's mother assures him sagely, but then his own mother can be just as unpredictable, so what's age got to do with it? Claude would like to know. But still he follows, uncomplaining.

Marguerite too has her faithful dog.

They pass the tower of the windmill. 'What is it *now?*' asks Marguerite.

'I heard a horse.'

'No, you didn't. It's a woodpecker. Listen.'

There is a woodpecker, sure enough, there's its drill, but what Claude had heard was different. Marguerite has gone down amongst the birch trees in the dell. Claude follows, at speed. The thin trees come at him too far apart for him to be able to tell if he's going deeper in amongst them or if it's just the same few trees he's stumbling round. 'Where are you?'

'Here,' she says. She comes out of nothing, right beside him, and her basket is full. There's the drill of the woodpecker again. Then behind her, movement, and a snort. He sees it take shape – four legs, the high head, rolling eye. The man in the saddle, leaning forward. Marguerite turns round, with a gasp. The man takes off his hat and, from horseback, makes them a bow.

'*Bonjour, les petits.*' His voice is soft. There's a silver badge on his shoulder, gleaming in the wet, and a cloth tied at his throat. He smiles at them. '*Je cherche la femme de Jean Fiskardo.*'

'Maman?'

He opens the door of the cottage with care. Sometimes there's a barricade of furniture behind it; sometimes she herself is waiting.

Behind him the dog subsides onto the path.

This time she's simply huddled in her chair before the fire, but she's let the fire die. 'Maman,' he says, taking her hands. They're chill as stone. Did she sit up all night? She has before.

Her eyes come round to him. 'Jack,' she says. Puts her hand over his, and pats it. 'I was talking –' and she looks around, and he sees her lose her place. 'I was talking to Papa.' A brief anxiety across her face. 'Did he go out?'

'Yes, Maman,' he says, quietly as before. 'Papa has gone.'

She settles back, her head against the mark where her head always goes. 'I thought he had,' she says. 'I heard him go.'

Don't think, he tells himself, *don't feel. Sort, act, do.*

'Maman, I'll lay the fire for you. Then I'll go up to the headland. Check the traps. Then we'll eat.'

No answer, and her eyes have already left his face. He knows better than to wait.

She's become used to hearing things, has Madame Marthe. The murmurs as she surfaces from sleep, and when she opens her pantry door, the ghost of a miaow. It means she makes the most of her own noise (but then everyone these days talks so quietly, no-one speaks up properly at all), and when she walks, her every step is marked with a good emphatic stab at the ground from the end of her stick. As now, stamping uphill to the first, the best of the season's precious crop of chanterelles, and in anticipation of the bounty to come, the twigs of her fingers grasp the twigs of her basket so tightly that her basket gasps.

And here's the first of them! The little golden trumpets, and she's not even at the dell! A bumper crop this year for sure. And here's another, and another – but what's this?

The mushrooms have already been plucked. Crumbs of chalky soil about the roots. Plucked and scattered all around her – sacrilege!

Who would do this?

That wretched boy. Only he, she thinks, of all the children in the village, only he would be as wicked, as wasteful as this. Bent double, cursing him, she thinks she'll glean as many as she can. There is a little clear space ahead of her grasping hand, where the curtain of the fog does not quite meet the ground, and in that space, as Madame Marthe moves forward, she sees a basket, still with a few chanterelles sheltering inside. And then there is a shoe. Bending closer she can see the fresh scar on the grass where it left its owner's foot. It's as she straightens up, the shoe in her hand, that she hears the scream – just one, on its own. Were it dusk, you'd think it no more than a vixen. Except something within the scream has set her own old dry heart pounding.

Madame Marthe moves forward, her stick held out in front of her. She feels she needs a weapon. She senses movement in the fog ahead of her and then she sees the man. She sees Anne's child, struggling in his grasp. She sees the blade at the child's throat. She sees Séraphine's child, stretched on the grass before them. The man has bared the girl's breast, but the girl is fighting him, kicking at the man's legs, clawing at his hands. The man sees Madam Marthe and seems to twist the girl away, and the child spins and falls to the ground, that white breast suddenly a bright and glistening red.

'You devil!' shrieks Madame Marthe, and throws the shoe. She takes a step toward him, stick upraised. Behind the man a horse – it must be his – momentarily lifts its head.

COLD ON THE HEADLAND, colder than anywhere. The fog makes him feel dulled, like when he first wakes, when sleep tries to pull him back, making its worthless promises: *Close your eyes. This is a dream. Wake again. All will be as it was.*

He feels his face harden.

The dog, too, is out of sorts, keeps looking back over its shoulder and giving interrogative whuffs at something only dog-eyes can see – or, given this dog, something only dog-brain can invent. An advantage of its blindness: the dog must be the only creature in Belle-Dame to whom the fog doesn't matter at all.

The first of his traps has been sprung, but the rabbit is only a baby, hardly as big as his hand. Clean over, snapped its neck.

That's good – he hates it when he finds them caught by a leg or an ear, hates approaching a trap and hearing their cry. This one is so small that he puts it in his pocket for the dog. Walks on. The dog, smelling the rabbit, follows, whining.

They need more firewood for a start. That means a rope, to haul the timber downhill from the wood –

He could get more rope from Didier-Marie, only last time he saw Didier-Marie, they had a fight –

So, fine, he will terrify Didier-Marie with threats of another beating if he doesn't take some of his father's fishing rope for Jacques, who is no longer Petit, nor ever of a humour to be trifled with, and now here's the bloody dog sticking its nose in his hand because it hasn't had its breakfast yet, so he takes the rabbit from his pocket and chucks it onto the grass. The dog throws itself down, paws either side of the little wet body, and he hears the first crunch, and looks back to where the cottage is, all his childhood, lost, and thinks with horrid adult clarity, *I cannot bear to do this any more.*

Oh, this does not look promising.

The roof of the cottage is green with moss; its shutters dangle. It puts him in mind of stories of those houses that retreat before the traveller, grow legs and skip away. He raps against the door, then leans an ear to it.

Ach, prok! Two, three, bright drops of blood upon his cuff. He pulls the sleeve of his coat down to cover them as the door opens by a crack.

A rats' nest of curls; grey, like tarnish, on the crown. Her head is bent; he can see only chin, tip of nose –

A pair of eyes, peering through the tangles. Squinting, scared.

Carlo leans his weight against the door. "Allo, *cherie*,' he says.

One little tap, that's all it took, and she'd retreated back across the room, as good as gold. A brief inspection, to assure him she was on her own.

What a pigsty. What a stink to the place. He'd closed the bedroom door, pulled up a chair for her. 'Sit,' he'd said, dusting the seat, but had to drag her to it, all the same. Now she's seated he stands back, to get a better look at her. Ah, was a beauty, this one, not a doubt. Now, though, she looks like a witch.

There's a window-seat or some such thing behind him. Carlo Fantom sits, takes off his hat. Fans to clear the air before his face.

'*Cherie*,' he says, 'this is no good. You know who I am?'

'Yes,' she says, slowly, dully, hand to her cheek. Her eyes meet his. 'I knew you'd come.'

'That's good, *cherie*. You not as crazy as you look, *korrekt*?'

A murmur, in reply. He cups a hand to his ear. 'What's that?'

'No,' she says. Draws a hand across her forehead, clearing the tangled curls. 'Not as crazy as I look.'

Carlo, getting comfortable, angling one leg on the other. 'You look bad, *cherie*. Very bad.' He sniffs. 'And you smell bad, too.' He could draw this out – it really is most comfortable sat here. For the first time he takes a look at what he's sitting on. Mattress. A pillow.

'What's this, *cherie*?' he says, getting to his feet. 'Someone else is sleeping here?'

Now she's half-standing too, as if trying to crawl off the chair. 'No – no,' she says. He wraps his fist in her hair, feels her fingers fighting his. 'Where are they, *cherie*? Whose bed is that, *hnn*?' For the first time, she's trying to escape, scraping at the front of his coat, scrabbling at him, like a cat trying to get up a wall. She has surprising strength. Another, bigger tap; it knocks the breath out of her. She's stuttering something. 'My b-b-boy.' The tears brim and spill. 'My boy. My beautiful boy.'

A child? 'Where is your boy, *cherie*?'

A great breath, shaking through her. 'He's gone, he's gone,' she says. 'I know, he's dead and gone.'

With his free hand, dragging her with him, Carlo Fantom

pulls back the cover on the bed. No linen. The mattress cold and hard. No-one has slept here in an age. *Ach so…* 'Your boy is dead?'

Tears, running through the grime on her cheeks. She nods her head. He puts his mouth against her ear. 'A mother should be with her baby, no?'

The tears cease. She knows. They all know, always, when the moment has come. Now, how to accomplish this?

He looks about. Above the table, a lantern, hanging from its hook.

When it's done, he's sweating a little. He rolls down his sleeves, re-dons his coat, retrieves his hat. He pictures the shock on the thick peasant faces when they discover her, but in truth this place, this thing, is behind him already.

Outside, he remounts his horse, lets it pick its way back to the road. Time to be gone from here, this place of peasants and their mud. He is about to spur his horse to a gallop when he sees, stepping out into the road, a man, another wretched hobbledehoy, wearing a strangely drooping flat grey hat. But however odd the man's appearance, he seems to know something of Carlo's business here; he must, because he steps directly out in front of the horse, and raises his arms.

Carlo runs his horse straight at him. The thud of contact, the horse stumbling, throwing up its head, and then the man is no more than a bundle left there in the road.

He'll be a mile into his journey before he hears a far-off church bell sounding out the news. But he'll be hours away before his hand, coming to rest on his jacket, finds the tiny tongue of leather where the silver wolf should be.

THEY'RE MAYBE HALFWAY down the hill, the dog and he, when it whuffs again, only this time the whuff is sharp, this one says definitely something's there. He is about to order it to heel when it launches a volley of barks at nothing and sets off down the slope at a run. He hears it crash through the undergrowth, tries calling it back – the half-wit bloody mutt, what's up with it?

The trees stand round him like a waiting crowd. But the only answer is more far-off barking.

Putain de merde –

He finds the dog at the end of the path, its hackles up like quills, a continuous savage growling coming from some place deeper in its chest than it has ever reached before. It pauses only when it must draw breath. When he reaches for it, it skips aside, but the growls don't cease. 'Come on then,' he says, walking forward, 'what is it?' But it won't go forward, either. It is glaring at the cottage. Is it something there?

With the dog still growling behind him he approaches the gate.

And sees the door of the cottage. Not quite shut.

The flame of his anger leaps up at once – what's she done *now*? He strides up the path, barges into the room. '*Maman*,' he says. His voice rings out – impatient, bullying.

The room takes the sound of his voice and lets it hang there, as only an empty room can do.

But the room isn't empty.

When he dreams of this, as he will do, off and on, for the rest of his life, it's the smallness of the sounds that haunt him. The gentle breathing of the fire, the collapse of her skirt about her legs as he grips her, as he clambers up onto the table; the squeak of the cloth on the hook. In the dreams he hides her face, he hides the hair caught in the knot behind her neck, he sees her hands only as he placed them, on her breast, not as they had knocked against his shoulders, as it had tried, poor inert thing that it is, to do what he wanted it to do, to come down, to answer to her name. He can't believe that he was ever strong enough to lift her, but he must have done; he steps into space with her in his arms and they land on the floor together.

He knows he speaks to her, but can never remember what he says – perhaps that he will be a better son to her, that he won't be angry with her anymore, won't leave her on her own, if only she won't do this, if only she will come back to him. Perhaps there are no words, just the incoherent noises of his grief. In his dreams he will see again how his hands had jerked this way and that as if he had the palsy, as he stroked the hair from her face, as he straightened her clothes, as he folded her hands. Was it then that he found it, gripped in her fist? Was it then?

He knows that he knelt there holding it, but not for how long. He knows he gripped it until he had forced the shaking of his own hands to cease. One of her eyes was open by a little, the eyelid stopped in its journey, and he knows that once his hands had steadied, with his thumb he had closed the eye, and that had felt as if he was releasing her; that now she was wholly gone. And he knows that he left the cottage, leaving the dog howling at its open door. He knows he goes down the lane with the silver wolf clutched in his fist, clutched so tightly his palm is sticky with blood. But it doesn't matter. Nothing is ever going to matter again. Everything is going to stop.

He pushes *Le Petit Jacques* out till he feels the current pull at his legs, tips himself in, drops her sail. Lying back, full-length, he listens to the water on the other side of her planks. When he is older, he'll think perhaps he had some idea of the river as the Styx. He's clear, always, to himself, what he had intended the ending of this journey to be.

The prow of the barge comes through the fog with such momentum that *Le Petit Jacques* caves in beneath it as under an axe. Jack opens his eyes to find a thick golden hawser above him, caught in some errant beam of sun, and the green sea pouring in through the V bitten into his boat's side. He's in water to his waist at once. The mast of his boat falls past him, the stern lifts up – now there's nothing under him at all. Above his head the hawser now runs straight along the side of the barge, and there are faces set above it, moving backwards as the sea rushes in over his head. It fills his eyes, it fills his ears, it's pouring in straight down his throat. He looks up, and the barge is still above him, big as a whale, with some great foaming commotion at its side; he looks down and there is the silver wolf, slipped through his fingers, falling away from him, falling fast. He tilts to reach it, and it's dark down there, dark beyond any colour he can imagine, and already he's grabbed at it, with a puff of blood in the green water as his hand closes over it again, and then his hands are reaching upward, and even the bubbles rising from his nose are streaking for the surface, and now his legs are scissoring themselves into movement too. He kicks. The great foaming commotion above his head is a net, hitting the water and sinking toward him. He kicks again.

PART III

July 1623–July 1630

CHAPTER ONE

Utopia

Of Intelligence:

'Every good commander must have these two grounds
for his actions: 1. The knowledge of his own forces and
wants… 2. The assurance of the condition and estate
of the enemie.'

John Cruso, *Militarie Instructions for the Cavallrie*

THEY MAKE AN ODD PAIR, no two ways round that – the
man so pale and wasted; and the boy so full of fire. Not
much liking lost between them, either, that Cyrius can
see – the Shadow Man is that acid, discomforting sort, while
the boy's temper would scare the very Devil. 'What *is* the story
there?' Cyrius asks, as he and Agetha lie together in the companionable dark, Utopia's canvas walls moving softly in and out
above them. And in the dark he feels Agetha smile, and rub her

face against him, and say, 'It's just the way of it, my man. It's the scouts. It's how they are.'

Because scouts *are* odd, who'd deny it? *March to a different drum*, thinks Cyrius, for whom such military turns of thought are still novelty enough to raise a smile, and live in a world that for their fellows simply isn't there. Once, walking together beyond the camp, Cyrius had Aesop list for him exactly what traffic had passed along the muddy track before them, and though Aesop was the mildest and most affable of men, the experience had been unnerving. 'It was like he was seeing ghosts,' Cyrius had reported back to Agetha. 'All these others I couldn't see at all.' An ox-cart; a drover with his herd of sheep; a goose-girl and her geese; and last of all, a gang of soldiers – all from the overlaying ruts and ruddles in the mud, a feather and a little plucked-up grass, the wounds along the branches of an overhanging tree.

'That's nothing,' Aesop had told him, as Cyrius expressed his amazement. 'The Shadow Man now, he'd see those cuts along the branches and he could tell you, was it the blade of a halberd did that, or was it a pike? For if it was the one, it might be no more than some officer's bodyguard a-swiping at the branches and making a much of themselves, as they do. But if it was a company of pikemen coming your way – why, that, my friend, would be a thing you'd wish to know. 'Tis a terrible weapon, a pike. There ain't no answer to it.'

Astounding, Cyrius thought it. 'How'd you come into this business, Aesop?' he'd asked, as they strolled back.

And Aesop, pulling at his ear, replied, 'Why, I suppose I have the disposition for it. More of a watcher than a one for action, me. And I've a good eye. Patience and watchfulness, that's what makes a scout.'

Cyrius could well believe it. There was a calmness to Aesop, something to do with the nigh-colourless frizz of his hair, and the way you never felt he fully wakened up. Indeed there was a calmness and a steadiness to all the scouts. Which of course made the presence of the boy, that young hell-hound, amongst them all the more of a puzzle.

The track led them downhill. Before them, on the wooded slope opposite (full of trees, this country, and fields let in amongst the trees as unexpectedly as patches on a coat), was their camp: some few dozen lazy infantry and the scouts – Aesop, Holger and Titus, the Shadow Man, the boy. The occasional messenger came calling, from some other company – Cyrius knew there were others out there, knew there was a great sweeping arc of looking and searching this way and that right through the whole of Lower Saxony – but this, this tiny clearing, this was home. And there was home, its sag-backed and ungainly profile like a helpful elephant kneeling down. Utopia.

And on the rise above it, him and that horse of his, there was the boy, standing sentinel. 'What about him?' Cyrius had asked, jerking a thumb. 'He got the makings of a scout, has he?'

'Him,' said Aesop, lowering his voice. 'What he's the makings of, I hope as I'm not there to see.' He shook his head. A change of subject: 'And what's your tale, my friend? What was your life, a-fore this one?'

'Why, I was a miller,' Cyrius replied.

'Oh yes? So what brought you into this fine war?'

'Some bugger burned down my mill.'

Everybody knows a joke about a miller. There was

If you hung every cheating miller, there would be no mills.

Or there was

Shake a miller, a weaver and a tailor in a sack, and the first to come out is a thief.

And of course

Bold as a miller's shirt, that every morning collars a rogue.

You grow a good thick skin as a miller. You time your days by the big, simple machinery of your mill, and if sometimes it seems to grind too slowly to endure, you pass an hour a-fishing in your millpond. You take on an apprentice, as you once were yourself. Fame and fortune leave you to one side, and Cupid don't come calling, either. Here you are, an old bachelor. Nearly forty.

And then one evening you're driving weary horse and creaking cart back to your mill, and the road seems strangely silent, and there's a taint of smoke in the air. And you come to the water-splash over the road, and there's your 'prentice, floating in it, and there, over the millstream, is your mill, smoke rolling from under its roof and soldiers in fancy shirts sat upon the ground all round it, watching.

Who raise themselves up as you drive down upon them, standing up in your cart like a charioteer, lashing left to right with your whip and calling down upon them every curse that you can lay a name to. And then you hear the woman's voice, saying, 'Make them pay.'

'I'll make them pay, never fear! They'll pay, right enough!'

He'd sounded hysterical. Later he would wonder if that was why she'd interrupted him. It would be like her – saving a man from the worst of himself. He'd looked down and there she was, a handcart tilted before her. That was the first thing he noticed, the cart. In some way it made her seem a miniature of him. The second thing was her eyes: their deep, sad, brown; and their expression – desperate, but determined. He looked at the cart again. There was a child sat in it, on a pile of folded canvas. Later he would discover this was all she had left in the world – her daughter, and the canvas that would become Utopia's skin. In this war there was always somebody worse off than you.

'Make them pay,' the woman said again. 'You've grain there in your cart, yes? And they've plunder. They didn't mean to fire your mill, what they want is food. But do the deal now, quick, before they work out they can just as easy rob you of it, too.'

'Who are you?' he asked, meaning not only who, but what, to travel with such men and know such things?

'Squirrel,' she replied. 'And Agetha.'

Confused, he found it easier to address the child, now on her hip, than her. "*Tag*, Agetha,' he said, gravely, holding out his hand.

The woman shook her head. 'No, no,' she said. 'We call my girl Squirrel. It was her father's name for her.' Which answered one question about her at least: a widow, not a whore. She met his eye. 'Agetha is me.'

Once it became clear that he would no longer be a miller, but would be setting up in the business of provisioning an army as a sutler, with a sutler's widow and a purse a-chink with Spanish silver, the first decision Cyrius had to make was about their sign. All sutlers had a sign, so Agetha informed him. Soldiers got to know their favourites, and looked for them again and again. Cyrius was quietly proud of theirs, which was, indeed, more elaborate than most: beneath the commonplace of wooden pretzel and swinging tankard, there hung a board painted with the name of their new enterprise – *UTOPIA* – then Agetha had the man add in beside the name the constellation of Orion, with the Dog Star picked out in gold leaf – Sirius, the brightest of them all.

The corporeal Cyrius sold candles, needles, wool and thread. Tapers, tobacco, playing cards. Sausage, pretzels, hard rations for the field. Beer in the summertime, and in winter, hot sugary grog. Utopia's construction could hardly have been simpler – two sturdy poles leaning together at the back, two rather higher at the front, crossed like the cruck-framed timbers of a house, and balanced between them, something long and light. A chestnut sapling was good, Cyrius found, or birch. Once all that had been dug and lashed securely into place, Utopia's canvas skin came over the top. Pull back the flap to make a doorway high enough for a soldier to enter without having to remove his hat, set up your tables, hang up the sign, and there you were. Open for business.

He still had his miller's cart. That, and his old horse, lived round the back. Still wore his commodious, smock-like miller's shirt as well, though these days over it he'd added a good long leather jerkin. He'd begun using the hem of the shirt to mop spills, a habit of which Agetha was trying to break him.

According to Agetha, it was their sign that had made them such a favourite with the scouts. 'It's in the stars,' she'd said, grinning, pointing up. 'Orion the hunter. A scout's a hunter. Sirius was his. And the scouts have dogs as well.'

Indeed they did. Great square-muzzled monsters, standing as high as your hip. Cyrius found that he spent a deal of his time making sure Squirrel never went anywhere near to them.

The rare occasions when the Shadow Man and his boy came into Utopia, to Cyrius's annoyance, very often one of their great dogs would lope in after them, throwing itself to the ground at the boy's feet with a smack of its fearsome jaws. The other matter, this particular evening, drawing Cyrius's eye to their table is the fact that the Shadow Man sits there in hugger-mugger conversation with a stranger, a man with a most delicately cared-for beard, and sticky-up hair, like a sprite. It was a moot point, in Cyrius's view, where the already risky business of a scout, a discoverer of intelligence, shaded into the even more knife-edge world of the spy. 'Aesop, who is that fellow?' Cyrius had asked, out the corner of his mouth, and Aesop answered, 'Ravello. Scouts under Anholt. General Tilly's chief of staff.'

'And what's he doing here?'

'Assaying of his intelligences,' said Aesop, sounding surprised that the question needed to be asked. 'Running 'em through with the Shadow Man, ain't he?'

For here was another mystery. Aesop, Titus, Holger, and every other scout who came into the camp, all of them consulting with this cinder of a man, who walked with one leg dragging and a crutch wedged under his arm. It was a wonder he did so at all, in Cyrius's view, a miracle how the man hauled himself from one day to the next. 'What drives him on?' Cyrius asked, in wonderment, and Aesop, *sotto voce*, had replied, 'Ah, there you have it, do you see? The answer to that question answers all.'

'What I heard,' Aesop begins, 'is this. One time, long ago, the Shadow Man, he had a comrade. A brother-in-arms.'

'Go on,' says Cyrius, wiping his counter. One eye on the boy, the stranger, Ravello, and the Shadow Man, there at the back.

'Now the Shadow Man –' (and Aesop lowers his head and his voice as well) '– you've heard as he's a Frenchie, I dare say?'

No, Cyrius had not.

'Oh yes. French as a fleur-de-lys. And his comrade was another, and both of them, they're in the army of King Henry of Navarre. Him what ends the wars in France when he trades Paris for a chicken in a pot. For they're a strange people, the French, and think only with their stomachs.'

'There was a King Henry what I heard of,' Cyrius begins, hesitantly, for he's wary of revealing how small the world of a miller can be, 'why, Lord, it was long years ago, but there was a King Henry I heard of, was done to death in Paris by a madman.'

Aesop tips his head forward. 'That's the one. And that's where the tale begins, for with King Henry dead, it's out with the old guard and in with the new, and the new power in the land becomes this man Concini. Now this Concini, he is one of those should never get to power, yet always seem to do. He taxes the people till they bleed, and he keeps the King's son all but prisoner –' (and Aesop drops his voice still further) '– and there's those say he took the King's place in the Queen's own bed, what's more. So amongst the old guard, a plan is hatched, to be rid of him. And the Shadow Man, he's a part of it – oh yes,' says Aesop, as Cyrius bugs his eyes in disbelief, 'don't think as he was always as you see him now. He was a good big part of it, and he brought his friend in on it too.

'Now the Shadow Man's a thinking sort,' Aesop continues, tapping a knuckle to his temple. 'The way it makes best sense to me, it's the friend is the man of action. For in all such enterprises, there's those as plan, and those as do, and it's the friend who's one of them as strikes the blow. Or fires the shot, as I believe it was. And that was the end of Concini.' He pauses, rubs his ear. 'You're sure you ain't heard none of this? Ah me,' says Aesop, cheerily. 'The mighty. How they do fall, eh?

'But this is where it all goes wrong. There is a plot around their plot, d'you see? Like an old egg – black on the shell, and if you break it open, stinking. And somehows or another, the friend there guesses how it truly is, and woe is him that he should ever do so, for while the Shadow Man is waiting one place, his friend is sent another, and no-one ever sees the man again. And by the time the Shadow Man has worked out some-thing's gone awry here, wrong as wrong can be, 'tis all up with the man's poor wife as well.'

'His wife?' exclaims Cyrius, thinking at once of Agetha.

'Aye, her too. Did away with herself is the tale, God rest her. Broke in heart and mind and soul. But,' says Aesop, holding up a finger in the air, '*but* – there was a child.'

'There was?'

'A boy. Now. Say you're the Shadow Man. How'd you be feeling?'

'I would be feeling,' answers Cyrius, thoughtful, glancing over to that table at the back, 'I would be feeling fair sick of myself, if truth be told. If it was I brought my friend in to this, I would be – I tell you what, Aesop,' says Cyrius, leaning forward, 'if there was a child left orphan out of this, by God, first thing I'd want would be to take him as my own.'

'Only,' says Aesop, laying the finger to his nose, 'you have to find him first.'

'Find him? Why, where's he gone?'

'That's the thing. No-one can tell you. Some say he's dead, some say he's lost, some say he's run away. But you're the Shadow Man, d'you see? If the boy's there to be found, if anyone can find him, then it's you. Patience and watchfulness.' The finger taps either side of the nose in turn, as if these are the very names of Aesop's orbs. 'So you keep these open.' Patience and Watchfulness again. 'You do what scouts do. You follow the trail – a name here, a memory there. And then one day, you're somewheres, and a word reaches you, and – well, my friend. Who d'you think that orphan child is now?'

The stranger, Ravello, thinks Cyrius, at once.

A rumpus from the table in the corner. The boy has got to his feet. Sent on some errand, it would appear, for Ravello is holding out a palmful of pence to sweeten the request, but the boy shoves past the hand and stalks out, lanky as a scarecrow and no doubt ill-intentioned as Hamelin's piper.

Oh, a nasty piece of work that one, and no mistake. Cyrius, looking back at Aesop for a clue, sees Watchfulness close and open slowly, in a wink.

'You don't mean – it's the *boy*?'

'In one,' says Aesop, smiling broadly. 'Why'd you think the Shadow Man keeps him so close? For pleasure of his company? It's so he knows the boy is safe. Why's he spend all that time with him, out in the field, when it's all the man can do to walk? He's teaching that boy every last thing he can.'

FOR A SUMMER'S MORNING, this one has a deal more grey in it than blue. And a blustering, indeed a battering wind, especially if you should be stood on a hilltop, under its crest of trees. As are Balthasar and Jack. The Shadow Man and his boy.

Balthasar, listing to windward, eases his weight against his crutch. Above, the clouds roll on, relentless, the underside of

waves on some almighty heavenly sea; and at his feet the landscape unreels in billows that mirror the stately roll of the clouds.
Swells and falls, swells and falls, an acre between each smooth
green billow, crest to crest.

'What do you see, Jacques? What do you see?'

Jack, looking; Balthasar, watching him look. The boy's pale
eyes – his father's eyes – flickering, ranging. The horizon, back.
The horizon, down. The stand of trees above them, how it puts
one foot downhill. The pine at the end of the foot, its crown
gone in some recent storm, and hanging down like the head of
something shot. The field below – young wheat, soft enough to
stream in the wind like ribbons. It would show every mark, as
clearly as the nap on velvet. More trees, filling the gaps between
the fields – oak, elm; a darkness amongst them that suggests
much growth of ivy, ancient and undisturbed.

Balthasar brings his crutch in under his chin. Beside him he
sees the boy's shoulders flex with irritation, like a horse throwing off flies. Time's up.

'Nothing could get across here,' Jack begins. 'The wheat is
so soft it would show, and there's no roads down there wide
enough for proper traffic. You'd have to split your force to move
'em through it. And no forage. Nothing but rabbits and pigeon,
that 'ud be it.'

He's warming to it now. Balthasar lets him run.

'Might be good ground to fight on. If you had the height,
like here, it would take something to move you. And you could
get some pace on a charge, downhill.' He stops. 'Well?'

'So if you'd men, you'd charge from here?' Balthasar asks,
carefully.

'I might. So?'

Balthasar pivots on his crutch. 'And the marsh at the bottom
there? That wouldn't worry you?'

The boy peers down the hill. Nothing at the bottom but
silken green. '*What* marsh?'

'Watch,' says Balthasar.

A swift, tilting across the field, little black arrow against the emerald wheat. That untidy fluttering fall. Then another – the same path, the same drop out of sight, the same soaring upward. Once you have them in focus it's impossible to miss them, as soon as one has gone another comes in to replace it.

'You get insects above mud,' says Balthasar, pleasantly. 'Run a company through that? I don't think so, do you?'

Silence from the boy. A soft breeze blows about them.

Then the snarl: 'You think I'm nothing, don't you?'

'Far from it,' says Balthasar, pulling his crutch free of the ground. 'But I also think you're only seventeen.'

'Who looked after me, before you showed up? Who kept me fed, who kept me alive?' And Jack might be taller, he might be bigger now, but Mungo Sant would recognize that face, that bottled fury. 'I did it. Me. The only thing I need from you is their names.'

'No,' says Balthasar, beginning his descent.

'I want their names. The one who knew my father's face, and the killer.'

'What, so you can go after them?' Balthasar asks, turning about. 'He killed your father, Jacques. Your father could fight like no man I have ever seen, and he lies in that graveyard in Picardy. No.'

The descent is sharp. Balthasar is almost out of sight. But he hears, nonetheless, the shout of rage, the sound of something – a dead branch, probably – being smashed against a tree.

Saxony, this is, the edge of the forest of the Teutoburg. Armies have marched through, fought across, breathed their last in this wooded country for centuries. Hanover north-east, Münster to the west, and Holland over the horizon, fifty miles straight that-a-way.

Somewhere between them and it, the army of a madman, running for its life.

*

Of an evening, it is the habit of the scouts to settle in Utopia and talk, picking and pulling the war apart in a manner that reminds Cyrius in an unsettling way of surgeons arguing over an anatomy. Lately, though, as far as subjects went, there'd been only one.

'Christian of Brunswick, that howler at the moon,' Holger begins. 'What do they say he has? Twenty thousand men, is it?'

'I heard it was twenty-five.' This from Titus.

'By God,' Holger comments, 'they may be rabble, but by God, that would be a force to reckon with.'

'It's Brunswick's three years' worth of loot I want to see. They say he's got two wagonsful of nowt but silver thalers. They say when his army went through Paderborn, there weren't a church left behind 'em with as much as a saucer.'

'They say, they say,' comes the Shadow Man's voice. 'What's this *they say*? It's sixteen thousand men Brunswick has, the same as we. Four of horse, twelve thousand foot. We meet, we'll be even.'

'Only we got to find the bastard, first,' Titus puts in.

Wind against the side of the tent. The canvas wall pushed in, sucked out. Cyrius raises an eye to his roof. He's a long pole of willow lashed in place up there, supporting the whole; it was light, but he'd had his doubts when he put it up there whether it would prove that strong.

We meet. He's never heard them speak of it like that before, a thing foretold and certain. *I've never seen a battle*, Cyrius thinks.

The wind again, strong enough now to have found a voice.

'Storm coming,' says Aesop, sounding cheery, 'I shouldn't be surprised.'

'And, *signore*, we have to ask, why is Brunswick here, in any case?' says Ravello, speaking as if to the air. 'He has no allies here. Here, he is on his own.'

'Those notices his troops nailed up,' says Holger. 'Fire and Blood! – remember those? God rot his eyes, he was good as his word. A wasteland, those men left behind them. And who they didn't kill, the plagues that they brought with them did.' A moment's gloomy silence at the thought. 'So yes, that is the question – why's he here?'

'*Ach*,' says Titus, breaking in. 'It's not *why* that matters. It's the *where*. Christian of Brunswick, the mad sod, him and his however many thousand men.' He throws wide an arm. 'Where the fuck are they?'

The storm, when it struck, did so with a roar that sounded to Cyrius like the whole world falling down. He and Agetha, with Squirrel pressed between them, watched from their bed as Utopia lifted off them and was hurled away. The sky so suddenly above them was split with lines of lightning that stretched from one horizon to the other, like paint being thrown off a stick. Titus and Holger, having drawn the short straw of a night patrol, came in at sunrise to find the camp as if trampled on by giants, with Utopia's canvas blown uphill and hanging from the trees like the moult of some gigantic insect. Aesop and Ravello were hurling grappling hooks into it, and a mud-stained Cyrius was doing his best to limit the damage they could inflict: 'Mind! There's a branch coming with it! It'll tear!'

Titus and Holger lend their weight to the ropes. One, two, three, *heave*!

Behind them the one-time contents of Utopia lie strewn across the slope. Agetha has already set up a sad corral of trestles and stools, and is now going over the ground anew, stooping to pick up this and that, placing them in the basket looped over her arm. Cyrius, turning his eyes from the noisy efforts of the scouts, sees Squirrel, bless her, copying her mother, crouched down, trying to work something free of the mud.

'Cyrius, look alive! Here it comes! Stand away!'

Cyrius jumps back. With a crack of breaking branches, Utopia hits the ground.

Way down the slope, Squirrel is about to burst into noisy tears. So great is the effort she's putting into her digging that her toes, wrinkled and fat as little carrots, grip the ground like ten more fingers, but all to naught.

A voice above her head: 'What you got there, Pennyweight?'

Squirrel stops, and blinks. Some tiny part of what she's been trying to free sticks out from the earth: a miniature battered casualty.

It takes Jack a moment to work out what it is. Her doll. Squirrel tilts her head and looks at him expectantly.

Jack crouches down, prises loose the doll and holds it out to her – muddy as a root.

Squirrel looks from the doll to him. Her lower lip pushes out. Her chin begins to pucker. There's a wet shine to her eye.

'I reckon,' says Jack hurriedly, 'as dolly needs a wash.' He holds out his hand. With utmost seriousness, Squirrel takes it – at least she wraps all her fingers round the one of his, and suffers herself to be led down the slope to the tumbling stream.

Jack gives Squirrel the strictest instructions to stay back from the edge and, crouching down again, holds the doll underwater till the mud is gone from its face and hair and clothes. 'There you go,' he says, handing it back, and Squirrel takes it, and presses it with both hands to her breast.

And there's her mother, calling her. Agetha of the gentle heart. Agetha of the great, dark, beautiful, downward-tilted eyes.

'You go back now,' says Jack, giving Squirrel a little push, to get her moving up the slope. He watches as she toils toward Agetha, doll clutched in one hand, nightgown held out of the mud with the other.

And there's Balthasar, limping along the edge of the stream toward him. He turns his back at once.

But Balthasar speaks, nonetheless. 'That was kindly,' he says.

'You and I,' says Jack, back still turned, 'you and I, unless you're about to give me them names, we ain't got a thing to say to each other.' *Ignore him*, he thinks. *Ignore him and he'll limp off elsewhere.*

But the voice behind him persists. 'She puts you in mind of Belle-Dame, that little one, doesn't she?'

He feels his anger flaming up at once. 'What do you know, about Belle-Dame? What do you know about anything?'

'Where do you think I went, after Beaune? Soon as I could keep my seat again upon a horse, I was in Belle-Dame. They think you're dead there, you know that? They found the wreckage of your boat, they think you drowned. Just one more death amongst so many. You want to know why I won't give you the names? That little thing you wear around your neck, that's why. The man who wore that killed your father. And then he killed your mother too.'

'My mother,' Jack begins, 'my mother killed herself.' The only way he can speak the words is as if they're weapons, as if they themselves could kill. 'She wanted to be with my father. She wanted to be with him more than she wanted to stay with me, so she killed herself.' He hears his voice rising. 'I *found* her, Balthasar, I should fucken know!'

But Balthasar is staring at him, open-mouthed. 'That's what you think? That she took her own life? Christ Almighty, boy. That woman loved you to her very soul; she would never have abandoned you. How can you think that?'

'I found her—' he begins, but Balthasar cuts him off.

'You found what he *left*. And you thought what he intended you to think. Jacques, the man who killed your father killed your mother too. Only she took that bloody little token from him, damn his soul, so somewhere, sometime, someone might know – who he was and what he'd done. I know you want those names, and I know what you would do if you had them. But he has taken from me every last person I ever loved. He is *not* going to get his hands on you. God above,' says Balthasar, shifting his weight with a groan, 'God above. You've not the first idea what truly happened in Belle-Dame that day, have you?'

Ain't that typical, thinks Cyrius. Everyone else sets to, putting the camp to rights, and what is it the boy does? Takes himself off like shit-fire. 'Hi, Kapitan!' yells Cyrius. It's not like him to criticize the military, but he has his arms full of torn and muddy canvas and God knows how many hours of work ahead. 'Kapitan, where's that boy of yours off to? We could do with him here!'

The Shadow Man turns. Boy and horse are disappearing at full gallop.

'Leave him be, Cyrius, leave him be. He needs time on his own.'

Oh, far easier, on your own. Easier no-one sees you fallen to your knees, tearing the silver wolf from round your neck, pounding your fists against the trees until the pain in them can vie with that around your heart, and you fall forward, keening like a child. For a moment he thinks he will throw it from him, deep into the trees – but it's all he has, it's all he has.

He killed them. He killed them all.

God should come striding through his forest now, grind him into the earth. The sky is crushing him; if he could open himself up, head to toe, still the howl would not be loud enough.

He killed them. He killed them all.

He can't find their faces, and starts sobbing again that he cannot. They're gone, all of them, lost to the sky, the sun, the turning of the days. The crumbling mould against his cheek might be their flesh. He can remember only her shape as she hung there; the solid marble of her forehead, the cold wall of her skull. And she one side of it. And he the other. *Forgive me. Forgive me.* Even to think of her knocks him to his knees again.

Every memory, all that he had pushed away for so long, crushing him beneath them – but isn't that all he deserves?

Forgive me. Forgive me.

The trees spread their arms out over him, as if asking, what do we do?

The coldness of the ground creeps upward, through his skin. At some point, his horse stands over him and breathes into his face.

They're gone. You're here. He killed them all.

Stars move along their paths above his head. A moon rises over the trees, gliding from one branch to the next as it peers down at him. Then it's gone. Or he sleeps.

There are creatures walking all around him in the dark, but perhaps he is invisible.

They're gone. You're here. He killed them all.

HERE'S A THING you won't see every day: a horse, saddled and bridled, standing in a clearing on its own.

Not that the horse seems troubled. As the sky has lightened, the horse has discovered abundant greenery all around it, and is making a hearty breakfast. From time to time it casts a glance at a mounding-up – the bulk of some kind of a thing – there in the shadows at the foot of that tree, but otherwise the strangeness of where it is and how it might have got there seems not to worry it at all.

The light strengthens. The first rays of the rising sun edge through the trees, like light angling down the aisle of a church, and the thing at the foot of the tree begins to stir. Puts out a hand. A leg. Sits up and rubs its face.

There are tracks through the dirt on its face that might make one think of tears, and trails of dried blood on its hands. The thing is in a mess, altogether. The horse comes over; this other creature gets to its feet (slowly, like it's achey from its night spent out-of-doors), and they stand together, forehead to fore-head, one on four legs, one on two. The horse lifts its muzzle and nibbles over the other's face. And the other gives a shaky sigh, and for the first time takes a look at its surroundings.

Trees. And more trees. And more after that. No sign of any path, nothing to say *way in* or *way out*.

The churr of a pheasant. The rattle of a deer.

Milano goes back to his interrupted breakfast. Jack, picking pieces of twig out of that ringletted mane, asks, wonderingly, 'How far did we come? Where are we?'

A walk together, he and Milano, through the trees. The ground tilts down, Jack can feel it as he walks, which is intri-guing, as he certainly doesn't recall a tilting-up on the way here. Inasmuch as he recalls any of getting here at all. There's a hole of some sort, opened in his memory, and last night lies at the bottom of it, black water at the bottom of some dark, dark well. So why not a walk through the woods? What else is there to do?

It's beech wood, here, and like all beech woods the ground is clean, and springy with beech-mast. Saplings struggle up wher-ever there is space – bright leaved, trembling with effort. Rocks burst through the soil, so split and fissured and bewigged with moss that they almost have faces, and something within Jack's senses has awakened, anticipating change.

The branches open overhead. Blue sky above, and almost at once the smell of woodsmoke and what he takes at first, so vivid and alien is its colour, to be a splash of fungus. Till it moves.

He drops to his knees immediately. The saplings before him make a kind of screen. Through it he sees the man raise an arm and stretch; that field of sentimental Brunswick hearts painted across the back of his coat in bloody gules. 'All for her' is Christian of Brunswick's motto, the 'her' in this instance being

Bohemia's exiled Queen. A vainglorious declaration, vainglorious and blasphemous, if you're as staunch a Catholic as old Father Tilly, who would probably give all the teeth still in his head to be looking at what Jack is looking at now.

The Brunswicker, finished with his morning stretch, gives a shout. An answering call, but from a good ways off. Jack is close enough to hear the first man muttering. You'd think the man would be close enough to hear the wild thudding of Jack's heart, in turn. Still crouched down, he creeps closer. There's a wagon, canvas-roofed and wicker-sided. Those shifting outlines, horses –

This was it, he knew it at once. The rearguard of that lost army.

The rising sun is warming his back. *So they're heading west*, he thinks. *But why?*

Milano, nosy as ever, sticks his head through the leaves and gives a snort and the sentry's head whips round, fast as a rattle.

Jack hears the man exclaim, '*Wod* the—' even as he hauls on Milano's reins. The plan comes into shape as he hurls himself out of sight behind the nearest tree. Pressed against its powdery green trunk he hears the Brunswicker marvel to himself, 'God in e'vin! Iss an 'orse!' Peering round the trunk, he sees the man approach Milano at an unsteady sway, holding out his hand as if Milano was a cat. 'Doo wanna come 'long me, 'orse?'

Drunk. A drunken sentinel. Even Milano gives a snort of contempt. 'Ooo come 'long me,' the sentry repeats, stooping for the reins as Jack steps up behind him, the branch in his hands, fresh-dropped in the storm and hard as a musket-stock. No, this is not the man who knew his father's face, nor is it the one who kills them all, but he'll do, he'll do.

Eins, he counts off, drawing the branch back. *Zwei –*

Heavier than you'd think, an unconscious sentinel, and tying his body over your horse, nothing like as easy as it ought to be.

He pats the man down, looking for weapons, but the dolt is not only drunk, he's not even armed himself. What he does have, however, is a glossy belt of Cordovan leather, studded all along its length with silver plaques. The story of some great hunt or other – the frantic deer, the huntsmen with their horns, the hounds flying over the ground like birds. Handsome. 'This your loot?' asks Jack, dangling it before the man's nose.

The man gives a groan.

'Life,' says Jack, buckling it about his waist. He picks up the branch again, stepping back, measuring the blow. Into his head a memory, unbidden: Paul, practising his swing at *kolf*. 'You just never know what it's going to land on you next.'

The first Cyrius knows of something up is Ravello, dashing past, and then the boy, followed by the infantrymen in a startled crowd. The reason for all this seeming to be whatever the boy has slung across his saddle. Cyrius, elbowing a way to the front, arrives just as the boy cuts loose the burden from his horse and lets it fall to the ground, where it rolls about, gurgling horribly.

A man. A man with a deal of blood on the back of his head, and as black in the face as if he had suffered a seizure, and wheezing like a pair of bellows because someone has connected the knots at the wrists, tied behind his back, to the loop twisted round the man's neck. A home-made *strappado*. 'Good God, did you do this?' Cyrius cries, and, without waiting for an answer, cuts the man loose. The man takes in a whoop of air. Rolls from his side to his front, still whooping. The strangest pattern of hearts on the back of the man's coat. Makes him look like the knave from a deck of cards.

'He wouldn't quit wriggling,' says the boy.

The crowd parts again. The Shadow Man is there, leaning on his crutch. 'Who's this?' he asks, as Cyrius helps the prisoner to his knees.

'Strange,' replies the boy, as offhand as before (though with an evil flame in his eye, now Cyrius is close enough to see it), 'I didn't ask the name.'

'Then *what* is it?'

'It's a Brunswick sentinel,' replies the boy. 'I've found 'em.'

AN INTERROGATION. Never a pretty thing, 'Come with us,' the scouts had said to Cyrius, in the highest of good humours, so go with them he did – two hours, back-country, to this place which strongly reminds him of one of the little dorps there'd been around his mill.

At least that's what it must have resembled before these hundreds upon hundreds of cavalry had arrived in it. Overturned wagons to block the village streets, filled fields and gardens with their tents. And hardly had the first roofs of the place come into sight than they'd been challenged – 'HALT! Give the word!' Not just a single sentinel, but a squad of them. One had ridden up on Ravello and the Shadow Man, who had the lead; the others, still within the trees, kept their carbines trained on Cyrius and the rest. Trying to sound light-hearted Cyrius had remarked, 'No sleepy-heads in that lot,' meaning the guards, and Aesop, laughing, had gestured to the horizon. 'Look up there.'

Outlined against the sky, a dozen or so trim, dark, glistening silhouettes.

'Dragoons,' Aesop informed him. 'Been tracking us this whole last hour.'

So was this place headquarters, then?

Aesop had laughed again. 'Tilly's headquarters? Father Tilly is another good two hour away. No, no. This is our vanguard. Anholt's men. And our friend there –' (he'd gestured to the prisoner) '– he's just what they've been waiting for.'

The interrogation takes place in the village pond. The Brunswick sentinel, pulled from his horse, is placed within it on his knees, hands bound. There'd clearly been as much rain here as in the camp, the water in the pond comes up to the man's chest, and to mid-thigh of those standing round him. Much taking off of boots and rolling up of breeches; much joking and joshing of the sentinel. Then at no sign at all that Cyrius can see, one of those stood behind the man cuffs him so hard around the head that he falls face-down into the water. Cyrius gives a gasp, but hardly is the man down than they haul him up, spluttering, by the hair. A bit more banter, back and forth, then they do the same again. More laughter. 'Aesop,' Cyrius exclaims, 'they'll drown him! Why don't he tell them what they want to know?'

'He will, he will. This ain't about withstanding. This is about saving face.'

An officer, in scarlet sash, has come to stand at the edge of the pond, and seems to have taken over the questioning. 'But what is it they want to know?' Cyrius asks.

'Why Brunswick's headed west. Makes no sense to me, but the boy was sure. Ah now, look at that. The fellow's had enough.'

The prisoner is making wild butting motions with his head. The officer takes a few fussy steps backward; the men around the prisoner stand off, to give him room. 'There now,' says Aesop. 'And once he's told all, him having proved to be so brave a fellow, the officer will sign him up. All friends. You'll see.'

'Sign him up?' Cyrius repeats, amazed.

'Surely. He can't hardly go back to his Brunswick brothers, can he? He left his post, the piss-head. They'd shoot him on sight.'

The prisoner is walking, on his knees, to the edge of the pond. More butting of the head; a twisting of his shoulders too, and suddenly a high-pitched order, yelped out by the officer. 'Ah Christ,' says Aesop, suddenly. 'I have it.'

'What? Tell me! *Tell!*'

'Christian of Brunswick, the mad bastard. That's why he's headed west. He's running for the border.'

CHAPTER TWO

The Tortoise and the Hare

'… how can it be better or otherwise where men are raised out of the scum of the people by princes who have no dominion over them, nor power, for want of pay, to punish them, nor means to reward them, living only upon rapine and spoil as they do?'

Lord Chichester, James I's envoy, on Brunswick's army

AUF *WIEDERSEHN* TO the Teutoburg. Goodbye, forest and rock; good day, hedgerow and farm. With the infantry leading the way they travel over it till sunset, then turn off the road into a pasture. As it grows dark Agetha lights the lantern suspended over their heads, then all three of them bed down in the back of the wagon. Cyrius is restless. His tailbone gripes after a day of being bounced along in the saddle, and his mind is uneasy.

'I don't like this.'

'What don't you like, my man?' Agetha asks, sleepily.

Cyrius puts himself up on one elbow, considering. What doesn't he like? Well, everything, really – the fact that Utopia, their home, is in tatters beneath them; and that everywhere about them has become so exposed – open fields, unprotected roads, and their solitary lantern, beaming like a glow-worm, under this vast, dark, alien sky. If it comes down to it, what use will they be, those lackadaisical infantrymen?

'Cyrius, you're letting in the cold!' Agetha complains.

'We ought to post guards. There ought to be sentries. We're out here on our own!'

'We ain't on our own,' Agetha tells him, through a yawn. 'Look about.'

What daylight had hidden, the darkness reveals: in every field, dancing lanterns, sparkling fires. Pinheads of light, as far as the eye can see.

'There?' says Agetha, through another comfortable yawn. 'All coming together. All the world.'

HE WAKES TO the sight of Squirrel jumping up and down, clapping her hands. 'Mutti, look! Mutti, look!' Still half-asleep, he raises his head.

'God in heaven! Holy God!'

Soldiers. The landscape live with them. Coming down off the low horizon, marching through the hedges, over the fields – not kept to a course like a river but coming over everything, like a flood. The green of the landscape turning dun. He hears a trumpet. Then another. He can hear drums. Four horses in two pairs, going past the opening to their field – creamy-white horses, tossing their plumed heads, and their riders in yellow tabards with the black Habsburg eagle spread across their fronts; the same black eagle on the long skirts of their kettledrums.

Down go the drumsticks: an eight-fold bam-*boom*-bam. Cyrius sticks his head over the side of the wagon: 'Aesop! Rouse yourself! It's the war!'

From under the wagon, Aesop's head appears. 'You what?'

'The war! It's here!'

Aesop rolls himself out from under the wagon and staggers to his feet. There are men pushing through the hedge at the top of the field; musketeers, using their muskets to break through. 'Well,' says Aesop, mildly, binding back his frizz of hair, as if that makes him ready for action too, 'you're right!'

'Cyrius! Cyrius!' Agetha has not even laced herself up, but there she is, struggling to hang their sign on the pole that held the lantern. 'Cyrius!' she calls again. 'Shift yourself! Be of use here! Hold this! Watch me!' She throws back the folded canvas. He's never heard her shout so loud.

'Now, my lads, who needs breakfast? We've beer, we've pretzels, good and salt – who's in need, lads, who's in need? This is Cyrius the sutler, here's our sign, and you remember it! Who's in need, lads, who's in need?'

All morning they watch the soldiers pass. Cavalry, infantry, banners of eagles and crosses, of saints and martyrs. Past noon, and still they come: a company of sappers, who stop to fill their flasks with Cyrius's schnapps. They have picks and shovels strapped to their shoulders and come from the coal mines of the Ruhr. Now they dig tunnels, or blow tunnels up. Once they are gone, their place around the wagon is taken by an artillery company, holding up mugs, empty bottles, flasks. They roll their guns with them, and the cannon seem to cluster round them, meek as livestock. Their banner shows St Barbara. 'In ancient times her father was an 'eretic,' says their fearsome-looking sergeant, 'a Lutheran, I don't doubt. And when he killed his daughter for her true faith, the lightning struck him down. And that's us,' the man declares, proudly. 'Thunder n' lightning. That's we.'

'It's a world within the world, dear heart,' Agetha tells Cyrius, seeing his face. 'Another universe.'

Every time he looks up, there she is – leaning over the edge of the wagon, bargaining, selling. The level of stock within the wagon is going down, and in Cyrius's imagination the coin, in little piles, is mounting up. What a partner she is. What a helpmeet. He's tried to do his bit – climbing in to stand beside her, waving a tankard over his head – but against Agetha, with her loosened hair and easy banter, he comes a poor second, clearly. 'Sooner buy off her, friend,' one cheery sapper tells him, 'if it's all the same to you!' So Cyrius takes himself off to sit on the ground, Utopia over his knees, and, with bodkin and yarn, starts patching and darning away as best as he can.

Late afternoon and the rearguard catches up with them. There are wagons like theirs, and a gang of washerwomen, who have their children with them, for Squirrel to run around with. Cyrius is watching the children scampering about in the evening sun like so many baby rabbits when he becomes aware of some heavy gaze laid upon him. He turns, and there's a man, stood off on his own. The man looks away, sharpish, and makes as if he's fully occupied in opening out the most prodigious-looking pack Cyrius has ever seen, a marvel of flaps and straps and pockets.

'You come a good ways, I see,' Cyrius calls over, politely, that seeming to be what such baggage might suggest. Nothing to give any inkling what this fellow's trade might be, whatsoever.

The man brings himself upright, and casts a slow, dramatic eye in Cyrius's direction. 'You serving?' he asks. The tone is suspicious. Serving? wonders Cyrius. Was the man asking what they had in the way of food and drink? Not the most courteous of addresses, perhaps, and in any case, Agetha, bless her, had sold them almost out.

Ah, *serving*. A soldier. 'Not I, friend,' Cyrius replies.

'Thought as much,' the man says, with a sniff. 'You get an eye.' He jerks his chin toward the wagon, where Agetha still stands, outlined against the paling sky. 'So that's yours, is it?'

''Tis so,' Cyrius replies.

'Horse and all?'

'My horse, too.'

'Mmph,' says the man, going back to his pack. Cyrius waits a moment. 'So,' he begins again, when no more is forthcoming, 'you serving yourself, I take it?'

'That I do, friend,' says the man, without turning his head. 'I serve my own affairs, is what I do. And mind 'em, too. And as a rule, I find that serves me well. You get me?'

Got you. Cyrius is about to respond (something along the lines of *There's a boy round here, you might know him, for he must have learned his manners the same place as you*) when he hears Agetha give a cry of welcome, and there's Aesop, hair stuck to his cheeks with sweat, and a grin on his face from ear to ear.

'*Tag*, Cyrius, my friend,' he says, walking up. 'You want to know what's going on?'

A lesson in geography. Aesop stands by the wagon, and takes from his pocket a stick of plumbago. Before Cyrius can stop him, on the dry and silvery wood of the cart, he draws a great-sized

X

'Hoi!' Cyrius begins, in protest.

'Hush,' whispers Agetha. 'This is important. Watch.'

Aesop has gathered a crowd. Even the stranger has come over, sticking out his chest and somehow contriving, or so it appears to Cyrius, to be making a great show of keeping himself that little bit apart.

'Now that,' says Aesop, pointing to the X, 'is us.' He moves a pace along the wagon, and draws a stick man wearing a feathered hat. Agetha, feeling Cyrius twitch, gives his hand a squeeze.

Aesop, with a grin, rubs out one of the stick man's arms. At once the washerwomen start a hissing, like cats. 'Brunswick,' continues Aesop. 'Thank you, ladies.' He strides to the far end of the wagon and slashes down it a hard black line. 'Border with the Dutch,' he tells them, strolling back. 'That's where Brunswick's headed. And if he should get over it, he's safe. Him and all them lovely silver thalers.' He turns about. Under the straggly wheat of his beard, the grin has returned. 'But this,' he says, 'this is what there is between him and it.'

Another line scribed on the cart, but this one wiggling and wavering. And another after that. Eight, in total. 'Now,' says Aesop. 'Who can tell me what these are?'

'Snakes,' suggests Squirrel, and the washerwomen laugh.

'Not snakes, little lamb,' says Aesop. He taps at the first. 'These are rivers. We've scouted the whole of it, and that's all this country is. Rivers and fields. So what this is, good people –' (and the grin grows broader yet) '– is the tortoise and the hare. Brunswick may have the lead of us, but there's seven more rivers to go, and he has to get all of his army and all of his wagons over each and every one. So each one, and he's closer to safety, but each one slows him down. And then we gain on him.' He taps the rivers in sequence. 'One, two, three, four, five, six – the Shadow Man, he's up country, he says it'll be here. Stadtlohn.'

There's a dry, sour taste in Cyrius's mouth. 'What'll be there?'

'Why,' says Aesop, blinking in surprise, 'our battleground.'

Dusk. The sour taste in Cyrius's mouth has been joined by a queasy fluttering in his belly. What would he give for sight of those raggle-taggle infantry now?

'My man?' Agetha puts a hand to his forehead. 'My man, you look unwell.'

He seizes the hand. 'Aggie, don't you think we should be gone?'

'Gone?' She sits back on her heels, amazed. 'Gone where? Gone why?'

'Somewhere else. Somewhere as won't have a battlefield for a neighbour.' His gaze is taken by the children – Squirrel, running and giggling with the rest, her cap fallen off, her brown curls bobbing. Into his head there comes the vision of his apprentice, face-down in the water-splash, the open surrender of the boy's outspread arms. He pulls Agetha toward him. 'Back country,' he says. 'Out of harm's way. We did well today, yes? We can set ourselves up. Start anew.'

'But we can't go yet, my man.' She shakes her head. 'They have to pay.'

He stares at her. Her purse – their takings – is there before him, looped through her belt. And the purse is fat – swollen like a little belly itself.

'What do you mean, they have to pay?'

'After the battle.' She sounds puzzled to be explaining this to him. 'They leave their mark with us for now, and then they pay us after.' Colour rises to her cheek. 'When they – when they have loot.'

'They pay us after?' He makes a snatch for the purse at her waist, but even as he seizes it, he can feel how horribly light it is. Pulling it open, he up-ends it into his lap. Out they come – scraps of paper, scraps of cloth; some signed with an initial, most with no more on them than the writer's mark. Some of the scraps – torn off from placket, say, or cuff – were marked with no more than a thumbprint, in what might have been no more than mud. There was a button. There was a piece of broken pipe. He thought of his schnapps, poured down their throats; the sausage sold off, slice by slice. The baccy, the pretzels, the cheese...

'Aggie!' he exclaims. 'Dear God, don't tell me. What have you done?'

*

Sunrise. Up it comes, relentless as ever. Cyrius opens to it one baleful, bloodshot eye. Up above him, in the wagon, Agetha was either sleeping or obdurately pretending so to do.

He'd called her a fool.

She's called him an addle-pot.

He'd accused her of not knowing her business.

She'd told him his millstones had more brains than he.

Never an angry word between them before, but now –

He lies where he is and lets the wrack of his good fortune wash about him.

A week ago, I was a man of business. Now look at us – on our bumbones. All but refugees.

Bruised from the hard ground, out he crawls, and lifts himself painfully to his feet.

The faintest sound, like a book dropping from a shelf. It comes again. The sun takes no notice, continues to rise; no dog has been set barking; the birds don't leave the trees. A cock-crow from across the fields is louder. So why is it that Cyrius, like every other soul that he can see, has come to the entrance of their fields, as to the doorways of their houses, to stand there, listening?

A grunt behind him. The stranger is there. Chops dark with stubble, and the rime of sleep dried round his mouth. But the man sticks his chest out, as if to prove he's more than equal to the cool of the day, and when the sound comes a third time, he cocks his head toward it and remarks, 'There'll be fortunes made out there today. Fortunes.'

'That so?' Cyrius replies.

'Ho yes. Fortunes. And I should know.'

A strange thing, how the idea of it should both terrify Cyrius, yet hearing that far-off noise, so pull at him. He turns to the stranger. 'You've seen a battle, have you?'

'Seen one? Seen one? Me?' The stranger looks about, as if checking for eavesdroppers. 'I've seen one. Se-ee-een 'em all,' the man says, rocking on his heels. Another glance about them. 'Not a thing I'd share with anyone, you understand, but –' He lowers his voice. 'Heard a bit of your trouble last night.' A nod toward the wagon.

'She's ruined us,' says Cyrius. Why shouldn't he admit it? What more did he have to lose? 'What little the storm left us, she's given away. And all she got off them is their *mark*.'

'There you have it,' says the stranger. 'Women. Can't leave 'em in charge of owt.' He leans closer. 'I said to myself, when I saw you, now there's a man could do with a change in his fortunes. Ain't that so? And out there –' (he nods again, this time toward the horizon) '– out there, with the right of kind of help, is where he would find it. That's where the wise man would take himself. Especially if he has a veteran in such matters. To assist. That's what the wise man would do.'

'If that's what the wise man would do, why don't he do it?' Cyrius snaps, and the man takes him by the shoulders, and turns him round. There is the wagon (still no stirrings from within). Tethered beside it, Cyrius's nag.

'Because the wise man,' the stranger is saying, 'would get himself, and his friend what knows, out there on a *horse*. Else how's he going to carry his loot?'

Loot. The stranger stands back, perhaps the better to observe the leafy sprouting of this notion in Cyrius's mind. Sticks out his hand. 'Korbl,' he says. 'At your service, friend. Don't pay it no mind, but I'm what you'll hear them calling hereabouts a crow.'

MID-MORNING, 5TH OF August, year of our Lord 1623. Thirty miles below the Dutch border. Tilly's vanguard (his premier troops, under the command of Field Marshal von Anholt) are watching the rear of Brunswick's army as it struggles across its second river of the day. Every so often the harrying attacks from

Anholt's cavalry draws out from Brunswick's musketeers a short, neat line, like a woolly hyphen, of fluffs of smoke; and a blink of time after, the crack of shot. From up above the river the noise becomes a word: *ra-tatta*. There's no thought, any longer, of heroic pursuit. Brunswick is travelling with sixteen thousand men and a baggage train of four thousand more; a greater number, all told, than the population of Berlin. When his army crosses a river, that river ceases to exist, becomes instead a flood plain of sunken fords and broken banks; as his army traverses the countryside, it leaves a track like the foot of a tornado. Tilly's troops are not about to lose him, and they know it.

Titus and Holger, watching with the vanguard, are puzzling on the subject of Brunswick's musketeers, or on their breed of muskets, rather. Titus, tilting his head to separate out the syllables of the *ra-tatta*, has just asked ruminatively, 'What are they? Why don't that sound right?' when the boy, stood behind him, says quietly, 'I reckon they're snaplocks.'

Snaplocks?

'I don't see no match,' the boy continues.

Sure enough, there is the smoke from the muskets themselves, but none of those tiny tell-tale pinpricks of red you'd expect from the musketeers' match-cord. Holger twists his head to address the Shadow Man behind him, leaning on his crutch. 'Shady,' he says. 'I do believe that boy of yours might have learned something, by God.'

A final castanet of shot, and the musketeers turn and wade their way across the river. The jeering of the cavalry reaches the watchers on the hill.

Stood a little apart from the rest is the Brunswick sentinel. To keep him from any foolish ideas of dashing off, the man has been tied round the waist to the stirrup of a cavalry horse. That tying him is an officer's wide silk sash. It gives the sentinel the look of having been done up as a present, something of the air of Hercules as dressed by Omphale.

The scouts' dogs circle and snarl at him. As the last of the musketeers completes the crossing, the Brunswick sentinel raises a hand in melancholy salute.

Here we are, on the banks of the river Vechte, a scant twenty miles from the border, at the tiny village of Stronfeld. Stronfeld itself is silent, all its people fled, but the fields before it are as live with movement as a tray of maggots. No-one in all of Brunswick's army dares to sleep. Instead they move around their watch-fires, from one group to the next. Every so often, from the outskirts of the encampment, there's the sound of shots. The marauders from Tilly's cavalry aren't sleeping, either.

In his tent, Christian of Brunswick lays his left arm across his forehead. It still doesn't feel as it should; the gesture has lost something of its speed, its flair – its *élan*. It used to be the right arm he would lay across his eyes like this, a gesture which he'd always felt spoke powerfully of a great one in private conference with his soul.

The good right arm was lost at Fleurus in the Spanish Netherlands almost a year ago, almost to the day. The limb came off to a fanfare. He had a medal cast. *Altera restat*, it read. The other remains.

He's owed a victory.

And he's been here before, snatched triumph from disaster as few less confident men might have done. Before Fleurus there was Hochst – another river crossing, yet he escaped, he, his cavalry, above all his precious baggage train, and from the same Imperial army, Tilly's army, too. How to change this to that?

Christian swings his feet down from the bed, and doubles his audience at once, as the sound wakes his servant. 'My slippers,' he says, pointing to his feet. 'My robe.'

The slippers are lined with miniver; the robe is smocked and striped: red, purple, gold. He's a handsome man, is Christian,

these rich clothes suit him, and there is security in them as well
as comfort. His movements, and the lighting of his lantern,
have set off further stirrings from outside: he hears his guards,
suddenly aware, out there at the tent's fringed doorway. Perhaps
throughout his army his soldiers turn to each other, not knowing
why, only that something has changed.

There is still light in the sky. He snaps his fingers. 'What's
the hour?'

'Past eight, most worthy.'

'Bring my secretary.'

Steal a march, he thinks, *and steal another victory.* In his mind's
eye he sees that ageing greybeard, Tilly, at the head of all his
troops, facing an empty field, while he, Christian, winters in
Holland, recruits, renews...

His secretary is there, but his audience is history, all Europe,
God himself.

Heavenly Father. Save me, I pray –

God is here. God is here. He watches his servant.

Save me from evil. Save me from sin. I put myself in Your care –

'Write,' Christian commands.

*– body and soul and all that I have. Let Your angels be with me,
amen.*

The secretary sits, board on his knees.

'To my marshals. Knyphausen. Isenberg. Sent by my hand, et
cetera et cetera.' He flaps a gold-striped cuff. 'The train shall be
ready to move in three hours. The troops are to follow immediately after.'

Long before sunrise, they will be gone.

Five miles back, or thereabouts, Balthasar sits propped against
his pack, face turned to that darkening sky. His cough has lately
sent a new root deep into his chest – or from his chest, there is
now a thorny shoot growing up into his throat. To sleep flat is
impossible.

In fact any sleep is impossible – all round him he hears men turn from side to side in search of it. The boy has abandoned all pretence at it; instead he's dropped into one of those open-eyed reveries of his. These alarm Balthasar – unless you look for the boy's breathing you'd almost think him dead – so he clears his throat (with his usual caution), and says, 'Your father would do that. I saw that, many a time.'

The boy's head turns toward him. It used to be that the opening to any conversation would be akin to the stick you might use to spring a trap, but in these last few days of the great pursuit, that has improved.

'My father?'

'Sleeping with his eyes open. A trick I've never mastered, I might say. He said it was when he did his thinking. Is that what you do, too?'

A shrug. 'I guess.'

'So what are you thinking?'

'Same as everybody else,' says the boy. But he's turned himself on his elbow, as if for further conversation. Those eyes shine up at Balthasar, pale as starlight. 'What'll happen tomorrow.'

Balthasar pulls his blanket higher up his chest. 'Whatever that is, it'll be no concern of ours.'

The pale eyes narrow. '*How*, no concern?' asks the boy.

'Not our place, a battlefield. Our job is done.'

A silence. It seems to Balthasar, watching the boy's face, that some small struggle is taking place within. If so, it is the briefest thing, because when the boy speaks, his voice is unchanged. 'Because we're scouts.'

'Indeed.'

'Not soldiers.'

Balthasar pulls the blanket to his chin. 'You have learned something.'

'Right,' says the boy.

*

Meantime...

Meantime, approaching river number three, following that fleeing army's track, Cyrius is being regaled with yet another chapter in Korbl's life-story.

'So there I was in Munich. Now, did I tell you of Munich? I did? By God I must trust that face of yours. There's not many I tell this tale to, that's a fact.'

Korbl, it seems, has found his tongue. Even Cyrius's nag has begun to hang its head.

Patience, Cyrius tells himself. *Think on them silver thalers.*

In his mind's eye he can see them – two innocent little bagsful. One for each pocket; he can almost feel the weight of them against his legs as he strides away. As he strides back to Agetha. He won't be greedy. A couple of bagsful, that's all he asks.

'And I never tell a lie, me, never,' comes Korbl's voice. 'Now, when I was in Frankfurt – Christ's stones, that was a time. You tell me what you make of this –'

The moon pours forth its radiance, stars wink upon them; in the fields ripe for harvest, the still corn bends its head. The night of the 5th of August, 1623. Before the night of the 6th, in the fields and woods around the village of Stadtlohn, eight thousand men will lie, dying or dead.

And when, hours after Korbl and Cyrius pass him, when Balthasar wakes in the gentle dawn, he will be aware of two things simultaneously: one, that he has to cough, and that as he coughs, his blanket is instantly marked with a feather of blood; and two, that the boy is gone.

THE ART OF breakfasting on horseback: another skill some never master, much like sleeping with your eyes open. Not Ravello, though. Ravello can eat, hold his horse, and scan the landscape ahead through that exciting new discovery, the spying-glass, all in one.

Che bella giornata. The sky seems rubbed with some soft powder, masking what will no doubt reveal itself as a fierce summer blue. Zephyrs of heat – or in this water-laden land-scape, of moisture, perhaps – already rise from the horizon, quivering against the spyglass's lens, and everywhere he turns its eye, the world seems washed and sparkling. It's the kind of morning makes a man glad that he's alive.

And here, at the fore-edge of the most formidable army in Europe.

Instead of with that chaotic rabble out there.

Through the lens he can see them: the infantry, the glinting uprights of the pikes, the cavalry horses – many, apparently, still unsaddled – and in the rear the wagons, with figures running behind them, hurling in bag and baggage... It's seven in the morning, that delicate haze already being burned away, and the watch-fires of Christian's army are still smouldering, aban-doned, there on the Vechte's far bank. Is it possible, Ravello asks himself, that what he sees out there is an army that has simply overslept? *Oh, Madonna mia* – what a joke, if so. What a bitter joke on some.

He takes another bite of his breakfast – thick rusk, new baked this morning, and made a little less of a jaw-breaker by having a cup of melted butter poured over it. The rusk is sweet and dry, the butter salt, and both came his way courtesy of the company of Anholt's dragoons there on the riverbank opposite, picking over the detritus of Christian's camp. He watches them (lifting this, poking under that), his head filled with the sound of his own jaws munching – and then he hears something else. He swings about, so abruptly that his horse takes a side-step in surprise. And there's the boy, one hand raised in greeting, the other shielding his eyes. "*Tag*,' the boy says, familiarly, riding alongside.

The boy intrigues Ravello. One, that he should be such a cold-hearted little rogue; two, that he's got that way so young, and three – well, three, everything else.

'*Buongiorno*,' Ravello responds.

'That them?' the boy asks, pointing ahead, where even to the naked eye the horizon is disordered by the press of Brunswick's fleeing army.

'Them indeed,' says Ravello, and passes the spyglass to him. As the boy holds the glass to his eye, and gives a whistle, a question occurs.

'You are alone? No Capitano Balthasar?'

'*Ach*, he ain't interested no more,' says the boy. He has the glass trained on the horizon still. 'Says his business is done.'

'But yours is not?'

'Look there,' says the boy in answer, passing the spyglass back.

Ravello looks. Far to the left, a body of horse is approaching. The shimmer coming off the ground lifts them as if they were floating. Unlike the dragoons, these riders are armoured as fully as lobsters, and each point of light – on helmets, on flanges at shoulders or knees – flares in turn along the line. They must be half a mile away or more, but some trick of the air has the drum of the horses' hooves bouncing around Ravello and the boy as if they were in their midst. As they pass, they seem to own the world.

The boy gives a grin. 'Don't tell the Shadow Man,' he says, 'but truth be told, I ain't no scout.'

A shout from across the river. As if the cavalry had been a signal, the dragoons are mounting up. 'Time to move?' Ravello calls in reply, and the captain of dragoons, who knows Ravello of old, calls back, 'First to the field, first to the glory!' Then the man looks again.

'Who's that with you?'

'Jag!' Ravello calls back. 'This is Jag!'

The cry comes back across the river. 'The lad who found 'em?'
'That's the one!'
'Bring him with you!' calls the captain. 'We like his luck!'

THEY REACH THE next river mid-morning. It's what, their
fourth? Brunswick is losing track. It's even shallower, this, than
the last. And there's a bridge – there, look, upstream.

A bridge so small, so thin and mean, it looks as if it's been
constructed out of pins. Put sixteen cats upon it and it would
collapse, let alone sixteen thousand men. How can these puny
things be such impediments? These foot-high bridges that give
way at once, these rivers that are scarcely more than drains –
they suck his guns into their mud, foul wheels and axles, slow
his progress to a crawl. His rearguard is now three long miles
away, and has been harassed with attacks all morning. Faint
cries, like birds, have tormented his progress for hours. *Those
tigers, those jackals, those wolves...* when he looks behind he can
see them, their mass on the horizon: what might be trees, or
brush, or scrub, dark like that, but moving ever forward.

God is his witness. God is here. It's so close, that border, now.

Christian of Brunswick urges his horse through his body-
guard, down the bank to stand in the stream, fetlock-deep. His
forehead burns. In just over a month, he will be twenty-four
years old. He lifts his sword.

'Onwards!'

They make the fifth crossing and by now it is obvious that what
is coming after them is not single companies of marauders, but
an entire army. As if the whole landscape was lifting itself up
like a wave. Noon, and they make the sixth crossing at a run.
Twenty thousand souls, running a race. Those at the back run
the fastest of all. They leave their spoor behind them: broken

shoes, packs and bundles, exhausted horses, the laggard and the lost. That great dark wave swallows it all.

And then, before him, like something from a dream, there is the village of Stadtlohn, with its bridge, its good stone bridge, and here, he thinks, here, is where we stand. Here we turn, here we fight. Like Hochst. The train goes through. His wagons, his silver – safe. The night comes down. And then?

We vanish from their sight.

He sends Knyphausen back to the sixth crossing, to face whatever may emerge from the woods on its far bank. At the seventh crossing, he puts his musketeers, and behind them, his infantry.

It is nearly two in the afternoon. His men are in Stadtlohn, they have the bridge. As he rides from the village with his body-guard and colonels, he rides with the protests of the villagers in his ears, as his men go about the business of plundering food. As he rides toward the sixth crossing, the end of the baggage train finally clears it.

And there is the crossing, and the woods beyond, and a small rise to the right of the woods, which he barely registers before the reaction of the troops in front of him – one he has seen so many times before, a kind of pulling upright, and shouts of notice, confirmation, as much as of alarm – tells him the first of Tilly's soldiers have come in sight.

CHAPTER THREE

Stadtlohn

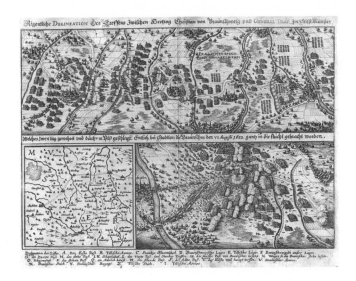

'Of all other military actions, the chiefest is that of embattelling, or ordering an army for combat…'

John Cruso, *Militarie Instructions for the Cavallrie*

WE CAME OUT of the wood –

Later, he will use those words exactly. Sitting with the scouts, as each recounts their day in turn, that's what he'll say. We came out of the wood.

There'd been this tumult up ahead of them all morning. They'd tracked it through trampled cornfields, over ground left as broken as if it had been ploughed. Its rump flashed sometimes white, when the baggage train was exposed, then dun, as Brunswick's infantry closed round it. And always, three, four fields ahead. They'd passed its leavings – horses wandering here or there, endless hats and coats as those who'd been wearing them grew hotter and hotter under the August sun. Apart from them, and what they tracked, the landscape was as if it had been emptied by a plague. Then they crossed the fifth river, and instead of that army being three, four fields ahead, it was only two. The dragoons sent up a roar; when the roar turned into singing –

Thou art a shie–ie–ie–ield for me

Alleluia

I – Will – Not – Be – Afraid

A-A-A-A-lell-UUUUUUIA

– they were close enough for the last in Brunswick's army to hear them, to turn about.

The captain of dragoons had cantered past. 'Stay with us, brothers! First to the riches! First to the glory!'

They were following a field path, with a cornfield over its hedge. As he kicked up Milano from a jog to a trot he saw there were women hiding in the corn, bobbing their capped heads up and down, like partridges. He called out to Ravello, 'Who are they?'

'Bad luck! *Molto male!* You've not seen them before?'

'Not seen nothing before!' The path rose in a gentle slope. He kicked up Milano again. He heard Ravello calling after him, 'What do you mean, you've not seen nothing?'

'Never been on a battlefield!' He pointed to himself. 'First time!'

Then they were over the crest of the slope, he and Milano, and two fields ahead the deep, deep green of a wood, with the last of Brunswick's army vanishing between the trees as if they were being pulled into it, like streamers.

*

The edge of the wood seemed to mark some kind of pause. The singing ceased. The first of the dragoons to reach it rode back and forth around its edge suspiciously. Only once they'd signalled all was clear did anyone dismount. Dragoons do their fighting on foot. There was a rough line of horses forming, tied between two trees. As he led Milano to it, Ravello caught him up.

'You've never been in battle before?'

'Never.' But all around them there was a tightening of sword-belts, a checking of pistols, a sharing-out of powder and shot. Too late to send him back now. 'Look,' he said. 'The way I see it, I don't do this, what's the point of me?'

Everything Ravello would like to say to him at that moment was right there in the man's face. But when Ravello finally spoke, it was only with the question, 'But you can fight – yes?'

'I'm handy with a sword. I ain't got one. I ain't never fired a pistol as yet neither, but when I was a kid with a catapult, I was a dead shot.' He felt the flutter of something way down in his gut. 'Yes, I can fight. And I'm going onto that field, with you or without.'

Ravello stared at the ground as if for inspiration; finding it not, he turned his gaze to the sky. 'With me,' he said, at last. 'But you stay as close as if you're glued to me, you hear?' He pointed to a spot by his ankle. 'I want you close to me as that. And I do this for one thing only, which is, I let you go out there on your own, the Shadow Man, he will kill me instead. And if you get *me* killed, I come back and *haunt* you, *capisce?*' A great breath. 'And now you follow me.'

Because in order to come out of a wood, first you must go in.

Into the trees – so dense with bramble that they had to wade with arms above their heads. There was laughter to begin with; gradually that ceased.

Innumerable tiny trailing threads of cobweb in the air. And no sound now, other than the pressing-down of boots on the carpet of stems. Then the noise of baying dogs, and then drums, and a hiss from Ravello – 'Jag, remember, you stay with me.' Ravello is half stooped-over, walking as if he were edging down a tunnel; Ravello, Jack sees, has sweat at the roots of his hair. Everyone is in that stooped half-crouch, he is so himself. He hears the dogs again, then there's a sudden whoop and then there's Holger, gripping the chain of one of the hounds, the chain wrapped round his fist, leaping as the dog leaps, and the dog, for so long silent, is up on its hind legs, baying and pawing the air. A cry of 'Steady, steady!' then someone shouting 'Muskets!' then a cry of 'Here!' and someone else goes crashing through the trees ahead.

It's a hunt. We're waiting for the quarry. Waiting for it to show.

His heart is beating so fast it's like a wire vibrating in the middle of his chest.

More shouting, weakly, further off, in front.

That wasn't us.

They're close as that.

I. Will. Not. Be. Afraid.

Was that more drumming, or was that his heartbeat still?

Left and right, in a line through the trees, they wait.

The drumming coming closer. More dog howls in reply. The drummers squeezing in between them, all making that same great *BAM-badda-bam.* 'Make a way, friend,' says one, elbowing past, then from directly ahead there comes the strangest sound, as if something in the trees had spat. The drummer yells an 'Oy!' of warning. To their left, one of the dragoons drops to his knees, points his musket upward, fires, and there's a yell and then the crash of a body falling through the branches. *Sniper,* Jack thinks, and then, *Sniper. Son of a bitch!* as the sound of the man's fall is drowned by a shout of furious rage, the same shout erupting from every throat, as if that one bullet had been aimed at the entire army. Every man who has one is banging on his breastplate, and if you have none, why then, you just throw your head back and roar.

And he roars with them. He hears their noise, their incredible noise, from further back than he can see. It seems impossible that anything could stand against them. He hears himself say '*Fuck*' and Ravello puts out an arm, as if to steady him. Holds out a flask. 'Drink,' Ravello says. 'You'll need it.'

The water in the flask is warm as blood. Something else is pushed into his grasp. A pistol, primed and ready. 'When you need it, steady it,' Ravello hisses. 'Steady it, and ease it.'

And now the drums again, and now he knows what's going to happen, everybody does, you hear it in the shouts, the groans and wailings of the dogs, the *BAM* of each drumbeat, the banging of your heart –

When the line stepped forward, he almost expected the trees to step forward with them.

And then they came out of the wood, and the world unfolded, instantly, to twenty times its proper size. That was the first shock. Surely no ground was ever this open, this wide. *Christ, we're ants...* And there, maybe two hundred yards away –

That's them. The enemy.

And there they were, with yet another river right behind them.

His first instinct was to run. Left or right, like a hare. With a sort of cold curiosity he saw what must be their captain, in yellow sash, half-raise his arm for the signal to fire.

From being an ant, now he was a giant. An unmissable target. The front of his body felt like it was the biggest thing on the field. There were cries again of 'Steady! Hold it steady there!' and he heard Ravello say, under his breath, 'Too far,' then cross himself. The figure in the yellow sash dropped his arm. Puff after puff of smoke – the top half of each musketeer disappeared behind it – and then the spitting noise again, but this time with an extra whistling top note.

And there, where the land dipped as the noise of that first volley broke, a flock of feeding birds of every size, every shape, took off from the ground.

He knew it as surely as if the Shadow Man had been there, whispering in his ear. *Marshland...*

Ravello pulled at his sleeve. 'Jag, over there! Look!'

He turned. There on the rise beside the woods, what he took at first to be black cattle. Only when he saw the men running back and forth between them did he realize what they were. Cannon. Their cannon, Tilly's cannon, positioned on the rise.

'Wait for the smoke!' Ravello was saying. 'Cover! When they fire!'

Some five or ten of the men they faced were running forward, bringing them into range. Jack glanced back at the cannon. Were they ready? Would they fire? He looked at the men running toward them, and saw one of them kneel, saw him adjust his sights, glance up, adjust again, and thought, *Not me you don't, you bastard, not today*, and as if the thought itself was enough to raise his arm, brought the pistol up. He took a line down the barrel. Steady and easy... The trigger was stiff as a key. Steady and easy... *the hell, how?*

A snap of noise, the *fzzt* of powder. The jolt sang down his wrist. He saw the barrel jerk as he fired and knew the shot went wide, went wide by yards, so he grabbed the pistol by the barrel and hurled it through the air, end over end over end, to wallop into the side of the musketeer's head. The man gave a yell, lost his hat, dropped his musket, went down.

From around him, a rough, astonished-sounding cheer that broke into separate shouts of warning. The rise had disappeared. A solid roll of white was tearing down upon them. Its speed was incredible; its thunder made you duck, made you shield yourself, crouch low. Curled, with their backs toward it, the white engulfed them in a blast of heat, hot as opening an oven door. A blur – no, merely the sense of one, of something hurtling overhead, as if you saw its speed, not it, and then the ground seemed to convulse. Pellets of earth came pattering down around him, then ceased. He was alone in this drifting world of white. He walked forward. Figures, like puppets behind a sheet. Somewhere, Ravello's voice. A dent in the ground ahead; the turf folded like a blanket, and on the other side of it, a boot. A little further ahead, something else, enclosed in dented clamshell of back and breastplate, like an enormous locket.

This is where those men were, he thinks, and then, *This is what cannon do.*

The white about him becomes grey. A man, running toward him out of the grey, musket held over his head. A wild and wavering cry came from the man's open mouth. Jack finds himself thinking *I can do better than that* and as the man runs at him he bellows into the man's face. The man swings the musket at him, Jack seizes it, and for an instant, over the barrel of the musket, their faces meet. He sees the stain left by the flash of black powder round the man's nose and mouth, the man's stubby lashes, the flaring colours of each iris. The man is puffing, trying to wrest the musket from Jack's grasp, so instead of pulling away, Jack shoves the musket into the man's chest. The man staggers backward, losing his grip. Jack lifts the musket up, and the man hurls himself against Jack's legs. They both fall flat. All Jack can think of is keeping the musket out of the man's reach, so he holds it away, with arms above his head, and from being round Jack's legs, now the man is crawling up him; the sort of rolling, breathless grappling you got with some of the children in Belle-Dame – the ones who couldn't fight.

The man's face appears over Jack's chest.

You idiot. He jerks the stock of the musket as hard as he can into the man's forehead.

A cry. The man's hands, which had been grasping Jack's shirt, clutch instead at his own skull. Jack brings the musket down again. The hands reopen and the man slides off him. Jack levers himself up. The man had been trying to crawl away; when he realizes Jack is standing over him, he curls himself into a ball. Looking down, Jack sees the stock of the musket has split. *Trash… their weapons are trash.*

And they can't fight.

And this, he realizes, is how it is. You're in this world of smoke and fire, your fellows might be all around you but you'll never see them, all you'll see will be what comes out of the smoke at you, and that's all you have to deal with. The thing in front. And now he does hear Ravello's voice, and calls back, 'Here! Here!' loud as he can. He holds the musket by the barrel, like a club. The smoke is thinning. He looks down. He is standing in water. He'd reached the river. Pebbles. Sparkles. He thinks he can see tiny fishlets, darting. He walks on.

HALF-THREE IN THE AFTERNOON, and Cyrius has just come in sight of his first battlefield. Nothing of it is as he had expected.

Ask Cyrius what he had expected – well, had you asked him so, before this afternoon – he'd have answered something like chess, perhaps, only with many life-size pieces, and all of them moving according to some clear, well-regulated plan; with choirs of trumpets, massed and gleaming ranks of men, the bending of legs and bowing of knees and combatants approaching one another as formally as great ones at a masque.

It would most certainly not have been this. These roiling clouds of grey and white. These whirling clots and straggling lines of men. The appalling lightning-like flashes in the smoke. The riderless horses, seeming in their terror not even to know to put the battlefield behind them. The cannon, there on the bald rise, hurling their shot overhead; the crowd at the battle-field's edge, God above, as if this was a prize-fight at a fair; and all about him, everywhere, this terrible noise, which is both one sound and has somehow distinguishable within it every scream and detonation of which it is made up... *This is hell*, Cyrius thinks. *This is what it sounds like down in hell.*

In a few years' time an engraver named Matthäus Merian will create a fine tri-partite study of Stadtlohn. Across the top half of the plate the long pursuit and all eight rivers; along the bottom, at the left, a map, to show those unfamiliar exactly where that long pursuit took place, and bottom right, a close-up of the battle. Artistic licence will reduce the blinding quantities of smoke to ostrich-feather puffs, and show battalions marching back and forth like so many squares of felt, all bristling with pike. Brunswick's great baggage train is shown as it was caught, desperately trying to get over the bridge below Stadtlohn, while the centre of the battle resembles some great termite nest, under attack. The bodies of the fallen – tiny, black and crushed – litter the field.

Cyrius does not of course have this engraving to help him make sense of what's happening in front of him and nor does he have Korbl. Korbl has marched himself straight down to the front rank of the jostling spectators, many of whom he seems to know.

All Cyrius has to help him is the dragoon's horse-master.

'Your first?'

Cyrius can do no more than nod.

'I thought so. You've that gob-swiped look.'

As the man speaks there are two of those lightning-like flashes from within the smoke, a matching pair, in brilliant sulphurous yellow, and two rocketing spires of smoke shoot upward, sharp as pine trees in a forest. The spectators at the field's edge set up a raucous cheering. They're women, mostly, and have the air of being in some sort of readiness. They have baskets on their backs, and many are gloved, the gloves as heavy as an iron-worker's. The few men in amongst them are sorry fellows, with hooks for hands or stumps for legs, and had looked on Korbl, pushing his way through them, with undisguised envy.

The flashes dull to red eyes, glaring through the grey. The pine trees of smoke fall back to earth. 'Ah, we're pressing 'em, we're pressing 'em,' comments the horse-master, approvingly. 'But if they don't stand, they die.' He coughs as the smoke drifts past, hocks out a mouthful of phlegm. 'Can't stay this way much longer, that's for sure.'

Behind them, visible through the trees, the lines of horses shift. There's the odd stray whicker, to which Cyrius's nag replies. 'He's a novice an' all, I take it,' the horse-master remarks, knowingly. 'Friend, out there an untried horse'll kill you faster'n a bullet. Schilling, and you leave him here with me. I'll keep an eye.'

The nag is pulling at its reins. 'Friend, I'd leave him with you if I could,' says Cyrius, 'but I ain't got as much as a pfennig. 'Tis the whole reason I'm here.'

A breeze moves the smoke from the nearest corner of the battlefield. The women at the edge of the crowd lean toward it; Korbl amongst them, that commodious pack hefted onto his shoulders.

'Down to your crusts, eh?' the horse-master is saying, sympathetically. 'I guessed as much. Saw you with your friend down there, and I thought to myself, there's one must have some pressing need. There's one whose face don't fit. Not with them.'

'Who are they?' Cyrius asks, in wonderment. 'What are they doing here?'

'Why, they're the crows, ain't they?' the horse-master replies. 'It's how they make a living. Wait till the fighting's done, then they go onto the field and pick over the dead.'

Meanwhile...

Meanwhile, Ravello. Who for the last ten minutes has been lying as flat to the ground as he can press himself, with the wheel of an enemy gun-carriage revolving above his head, and two dead oxen lying in front of him. There are also four gabions – great baskets of packed earth – which should have been wedging the gun-carriage into place, except that last time this cannon was fired, it burst. It lies there now, looking like Vulcan put his thumbs down the barrel and ripped it apart. Beyond the oxen, which took half the blast, lie the remains of the gun-crew, who took the rest of it. One of them is no more than a pair of eloquently misaligned forearms.

No matter. This cannon may have had it, but Brunswick has plenty more, and from the scant and hasty cover they hurled themselves into here, Ravello and the dragoons can watch as the cannonballs fly shrieking over their heads, arc down behind them to strike the hard summer ground, and lift again to go bounding through the companies of Anholt's foot. And between them and the guns, what might be a whole battalion of Brunswick's infantry, who are putting so much lead into the air that the wheel of the gun-carriage is being spun about by it, like a child's top.

They'd come too far. The smoke had lifted, and there they were, almost in the enemy's front line. Nothing but a field-drain between them and it. They can hear one of the dogs down in the drain now, howling like Cerberus, its chain caught under Holger's body – Holger, who was first out the smoke, poor unlucky soul, and lies now with his head in a trickle of water, pillowed on broken brick. Ravello will mourn Holger, they all will, but right now all he wants is for the accursed howling to cease.

The captain of dragoons, to Ravello's left, points behind them to where there is an abandoned wagon, yet another from Brunswick's baggage train. Rather than speech, the man scuttles the fingers of one hand over the palm of the other. *Good, yes,* Ravello signs back. He reaches for the boy, who's pressed flat beside him. The din about them is beyond deafness, it rolls from one side of your skull to the other without cease. He mouths, as much as speaks it: *Time to go.*

The boy twists his head about. His hat is long gone, face and neck are black with smoke and one ear has been chipped, with a finger of sticky blood trickling its way down to the boy's shirt and spreading itself about there, as such wounds are wont to do. Another rattle of shot. The wheel of the gun-carriage spins and sings. Ravello puts his mouth against that bloodied ear and shouts, '*Andiamo!* We go!' He points back behind them to the wagon. 'On your belly! Follow me!'

But the boy pulls himself free. 'NO,' he shouts. 'NO, Ravello, wait!'

Shot is making the gabions rock above Ravello's head. There's a sharp yelp from one of the dragoons, then the man does that smooth leaning over to one side that Ravello recognizes all too well. Long before Anholt's men can get here, they'll be no more than so much bloodied earth. Wait? Wait for what? *Pazzo! Imbecile!* 'Jag, we have to move back! *Ci ritiriamo!*

'NO!' the boy shouts again. He takes Ravello's hand and presses it flat against the ground. 'Listen!' the boy bellows. He's staring into Ravello's face, waiting for him to feel it too.

Mother of God. It feels as if the earth –

It feels as if the earth is *bouncing*.

'What IS that?' the boy yells, above the tumult, and then, 'What the hell, ain't no-one going down to get the dog?'

Crows, Cyrius is thinking. Crows. Of course. And there was he, imagining the lowest he could ever feel had been on waking that morning.

'Not as I judge,' the horse-master is saying, 'soldiers' widders – not an easy life. And the old'uns, what ain't whole no more – who can they prevail upon, other than the dead? But one such as your friend there, with all his limbs and strength?' The man shakes his head. '*Ach*, the whole world's dreaming on them silver thalers, you ask me.'

'But you wouldn't do it, would you?' Cyrius exclaims, bitterly.

The horse-master gives a bellow of laughter and takes off his hat. His hair comes with it. The top of his head is cratered as the moon, seamed ear to ear with scars. 'Fleurus,' the horse-master says, by way of explanation. 'No, no. Back here with the horses, that's the place for me. Plenty of thieving hands up here, and all.' He casts a glance behind him as he says it, then exclaims, 'Damn me! Look at that fellow! What was my very words?'

There is a man at the line of horses. The horse-master, with a shout of 'Hoi!', runs toward him. But instead of taking off, the man comes forward. It seems he has a question. As Cyrius watches, the horse-master points to the battlefield. The man falls back a step, then seems to gather himself. The horse-master is thanked. The man turns away.

'Poor old sod,' says the horse-master, coming back.

'Not thieving, then?' Cyrius can still just make out the prog-ress of that solitary figure, who appears to be walking straight onto the battlefield. He has to lift his voice. The noise behind them, which Cyrius had thought at first was rustling leaves, is now a stream in sudden spate, tumbling over pebbles.

'Looking for someone. Told me as he recognized one of the 'orses. Told him, whoever it was, was riding it, they went with the dragoons.'

A strange thing – the figure has now wholly disappeared within the veils of smoke, but from its halting, corkscrewed gait, Cyrius could have sworn it was the Shadow Man. 'Did he say—' he begins – and then stops. The sound of the stream is now that of applause – a thousand handclaps, an audience out of sight. Even the crows have heard it.

When it comes into view, stilling the guns, shaking the earth, what it looks like to Cyrius is a landslide. Great columns of movement, articulated in some way that is so smooth it has to be organic, and so exact it must be a machine. They are like segments of one single creature: six ranks deep and thirty men across, four such divisions at a time. No human noise comes from them, just bugle calls, and the answering volume of thousands upon thousands of iron-shod hooves, the rattle of thousands of armour-cased riders. As Cyrius watches, open-mouthed, the ranks change shape. They lengthen, they spread – one line, one-hundred-and-twenty across, and then another, and another after that. The crows know what this is at once – endgame – but to Cyrius, they are the most perfectly ordered thing he's ever seen, all the pomp and state he had imagined.

And for Ravello, half a mile away, as he realizes what is coming up through the ground into the palm of his hand, they are the remote possibility that they might just be getting out of this alive. He turns to the boy – and finds himself facing empty air. The boy is negotiating his way sideways down the bank into the drain. Ravello, panic-stricken, shrieks his name, and then to his amazement sees the whole of the front line of infantry pause in their firing and, in violent and inexplicable disorder, break ranks.

Down in the culvert, the boy is greeted by a volley of delighted barks. Beside Ravello, the captain of dragoons has dared to lift himself to his knees. Ravello hears the man ask, as if to himself, 'What the devil—' and then with a shout stand up, because here they come, here they come, right now: Tilly's great cavalry, all three thousand of them. Every single one of them rolling down on Brunswick's baggage train, and his forgotten and unprotected right flank.

All the same. In Ravello's head there is still that moment when the air was thick with shot, *thick* with it, like flies round a horse, and the boy had walked down into it, untouched, unscathed, as if it were no more than gentle summer rain.

FIVE IN THE AFTERNOON. The battle of Stadtlohn is almost done. Those with the stomach for it are entertaining themselves at the top end of the field, where the remains of Brunswick's infantry had tried to flee across the marsh. Those (many more)

hungry for loot are at the bridge, tearing Brunswick's baggage train apart. But below the bridge, where the river makes a curve, under the shade of the trees, Jack is taking his ease. There is any amount of noise drifting his way from the baggage train – shouts of glee or furious altercation, shots, shrieks, the crack of axles giving way – but here under the trees, the only sound is that of a dog's contented lapping.

The water comes from a barrel Jack holds on his lap; the dog's bowl is a nautilus shell. It came, in turn, from the iron-bound trunk some trooper dragged this far, then decided was too heavy to drag further. The contents of the trunk lie strewn about – books, bed-linen, a nightshirt (caught on the grass, blowing about like a wraith), a fine hat, the jewel ripped from its hatband, and a pair of bead-embroidered gloves, whose leather is delicately scented with vanilla. Jack is considering taking these back for Agetha.

The impact of the cavalry charge had spread across the field from one end to the other. Within moments the infantry battalion in front of them had cleared, running away in panic. As the officers tried to force their troops to hold a line, a powder wagon had exploded. A whole forest of pine trees, rocketing into the sky. The crater it left in the field is fifty feet across, and ringed with body-parts, something Jack no longer views with any amazement at all. Meat and bones, he's thinking. Meat and bones.

Half Brunswick's army lies dead on the field. Four thousand more will be taken prisoner, and the survivors chased across country till dawn. Brunswick himself will cross the Dutch border with a scant two thousand men. He will lose sixteen guns and four mortars, all of which Tilly will put on display in the marketplace at Coesfeld, twelve miles away. He will lose the whole of his baggage train.

Tilly will lose about a thousand men.

There is a singing in Jack's ears and his thoughts have reached some strange place of their own. Thus: how quickly blood dries up, on summer earth; how curious the jelly that it leaves. How simple a thing death is. How instantly it unpicks everything. What neat containers boots make, for those feet. And how (and this is the strangest thought of all) this is the first place since the turnpike where he has had that sense of complete belonging, of home.

The dog, thirst slaked, gives a hound-yawn so loud it sounds like its jaws need oiling. It's the black one this, with the white mark on its chest. As it watches, one ear cocked, Jack lifts the barrel and pours water over his face. Never been so dry. Out on the field, his lips had been sticking to his teeth; when he next finds himself before a looking-glass the inside of his lower lip will show a purple line as if he'd been punched in the mouth. Then there is this mysterious broken blister across the fingers of his right hand, which makes no sense at all until he remembers throwing that pistol, the heat of its muzzle, just fired.

He chucks the barrel one way, and the nautilus shell the other. Whoever wants such lumber is welcome to it. Whistles up the dog, and sets off along the curve of the riverbank, with the dog doing its bouncing hound-trot ahead of him. As he walks, he makes a gentle clinking sound. There are places you can pick silver thalers off the ground hereabouts like daisies. He is not totally indifferent to the idea of booty.

What he plans is to follow the river into Stadtlohn, find the horse-master, reclaim Milano, buy a billet, and sleep for a week. He thinks that he has never been so tired. If his legs are still walking forward, it is only because that is all they can remember to do. Nor has he ever been so hungry; as he walks he tears hunks from a wheel of rye bread, loaves of which can also be found, scattered across the ground and burned to charcoal on one side. Slowly coming into focus, as his hunger fades, is the notion that he might – *might* – nerve himself to try to find a girl tonight.

In one day his life, which was so complicated and so heavy to support, has become as weightless as a dandelion-clock. Soldiering. This is what you do, this field is where you do it, and the dragoons, or Ravello, or even the Shadow Man, are the brothers you do it with. Simple. *And I killed no-one*, he thinks. He had walked through a battlefield, through his first, and his hands are clean. He hears himself snort with laughter. The dog peers back at him, as if asking *what's the joke?*

'My father,' he tells it. His voice is so hoarse he's amazed that using it don't hurt. 'This is so simple. He was right.'

And head up, grinning like a lunatic, he lets his steps wander toward that wagon on its own over there for no reason at all, really, other than that the dog is tracking toward it, nose to the ground, and that the wagon, with its wicker sides, does look so curiously familiar.

'But the dead,' Korbl is saying, in pleading tone. 'Not them as is wounded, fair enough, a'cause they can be desperate vicious, them, but the dead – you tell me, what's the difference to them?'

'*Not* the dead,' Cyrius repeats, striding forward. As he walks, he's skirting them, wherever he sees them (which is everywhere) – the white of a shirt-front, the red or rose pink of a sash. All buried in the summer grasses. Flowers in a meadow.

His and Korbl's progress is a meandering, back-and-forth thing.

'But they're dead—'

'*Loot*, you said,' bellows Cyrius, rounding on him. 'Silver thalers. In the wagons. Proper *loot*.'

Now it is Korbl who looks horrified. 'You mad?' He points to the baggage train. 'You out your sodding *mind*? There's *soldiers* there. Armed men!'

'My *horse*,' thunders Cyrius, tugging the nag behind him, to make the point. 'You want the use of him, then *not* the *dead*. If it's on the ground, fair enough, but we ain't a-stealing off the *dead*.'

'Oh, I might'a known,' Korbl begins. 'Think you're too good for this, do yer? Look, it's nothing! There's no difference, if you take it from a pocket or you pick it off the ground! Everything out here has blood on it, all of it the same!' Now there's a wheedling note to his voice. 'Dead is dead, innit? We turn a few over, that's all.' He seems to see that he is getting nowhere. His tone changes. 'You don't even have the balls to bloody look at 'em, do yer?' He's heading toward a wagon marooned above the riverbank, its wickerwork sides bowed out, canvas roof ripped and trailing on the ground. 'Waste of my sodding time—'

He stops. His back is to Cyrius, but there's something in how he came to a stop that has Cyrius slow down as well. 'Korbl?' he asks.

Korbl is now walking backwards toward him.

'Korbl?'

Korbl has both hands at his belly. There's a noise in the air, a slaughterhouse squealing.

Around the corner of the wagon comes the Brunswick sentinel. The remains of an officer's silken sash still flutters at his waist, and he's wielding a pike that must be five yards long. And he marches past Cyrius; he one end of the pike, Korbl the other. The two of them joined by its fifteen-foot haft.

'Ah, God!' cries Cyrius. 'Ah, God!'

The sentinel sees Cyrius, starts trying to shake Korbl off the pike. Korbl releases his hands and falls, with a long and awful cry, into the grass. The head of the pike, winged like a bat, flashes past Cyrius so close he hears its sigh. He jumps back. His horse, startled, shakes itself loose from his grasp, cantering sideways. The sigh comes after Cyrius again. He'd never considered meeting a pike. Stopping a bullet, yes, some last stray shot, into eternity in an instant, but not this, this being sent there gaffed and helpless. Now he knows what Aesop meant, and no, there is no answer to it, no getting near the sentinel and no disarming the man without. Face him, he'll impale you. Turn

your back, run away, the same. Something is clutching at his
leg. He looks down, and there is Korbl, mouth stretched wider
than should ever be possible and his bowels – his *bowels* – are
there beside him in the grass, creamy-coloured, shining, neatly
coiled. Korbl's gut has been ripped open like a bag.

And then from somewhere nearby comes a murderous growling. The sentinel twists about, and there, bounding up on him,
is one of those monstrous dogs and this figure behind it, this
hideous scarecrow, tattered and bloody, who sees the pike just
in time to dance beyond its reach.

The dog lets off a fusillade of barks and jumps this way and
that, as if it thought the sentinel was about to throw the pike
for it, like a stick.

Now the two of them are targets. The sentinel lunges at
Cyrius, and the scarecrow jumps into range. 'The battle's over,'
the scarecrow yells. 'The fighting's done.'

The sentinel's only response is another stab.

'Put it down,' the scarecrow urges. 'Put it down, walk away.'

The sentinel seems to be deciding between them. The dog is
dancing back and forth round Cyrius's feet. A canine yelp as it
runs into the back of his legs and Cyrius is on the ground, on
the ground and helpless. He sees the sentinel approach, over
the waving tops of the grasses. The man has made his decision.
'Help me, help me!' Cyrius screams, scrambling backwards. But
all the scarecrow does is remove its belt. The sentinel is coming
closer. Jab, jab, jab. Then, of a sudden, he throws up an elbow,
like a man beset by a wasp. Then he does it again. The scarecrow is throwing something at him, something that winks silver
in the air. The sentinel swings about, with an oath, and like the
needle on a compass, now the pike points at the scarecrow. The
head of the pike stabs at its face, and Cyrius sees the scarecrow
sling its belt around the pike, behind the wings on the blade,
and run toward the sentinel, belt looped around the shaft like a
man sliding down a wire. It launches itself, both feet, into the

sentinel's chest. The noise of the pike falling to earth. A wrestling match: feet, elbows, one uppermost, then the other. Then nothing. Nothing but the grass-heads against the sky.

Cyrius pushes himself up.

The scarecrow is sat back on its heels, wiping its knife on its leg. Something lies beside it in the grass.

'There's another,' Cyrius says, looking about. 'He's hurt – he's hereabouts. He's somewhere.'

'He's over there,' the scarecrow answers, pointing. Its voice is so deep and raw it hurts to hear it. 'He's dead.'

Cyrius gets unsteadily to his feet, takes a step or two forward, and there is Korbl, legs drawn up, face blue. The nag, entirely unconcerned, is grazing. The dog has sat down, wagging its tail. The scarecrow gets to its feet. It turns toward him. It says, 'Cyrius.' It says, 'I was coming off this field *clean*.'

And only then does Cyrius recognize who this is.

The Shadow Man's boy shoves him in the shoulder. 'Cyrius, what the *fuck* –'

The boy shoves him again. Cyrius is once more on the ground. The boy leans over him, like a sailor leaning into the wind.

'– the *fuck* d'you think you're doing here, you God-damned sodding shit-head half-wit, you think you're some kind of fucking hard-arse, coming out here? You think this is any kind of place for you? The *fuck* are you at?'

Never faced a mouthful like it. He's ready to reply – some burst of invective of his own – but he looks at the boy for the first time, closely – the blood on neck and shirt, the dirt on him, and – 'I don't know,' Cyrius replies, meekly. He feels amazed at his own honesty. He finds he's staring at the boy again. He can't work out what's happened to him – is the boy hurt? He hears himself say, 'There's blood on you.'

'Yeah,' says the boy. 'And some of it's even mine.' The air is thickening around them. Smoke from the last of the battle, from its death-throes. The boy turns about. He walks stiffly, like now he feels his hurts. Whistles up the dog. 'You don't belong here, Cyrius,' the boy says, wearily. 'I'll take you into Stadtlohn.'

The smoke drifts between them, wreathing its treacherous way. Cyrius has to put his sleeve over his mouth. He calls out, 'Jag! The Shadow Man! Did he find you? He was out here too!'

The boy erupts out of the whiteness. 'He was *WHAT*?'

HERE IS THE MARSH. It let the first of Christian's panic-stricken army pass over it, then it began to liquefy. Pounding feet will do that, likewise horses' hooves, likewise the reverberations of artillery. Now it was a trap. Tilly's cavalry began to herd all those still on the field toward it. The guns on the rise turned their mouths toward it. Now, it was a killing ground. The irony of being caught in it would be very present for Balthasar, were he not in such agony that simply making it from one breath to the next is taking all he has.

There are other figures round him, calling to each other, crying for help, trying to pull themselves free. The mud sucks you in, shin deep, and closes round you, cold and tight. He's never thought of the earth as having an embrace, but if it does, then this is it. Oh Christ, air, *air*, he has to breathe! His heart feels white-hot in his chest, his ribcage in such extremis that his ribs must surely burst into flame. He has no sense any longer of where he is, what is before him, or behind; the whole world had shrunk down to this – the bellows working in his chest, the expansion of his heart, that scalding throb, the pain in everything, the taste of the smoke, the awful impact of the guns. When the cannonballs strike, they throw up a black spout of mud, and where they strike, the shouts become staccato screaming. Some of the dead are left standing, rooted like shattered trees. *We are the army sprung from dragon's teeth*, he thinks, *but now the earth won't let us go.* Another round from the guns.

More screaming. He feels the tide of lava lift in his chest. Now there is other movement in the smoke. Creeping shapes, bent like hunters. He hears a single shot, he thinks at once, *a coup de grâce*. Sometimes there are riders, silhouetted, sword-arm raised. *Let me die*, begs Balthasar, *but let the boy live*. One of those creeping shapes is even that of a dog – tail up, quartering the ground, and a figure behind it, urging it on. Now he thinks he hears it bark, urgent and enthusiastic, a hound upon the scent. A bank of smoke drifts past him like a whale. And then he sees it, bounding toward him, that white blaze on its chest –

And the dog leaps at him, great wet tongue lashing Balthasar's face, and then there's the boy behind it, standing there, hands on his hips, and saying, 'You're going to lose them boots.'

Balthasar feels the tears erupting down his face. He tries to speak, to tell the boy to *Go, go, go*, but all he can do is weep and hold out his hands.

The boy bends toward him. 'Stop fucken giving me them fucken orders,' he says, calmly. Balthasar feels the boy's long arms go round him, then gives a whoop as the boy's shoulder lodges against his breastbone.

'Brace yourself, Shadow Man,' says the boy. 'And point your toes.'

THE EVENING OF the 6th of August, 1623. There are tents, now, out in the fields before the village of Stadtlohn, and bonfires too – raging, some of them, spouting firefly trails into the darkening sky. Soon it will get noisy. Soon, when it has Christian of Brunswick's treasury being strewn about its streets, the tiny village of Stadtlohn will become, for one night only, perhaps the richest place in Europe. A silver thaler for a jug of beer. A diamond ring for a plate of meat. The silk robes of a colonel's lady for a cuddle with a farmer's wench.

The scouts are gathered in the graveyard of Stadtlohn's church, as befits so vigilant and discreet a group of men, and suits Cyrius also, very well. Cyrius would be happy if nothing ever happens to him again from now on for the rest of his life.

Get into Stadtlohn, the boy had said, so he did. *Find the horse-master*, the boy had said, pressing coins into Cyrius's palm. *Get me back Milano*. So he had, although he recognized the horse-master only when the man, standing right before him, had once again removed his hat.

You all right, friend? the horse-master had asked. You look a little wobbly there.

Wobbly. That was right.

He'd sat by the fence to a cottage garden, one horse in one hand, one in the other. After a while, the cottager had come out to see if he was alive or dead. Finding it was the former, the man brought him a cup of water. Cyrius spilled most of it, just getting it to his lips. Who won? the man had asked, and Cyrius could only shake his head, and whisper, I don't know. Every time he closed his eyes, the battle flashed before him: the street a whirl of smoke, of arms and legs. Screams in his ears.

The man returned, proffered the cup again. You, he said. You won. We reckon it was you.

Strange sights went past him. A man, laughing madly, wrapped in a cloak, surrounded by his fellows, but leaving a steady dribble of blood on the ground. A girl – very young – her skirt pegged up, lugging a basket of hats, *and each one*, Cyrius thought, *each one of those, a man*. A wagon loaded with the dead, *and how strange it is*, he thought, as he watched the corpses jostling together, *I know at once there is no life in any of 'em*. Their colour, that blue-white. He thought of Korbl, closed his eyes. He tried very hard to summon up Agetha's face; when it appeared before him, with the living woman underneath, for a moment he had no idea if he should trust that it was real or no, but then the living woman slapped him, so it seemed most likely that it was. 'You took the *horse*,' she said. 'You took the *horse*.' No 'Thank God you're alive.' 'You took the *horse*.' Aesop rode up behind her, and somehow, their good old wagon behind him, still marked with Aesop's map upon its side, and its poles now lashed to Aesop's stirrups. 'You're here,' Cyrius heard himself murmur in amazement, 'you're here.' His trembling hands had fluttered to Agetha's shoulders, landed there, and *by God*, he thought, *I am never moving them again*. He has one arm about her still, and the scouts – unmarried men, one and all – are leaving a little space around them. Tactful, Cyrius calls that.

Titus is saying, 'Our man Holger, bless his soul.' He gives a gulp. 'He always said as Brunswick's men, they never hold their lines, and he was right. They lost it once that powder wagon blew. It was all *Run, run, run!* with them thereafter.'

'No, no,' says Aesop. 'Brunswick lost it when he didn't guard his right.'

'They lost it soon as it was our guns on that rise. Soon as I saw it was our guns there, I knew the day 'ud be ours too. It was ours soon as we came out of the wood.'

For a moment, no-one replies. No-one seems to quite know how to deal with the boy any more. To have saved Cyrius was one thing; to walk in here and let the Shadow Man fall from his back was quite another. 'Is it true?' Ravello had asked, drawing Cyrius to one side. 'The boy went back onto the field to find him?' Now Aesop breaks the silence, asking, 'Jag, you had a word of thanks out of him yet?'

The Shadow Man sits between Cyrius and the boy. He holds a cloth to his lips and coughs in it continually, folding it over and starting again; little dry coughs, like a man with a catch in his throat, rather than the smoke of half a battlefield.

The boy laughs, then he too has to cough into his hand. 'No,' he manages, at last.

'Shady,' says Aesop. 'Shame on you.'

And now, very slowly, the Shadow Man gets to his feet. His crutch is gone, he has to use Cyrius to push himself up, in fact Cyrius has to stand up with him – those broad miller's shoulders, those strong miller's hands.

'One,' the Shadow Man begins. 'One, he left his place.' A wheeze of breath. 'And two, he disobeyed his orders.' Another wheeze. 'A worser hothead, I never served with.' A cough. 'But,' says the Shadow Man, 'I'll grant you this. He is his father's son.' He turns to the boy. 'Jag,' he begins, and then another fit of coughing, and then suddenly there is a little blood upon his chin. The Shadow Man raises his hand to it, looks at the smear in wonderment, staggers against Cyrius and then before they've even laid him on the ground he's as bloody as if he'd been stabbed. When Cyrius tries to lift his head, the froth pours from his mouth like water rising from a spring. The boy is on his knees beside him, the Shadow Man's hands held to his heart. 'Balthasar!' he's saying. 'Balthasar!'

The Shadow Man opens his eyes. Another wracking, choking cough. One hand seems to be trying to find the boy's head. 'Jag,' he whispers. Another flow of blood. 'Jag.' A fight to clear his mouth. Cyrius tries to lifts him, and the Shadow Man's head rolls on his shoulder. Warmth on Cyrius's shirt, cooling on his skin. The Shadow Man gives a long tired sigh, then says, 'The first—' A click as he swallows.

'Stop it,' the boy says. 'Stop trying to talk, you're making it worse.'

Another thick wet click. More warmth, spreading over Cyrius's shoulder. A spasm shakes the body in his arms. 'Please don't,' the boy is saying. 'Please, please don't. Don't go, don't leave me, please.'

The Shadow Man's eyes close. A sort of stretching shudder. He opens them again, gazes at the boy. 'Jag,' he says, 'Jag.'

And then a change. A gentle change, in its own time. Cyrius, looking down into the Shadow Man's face, has long enough to work out what is happening; then it's done.

Ravello is the first to move. 'Jag,' he says, softly.

'I know,' says the boy. 'I know.'

SUNRISE, and a breeze has found its way into Stadtlohn. It wakes the first of the tumbled sleepers in the streets, and turns the weathercock upon the spire, and presses against the huddle in the churchyard, as if to see what's going on.

The Shadow Man lies in his grave, wrapped in his cloak, which is stained with his blood. The same dark stains are on Cyrius's shirt, where he stands, spade in hand. Cyrius had elected to act as gravedigger, and the grave he dug is deep and wide – *Cyrius-sized*, thinks Jack. More than enough space for a husk like the Shadow Man.

The breeze presses the cloak flat to the face underneath, like a passing hand, then goes on its way.

Titus is reciting a prayer. 'Oh God,' he begins. 'Oh God, who knowest us to be set in the midst of peril, grant we may overcome.'

Aesop gives him a nudge. 'That's a battle prayer.'

Titus tries again. 'Lord, all my hopes and consolations, all my trials and miseries—'

'So's that.'

'They're all I know.'

Beside him, Jack feels Squirrel slip her hand into his.

Cyrius stabs the spade into the ground. 'Lord,' he says, gruffly, 'receive Thy servant. There.'

The scouts, in turn, take up handfuls of earth. Ravello is the first to throw his in. Then a good spadeful from Cyrius. Jack closes his eyes. The dead to the clay. All of a sudden he needs to feel the earth beneath him, to know the world is still there. So he sits down on the dew-wet grass, and Squirrel puts her arms around his neck, and with her noisy childish breathing at his ear, and with the hound leaning against him from the other side, he listens to them burying the Shadow Man. And with the man, all his secrets too.

It's everyone, he thinks. *Everyone I have to do with, dies.*

When he opens his eyes again, the thing is done. There's Cyrius, sweaty of forehead, bending toward him, and Agetha, she of those beautiful great dark eyes. He wants to tell them how lucky they are.

'What will you do, Jag?' Agetha is asking. 'Will you go with the army? Ravello is going with them. Will you ride with him?'

'No,' he says. 'Not me.' He pushes himself up, pushes past them, goes to Milano. The dog follows him. Behind him he hears Agetha, voice upraised in protest.

You ain't any part of me, nor I of you.

Titus and Aesop ride past, heading out to find Holger's body. Once again, everyone else has a thing to do, a place in the world. *And me*, he thinks, *and me? What do I do?*

He leans against his horse, closes his eyes. The dog, beside him, gives a whine. What was that hopeless little figure, on its own?

Colin-Maillard.

No, he thinks, *no. Sort, act, do.* Checks his pack. Then water-bottle, bed-roll, girth good and tight. *But what for? What is any of this for? Balthasar is dead; the names are there in the grave with him.*

A trooper, half-drunk, has come staggering across the road to the churchyard, is leaning, swaying, on its gate. He calls out, 'You Cyrius the sutler?'

'I am,' comes Cyrius's reply.

'Ought to get your sign out, friend. We might'a missed you.' The man digs about for his pocket, finds it at last, and comes out with a handful of silver. He staggers backward and coins go scattering across the road. 'Owe you summat,' the man declares, steadying himself with a few unplanned steps. The gate creaks as he leans against it. He turns about: there's a knot of his fellows, waiting behind him. 'Here you go, mates!' he calls out, cheerily. 'Found 'im!' He turns back, face split by a boozy smile. 'Come to pay.'

Then over Milano's back, there is Ravello.

'*Saluti*, Fiskardo,' says Ravello. 'If I may, a word.'

Oh, the things a man will do for the woman he loves. 'Go talk with him,' Agetha had said. A line of men in front of her, all meekly waiting to pay. One was holding out his buttonless cuff to her: 'See, missus? Remember me?' A smile to the eager petitioner; out the corner of her mouth she'd hissed at Cyrius, 'You'd be dead out on that field yourself if it weren't for him. We can't just go and leave him on his own. Go talk with him again.' So off Cyrius goes, back across the churchyard, back to the boy. 'Now look'ee, lad,' he begins. Never felt so flat-footed in every way. The dog is nosing at him; he bats its muzzle away. Points over to Agetha. 'She's in enough of a fret about you as it is. Give me something I can tell her, to set her heart at ease.'

But this time when the boy turns to face him, he's smiling. 'Yeah,' he says. 'Yeah, here's something for you.' And he takes the hound by its collar and pushes it against Cyrius. Cyrius looks down at the animal in horror. 'No, you take him,' the boy says. 'He can look out for Agetha and Squirrel. In case you decide to go off soldiering again.'

Cyrius feels the colour come into his face. 'But you can't set off on your own—'

'Yes I can,' comes the reply. And now the boy is holding out his hand, as if ending the conversation. Cyrius, nonplussed, holds out his own, still grimed with earth, but as their hands meet, the boy pulls Cyrius in against him. 'You take care of 'em, you hear?' he hisses, once their heads are close. 'I want to come into camp some day and find you an old greybeard and Agetha in the kitchen and Squirrel serving the beer. Don't you waste what I did. You understand me?' And he doesn't release the hand until he sees, from the shamed and downward flick of Cyrius's eyes, that he does.

'So what will you do, lad? I saw you and Ravello talking. You set to try life as a scout?'

'One day,' the boy replies. He swings himself up into the saddle. His horse shakes its head of unlikely curls. He looks down at Cyrius. 'Right now, I'm going hunting.'

'The Shadow Man was wrong about you,' Ravello had begun. 'He was wrong about you, and at the end he knew it. You've a right to know who killed your parents, and they've a right to be avenged. You want that to be your path, nod your head.' And he had waited.

And then '*Bene,*' Ravello said. A glance to left and right. '*Allora.* So, the first, he's one Enric Maduna. The regiment he's in came out of Styria, and it has the Virgin on its flag. My guess is, Maduna's of the family who raised it – and with that flag and that name, maybe he has command of it, too. But of the second, the assassin, all we ever had for him was a nickname. Charles the Ghost. You find the first, Maduna, maybe you'll find out more. Good luck, Jacques. You know how we say that, where I come from? *In bocca al lupo.* In the mouth of the wolf.'

CHAPTER FOUR

Jag

'It is the property of horsemen not to attend the enemie's coming, but to go & affront him...'

John Cruso, *Militarie Instructions for the Cavallrie*

ANOTHER DAWN, another place, another day. Hans, first to wake as ever, watches the pink globe of the sun slide up the outside of the tent.

– *Morning, Wilhelm.*

– *Morning, little brother.*

– *What's the weather going to be today?*

– *Get off your arse*, says Wilhelm, inside Hans's head, *and go an' 'ave a look.*

With a practised wriggle, Hans frees himself of his blanket. Gunter and Matz, two of the other sleepers in the tent, are supine, dead to the world. Only Stuzzi, lying across the entrance, produces a whimper as Hans clambers over him.

Outside, the sun is climbing a sky as flat a blue as paint. Hans gets to his feet and takes a reading of the day. There's the camp, all just as ever. Funny how they always seem larger by night. *Going to be another hot one, Will.*

But Will has gone, back to his distant netherworld.

Ach, it's good country, this. The war has hardly touched Bavaria, you can tell – these great green plains, high and wide and full of sunlight, are full of crops and villages too; the roads are peopled, the fields kept neat. And the camp is a good one too, and their spot within it, one of the best. Their tent sits on a rise, so it's stayed dry, and there's a couple of trees, where he and Matz had improvised a hitching-rail the night before. Quick spot-check of the horses: the Holstein mare, the three pack horses, the gelding hack –

And there's a sixth. Hans is so taken aback he has to count again: onetwothreefourfive and there at the end this handsome little bay, with a long black mane and tail in heavy ringlets, like a woman's hair.

Shit, thinks Hans. *This is going to take some sorting out.* And glances at once at the other tent, a few yards to his right. As a rough indication of the status of its occupant, look at a tent's geometry. The tent where Hans, Gunter, Matz and Stuzzi sleep is a simple triangle; as a cavalry crew they aren't quite at the bottom of the pile (the drummer boys frequently find themselves sleeping out in the open air), but they're pretty low. The tent to the right is a hexagon, with double-layer side walls, and the pitch of its roof high enough for a man to be able to sit on a camp-bed underneath it.

Lying snoring on his camp-bed underneath it at this present moment is their captain, Herzog Heinrich.

For the boys who serve him as his crew, Heinrich is not so much a man as a collection of phenomena. His heart-stopping bellow. The impact of his fists. The veins snaking over his close-cropped scalp. If Herzog Heinrich finds they've somehow grown another horse overnight, there's going to be hell to pay.

Oh, shit shit shit, thinks Hans, panicking now, when his eye is caught by the sight of a figure walking up the incline toward him, lugging a bucket of water. The bucket has a B stamped on it, for their colonel, Bronheim; the drawing of a tower, for Bronheim's home in far-off Styria; all over-hovered by the Holy Virgin Lady, like their flag; and round the rim the lettering Hans had put there himself: THESE IS OWERS GO TO HEL AND GET YER OWN.

The stranger approaches. A long lean lad, lean as a twig, in a shirt as patched as a hurdy-gurdy man's and a tip-tilted hat with a feather hanging off it, strolling up through the camp as if he owned the place. Seeing Hans staring at him, the hat is tipped back a little further. A greeting:

'*Grüss Gott.*'

Southerner, thinks Hans at once. To his amazement the boy continues past him, straight to that handsome little bay. Plonks the bucket down before the horse, which starts to drink, and stands there, rubbing its neck.

Strangers in a camp are rare, attack the best form of defence. 'Who the frigginell are you?' Hans demands.

'Jag,' the boy replies. At least, that's what it sounds like.

Hans takes a good long squint at him. Boots down at heel, hair in his eyes, and brown as a shepherd. And the notch of an old scar on his cheek, high on the bone, like a starburst.

'Them's our buckets,' Hans says, as aggressively as before. 'Our buckets, for our horses.'

'I know,' comes the reply. 'I've done yours.'

A commotion from the triangular tent: Gunter and Matz, with Stuzzi trailing a little way behind. The stranger takes off his hat and sweeps them a bow. His eyes are startlingly pale, pale as a ghost's, and while Hans wouldn't say he was squaring off, there's something there suggests it might be wise to be polite.

'Who's this?' asks Matz.

'This here is Jag,' Hans replies.

'And this here,' says Jag, pointing to the bay horse, 'is Milano.'

Herzog Heinrich, waking to the sound of voices, opens the lacings at the corner of the tent. He sees his crew, bunched together, and the fifth figure, of the stranger. The new recruit. And Heinrich's new mount, looking even prettier than it had the day before. He'd come out of the tavern (Heinrich likes a drink. Drink makes him feel the way he thinks he should – potent, unassailable, a man of account), and his eye had been drawn at once to the sheen on the bay's flanks. Then he'd seen the boy. Crouched down beside it, sorting through his pack. The narrow waist, the wash-dead, threadbare shirt, those big, amphibian-looking, adolescent hands. Lovely...

Heinrich knows that what he does is wrong – is, in fact, a capital offence. But when he does it, then it seems no more than his due, a perk, almost. Showing his lads what makes a man. 'That your horse?' he'd begun, strolling over.

The boy had stood to face him. Taller than Heinrich had been expecting, and something else he hadn't been expecting either, the icy eyes, the flick of warning: *Try it. See how far you'd get.*

'Yeah,' the boy had answered. 'Yeah, he's mine.'

If the boy had been only a couple of years younger. But the ones who'd fight back, make a noise, you don't want them. A swift reverse in Heinrich's attention, from the boy back to the horse. 'Want to sell him?'

'Nope,' said the boy, 'I want a place in a crew. He comes with me.'

Oh, got an edge on him, this one. 'What've you done?' Heinrich had asked, meaning, what action have you seen?

'Joined up at Heidelberg in twenty-two,' the boy replied. 'I was a scout.'

Heinrich had been only half-sure he believed this. Scouting would have been pretty stiff work for a lad this age. 'Who's your officer?' he'd asked, thinking *Let's check this out*. 'He about here, is he?'

'Nope,' said the boy. 'Bought the farm.'

One of those farms you hear so much about these days: three foot wide, six foot long, six foot deep. Heinrich gave a friendly smile. 'A scout, eh?' he'd said. 'That's good enough for me. I pay eight gulden a month—'

'Fifteen,' the boy said. 'I get fifteen.'

Heinrich, knocked back, replied at once, 'I ain't interested for fifteen.'

'Then nor am I,' said the boy, making to strap the pack behind his saddle. Light as a sunbeam, the suggestion floated amongst Heinrich's thoughts: would it be worth taking this lad onto his crew simply to have the opportunity of knocking the jelly out of him? 'Who's *your* officer?' the boy demanded, interrupting.

'Bronheim,' said Heinrich, automatically – before the insolence of the question registered.

'Never heard of him.'

At that, Heinrich found himself becoming truly riled, as well as tempted. Something about the turn of the boy's shoulders, the way he, Heinrich, had apparently been dismissed. His eyes slid over the bay once more. He liked the idea of himself, atop of that.

Heinrich is paid one hundred and fifty gulden a month – as much as any captain in the regiment. But out of that he has to find for his kit, his horses, his four boys, not to mention his pleasures, none of which come cheap… Never mind. There's always some new ruse, to keep his crew's wages in his hands. 'All right, fifteen then,' he'd said. 'Fifteen gulden a month, and you'd better be worth it.'

*

Now Heinrich rises, stretches, scratches over jaw and scalp. Fifteen gulden. *Got one over on me there, the little shit.*

He pulls on his boots, draws aside the flaps of his tent and emerges into the day. Swaggers across. Sees the group break apart at his approach. 'You introduced yourselves, have you?'

'I didn't know we was getting no-one new,' says Matz, sounding sulky.

'Didn't you?' says Heinrich, all concern. 'But then you don't know fuck all about nothing, so what's the odds? Now –' He surveys them. Flicks a hand at Gunter, but only for the pleasure of seeing the boy jump. And where's his cherub? There he is, there's Stuzzi, hiding at the back. Heinrich has never hit Stuzzi (you don't go spoiling your molly), with the consequence that Stuzzi is maybe three times as terrified of him as the rest. God's in his heaven, Heinrich's right with the world. 'You got my new horse ready for me yet?'

Heinrich mounts up. Milano, feeling this unaccustomed weight upon his back, takes offence, immediately. He sucks in his belly and the girth slips. Heinrich dismounts. The girth is tightened; Milano lets out his breath, and begins a terrible wheezing, as if its tightness is now suffocating him. Heinrich dismounts again, the girth is adjusted. Milano glances at his boy, reads what he sees there as approval, and as Heinrich attempts to mount up a third time, takes a couple of shambling steps backward. As a final touch he splays his back legs and lowers his rump. He feels the saddle start to slide...

'God-damned piss-poor useless God-damned jade!' Heinrich roars, dismounting. Ride this horse? He'd be a laughing stock. The nearest thing to hand is Hans, so he kicks him in the backside. 'You can use that useless God-damned dung-bag to carry my tent!'

*

At noon, the order comes to break camp. Jag takes down Heinrich's tent himself, stowing its cumbrous bulk behind his saddle without a word. Hans, Gunter, Stuzzi, Matz, loading the packhorses, watch him out the corners of their eyes. Gunter, who has a nervous turn of mind, with raw red patches on his forearms (Heinrich's nickname for him is 'The Leper'), whispers, 'Where'd you reckon he got that horse, then?'

'Nicked it,' Matz replies, with all the authority of the born recidivist.

Heinrich, breakfast in a bottle in his fist, is watching too, watching for the chance to show the little shit who's boss. Hans, whose backside is extremely sore, is ashamed to find he's hoping Heinrich gets it. They're a tight old gang, Matz and Gunter and Stuzzi and he, and none too certain of this new fellow, with his sure-footed air.

The tent, lashed into place, makes an unsteady load. It's rocking like a howdah. Matz puts his elbow into Hans's ribs. 'Can't wait to see this,' he comments.

The new recruit steps up to his horse – and next minute he's on its back. Floats up there like a bird. Hans is open-mouthed. *That's a proper horseman*, he thinks. *That's the thing itself.* Matz, jog-trotting past, leans down and jerks a thumb. 'He'll do,' he says.

Hans is not so sure.

A regiment on the march: three hundred soldiers, six hundred horses, two hundred boys, and somewhere in the centre, like a queen within her hive, their colonel, Bronheim. On the hard dry summer road the noise they make is frightening, their approach sounds like a river, a river full of rocks. The dust they raise is frightening too, coating everything on the road and ten feet back from it, like ash. Through the dust there is the occasional flash of steel as the sun catches on helmet or breastplate, and the glow of their charming, delicate, gold-fringed standard, the

Virgin Mary rayed in all her pearly glory, carried aloft above the clouds of dust by Bronheim's ensign, and to which the pale eyes of the new recruit return over and over again. Bringing up the rear, the baggage train: blacksmith, quartermaster, paymaster, mongrel dogs, mongrel children, wives and whores.

Hans, down in the dust, has his handkerchief tied over his face. Leading the Holstein mare is meant to be an honour, but rarely feels that way. Sixteen hands, five foot four at the shoulder, weighing in at half a ton, and barmy as a cat. She pulls to the left, she pulls to the right, and skitters if so much as a pebble rolls beneath her shoe.

Clippety-clop behind him: Milano draws level, moves past. A voice above Hans's head: 'Want a ride?'

Head down, Hans gestures over his shoulder. 'Leading her. It's my job.' *Bugger off,* he thinks.

'Yeah, but she don't like being led. Some of 'em don't. What she wants is an escort.'

'Huh?' says Hans, looking up.

'I'll show you.' And the boy leans down, scoops an arm under Hans's own and with a bit of a scramble Hans too is hefted atop Milano. *Frigginell,* Hans thinks, rubbing the underside of his arm. Their new recruit possesses a savage grip.

The boy leans over again, hooks up the dangling reins of the Holstein mare, and clucks his tongue. The Holstein mare picks up the pace, moves alongside Milano, and settles down to a stately trot.

'Told you,' says the new recruit.

Milano gives a whinny. *Good morning, madame.*

That's a bright lad you've got there, says the Holstein mare.

A diamond, madame. A diamond.

Three hundred soldiers, six hundred horses, two hundred boys. They all have tales to tell.

*

On they go, the great road north, never a thought to where or why –

Although to be honest, where hardly matters any more. To the north, the people of Mecklenburg and Pomerania are still being terrorized by the remnants of Brunswick's army, unpaid and ungovernable; and these poor territories being so weakened, now there are rumours the Danes have their eye on them too. To the west, the Spanish are besieging the Dutch city of Breda, just to drive home the message to the Dutch of their foolhardiness in offering refuge to Spain's enemies, and will still be doing so ten months from now. With Spain so occupied, to the south France has just marched its troops into the mountain passes of the Valtelline, to the dismay of the Pope and the fury of the whole of northern Italy. While up the east, in the Baltic hinterlands, having fought Bethlen Gabor, Prince of Transylvania, the Turkish army and the Russians, Poland suddenly finds another enemy on its side of the Baltic pond: the Swedish King, pop-eyed Gustavus Adolphus. A Viking throwback – vigorously martial, zealously Lutheran, battle-hard and fierce beyond belief. Bronheim could march his troops to any point on the compass and find a foe there waiting; any of them could do the same. That habit of expansion: one becomes two becomes four becomes more than a body can count.

Hans enjoys a good march. Riding pillion, above the dust, he feels his spirits rise. He's fascinated by Milano's piratical mane, and in the mood for conversation. Leaning forward, he shouts into Jag's ear, 'I've never seen a horse with curls in its hair before.'

'Nor had I,' comes the reply.

This is encouragingly human. Hans leans forward again. 'So where'd you learn to ride?'

'Don't remember.'

'You don't remember where?'

'Don't remember learning.' And the new recruit turns his head about and grins, so Hans knows not to take this too seriously. 'Tell me,' he begins. 'Your colonel. This Bronheim. Tell me about him.'

Bronheim is as remote from Hans as is the moon, but Hans is eager to please. 'What d'you want to know?' he asks.

'Where's he from, for a start. That his true name?' The regiment, approaching a bridge, has slimmed down to single file, with a few precautionary guards stationed on either bank. Amongst the guards Bronheim's crew, lords of their little world, lounge back upon their mounts and watch their regiment pass. Bronheim's crew is hand-picked, older than the other boys, better paid and better fed, and when they say their regiment, they mean it. And they've spied Milano. ''Ere,' comes the shout. 'Where'd those scuts get a horse like that?'

Shit, thinks Hans. His spirits plummet. Trouble, trouble, trouble.

The regiment makes camp at sundown; to the outsider, a noisy and confused affair. There are disputes over tent-sites, things have been left behind, misplaced, gone missing altogether. Rich pickings for the light-fingered and sharp-eyed. 'Look at this,' says Matz, returning proudly, and pulling open his jacket reveals, in unhygienic proximity to his armpit, a whole bacon-hock.

Who cares for hygiene? A hock of bacon is as much meat as they see in a week.

Hans is their cook. He likes chopping, mixing, baking things; that all seems eminently straightforward compared to so much else in life. The fire beneath their cooking pot is going nicely, the water on the boil; they've onions, cabbage –

– and an audience. Hans reaches for the bacon and his fingers close on nothing. Bronheim's crew, all eight of them, surround him, grinning; their leader, Bertholdt, waves their supper in the air. Hans sits back on his heels. *Knew it*. Gunter, Stuzzi, Matz look on, resigned. If the worst they come out of this with is the loss of their supper, they'll be getting off lightly.

Bertholdt pulls a bite out of the bacon, chews it up in front of them, mouth open, spits it out. 'You eat this kack?' he asks. Laughter from his crew. 'Now,' Bertholdt continues, 'it seems to me some folk have forgot their manners. Forgot who gets the prime mounts hereabouts.' He takes another bite.

Jag stands up.

To Hans, it looks like he's ashamed of them, or just wants out of this, because that's how he stands, as if he's bored, as if this isn't worth his time. Then he speaks. He says, 'Give it back.'

Bertholdt gives a sort of crow of disbelief. 'Make me,' he says.

And Hans sees Jag's face go *fair enough, if you insist*, and he takes a step forward – and belts Bertholdt across the mouth. It's not even a proper punch, like you'd throw at another man; it reminds Hans of the sort of slap he used to get from his mum, when he was little and had been leading her a dance and her doing the laundry, or any of the other things put women in such bad temper, it's like that, only it's like that to the power of ten. Bertholdt's head snaps right, his feet go out from under him, and he goes down face-down in the dirt, out cold before he even hits the ground. The hock of bacon rolls from his grasp.

'Oh dear,' says Jag, commiserating. Picks up the bacon, wipes the grass off it, and bouncing it idly in his palm, like Samson with the jawbone of the ass, turns to the rest of Bronheim's crew and enquires, 'Want some?'

No, they do not. After a second or two, a couple of them slink forward, and with Jag watching their every move, they pick Bertholdt up by the heels and drag him off.

Lesson one: do not pick fights with Jag.

Gets you wondering about that scar, too.

It's a fine warm night, and Heinrich's crew are lying stretched out on the ground, replete to bursting. Gunter and Matz are snoring lightly. Hans, stuffed full of bacon and cabbage, head propped against a tussock, is awash with a rare sense of complete invincibility. His stomach is so bloated he can't even see his feet. He belches quietly.

'That was good.'

'Yeah,' comes the reply. Jag is lying on his back, head pillowed on one arm, gazing up at the stars. 'I ain't ate like that in an age.'

'No, I mean you smacking Bertholdt one. That was good.'

'He asked for it, he got it.' The way it's said sounds almost philosophical. 'Look, there's another.'

A shooting star has arced across the heavens. Hans levers himself up onto his elbows. 'What d'you think they mean?'

'Not much.'

There are rules in a cavalry crew, the first of which is, when there's a new face about, he tells you who he is and where he's from. Thus far, the amount they know about their new recruit could be written on a fingernail. Hans decides it's up to him to set this right. 'I'm from Münster,' he begins.

'I know,' says Jag. 'You can hear it in your voice.'

Hans's Westphalian accent is indeed noticeably strong. 'Old Herzog Heinrich, he calls me the Münster Cowpat,' Hans admits, colouring up.

'Why'd you all call him *Herzog* Heinrich? If he's a duke, then I'm a mermaid.'

'It's all them airs he gives himself,' Hans replies. 'Him and Bronheim, how we ought'a see them as the same. The Holstein mare, how she cost five hundred thaler. His Spanish saddle, how it cost eighty. And that tent of his.' Hans has lowered his voice; Heinrich hasn't showed so far, but he could be anywhere, listening, ready to come down upon them like the wrath of God.

A soft laugh. 'Yeah, that fucken tent. Something tells me that tent of his is going to suffer a sad accident, one of these days.'

Hans sits up. 'Don't get on his bad side, friend. He'll make your life a hell.'

'He's got a bad side?' Rolled on his side, those pale eyes glinting. 'And what's all this about your brother?'

There, thinks Hans. *So they do still talk about old Will. Behind my back.* 'I joined up with him. Only reason I'm here. He was doing the training – you know, the training for a cavalryman –'

'Yeah, I know it,' comes the reply, softly again, but in a different manner to before. Is that sympathy? Hans's eyes have started to prickle.

'– so he was doing the training, they were doing the drill with pistols, and he made to push his hat back with the pistol in his hand. It was still loaded –'

An almost audible wince.

'– went off in his face.'

A year ago. Standing with a crowd around him, staring at his brother's corpse. The bullet for a cavalryman's pistol is a ball of soft lead, a half-inch in diameter. The top of Wilhelm's head had been no more than a broken bowl of bone, a puddle of blood at its sump. Hans has heard men who have lost a limb speak of it still aching, but with him it feels more as if he's the one who'd been amputated, a branch dropped from a tree. There was a connection, now it's gone. It hurts. It isn't there. 'He just weren't very smart, old Will. Matz'll tell you. Matz says you'd have to be brainless anyway, to do that to yourself.'

'Does he?' says the new recruit, considering.

Hans wipes a hand over his face. *It's all right*, he tells himself roughly, *it's dark. He won't know I'm crying like a girl.*

'And where's Matz from?' the voice continues, after a pause.

'Suhl. He'd a job with his uncle, in one of the foundries. But they threw him out.'

'Why'd they do that?'

'Nicking stuff, I reckon.'

'And Gunter?'

'Oh, he's got family. Bavaria. His dad soldiered, his granddad too – it's like that with them. Old-fashioned. Ever after. You know.'

'And Stuzzi?'

'His folks had a farm.'

A chuckle. 'Never.' Stuzzi looks so much like a farm-boy it's a joke – the yellow curls, the big blue eyes, the big pink mouth forever hanging open, catching flies. Hans is suddenly reminded why he began this conversation in the first place.

'So where are your folks, Jag?'

'No place,' comes the reply. 'They're dead.'

Lesson two: no histories. Out of nowhere, another shooting star.

RUMOUR BLOWS ABOUT the camps continuously, like a gritty summer wind. Sometimes it is useful: 'You hear about the drummer boy, who had the fever? Now they say he's got the rash.' 'Christ. Stay clear of him, then.' Sometimes it is fantastical: 'No. God's my witness, right after that comet, they cut the crop and there was blood in every stem. In every one. I'm telling you, it's end-times. No mistake!' And sometimes it is a matter of record: 'That new lad in Heinrich's crew? You heard what he did?'

Inevitably, some of the lighter dust gets blown into the colonel's ears.

Heinrich is in a card game, a drum for a table. Thanks to a pair of deuces tucked inside his boot, he's going to win. Someone approaches behind him, the other players jump up – Heinrich, annoyed, jumps up as well, and manages just in time to turn it into a smart salute. Bronheim.

'Don't let me disturb the game.' And disturbs it irreparably, at once. 'Heinrich, a word with you.'

This is unexpected, and the unexpected is rarely good. Rumour only has to open her mouth that bit too wide the once, and Heinrich's dancing on the end of a rope.

'Hear you've a proper little David in your crew.'

David? thinks Heinrich. A very nasty moment. David and Jonathan?

'Had a fight with one of my lads.'

David and Goliath. Scripture is not Heinrich's strongest suit. Brandy, bullying, buggery, yes, but Bible study, no. 'Oh, him!' says Heinrich with relief.

'Wondered if you knew,' says Bronheim. 'Thought I'd mention it.'

Is his colonel angry? Bronheim makes Heinrich nervous. You'd think talking with a cousin would be an easier thing, but no. 'Oh, him, yes, I knew. Going to put him on half-rations. Stop his pay.' *Now that's a thought.* 'I'll sort him out,' Heinrich announces, with growing confidence, and cracks his knuckles.

'Really?' says Bronheim. 'Well, I'd watch yourself, if I were you. He all but broke my lad's jaw.'

And the other players in the card game laugh. Bronheim is popular, Heinrich is not. Besides, he's their colonel. Your colonel makes a joke, you laugh, that's all it is.

But not to Heinrich.

A rebuke. In front of an audience. A rebuke from Lord High All-The-World-Is-Mine... Where is the little shit? I'll give him David. I'll give him Goliath!

Striding up through the camp, up through the rows of tents. A kick at a straying dog: God-damned no-name little cur... make me a butt, a joke? Fists clenching and unclenching, hammers on a machine. Hans, sat outside their tent, working over Heinrich's breastplate with a pounce-bag of dry sand, has just enough time to look up – me? Not me – and call a warning – 'Jag!' – before Heinrich sends him over backwards. Hans knows that stride, the expression on Heinrich's face, the swinging rhythm of those fists. He hears Jag, over with the horses, call back, 'What?' then those giant fists going *wham wham wham* –

Massaging the knuckles of one fist in the palm of the other, Heinrich returns the way that he had come. Hans waits for the whistling in his head to cease, then picks himself up and goes to find Jag. One good blow from Heinrich, you'd be black and blue for days. And he got in three of them…

Jag has raised himself unsteadily onto one knee. 'What the fuck was that?' he says, as Hans helps him stand.

'He must'a heard,' says Hans, miserably.

'Heard what?' says Jag, rubbing his gut.

'About you belting Bertholdt one. That would'a been to show you who's the boss.'

Jag stares at him in amazement, then puts back his head and roars with laughter. It's a huge laugh, a giant of a laugh, wacky as a loon. 'Hans,' he says, wiping his eyes (one is already swelling shut), 'you got to show someone you're the boss, surely you ain't?'

A revelation. Hans has never thought of it that way before.

Evening. Heinrich, in his tent, his lair. He's not done yet.

Hans and Stuzzi are walking up through the camp, lugging a bucket of water apiece. They pass the flap of Heinrich's tent. 'Leave that,' comes the voice, thick with drink. 'Hans can do that. Stuzzi, you come on over here. I've got a job for you.'

Stuzzi stops dead.

'Act like you ain't heard him,' says Hans, in an urgent whisper. 'Come sit with the rest of us, he ain't about to come for you with all of us about.'

Stuzzi is motionless. Blue eyes wide, mouth hanging open, like a dog told to do two things at once. Always, always, he goes.

Suppertime. Hans is acutely aware of the gap where Stuzzi ought to be, beside him, yet no-one says a thing – at least, not until Matz reaches across and makes to spoon the final portion from the cooking pot onto his plate. Jag, who has a black eye the size of a poached egg, puts out a hand to stop him. 'That's Stuzzi's, ain't it?'

They don't eat so well tonight. What is meant to be dried fish, but could be dried anything, some lumps of bread, the greasy heel of a cheese, all cooked up together. The march has been a long one, provisions are running low.

'Huh,' says Matz, and points with his spoon toward Heinrich's tent. 'We won't be seeing Stuzzi tonight.'

Jag too looks down at Heinrich's tent – a black silhouette, flaps tightly closed. 'He could be hung,' he says.

'And Stuzzi would be as well,' Hans points out, quickly. Military law: there's no such thing as an innocent victim, there's just the sin, committed, and the guilty sinners, groaning on a gallows. They know it, Heinrich knows they know it, no-one says a word. Heinrich only had to lay a finger on Stuzzi and he had him, every way.

Jag is silent for a while. Then – 'He's a bit of a cunt, your captain, isn't he?' he says, thoughtfully.

'He's yours too, now,' says Matz.

Three days later, when they are camped beside a wood, a dog-fox finds its way into Heinrich's tent. Having sprayed the tent with essence of Reynard – the tent and everything in it – the animal departs, as mysteriously as it had arrived.

Bronheim, at a halt on that day's march, is consulting with his captains, map spread out upon the road. There is a rendez-vous approaching, a great camp, a leaguer – or there should be, if the map can be believed. Military cartography is a rough science at best, decisions over route, direction, require consider-able concentration, and Bronheim's is not being helped by the stink coming from somewhere in the crowd of waiting troops. 'What is that unholy stench?'

'Begging your pardon, sir,' comes the cheery reply, 'I reckon that it's us.'

Bronheim looks about, and spies at the edge of the crowd a crew of boys, dismounted. One of them, the tallest, is beaming a sunny smile. His horse has the most unhandy, swaying bundle on its back. 'Apologies, Colonel,' the boy says. 'Fox got into our captain's tent. We tried to wash it, but the stink won't budge.'

Heinrich is glowering at the boy. So this is the one, is it? And the lad has a black eye – one half his face in mourning, as they say. Has Bertholdt been trying to even the score? *Good God*, thinks Bronheim, *isn't there enough conflict in the world already?* A moment's irritation, but it adds to all the rest: the sweat tickling his back, the untrustworthiness of their maps, the imperative of reaching the great camp... 'Heinrich, what's this?'

'It's like the boy says,' Heinrich replies. 'Nothing I can do.' Heinrich isn't feeling at his best, he's woken with a nasty case of fizzing guts, and though he's been dosing himself with nips from his flask all day, even that doesn't seem to be helping. The brandy has a spiky after-taste, and his tongue feels coated and dry.

Something Bronheim can do, however. 'Burn it.'

'My Colonel!' Heinrich is aghast. 'But that's the finest tent I've had!'

'Burn it. Get a chit from the quartermaster-general when we've made the rendezvous. God's nails, you think I'm leading my company in, stinking like a brewer's fart? Burn it. That's an order.'

The regiment moves on. The crew of boys is left beside the road, with Milano and the tent.

Combusting a thick canvas tent isn't easy, but they use their knives to rip it into strips and, under Jag's instructions, start the blaze with bracken and handfuls of dry moss. No tent, no lair. 'Stuzzi,' orders Jag, 'say *Wiedersehn* to the tent.'

'Bye-bye, tent,' says Stuzzi, almost the only words he's spoken in three days. Then he glances anxiously from one face to the next, trying to work out if this was indeed meant seriously, or was it just another joke at his expense?

'Man,' says Matz, admiringly. 'If Heinrich could see this, he'd make salmagundi out of you.'

'Yeah?' answers Jag. 'You want to know what I think of that?'

Milano is a very puzzled horse. He'd been carrying that thing all this time, now they unload it off him and set it on fire. Then his boy had pissed on its remains. Then they'd all made water on it, standing round it, cackling like cockerels. Then off they'd set again. They've been walking now for the best part of two hours. Dusk is darkening the fields to either side; there are shadows stretching out across the road. He gives an anxious whicker. *Friends, it's late.*

Milano is not the only one to have noticed the shadows creeping in. 'Shouldn't we have caught up with 'em by now?' Gunter is asking, nervously.

'We'll find 'em,' says Jag. 'Look at the road.'

Pocked with hoofmarks. A lot more than a single regiment has been this way.

Stuzzi, aloft on Milano, is nodding off to sleep. Eyelids heavy, closing, closing... what's that? He shakes his eyes open and squints. Someone's laid a patchwork counterpane across a hill out there. He remembers a counterpane like that upon his bed when he was little... Hang on there – a counterpane?

Gunter has gone running forward. 'Hey!' he calls. 'Christ a'mighty! Come and look!'

They stand there, staring out at it. Matz is the first to speak. He gives a low whistle. 'Jesus,' he says. 'I never dreamed the war had got as big as this.'

CHAPTER FIVE

The Venus

'Come, sweetheart, wilt thou do a little? The fitt's come on me now. I will show thee a pure pair of naked breasts, smooth buttocks, lovely and ivory thighs whiter than untrod snow...'

John Garfield, *The Wand'ring Whore*

THE GREAT CAMP. The lines of tents, radiating further than they can see, the pennants for each regiment flapping in the breeze. The bald acre of the parade ground. The bugle calls. The barking dogs. The roundelay of horse-talk, flickering back and forth across the camp like summer lightning. And the continual muted noise of thousands upon thousands of men.

It takes them till almost dark to find their regiment within it. Even when they do, even when amongst this colossal ant-heap they are again surrounded by faces they recognize, there's still no sign of Heinrich. Hans, politely quizzing the muster-sergeant, comes back with the news that Heinrich's in the cranken-house, signed off sick. 'Yeah, I don't reckon we'll see him for a while,' comments Jag.

Heinrich had seemed indestructible. 'What makes you think that?' Hans asks, puzzled.

'Just a feeling.' That and the knife-tip of saltpetre he'd shaken up in Heinrich's flask; saltpetre that not only puts the bang into black powder, but will very handily tie your guts up into knots as well. He had considered making it more, settle the old sod's hash for good and all, but any bigger dose and the taste would have been unmistakable. Besides, that would have meant the crew being broken up, any number of complications, none of which would have served his ends at all.

It has to be this regiment. All the months of travelling and looking, there was not one other with the Virgin on its flag. It's this one; he's sure of that.

So why is the sodding colonel's blasted name Bronheim, and not Maduna?

Patience. Watchfulness.

Right.

The camp is like a city – greater than Münster, unimaginably vast compared to the tiny dorps where Gunter and Stuzzi grew up. Brewhouses, bakehouses, guardrooms big as barns. Field kitchens the size of altars. A tent so huge it has a whole bed inside it. 'Four posts and all, and a proper table laid out with silver and plate,' Hans reports back, marvelling.

'Why didn't you nick something from it?' Matz wants to know.

'I didn't like to,' Hans replies, blushing. 'Would'a spoiled it.'

Jag discovers a horse. Not just any horse, mind, but a coal-black giantess, seventeen hands high, seven hundred thalers' worth, according to her groom. Most soldiers' horses are geldings or mares, only the entirely mad (Bethlen Gabor) or those experimenting with shock tactics almost entirely unknown (the King of Sweden) take stallions onto the field. With Jag close-questioning the man – what does she eat? What bit does he use? – the others lounge about them, arguing in a lackadaisical fashion if even a horse made of gold could be worth as much as that. 'She got Arab blood?' asks Jag, squinting at the horse with his head on one side.

The groom is impressed. 'You've got an eye, ain't you? What makes you think that?'

'She's got them little flicky ears.'

Unusual that the boy should even have seen a horse with Arab blood before, let alone made note of it. 'Where you from, lad?' asks the groom. Hans sits up, starts to pay attention.

And is left as disappointed as before. Jag gives the man one of his beaming smiles. 'Over there,' he answers, jerking a thumb in the direction of their tent.

They walk back to the tent together as the sun goes down. 'I'm going to have a horse like that one day,' says Jag, unguardedly, with a last glance at Her Seven-Hundred-Thaler Highness, peacefully cropping the grass.

'Yeah, right,' says Matz.

Yeah, right, thinks Milano, when his lad turns up with his nosebag – late, and laden with some other horse's scent – and nips him on the arm.

Gunter, Stuzzi, Hans and Matz inspect the wound. A visit to the surgeon's tent, the cranken-house? 'I don't think so,' says Jag, with a laugh, binding it up. 'You ever been in one of them places?'

It's the smell that's the worst, thinks Heinrich. Once you get used to the smell – a fair portion of which he's contributed himself, in the last couple of weeks – it's almost homely. And once he'd stopped casting up his guts, and was no longer convinced he was about to become a victim of typhus, dysentery, the plague, the bloody flux, any of the enteric disasters that lie in wait in every cooking pot, on every spoon and bowl – he'd quite begun to enjoy himself. Regular meals, orderlies to wait upon your every whim, no little tykes to keep in line (*no Stuzzi*, he thinks mournfully – oh, he is feeling better by the day), no ice-eyed little bastard drilling ice-holes into Heinrich's back.

Meantime, plenty to occupy him. Amongst the otherwise motionless, sweating, raving, dying or dead inhabitants of the surgeon's tent, there's a gunnery sergeant with a hernia (occupational hazard); a quartermaster recovering from a dose of the French pox; a messenger with a strange complaint diagnosed as wandering ague; and a sentry who had the bad luck to discharge his weapon into his own foot. The bullet went straight through, but the wound refuses to heal. It's sloughing now, the remaining skin a moist, unhealthy grey. 'You got a stinker there, mate,' says Heinrich, settling on the man's bed. 'Who's for a hand of piquet?'

The quartermaster has a sideline in purloined booze. He has one of his lads tap a barrel, fill a couple of jugs, and make up the loss with anything to hand – what, even Heinrich quails to think, but the stuff that comes into the ward is excellent, liquor that can knock any but the hardened drinker out cold, and is purchased by the surgeons to act as antisepsis, anaesthetic, what you will. They make quite a party of it, most days. 'You joining us, mate?' Heinrich calls out genially to the latest newcomer – a groom who was kicked by his charge and is now nursing a broken shoulder. Some general or other is paying for his care; as a result the man seems to think he is too good to play with them. This annoys Heinrich, but with a couple of glasses inside him he's a friend to anyone.

'No, no,' the fellow says, as always. 'You're too sharp for me. I'll watch.'

As the cards slap down upon the sheets, the usual litany of complaints comes into shape above them. The sentry still has three months' pay outstanding from last year, the gunnery sergeant's wife ran off last spring, the quartermaster, congratulated upon the quality of his latest batch of booze, gives it as his opinion that if his lad is bringing two jugs in to them, he'll be selling off three on his own account. 'Yeah, I got a lad in my crew, giving me grief,' says Heinrich.

'Stealing from you, is he?'

'No, but I got another one does that and all.' Halfway down the jug and Heinrich has reached the stage of intoxication where all the sunlight vanishes from the world, he is the man of sorrows, did ever gallant soldier have as many cares as he? 'This lad,' he begins, 'I pick him up along the road, and first thing he does is start a fight with my colonel's crew. I get him out of that, he starts on my old mare. Has her come when he whistles, like some performing dog.' He shakes his head. Treachery, betrayal – a man can't even call his horse his own.

'You ought to sort him out,' says the sergeant.

'Oh, I've tried,' says Heinrich. 'Oh-ho, I've tried, don't think I ain't. Him and that fish-stare of his, giving me the evil eye—'

'I think I know this lad of yours,' says the groom, leaning forward. 'Bronheim's cavalry, ain't you?'

'That's us,' says Heinrich, gloomily.

'Good tall lad. Got a scar,' says the man, touching a hand to his cheek.

'That's him. I'll even up with him, when I get out of here.'

'That so?' says the groom, sitting back. 'You don't want him, I'll take him off your hands. He's as good an eye for horse-flesh as I've seen in a long while. Where'd he come from?'

'Fuck knows,' Heinrich replies, irritated. 'But I know where he's headed. Hell in a handcart, that one.'

'You reckon, do you?' says the groom.

And there it is again. Heinrich doesn't get it: he looks at the boy and sees the usual no-name, no-account little cur; the rest of the world looks at him, and warns Heinrich off.

'Blank-oh,' says the quartermaster. 'Ten points,' he adds, to the messenger, who's keeping score. They draw again.

It's just that you can never tell what the little bastard's thinking, Heinrich decides. Those eyes of his. They ought to be as easy to see through as glass, but trying to work out what's going on behind 'em is like trying to look into the sun. He glances at the new cards in his hand. 'I got five diamonds,' says the quartermaster. 'Ten points to me.'

The sentry sighs, and shifts his rotting foot to a more comfortable position. Foul smells spread diseases, everyone knows that, so the surgeon's tent is situated well away from the rest of the camp, down by a stand of trees, where a slow-moving river daydreams its way along. Rafts of mosquito larvae pimple the smooth skin of its shallows. Mosquitoes also spread diseases; unfortunately nobody knows this. There's one whining now over Heinrich's head.

Heinrich thumbs his cards into a fan. The mosquito settles on the sheet. Heinrich eyes it, stealthily.

What is he thinking of? He's their captain, they're his crew, his power over them is that of life or death. He holds all the aces in his hand. He slaps them down. The mosquito is a blot, a smear. 'There,' he says, triumphantly. 'Beat that.'

The river may trail with weed and hum with insect life, but if you can't afford to have it done for you, it's the only place in camp to tackle your laundry. It's hot; so hot the horizon is quivering, and there's a deal of splashy tomfoolery as well as laundry going on. Hans, lying on the bank, shirt drying on a bush above his head, has his ease suddenly disturbed by a louder yelp from Matz, out in mid-stream, peering round the river's lazy bend: 'Fuck me!' He lifts his head. Jag, also hauled out on the bank, has turned to look as well. Matz, waist-deep in the water, is wading away from them, fast as the weed will let him, waving his arms above his head: 'Ladies! *Ladies!*'

Ladies? 'What's going on?' Gunter asks, uneasily.

'Damned if I know,' says Jag, and raises his voice in a roar that in a year or so, thinks Hans, is going to rival one of Heinrich's. *'MATZ!'*

A furious splashing. Matz reappears, forcing his way back downstream. 'There's women!'

'What?'

'I said, there's *women!* On the other bank! There's a whole other camp!'

'Matz, I can't believe you've never seen a leaguer bitch before,' says Jag, subsiding back onto his elbows.

'You don't understand!' says Matz. He's come to a halt, is gesturing frantically behind him. 'These ain't like ours –' (meaning the regimental wives and sweethearts) '– these here's the real deal! They're huge great –' (his arms describe impossible proportions in the air) '– huge great things! Wild-looking! And some of 'em *ain't even dressed!*'

'Not dressed?' repeats Hans, mouth agape.

'No! Naked as friggin' Venus, half of 'em! Oh, come on, lads, you got to see!' And Matz starts wading out for the opposite bank.

Jag hasn't moved. 'Trust me,' he says, lying back, grass-stalk in his mouth. 'They ain't none of 'em going to be interested in you.'

'I ain't going, nohow,' says Stuzzi, mid-stream, sat astride a rock. Stuzzi has recently astounded them by coming up with some decided opinions of his own. 'I've seen them camps before. They all come out and pull my hair. Call me a molly. Tell me I ought to be wearing a dress.'

The response Matz had been anticipating would have been something along the lines of a quick *the hell, well spotted, mate!* and *where?* He turns about, a thick green wake of churned-up muck stretching between him and them. The river is unexpectedly cold, its bed unpleasantly soft, weed keeps wrapping round his calves like bandages. He's fed up with Jag, always taking charge, and as for Stuzzi, he's a fucken joke. 'You *are* a molly,' he shouts back, furious, and Stuzzi's face acquires its soft, lost, beaten look of old. 'God, you're all heart you are, Matz, ain't you?' comments Jag, then, soothingly, 'It's all right, Stuzzi, you don't want to go, no-one's going to make you.'

'Yah!' shouts Matz, striking the water with his hand. 'You're scared, you are. A yellow dog!'

'Shall we go, then?' Gunter asks, clearing his throat. He sounds, thinks Hans, completely terrified, but then Hans's own pulses have set up a pretty hard hammering too. Naked women! Hans has never seen a naked woman before. So why, now, does he want to see one so badly? He has no idea.

Jag stretches out, arms behind his head. He's sunk so deep in the grass of the riverbank that Hans can hardly see him. 'I ain't stopping you.'

Matz strikes out at once for the opposite bank. Gunter follows, with a shriek – 'Christ! It's freezing!' After a moment, Hans follows too.

In the silence, once they've gone, a bird begins to sing in the trees above Jag's head. Stuzzi hears him give a sigh. *Jag, scared?* thinks Stuzzi. *Why, that's just Matz being a—* (Once upon another life ago, Stuzzi was taught that bad words made the angels weep, and he still tries very hard not to use, even in his thoughts, the robust shorthand with which his mates – indeed every soldier in the entire God-damned, God-rot-it fucken army – litter their conversation, as casually as they salt their meat, but thinking the blanks gives him a satisfying frisson nonetheless.) All the same, he can't help feeling something here has gone a bit awry. 'Don't you think you ought to go with 'em?'

A chuckle. 'Ten minutes. They'll be back. The women in those camps – they ain't keen on sightseers.'

Silence. Jag lifts his head. Stuzzi's understanding is so simple you can almost see it happening in front of you, conclusions ranged like precious objects on a shelf, not to be touched.

'Jag?'

'That's my name, don't wear it out.'

'So have you been in them camps before, as well?'

'You might say that.' He stretches further, fingertips entwined. Beneath him he can feel the dry earth beating like a heart. 'Took my first steps in one of 'em.'

That's another thing about Stuzzi. No-one else appreciates this, but because it would never occur to Stuzzi that he knows anything, he's actually very discreet.

It could be the approach to a village, a dorp, thinks Hans. There are chickens scratching about, the odd tethered hog. Lines of washing. The heat, once they'd emerged from the trees, had been stunning.

They're coming up to the first in a clutter of tents. Only the tents aren't set in rows, like they should be, they're rigged up anyhow. There's even the odd wagon, also plainly serving as a home. There's cooking smells. 'Like old times, this, ain't it?' says Matz, in high good humour, meaning before Jag turned up. He's adopted a swagger. 'Oh Lord. Oh my Lord. Told you. Look at that.'

There's a woman walking toward them. She's wearing petticoats – no skirts – and without her corsets, too. Nothing over her breasts but a chemise. Her breasts are big. They wobble as she walks. Her nipples look to be the size of plums. 'Oh my,' Gunter whispers.

"*Tag!*' Matz calls out, as the woman comes nearer.

The woman eyes him up and down. 'Listen, little cherry,' she says, 'come back when you ain't so frigging green.' And proceeds upon her way.

'Yeah, well, some of 'em is bound to be like that,' Matz declares, recovering himself. 'Downright common, some of 'em.' He points toward a rambling path, leading between the higgledy-piggledy tents. 'Let's try down here.'

*

The bird has stopped singing. A hot, dry breeze is worrying the leaves. 'Jag?' Stuzzi calls out. 'Jag, it's been a whole lot longer'n ten minutes now.'

'We're lost, ain't we?' says Hans. 'Admit it. We're lost.'

The camp is a maze. Even the paths don't seem to know where they're headed, you walk down one, dead end, try another, come out in a circle where you were before.

'We're not lost,' says Matz, furious. 'We're just – we're finding our way, that's what. Look, let's try this one. We ain't been down here before, I'm sure of it.'

Bollocks, thinks Hans. Tucked in behind him, Gunter whimpers, 'I wish Jag was here!'

'Jesus!' Matz exclaims. 'Will you stop going on about Jag! What's so great about him, all of a sudden?'

'He wouldn't have got us *lost*,' Gunter replies, with some acerbity, and then, 'Oh Christ, there's another of 'em.'

'Just keep going,' says Hans. 'Keep going, don't look at her.'

Another shabby little tent, another woman sat outside it. This one wears a leather corselet, half-unlaced, displaying a cleavage like a cloven hoof. She's built like a pikeman. She's even smoking a pipe. She sits back, pushes out her breasts as if ready to make them explode. Oh God in heaven, how not to look?

She's seen them. Here it comes –

'What are YOU staring at, you God-damn string-dick snot-nose little runt?' And another shout, as they scurry past: 'Ow, look at the little chickens. Scared of being *plucked*.'

Just get us out of here, Hans thinks. *I'll be a monk, I'll never look at another whore again, long as I live. Please God, just get us out of here, just get us out of here alive...*

'Down here,' says Matz. 'We're on the right track now.' And stops dead.

A girl has emerged from one of the tents before them.

She's like a being from another race. White-skinned, long-limbed, delicate as a doe. She pauses in the doorway, raising her arms, lifting her hair from the back of her neck. She has a long pin in her hand, and as she draws the pin between her lips and skewers it through her curls, Hans feels it as if she had skewered him through the heart. She starts to walk toward them. Her walk (thinks Hans) is like her whole body is saying *hello*. She's wearing nothing but a little shift. The sun is shining through it. It's like she's wearing nothing but a cobweb. It's more than if she were naked. It's worse than if she were naked. He can see –

Those. He can see –

That.

Oh, fucken hell.

Hans feels a wavering disaster of a smile bloom across his face, and a blush that seems to cover his whole body. He is excruciatingly aware of the need to cover his lap. He sees the same helpless goggling on Gunter's face as well –

'Didn't I tell you?' says Matz, exultant, and, marching up, blocks the girl's path. 'Excuse me, miss!'

Her smile has gone. She watches Matz approach with the same hostility as her sisters.

'Excuse me, miss! My friends here think we're lost.' A wink at Gunter and Hans. 'Would you be so good as to direct us back to the cavalry tents? Maybe you could show us the way?'

The girl's eyes flick over them. Matz is now so close to her he's almost standing on her toes. The expression on her face takes on a freezing quality. 'Oooh, she's going to knee him,' whispers Gunter, in agony. 'Watch.'

Hans is watching, but not the girl. Someone else has come out of the tent where she had been.

Bronheim.

Fuzzed with sleep, wearing nothing but his boots and shirt, and looking about to see where his little whore has got to.

'Matz!' hisses Hans. Matz waves him off.

'Matz!' Gunter has joined in. Matz puts two fingers up at them. He's seeing nothing but the girl. The scene has all the sticky qualities of nightmare. Hans closes his eyes. They're going to get flogged for this, all of them, if not worse. What's the penalty for flirting with your colonel's whore? He can't remember ever hearing it – obviously a crime of such heinous stature it's not even on the books.

'Having fun?' asks Jag, strolling up. He's got that big grin on his face again. Then he spies the girl. 'Oh *ho*. Thought something must be keeping you.'

'Bronheim!' gasps Hans.

'Is it?' says Jag, peering exaggeratedly ahead. 'Lordy, so it is.'

'And Matz!' Does this disaster need more explanation than that?

'Damn me,' says Jag. He sounds impressed. 'Well I never.'

'Jag, we've got to do something!'

'Matz wants to try it on with Bronheim's Venus, good luck to him.' But there's a sparkle in his eye.

'Jag, *please!*' says Hans, entreating.

The sparkle has grown warmer. 'She *is* a Venus, ain't she?' says Jag, softly. 'Oh, very well then. Do me best.'

He saunters forward. Taps Matz on the shoulder. Matz spins around, Jag elbows him aside ('Hey!' cries Matz, outraged). Jag gives the girl that beaming smile, puts his hands about her waist and lifts her up into the air with a suddenness that makes her squeal.

'What's your name, little bird?' they hear him ask. 'And make it quick.'

The girl's expression has changed too, and not only (so it appears to Hans) because she too has now seen Bronheim, striding down upon them with a face like Jove about to hurl a thunderbolt. 'Gretchen,' comes her reply. She has her hands on Jag's shoulders, bracing herself. Bronheim has reached them.

'WHAT THE DEVIL'S THIS?'

Jag lowers the girl to the ground. There's a breeze playing round them, lifting Bronheim's shirt-tail – another good question, what's the penalty for seeing your colonel's great white hairy arse?

'Our service, sir,' Hans hears Jag announce, 'and by your leave, but this here is my cousin.'

'Your *cousin*?' It's clear Bronheim does not believe this for a minute.

'Yes sir,' says Jag. There's that giant grin again. 'My cousin Gretchen.'

The little whore has wound herself round Bronheim's arm. 'Only we ain't seen each other in an age,' she says, smiling fondly, and displaying a deal more wit than Hans, for one, had given her credit for.

'Is that a fact?' says Bronheim. Only sounding rather less certain now that it is not.

'Yes sir,' Jag answers, smartly. 'I heard she might be here, so came to look for her. But seeing she has so much better company than us, sir, shan't impose no more. Gretchen –' (the girl dips her eyelids at him) '– it's grand to see you look so well.' A neat salute to Bronheim. He turns about. 'Come, lads,' he says, briskly. 'There's work to do.'

'Bye, cuz,' the girl calls after them.

Back at the tent. 'But I don't understand,' says Stuzzi. 'How come if she's your cuz, you didn't know as she was Bronheim's whore?'

'You'll have to ask Matz that.'

Matz scowls at them, furious. 'You wait,' he says. 'You just sodding wait. And I was the one who saw her, just remember that.'

'That's right, mate, so you did. Only trouble is—'

'Bronheim saw her first!' Helpless with glee, Hans collapses to the ground. He hears Gunter's cackle, 'Oh, Matz – oh my – your face, when you saw that it was Bronheim –'

Hiccupping with laughter, Hans gazes at the sky. No shooting stars tonight. Instead great banks of cloud rolling over
each other, thunderous, disturbed. 'Hey,' says Hans, sitting
up. 'It's raining!'

Rain tightens the curls in Milano's mane, makes all the horses
frisky. The great commanders sit in their tents and plot and
plan; outside the rain falls on the great and small alike.

It's the age-old problem: you muster up an army, then
you have to keep it fed. Those thousands of horses consume
hundreds of acres of fodder a day; feeding the men has required
the slaughter of hundreds of animals a week. A camp lives off
the land for as long as it can, and then it moves. The army that
stops moving starves and dies. But in the autumn, when the
rains come down, moving all those men as one is an impossibility. Put even a single regiment of horse down some muddy
autumn road and you render it impassable by anything else for
days; those troops left to follow after are stranded, the peasants
whose cattle you helped yourself to start nipping round your
heels, and pretty soon your brave army is just one harried, starving mess.

The solution is to split your army up, send them off to winter
billets in some lucky town. No-one makes war in wintertime,
it's understood.

Some regiments from the great camp are being sent west,
to mop up the last desperate resistors in the Palatine. Some
are being sent to winter in the great bread-basket of Bohemia.
Bronheim, however, draws a rather shorter straw.

The groom is giving Her Seven-Hundred-Thaler Highness a
last once-over before setting off when he realizes he has, again,
an audience. 'Come to say goodbye?'

'Yeah, I guess,' says the boy, coming closer. 'Thought she
might like this.'

A final apple, carefully quartered. The mare munches it out of his hand as the boy rubs at the star on her forehead. 'She really seven hundred thalers' worth?' he asks, wistfully, as if even a hundred less might put her within his reach.

'Every pfennig,' says the groom. 'War's putting the prices up of everything.'

'Everything 'cept wages,' says the boy, with a rueful grin.

Well now, thinks the groom. *Is that a hint?* 'How much do you get?'

'Fifteen a month. When I get it.'

It is, the groom decides. The boy has certainly left it late enough. What was the camp (and before that, meadow, pastureland) is mud as far as the eye can see, a few patches of yellowed grass marking where the largest tents had stood. 'I could double that.'

From the remaining cavalry tents, marooned amongst the sea of mud, a shout of rage. Heinrich has returned. The boy makes a face. 'Can't do it,' he says. 'Appreciate the offer, though.'

Bad timing. The groom is disappointed. 'You ain't going to stay part of that crew forever, are you?' he asks.

'I ain't made plans that far ahead,' says the boy.

Which is odd, because if ever there was a lad looked like he had a future in this game… Ah well. 'So where are they sending you off to now?'

'Some place up in Pomerania. Up on the Polish border.'

Now it's the groom's turn to pull a face. 'Then you watch out for yourself, young man. That's a long march. And that captain of yours – he don't seem over-fond of you.'

'I guess that makes us quits then, don't it?' says the boy, unconcernedly. He gives the horse's neck one final pat. 'Good to have met you. Sir.'

It's rare for a groom to hear himself addressed as *sir*. 'I tell you what,' the groom calls out to the departing figure, tromping through the mud, 'If it comes down to it, between you and that captain of yours –' (because it really is going to irk him, this, he can feel it already) '– I guess you can look out for yourself, hey?'

He'd meant it only as a response to the compliment to him, and a small boost to the boy's morale, perhaps, with that march ahead of him, so the reply he gets is a surprise.

The boy's smile is as broad as it can be. 'Sometimes I think that's all I'm waiting for.'

CHAPTER SIX

This Right Smart Little Town

'We see the Eagle spreading her Wings in Germany, reaching with her Talons as far as the Sound of the Baltick Sea...'

John Rushworth, *Historical Collections of Private Passages of State*

HANS IS COMPOSING a letter to the folks back home:

Dearest Mutti

Like all of his letters, it will never be sent. Composition takes place solely in his head.

My willing service to you. This is a greeting from your son the soldier-boy.

I guess by now you have my other letter, telling you of poor Wilhelm.

She does not, of course. When Hans next sees his mother she'll still be expecting to hold two sons in her arms.

Dearest Mutti, you must understand that when you're soldiering, these things happen.

An awkward wriggle on his perch. He's composing this sat on the top step of a market cross. There ought to be more to say on the subject of Wilhelm, but dredging his imagination, it seems that there is not.

I am in good health.

He looks about him.

We are in Grauburg now, Mutti, in our winter quarters for this year. Grauburg is a long, long way from you.

Start again.

Grauburg is this right smart little town. We thought it 'ud be some borderland shit-hole (his mother will never be reading this, after all) *and the march to get here was a bastard – sleet and rain the whole damn way – but here we are, all safe accomplished, as they say, us and a troop of infantry, a squad of gunners and a company of musketeers. You would like it here. They've got this walkway on the walls all round the town, and a proper market, and what must be a dozen churches, easy. We've been here a month now, right comfortable.*

Now, what else?

Mutti, we've this new lad in our crew. Well, I say new, but he ain't no more, it feels like he's been there forever.

He stops.

It's like he's made of something different. He ain't the same as us at all.

He stops again. Is this the kind of thing a mother would be interested in, or even understand? Hans is far from sure he understands it himself.

Anyway, Mutti, this here is where we are. We never thought we'd get a billet – by the time the officers had taken over all the houses on the square, and the gunners had put their guns onto the walls, and moved themselves into the taverns, and the infantry had taken over anywhere left with a roof, there weren't a barn nor a shed to be had.

So we've ended up in this fruit loft at the end of someone's garden, down toward the West Gate, as they call it, with the horses stabled underneath, and our kit laid out in the room above. It's good and warm that way.

At least, it is when Stuzzi remembers to close the door.

So here we'll sit and wait it out till spring. There's hills all round the town, and you can see the snow on them already. Mutti, I will sign off now. Ever your loving and obedient son –

Hans

Hunker down and wait till spring. Pass the days in doing what any army does out of the field in wintertime – dicing, drinking, petty theft, harassing the good citizens' daughters and wives (any man who thinks he can get away with it), target practice off the weathervanes (the musketeers) and idle vandalism. Graffiti is especially popular; every army likes to leave its mark. The market cross is sheltered by a little roof, supported on four slender Gothic columns, one of which now bears the recently incised inscription:

H.J.M.G.S.

*

1624

Across the square a company of musketeers is readying themselves. They've swapped their muskets and stands for pistols and knives, and instead of rattling bandoliers of wooden powder flasks criss-crossed over their chests (twelve to a man – the musketeers call them their apostles, and in moments of stress count them off like a rosary), each has a leather satchel. *A hunting party*, thinks Hans. Most musketeers were hunters in their other life; they make the best marksmen. Must have tired of shooting weathercocks.

Hans heaves a sigh and folds his penknife. *Point of fact, Mutti, being out the field? It's proper boring.*

Less boring for some than for others, perhaps.

In the biggest room of the finest house on the square, the one with a balcony, so he can keep an eye on what his troops are getting up to, Bronheim lies in bed. He's half-hard, half-asleep, and is watching Gretchen wash herself. Her tiny pale pink nipples bob up and down as she sponges between her legs; she's still so young her breasts point left and right, and in bed her nipples quest this way and that like the noses on a pair of kittens. She doesn't have much pubic hair, but what she has, when wet, forms the most enchanting little quiff, silhouetted now against her thigh. His thoughts are lazy, overlapping, but are slowly moving him toward the conclusion that this, given the vagaries of fortune, the unknowability of Fate, the imperfect nature of the world and the sinful flaws of man, is probably as good as it can get.

Gretchen has the wickedest, most minxish little smile as well. 'You're looking pleased with yourself.'

'I'm a very happy man,' he replies.

Got you, says Fate, waiting by the door.

A knock. Now who the devil's that?

'Colonel?'

His ensign's voice. 'Sir?' And clear the man knows full well Bronheim's not alone.

'What is it?' Bronheim struggles out of bed, and points to Gretchen to get in. Pulling on his shirt and breeches, he lets down the curtains round the bed (a wicked giggle from within – all his staff know their colonel brought his new whore with him, and half of them have done the same, but damn it, a man in his position has to observe the proprieties. 'Quiet, you,' he tells her), and opens the door. 'What is it now?'

'Sir, it's the captain of the musketeers. Says he needs to speak with you. Sir, they've been up in the hills. Found something.'

*

A path cut through the trees, and plenty of traffic been along it too. And done recently, the broken branches still oozing sap.

'Any sign who did it?' Bronheim asks.

'No sir,' the captain says. 'But one of my men says someone took a shot at him. Shot off his hat.'

Probably caught it on a twig, thinks Bronheim, who has the usual cavalryman's god-like contempt for any other section of the military. *They plucked me out of bed for this?*

But two nights later, it's the gunners, on the walkway, on the walls. 'You see that?' they say, pointing off into the dark. 'Lights. Up there in the hills.'

Bronheim can feel the cold striking up through the soles of his boots, he can hear the soft secret murmuring of the trees (so many trees, it's like the land beyond the walls has been replaced by some mysterious inland sea), but he can't see anything. Nothing but pitch black.

Gunners are odd fellows, everyone agrees. Superstitious as old maids. While Bronheim is ready to excuse this in men who live but one stray spark away from being blown to kingdom come, it's rather harder to excuse being made to stand out here, shivering, peering into nothingness, searching for what? A will-o'-the-wisp.

Whatever it was, there's nothing now. Daybreak tomorrow, send out a patrol.

'You found a *what?*'

'A camp, sir,' says the lieutenant, turning his hat in his hands. He seems horribly embarrassed to be the bearer of such bad news. 'We found where there had been a fire, sir. A pile of ash. Ten foot across. Still warm.'

'Charcoal burners?' Bronheim suggests, looking round the

table to see if anyone else agrees. The usual murmurs: that'll be it, sir, bound to be.

'Eickholz, did you *see* anyone?'

Lieutenant Eickholz shakes his head.

'Well then,' says Bronheim, pushing back his chair. 'Charcoal burners. Hah!' He's only giving this half his attention, but then it only deserves half. The rest goes to Gretchen, the image of her, lying as he left her, bare rump upward in their tumbled bed.

'There's more,' says Eickholz, suddenly. 'We lost a man.'

'You lost a man? What do you mean, you lost him? You mean he's dead? You were attacked?'

'No sir,' Eickholz replies. 'We simply lost him. One minute he was there, the next he weren't.'

'You mean there's some poor soul still wandering about up there?' It's almost comical. Not if one were the man concerned, of course, but here in this strong, handsome house, a fire burning, wine on the table, Gretchen waiting in the bed upstairs, it is definitely worth a smile.

'Yes sir,' says Eickholz, twisting the brim of his hat into a fat felt roll.

'Then you'd best go back up there and find him, hadn't you?'

'Market day today,' sings Gunter, merrily. 'Market day today.' And they've been paid as well. 'I'm going to buy me some of them sugar buns.' Gunter is turning into a bit of a glutton. 'Them sugar buns, with the butter glaze on top. What are you going to buy, Jag?'

'New socks,' says Jag, waggling his fingers through the holes in his current pair. 'Unless any one of you is handy with a darning needle.'

Stuzzi is longing to say *I'll mend 'em for you, Jag,* but Matz is watching, so he bites his tongue.

They leave their billet together. Gunter dancing ahead of them, capering in time. Two old biddies, gentlewomen of the town, stop to give him a sour look: little ruffian, no manners, all that noise. 'MAR-AR-KET DAY-AY TODAY,' Gunter sings, capering to the corner. He stops. 'Here,' he exclaims, 'where's it gone?'

At the same moment, on the other side of the square, Bronheim, puzzled by the continuing quiet outside, strolls onto his balcony. Looks out, and down, and all around –

No baker's cart, no sugar buns. No pens of pigs, no crates of chickens. No haggling quartermaster. No peasant farmers. No crowds of shoppers – nothing. Clusters of baffled townsfolk. Bronheim can see right across the square.

No market.

The sound of horses coming into the square, at a slow trot. Gunter has seized Hans by the arm. 'What is it? What's going on? Who are they?'

The man in the lead of those now shambling past – hatless, face bloodied – has the wild and staring look of a man just waking from a nightmare. The horse behind him has its rider strapped across its back, arms dangling. Then two more, swinging in their saddles – as Hans watches, one leans slowly sideways and falls from his mount in a tangle of boots and reins that puts you in mind of thatch falling from a roof, a knot pulled from your hair.

'Oh Jesus,' says Hans. 'That's our patrol.'

Three men wounded, two more missing, two shot dead. This from a patrol of twenty. One end of the market has become a mortuary, the other, a hospital; the downstairs parlour in Bronheim's billet the setting for a council of war.

'And you saw *nothing*?' Bronheim can't believe it.

'Nothing.' Eickholz reeks of brandy – not his fault, they had to pour half a bottle into him before he could speak at all. 'I know we got one. I heard him cry. I heard him fall. But we saw nothing. They threw flares down on us, and then this hail of shot – it was black, sir. Pitch black. Dark as hell. Oh my God.'

From outside an animal howl. The wounded are below the parlour window; all will be dead by morning. Two are insensible; the third, with a bullet lodged in his pelvis, is not. Seven men, out of twenty. Who would do this? Grauburg holds three hundred cavalry, forty gunners and their guns, a hundred infantry, four dozen musketeers. The population of the town rose by a quarter as soon as they entered it, *who would damned well dare?*

His officers are waiting. Stooping, ear to keyhole in the hallway, the owner of the house waits too, wife and children lined up anxiously behind him.

And Bronheim, finally, wakes up. 'I want two patrols,' he says. 'No, make that four. We send 'em out, north, south, east, west. My cavalry. The infantry. Split the musketeers between them. I want every farm between here and the border turned inside out. I want every God-damn peasant to tell us what he's seen and what he knows, and if they won't talk, make them. Where's Heinrich? Him. Use him.' Forget Gretchen, forget that warm accommodating bed, and bye-bye spending winter idling, out the field. The war has travelled with them, has it? Fine, then they'll turn and face it once again. 'I want to know who's out there. I want to know who's done this and I want them made to *pay.*'

They've lit fires around the marketplace, as much for light as heat, so every figure in the crowd casts his twin in shadow on the flame-lit wall. Someone forgot to issue them with a surgeon, so what attention can be given to the wounded comes from their blacksmith, who has a sideline in veterinary medicine, and who is now attempting, with pincers designed for bending iron, to extract the musket ball from the wounded man's hip.

That animal howl again. Stuzzi has his fingers in his ears.

The blacksmith wipes his face and tries once more. The man stubbornly refuses to lose consciousness; he's going to die with his eyes open, this one, watching it circle near. Two of the sergeants are holding him down, at his head a kneeling woman weeps over his face.

'They should finish him off,' Matz whispers, savagely. Matz's way of dealing with any strong emotion is to attack it head-on. 'Someone should just do it. Oh, fucken *hell* –'

The man is flailing at the air, as if trying to beat something off. The woman gives a wail. The man arches up from the pavement, flops back, and she throws herself upon him, calling out his name, cradling his shoulders, trying to hold up his head, shrieking, over and over again. She sounds like a thing caught in a snare. Women's grief is scary. At last a few of her sisters slip forward from the crowd, and half-lead, half-drag her away. And Jag, in a voice very different to his usual tone, says quietly, 'They should keep an eye on her. Sometimes, when they go like that, they don't come back.'

He says it almost to himself. Hans, peering at him, is doubly startled, not only by the compassion in the speaker's voice, but by the grief in his face as well. Where did that come from?

Matz is dumbstruck with contempt. It was the soldier who mattered, not the whore.

Bring on the bully-boys.

This is what a man enlists for – to go flying through the countryside, walled in with back- and breastplate, sword at your hip, pistol at each knee, hurtling along on a horse so big, so heavy, that it shakes the ground. Fifty men galloping behind you and nothing more worrying in front of you than some little farmstead. This is the third today. The others have produced nothing more than the usual protestations of innocence and the usual complaints, as Heinrich's squad worked through henhouse and barn, that now they'll starve, that now they've nothing (bare-arsed lies, as everybody knows, all peasants always have a hidden pot of gold) – but this one might be different. This one is uncomfortably close to a flank of those wooded hills.

The squad clatters into the farmyard. The Holstein mare, champing on the biggest bit Heinrich could get in her mouth, has flecks of foam around her jaws like a rabid dog. He hauls her to a stop, sticks the spurs in her sides, and she rears, eyes rolling. Heinrich takes a pistol from the holster at his knee and fires it off into the air. 'Come on out!' he bellows. 'I said come on out you God-damned boors, show yourselves!'

Nothing. The horses wheel and rear. Heinrich clonks the Holstein mare across the back of the neck with the butt of his pistol and she crashes back to earth. He takes a long, slow look at the farmhouse itself. No smoke from its chimney. Windows shuttered. Heinrich dismounts. 'Try in there,' he orders, pointing at the barn. Peasants are like rats, they always have some hole down which they hide.

Kicking in the farmhouse door is the work of a moment. Beyond the door, two rooms, bracketed around a chimney-breast, a wooden ladder leading to the attics. Heinrich moves from one room to the other, comes back to the first, holds his hand over the sooty hearth, peers up the chimney at the sky. Stands in the centre of the room, perplexed. The place is empty. Nothing left. Not a stool, not a cup. And it's clean – the floor swept, the oven clear of ash. What terrifies a peasant so much that he'll desert his hole, yet gives him time to empty it first?

The sergeant pokes his head around the door. 'Well?' Heinrich demands, and the man shakes his head.

'Just like this, sir. Whole barn's cleaned out. Not so much left as an egg.'

And there's a shout. 'Captain! Something here!'

The squad is in the orchard, standing round an oval of bare earth. 'Well now,' says Heinrich, stooping down, patting the ground. 'What have we here?' He stands up, smiling. 'Few bottles of wine, maybe? Cheeses? Bit of plate?'

'Pot of gold?' the sergeant suggests.

Heinrich's smile grows broader, shows his teeth. 'Get digging.'

The first sign that they've got this wrong is the smell, creeping up between the clods of earth, strong enough to bring the juice into your mouth. Heinrich holds his cuff across his nose. 'Keep going,' he orders, but he knows what this will be even before the hand emerges, nacreous with rot. Then the arm, still clothed, and then the matted hair.

They bring him out and clear the dirt from his face – 'That's Gottfried,' one man offers. 'Him what was in the patrol.'

Fuck, thinks Heinrich. He glances at the hills, where the trees seem to be creeping closer. Then one of the men standing round the hole, the pit, the grave, gives a yelp: 'There's another one in there!'

There are three in total. They lay them down upon the grass – that poor bastard first went missing in the hills, and the two from the patrol. All three dispatched with a shot through the back of the head.

'We need to tell the colonel,' says the sergeant, breaking the silence.

'Yeah, we need to tell the colonel,' Heinrich parrots, but what? God-damned peasants wouldn't do this, wouldn't dare, they don't have pistols, they have flails and scythes... He glances at the hills again. What is it? What is up there?

'Sir!' A shout from the other side of the orchard. 'Sir, there's another grave!'

And so there is. Unmistakable, this one, neatly rounded, neatly patted down, under the apple trees, facing the hills... not such a bad place to wait out Judgement Day. Chosen with care. Chosen, one might almost say, with love. A cross of pebbles pressed into the mound, a garland of withered leaves.

'Dig it up,' says Heinrich.

It isn't deep. The ground's too cold. It comes up in a winding sheet, tucked neatly in at head and toes. Heinrich sniffs it.

Fresh. There's something wrapped around its head, blue cloth, heavy with half-frozen clay.

'Hold him up.' Heinrich advances. 'Let's see what we have here.'

He puts his hands on the winding sheet and pulls. The corpse falls forward, unwrapping as it rolls. The men holding it leap away. Heinrich staggers back. 'Mother of God!'

The cloth – the flag – unfurls across the ground. Bold blue and yellow. Three gold crowns. The three gods of the Uppsala. The crowns of the holy kings. Or those of the three kingdoms, united under one: Norway, Scania, *Sweden*.

HERE WE ARE AGAIN, that panelled parlour, fire banked even higher than before, more wine on the table, more chairs (and men) around it too. Another council of war. But this time, the room is fizzing with bravado. 'The Swedish,' says Bronheim, leaning back, tenting his fingertips. 'Who knows something about them?'

A clamour of answers. Captain Mannfred – good fellow, good, good fellow, solid as they come – gets in first. 'God-damned Lutheran heretics,' he says, and the room rumbles its agreement. 'To a man,' Mannfred continues, growing bolder. 'To a *babe*.'

'They live in darkness,' says a voice. *Are we speaking theologically?* Bronheim wonders. 'Perpetual midnight,' the voice continues. 'Sun never shows its face up there, I've heard. Whole country is accursed.'

'They've all got webbed feet, and six fingers.'

'That's 'cause they fuck their sisters.'

A rather more salacious-sounding rumble than before. Those sitting round the table all lean forward, look the speaker's way. The speaker, captain of the musketeers, has flushed up like a girl. 'Can't tell which man's wife is whose, I guess. Too damned dark!'

A pause for laughter. Bronheim lets them laugh. And then the voices go on as before:

'Greater sots and drinkers even than the English, so folk say.'

'And they ride *reindeer*. Never heard of horses. There ain't a decent mount to be found in the entire country.'

Webbed feet? Six fingers? Greater drinkers than the English? His men are coming off their hooks. 'I rather meant,' says Bronheim, leaning forward, 'who can tell me something of them militarily?'

The rumble grows darker. Well, as to that, Colonel, as to that –

'They're none so easy to beat, I'll tell you that.' Now, who's this? One of those squashed in at the far end. Bronheim raises an enquiring eyebrow at his ensign. Captain in the infantry, is it? No wonder Bronheim doesn't know the man's name. 'I knew a sergeant,' the man goes on. 'Served at Riga. Came up against the Swedish. They all but wiped his unit out.'

'And Riga fell,' says Bronheim, musingly. 'Is that what we have up there, in the woods?'

Roars of defiance. 'What we have up there,' says Mannfred, his voice once more drowning out the rest, 'is a pack of freebooting no-account hireling God-damn *slaves*.' The room, impressed, falls quiet. 'Swedish army'll take anyone,' says Mannfred. 'Scratchings and scrapings of every country on earth. It's a well-known fact.'

Thank you, Mannfred, Bronheim says – or is about to say, when he spies Eickholz shifting in his seat. 'Lieutenant?'

'No, nothing of importance, sir,' says Eickholz, uncomfortably. Eickholz is the only one here whose rank is a lowly lieutenant; if Bronheim's cavalry were less in number, it wouldn't even be that.

'Tell us.' Bronheim spreads his arms out wide. 'We're all brothers here.'

'Well – I've come up against them, sir. As you know.'

The room does know, and privately each individual believes they could have done better than Eickholz, in such a fierce and sudden piece of action. Wasted on a lieutenant, a clash of arms like that.

'And they – well, sir, they'd a prodigious rate of fire.'

'How *prodigious*?' asks Bronheim.

Eickholz drops his head. 'I reckon they were getting off a round a minute.'

Brothers or no, this is not what Bronheim wants to hear. 'Captain?' he says, looking down the table. 'Our best is?'

'And,' says Eickholz, 'their first shot, took Gottfried out the saddle? They were plus two hundred yards away.'

A round a minute, and a range of two hundred yards? The sharpest of Bronheim's sharp-shooters is unreliable beyond a hundred yards; at two hundred their bullets would hardly raise a bruise.

'And they have horses,' Eickholz continues. 'We heard them. In the woods.'

'So how many do we think they have up there?' Bronheim asks, coming to the point.

No-one seems willing to commit themselves. 'An 'undred men,' the captain of the musketeers offers at last.

'More,' Eickholz says at once.

'Come off it. Old Sven-rag-and-tag up there? How? How, if he's that sodding handy at hiding himself? How can he have more than that?'

But Eickholz will not be silenced. 'Two hundred men,' he says, stubbornly, and is about to add 'at the least', when the infantry captain, with a ruminative air, begins, 'That sergeant that I spoke of. He said they had these axemen in their force. Hackwells, he called 'em. That's their cry. That's what they're shouting, when they come at you. *Hack well! Hack well!* And the man makes a sweeping, chopping motion with his hand – and upends his glass into Heinrich's lap.

Herzog Heinrich has been listening (half-listening) with lowering brows and shortening temper. Isn't he the one who found it was the Swedish in the first place? It should be him holding forth here; instead it's that scut Eickholz and this no-name dog from the infantry. He rises, slowly, majestically (the sound of chairs scraping back – those nearest are getting themselves out of harm's way). He looks down at the stain spreading across his breeches, the infantry captain quaking in his seat – 'S'a God-damn disgrace,' Heinrich finds himself saying. His tongue seems to be taking longer than usual to find its way around his mouth. 'S'a God-damn –' (he bangs his fist upon the table, as much to bring his tongue to order as anything else) '– God-damn disgrace!' He squints to bring Bronheim into focus. 'You listen to –' (he points at Mannfred, whose name has suddenly escaped him) '– You listen to *him, there!*' His fist strikes the table once again. 'Fucken Swedish, they couldn't hit Monday from Sunday.'

With growing amazement, Bronheim realizes that Heinrich has dared present himself at his colonel's table already drunk. He looks at his ensign, as if for explanation; the ensign merely rolls his eyes to heaven. In his opinion, even if Heinrich and Bronheim do share blood, they should have left the old sot back at the great camp.

'There ain't no more'n a bunch of God-damned herring-eating trolls up in those woods,' Heinrich continues, righting himself. The ensign rolls his eyes again, Heinrich sees him do it, thinks, *Fucken little flag-folder*, points a finger so he can be sure that he has Bronheim's full attention. 'You want my advice? You leave 'em up there. You won't hear no more of 'em in a week or two. You leave 'em up there till they're frozen into *blocks.* Then I'll go, I'll go, *I'll go* hack 'em up meself.'

'Thank you, Heinrich,' says Bronheim, and moves the pointing finger a little away from his face. 'Gentlemen,' he begins, with commendable restraint, then, abruptly, 'Damn you,

Bertholdt, what is it you want, hey?' The leader of his crew is mooching by the door; how much of Heinrich's ravings had the little sod just seen? 'Damn your eyes, you stand straight when you speak with me!'

'Begging your pardon, sir,' says Bertholdt, coming away from his slouch against the door jamb, and clearly not caring whether he's pardoned or no. (But then why should he? Bertholdt's has been a sorry fall. Publicly bested by that lanky bastard in Heinrich's crew, pushed yet further down the pecking order by the advent of Bronheim's cat-faced little whore.) 'Only the gunners say there's an 'orsemen come outta the wood. And he's asking for a word with you.'

Gretchen, lying on the bed, grouping the knots in the panelling above her head: little ones like cherry pips, big oysters, triplets, twins. Some of them make families; oh, she's bored.

Oh, she is bored. This is no place to be young in. She's fed up with this town, she's fed up with this room (which had seemed, when she first saw it, splendid as a room within a palace, or her imaginings of one), she's fed up with the lady of the house drawing back her skirts whenever she and Gretchen coincide, she's fed up, most of all, with counting them damn knots above her head while Bronheim labours over her. Night after night she's done it, if she has to do it but once more she'll scream.

She twiddles a ringlet round one fingertip, tilts her head, directs her hearing down. There's a grand commotion of some sort going on down there. Doors banging, booted feet running about, shouted orders.

Oh, who cares?

More ringlet twiddling and smoothing. Gradually, it dawns on her the house is quiet. *They're gone.*

Gretchen sits up. Goes to the window, swings it open, waiting, willing, in the wintry air – *oh please be there, oh please…*

Two soft warbling notes: a gentle mourning, winter's here. Gretchen stiffens at the sound; the back of her neck tingles as if it were being stroked.

The two notes come again.

Gretchen plucks her shawl from a chair, rootles her shoes from under the bed (a gift from Bronheim, buttery doeskin, high of heel, toes squared off like the muzzle of a fawn), and runs for the door. The lady of the house, sniffing about in the hallway, draws back her skirts in her usual manner as Gretchen hops, skips, runs and jumps it down her stairs, but this time Gretchen doesn't care. Plenty of soldiers (Eickholz, for one) loiter round the house in hopes of catching sight of her; but only one puts that sparkle in her eye. And only one who always, always seems to know when she's left on her own.

Behind the house there's the lane to the stables, sheltered by high walls. Gretchen skitters down it, calls an answering warbling note. She's not as good at this as him, but she's learning.

And there he is. And smiling. She does like that smile. She'd tried to tell him once that he was handsome, because ain't that what you do? but he'd denied it. 'I was pretty enough when I was little,' he'd said, laughing, shaking his head, 'but I'm going to be a big ugly bastard, that's the truth.'

Here he comes, shaking the hair from his eyes. 'Hello, you big ugly bastard,' she greets him, giggling, halting on one squared-off toe.

He has a nickname for her too. 'Hello-o, little bird.'

Viewed through a spyglass, the horseman waiting out beyond the East Gate, leaning forward on the pommel of his saddle, has a solid reality that rather takes Bronheim aback. Moreover the man's mount, pulling at the frost-stiffened grass, looks more than respectable, if very shaggy in its winter coat. There's something about the pair, even that far off, not to be argued with. They look like they could last up in those woods for years.

'We ready yet?' Lashing the softening body of the Swedish soldier to a packhorse has taken a while, and the wet, cold stink of it, like rancid bacon fat, is fast becoming unmistakable.

'Yes sir,' says Mannfred, holding his nose. 'Ready now.'

So much for his escort of Praetorians. All his captains, all abreast (yes, Heinrich too, on that fancy mare of his – the man's a sot, he may be worse, but if you want to make your enemy think twice, it's the Heinrichs of this world you put in front of them), all pulling faces at the odour of a corpse. But there are also the musketeers, climbing into position in the attics of the houses by the gate, there are his gunners on the walls – what, go out there and parlay, naked? He's not such a fool as that.

'Right,' Bronheim says. 'Open the gates.'

And now Gretchen, withdrawing from a first chilled kiss, knitting her fingers together in the warmth at the small of her lover's back, under his shirt. 'You're mad about me, ain't you, Jag?' she says, nudging her face against his neck.

He gives a yelp. 'Everything but them little frozen paws.'

He's right, her hands are frozen. It's far too chill to stay outdoors. They used to go up to the hayloft (the horses in Bronheim's stable have known all about this for weeks); but last time as they lay there, curled root to notch, tight as the two halves of a chickpea, they'd heard the stable door open and Bertholdt walking about beneath them. '*I said brush her, damn your eyes, not tickle her.* Ho yes sir. Ho yes, your great magnificence. *And stand straight, damn you. God's nails, I'll put some backbone in you if it's the last thing I do.*' He was imitating Bronheim, the snap when Bronheim was annoyed, and not a half-bad imitation either, Gretchen had been amazed that Bertholdt had the wit, and then, thinking of him down there and them up here, the look there'd be on Bertholdt's face if he could see them now, had realized she was going to get the giggles. The repercussions of discovery hadn't occurred to her at all, the only thought in her head was that this was funny, and that if she laughed, and gave them away, it would be funnier still. She could feel the laughter rippling beneath her ribs; given how they were joined at that moment, Jag must have felt it too. He'd put his hand across her mouth.

His hand had smelt of apples, like a horse, and tasted of leather. She'd bitten it, bitten it hard. She can taste it still. She'd thought he'd stand it till Bertholdt left, then whip the hand away, which would be even funnier; but he had not. At the back of his eyes, something had ignited. She'd sensed it was the first time she'd done something that truly interested him. And he'd fucked her, hand across her mouth, her teeth grinding his flesh, her breath coming in tiny desperate puffs down her nose and Bertholdt moving about beneath them, and all the while that flare in his eye, like the end of a fuse, disappearing off into the dark.

He's bad, is Jag. He's scary, that's the word. Gretchen knows that there are rules (she also knows that with a man of sufficient rank beside you, you can ignore most of 'em), but Jag behaves as if they just weren't there at all – leastways, not for him. He has to be mad, trying it on with her. She's his colonel's whore, for heaven's sake.

But then this doesn't feel the way it does when Bronheim squashes her against the bed, this feels more like what it's all about. Up in the hayloft, held, suspended, falling, all at once, washed hot and cold, hot and cold, pressed to his shuddering heart, she'd felt as if she'd float right through him; everything so good she couldn't tell where she ended and he began. She'd been pink as a rose when they'd finished, giggling still. And he, flopped on his back, smiling that giant smile of his, had drawn her to him. 'Tell me about Bronheim,' he'd said.

Now, though, she draws back her head, puts her hand over his great beak of a nose. 'Your nose is cold as a dog's!'

'Yeah, it is,' he'd said. 'And so's the rest of me.'

And she with that great fire in her room, pumping out heat; and all that food as well – nuts and sweetmeats, little cakes.

All that commotion, they'll be gone for hours yet.

'You come with me,' she says, the minx. 'I've got an idea.'

Dear God, it's cold out here beyond the gates. The wind has teeth, the ground is fanged as well; this field was ploughed before it froze and now the most delicate plough-turned rim of earth stands up as hard as if it had been cast in iron.

Here he comes. Urging his horse forward, to a trot.

'*Hallå*, Deutscher!'

The greeting is ringingly clear – must be the air, thinks Bronheim, the desiccating chill. He's never heard a Scandinavian accent before, that whale-song lilt, and doesn't care for it. His horse has put her ears back too, must feel his nerves.

'*Hallå*, Deutscher! *Very* kolt!'

Not to be outdone, Bronheim summons up a good loud shout of his own. 'Keep you waiting, did we?'

'Yah, Deutscher –' (the man is coming closer, lowering his voice; a little steel within it now) '– Yah, Deutscher, so you did.'

Well, thinks Bronheim, *ain't we just broken-hearted to hear that.*

'I was thinking, maybe they are scared.'

The fellow has pluck, give him that. The line of horsemen behind Bronheim, and he doesn't turn a hair.

Close enough now to get a proper look at him. Breastplate, studded gauntlets, boots turned up above his knees, and a long cloak of fur spreading out across his horse's back. Yellow hair in a plait looped round one shoulder. *Like a woman*, thinks Bronheim, with distaste.

The Swedish horseman reins his horse to a halt. 'So, Deutscher,' he says, through a cloud of breath. 'You got my boy?'

At Bronheim's signal, the packhorse is cut loose and wanders forward. The horseman steers his mount up to it, like a sailor coming upon some small abandoned craft. He lifts, with one gauntleted hand, the cloth they'd folded round the young man's face. 'Elof,' he says, softly, and rests a finger on its forehead, as if in admonition, as if to say *I told you no good would come of this.*

Bronheim feels caught out in some action that should have been beneath him. 'You have your dead,' he says, brusquely. 'We have ours. Ours have been decently buried; you may do as you wish with that.'

The horseman, bending, scoops up the packhorse's reins. 'We had him buried once,' he points out, softly as before. 'Who was it dig him up, Deutscher? You?' That studded fist, flashing like a mirror in the slanting winter sun, roams left, to indicate the escort. 'One of these? What if I say I want him too?'

The escort of Praetorians reins back. Heinrich gives himself away at once, loses a stirrup. Bronheim, spluttering with fury, bursts out, 'My men need be no concern of yours!'

'Oh, but they are, Deutscher. They are. How many more you got inside those walls?' And when Bronheim, open-mouthed at the effrontery of this, fails to reply, the voice goes on, 'Your men, you know, they talk, before they die. Eight guns, a regiment of horse, a company of infantry – you got five hundred, Deutscher. At the most.'

The accuracy of the assessment is staggering. 'You get yourself out of here!' Bronheim exclaims, threatening in turn. 'You get yourself out of here while you can.'

'You going to shoot me in the back?' The voice is soft with menace now. 'I wouldn't, Deutscher. Not if I was you.' And the man is smiling, one eye on Bronheim, one eye on those big, dark trees. *Damn his arrogance*, thinks Bronheim, whose gaze (he cannot stop it) has also wandered to the shoreline of the wood, those cinnamon-coloured trunks, score upon score of 'em, line upon line. *How long have they been watching us? What do they know?*

'You listen to me,' he begins – when the man once more holds up his hand.

'No, you listen, Deutscher,' the man says, so low he might be making the arrangements for a tryst, and close enough now for Bronheim to espy the single pearl, knotted into either end of his moustache. 'This is our domain. We winter here. The snows come soon and there is not enough for you as well. You march your men out, we let you go. You stay, you're going to die. You understand?' He wheels his horse about; the pack-horse follows meekly. The cloak of dark fur ripples as he turns. A Parthian shot. 'You think about it, Deutscher. We give you till tonight.'

So here they are in that great bed, that panelled room. Gretchen's mouth is sticky with plum wine, and Jag is moving back and forth between her mouth and breasts, and his voice, a-rumble with amusement, is saying, 'God, I hope Bronheim knows how lucky he is.'

It annoys her, just a little, how often Bronheim is the thing they talk about. She's not sure how it happens, but they do. She says dreamily, 'I think you want to be like him.'

'What, colonel of a regiment?' He laughs. 'It's an idea, give you that.'

'Then you need a rich old uncle. And he has to die, and leave you his fortune, and his regiment, and his castle. That's how Bronheim did it.'

One fingernail, tracing a maze around her navel. It's like there's a golden thread inside her, spooling from within her belly to down between her legs.

'Did he so?' She can tell he's smiling, just from the sound of it. 'Swift.' One path of the maze is wandering downwards. Gretchen presses herself back against the pillows.

'It's why… oh, Jag.'

His voice, rich with amusement. That growling under-note of arousal, too. 'Go on.'

'It's why Heinrich is so jealous of him. Because they're cousins. But the old…oh… but the old uncle left Bronheim everything.'

'So Heinrich's a Bronheim? I'll be damned.'

'Yes... oh.' She's starting to push with her feet against the covers at the bottom of the bed. 'No, it's the other way... Bronheim he took... his uncle's name. It used to be the same as Heinrich's. Like Our Lady. The Madonna. On our flag.'

He's stopped.

'Enric Maduna.'

His voice is different. Gretchen opens her eyes. His face has changed, too.

'That's right.' The change is startling. She sits up. 'How'd you know that?'

The fall of the bar across the gates behind them, and all the brave talk starts rolling out at once.

'You hear him? Fucken troll.'

'By God, he and I will know each other, if we meet again.'

'He knew old Heinrich. Got a price on your head there I reckon, my friend.'

'I'd sleep with one eye open, I was you.'

'Especially tonight.'

'Oh my Lord yes. You got them hundred herring-eating trolls tonight, remember?'

'Hah! Any God-damn Sveder shows his face down here...' The threat dies away in a growl. 'Need a drink,' Heinrich announces. He looks distinctly unsettled. But then (thinks Bronheim), he has to admit, his own nerves had been jangling out there too. If those men up in the woods were to throw all their two hundred, whatever it is, into a raiding party, they could hardly do much damage, but they could be a cursed nuisance. *Put an extra guard upon the walls tonight*, he's thinking, as they come into the square. *Can't hurt...*

The shops are putting up their shutters, housewives hurrying to brewhouse, bakehouse, the early winter dusk already closing in. As one, the troop turns toward the tavern in the square.

'Colonel,' comes Mannfred's voice. 'Join us for a warmer. Christ, it was colder'n Gabriel's bollocks out there.'

'Later.'

And feels their knowing glances. *Oh, he's got something better than drink to warm himself with.*

Well, let them smirk. Isn't this the one thing that it's all about, to come back safe and whole, to a woman waiting for you? thinks Bronheim, as he ties up his horse.

'Bertholdt!' Damn his eyes, where is the boy?

Isn't this the one thing that a man comes home for, something soft and clean? It's a damn cold world out there, a damn cold hard and unforgiving world, a man battles through it... *little Gretchen*, he thinks, picturing her skin, her eyes. Why, he might almost be in love with her.

And why not, he asks himself, as he climbs the stairs, snuffs the scent of supper rising from the kitchen. Halts on the landing. *I'll surprise her.* Takes off his boots, and in his stockinged feet pads up the last flight.

There's many a warrior has made an honest woman of his whore. They make the best wives for a soldier, anyone can tell you that.

He opens the door.

The babes in the wood, is his first thought on seeing them. Ridiculous, but his instinct is almost to apologize, for plainly he has just walked in on some moment of great import: there's the boy, kneeling on the bed, and Gretchen, naked as the day she was made, and unmistakably one has just said something of huge consequence, though what to who –

After that there is just time enough to wonder what it is, exactly, that he feels – howling anguish? Blazing wrath? – before Gretchen, with a series of tiny shrieks, starts snatching up the bedclothes to cover her nakedness, and the boy, giving Bronheim one cool look, slides from the bed and stands there, squaring off.

CHAPTER SEVEN

In the Mouth of the Wolf

'…both in Ancient and Modern times, Cities and Forts
have been surpriz'd, when those within thought themselves secure…'

James Turner, *Pallas Armata*

NIGHTFALL. Out in the square every crew (bar one) has
gathered at the market cross. Rumour twists amongst
them. Her breath is sticky, clings like frost.

'Is it true? All this time? Pressing the sheets with the colonel's whore?'

'Found him right at it, so I heard.'

'Fuck me. Fucken 'ell!'

'What'll happen to him?'

'He'll be shot.'

'He'll be hung.'

'He'll be drawed and quartered.'

'Holy saints.' Then, with commiseration, 'The hell, I hope as she was worth it.' And then a pause. 'So what'll happen to her?'

Light as a whisper, Rumour is, fleet as a cat. Up she flies, up the façade of that fine house, the finest on the square, up to its balcony. What's going on in there?

Far too much noise coming from inside for anyone to take notice of her.

Gretchen, toga'ed in a sheet, is huddled in the corner, hands shielding her head. Bronheim had thrown her shoes at her (Heinrich, waiting downstairs, horribly sobered, heard the double thump and thought, *Christ, if he's using his fists on her, what's he got in store for me?*). There's blood on her lip, and one pearly shoulder, peeping from under the sheet, is an angry red.

'I'LL HAVE YOU WHIPPED! WHIPPED BLOODY, DO YOU HEAR?' Bronheim is making circuits of the room; every time he comes back to her he starts shouting anew. 'DO YOU CARE NOTHING FOR ME – FOR MY NAME – AT ALL?'

Well, yes, she does, and no, she don't. He's making such an ape of himself, shouting and slamming about. And he had hurt her, and she knows that once that's started, it don't stop. Gretchen may flinch as Bronheim stands over her, but something within her has gone cold as ice and hard as diamonds. She'll have to come up with something extra special for him, she thinks. Take her punishment, sit on his knee, kiss his ear, be penitent, contrite. She dares a peek upward, as a tentative first step.

He's still there, blowing like a bull. 'How many times?'

She stares at him. What difference would how many make? There are times men make no sense at all. 'You mean – today?' she asks.

Bronheim puts his hands on either side of her face and, roaring with fury, pulls her to her feet. 'HOW MANY TIMES? *HOW LONG HAVE YOU BEEN PUTTING HORNS ON ME?*'

His voice is close to breaking. If he doesn't possess himself, he'll throttle her, he knows he will. How can she have done this to him? How can his little love, his downy rose, have played him false? Look at her, those eyes, that little mouth half-open, God above, how many times has he looked down and seen her just like that, her tongue, her head pressed back... and played him false with what? Another officer? A better man? Christ, he could tear her limb from limb!

But what is he to do with her? Throw her out, and see her on some other man's arm, hear his own name made the stuff of guardroom ribaldry?

But how can he possibly keep her with him now?

It's like a voice at his ear, coldly insinuating: *You can. You can if you can say she's not at fault.*

His breathing slows, his mind starts working. The hell with it, she could be as guilty as Jezebel, all she need do is pretend.

He forces himself to make his voice low and calm. 'He forced you. Forced his way in here and then –'

Gretchen, mightily startled, has lowered her hands from her face. Her eyes are so wide with shock he can see the white around each iris.

'Didn't he?' God knows, the boy has been strong enough. It had taken him, Bertholdt, his whole crew, all combined, to get the boy from the room. 'Didn't he?' He pulls the sheet from her. On reflex, Gretchen crosses her arms across her naked self. He grabs her arms and shakes her, her head jerks back and forth, he'll shake what he wants to hear out of her if he has to. 'Say YES! *ANSWER ME!*

And Gretchen, with a sudden dismayed understanding that the consequences of this could go on forever, that nothing she can say will be right, that everything she might say will be wrong, eschews further speech altogether, and does what many a smarter girl has done before her. Bursts into tears.

*

Down in the tavern, tropical with heat from the immense tiled stove, Captain Mannfred lifts his tankard and with its lid salutes – what? On the opposite side of the room, the first drinking song of the evening is in full swing, with a serving girl, tittering with terror, being passed from hand to hand and lap to lap, like a human pass-the-parcel. The last lap she lands upon is Eickholz's, who jumps to his feet, dumping the girl on the floor and exiting abruptly. Mannfred roars with glee. 'No, straight up,' he says, raising his voice to address his gloomy companion, as the girl picks herself off the floor. 'Give 'im 'is due, Heinrich. Most of the little tykes join up these days, still wet from the tit, the half of 'em. I take my hat off to the rogue, I do truly.'

Heinrich lays his head down on his arms. 'He ain't cost you your crew.'

Across the square and down an alley. Here's a little fruit loft. What's this? What's happening here?

'Right,' says Bertholdt, striding about, smacking his palm with the handle of his whip. 'There is going to be some changes made round here.' He pauses for effect: Lord, they're a sorry-looking bunch, this lot, now that their leader's gone (and they won't be seeing him again). The little yellow-headed one, the catamite, he's outright weeping. Bertholdt gives his sash a tug; he hasn't quite mastered how to tie it, but the sash is the insignia of an officer and Bertholdt has recently been given a promotion. One falls, another rises by his fall.

'There is going to be no more of this running wild.' He brings the whip down *crack* against his thigh. 'There is going to be no more of this *pleasing* of *yourselves*.' *Crack!* 'There's rules in an army, there's how things is done, and by God, while you're my crew, you'll do 'em to my liking, understand? Now –' (he pauses to draw breath) '– our colonel – remember him? Him what you owe a little to in better *manners*? Him what you owe a little to in plain *respect*? He's looking for an extra guard upon the walls tonight. And *I'm* looking for *volunteers*.'

And where's the cause of all of this?

Locked in a cellar in the quartermaster's stores, that's where, coming to upon a cold stone floor. There's a noise in his head. It takes him a moment to identify it as one of Gretchen's shrieks of terror.

You fool. You idiot. Thinking you could live like the rest of them –

You never do that, not for a second, you witless fucken dolt.

It's not as if he even dislikes Bronheim. He thinks Bronheim spends a deal too much time listening to his captains, and not enough finding out for himself, but dislike the man? Not at all. Nothing, for example, compared to the fury that the thought of Bertholdt now sets off in him – Bertholdt's boot swinging into his balls, and the rain of blows upon his head, his back...

Or Heinrich. Enric. *Right in front of you. All this time, right before your eyes... You blind stupid witless fucken dolt* –

Enough. This is getting him nowhere. He brings his knee into his chest and pushes himself up, so that he is at least sitting, rather than lying, on that cold stone floor. Above his head, at street level, a barred window gives onto the dark outside; even as he watches, spiricles of frost blow in between the bars. His head is ringing; Bronheim's crew had used it, as they carried him in to the quartermaster, to open the door. He remembers the quartermaster, leaping up, demanding, 'The devil's this?' and the fuzz of voices as they threw him in here. Through the blur in his head he'd caught the words *nailing the colonel's whore*, and the quartermaster's startled exclamation: 'He did *what*?'

It hurts to breathe. It seems entirely likely that his nose is bust again. His arms are tied so tight behind his back they're going numb.

Doesn't matter. Push it away. Pain is not the thing to be scared of. He understands pain. You press against it, set it whirling like a whetstone, use it to put your edges back.

Right. Sharpen up. He tilts forward and, bent over like a crookback, makes it to his feet.

Next thing. *How am I getting out of here?*

He scans the room, looking for the weak spot. He can do this to a road, a line of trees, a man's face; he can certainly do it to four walls and a floor – and a window.

He rocks back on his heels, surveying it. Barred, but only vertically, and the bars set none too closely, either. This room was never meant as a jail. Could he squeeze out through there?

Going to damn well have to, I reckon.

But the window is still eight feet or more from the floor.

So how am I getting up to it?

Not roped like this, that's for damn sure.

Rope...

Beyond the door he hears the heavy creak as the quartermaster settles his bulk on the bench. He tries to conjure up all that he saw as they carried him in – the quartermaster jumping up, bench, table, jug of beer, the quartermaster's supper, on a pewter plate –

That'll do.

'HOI, MATE!'

His voice is hoarse, but then quartermasters spend their days bellowing and roaring, delicacy of tone is unknown to them.

Another creak. 'HOI, *MATE*! You out there, are you?'

A voice beyond the door. 'You pipe down, you.'

'But I'm like to freeze to death in here!'

A growl. 'Cheat the fucken 'angman if you do.'

Hunched down, he puts his mouth against the lock. 'You got anything to eat out there?'

A hack of laughter. 'No, I'm the quartermaster, ain't you heard? I just sits 'ere in an empty *shed*.'

'You have, I saw it. On your table. Oh, come on, mate, you know how it is. You finish nailing 'em, you're starving, ain't yer?'

For a moment there's no response at all. Then the voice comes back. 'You got some balls on you, young'un, I'll say that.' A final creak, then footsteps. ''Ere. Stand away from the door.'

He lollops backward. The door opens wide enough for the pewter plate to skid across the floor, spilling a detritus of cheese rinds, crusts of bread, the bone of a leg of mutton. 'You pick at that, you little sod.'

'Thanks, mate!'

Thank you indeed. It's useful stuff, pewter, no doubt why so much is made from it – buttons, badges, spoons – and plates like this. Very willing metal, in its nature. Too willing. Bang it, and it takes a dent at once, bend it back and forth, it splits.

He puts one foot on the plate and tips it up. Juggling it upright, against his ankle, he puts his other foot upon it, presses down. The rim is surprisingly sharp, but the pewter starts to fold. Juggling it again, he turns it over, presses it the other way. The plate is bent in two. Flips it once more, presses down on it again – the pewter snaps. Bit more bending and juggling and the plate is in two halves on the floor.

Down on his knees, feeling behind him, he picks up one half and, carrying it across the room, wedges it at waist-height above the hinge of the door. Backs up against it, till he can feel the edge, and starts to saw.

It takes a damn sight longer than he'd thought. The edge keeps folding over and the ropes are thick, they're skinning his arms as he saws at them, and when at last the final thread pops, almost audibly, the rush of blood back to his fingers has him hopping up and down. His forearms prickle with heat and hurt, and his fingers are swollen, useless. He works them back and forth until they feel like they belong to him again. He hears a clock strike ten. Time to go. What he needs now is something that'll get the rope up there...

He picks up the mutton-bone, weighs it in his hand. A good size. A good weight. The whole thigh-bone. Two thoughts: *Christ, quartermasters do themselves well enough and no mistake,* and then that old memory of Bertholdt face-down in the dirt. Almost unconsciously his lips come back from his teeth in a snarl; but that one's going to have to wait. He takes the rope, ties it in a good tight double-hitch about the bone and hurls it, aiming at the space between the bars.

And misses. The bone bounces against the iron, drops to the floor. Tries again. Misses again. His arms are still not working right, and after three more goes they're getting tired. Also that may just have been the quartermaster, stirring in his sleep. Them sodding bars, so cold you hit them and they ring like bells.

He stands beneath the window, lets his head fall forward, closes his eyes. He feels the cold air flowing over him. In his head he sees the space between the bars. Holds up the leg-bone, whirls it like a sling-shot over his head, lets the rope go, and as it goes he sees it, in his head, disappearing through the gap –

No crack upon the floor. The rope does not go slack. Opens his eyes and there it is, lodged across the bars like a grappling iron. He tugs the rope. Puts one foot against the wall.

Now then. How strong is the bone in a leg of mutton?

GRAUBURG IS QUIET NOW. Bats settle in its many belfries, children wrap themselves up tighter in their beds. The drinkers in the tavern have their heads down on its tables, lie stretched out on the benches, on the floor, amongst the cards, the broken pipes, the counters from a draughts-board. Rumour, floating in the veils of pipe smoke up above their heads, is snoozing too. Out on the walls the last watch of the day is coming to an end, and settling down to supper – barley porridge, cooked up with a cup of schnapps, get a bit of blood moving in all those frozen fingers and toes. In that fine house on the square, in the four-poster bed, Gretchen is pretending she's asleep, while Bronheim, as quietly as he can, is exiting their darkened room. A public trial, a public execution? *I beg to differ*, Bronheim had decided, *I think not.*

He picks his way down the stairs. As he opens the front door, the freezing air hits him like an accusation. The temperature has collapsed, a reminder of how far north they've come. Frost has laid a fleece across the square; he's going to leave a track.

At the far side of the square, under the lantern marking the door to the quartermaster's stores, he stops, takes the wheel-lock pistol from under his coat. True, he may feel guilty later, but once it's done... and that's the great thing about a wheel-lock, thinks Bronheim, as he winds the key, as the flint nudges back, back, back. They don't admit of second thoughts.

And up above the town those thousands of trees are stirring in the wind – *shhhhh.* Quietly does it. The horses with their jangling harnesses bound up with cloth, the men threading through the trees, hands raised in greeting, whispered cautions passed back down the line. No easy thing this, bringing near-enough seven hundred men together, in the dark.

At the side of the path one man stands intent, peering down the slope. Something the size and weight of a church bell is being lowered down that slope, the ropes restraining it squeaking as they rub against the trees. Most of his cannon are light field-pieces, as you'd expect of such a mobile unit, but what is being coaxed, cajoled and eased so gingerly down that slope, inch by agonizing inch, is something different. This is a one-shot, one-chance show-stopper. This is a petard. Packed to the brim with the most potent, fine-grained powder, and layered into it, like the prizes in a bran-tub, horse shoes, broken weapons, rusted armour, nails...

The swell of men passing behind him has increased. '*Tysta! Var tyst!*' Bit of God-damn quiet, if you please!

At the absolute limit of his vision, he can see the town, the few odd lights like sparkles on a puddle in the dark. No moon as yet, and hardly a star; they chose tonight with care. And with the eye of faith, he's sure he can make out the faint outline of the walls, the higher, squared-off bastions, the watch-fires and a set of gates. A petard has one purpose only: blow those gates to smithereens.

He watches. The wheels turn, the ropes squeak. Down it goes.

The quartermaster, slumbering, head down on his chest, is woken by the unexpected but delightful sound of a silver thaler being placed on his table; then brought fully awake by the unwelcome sight of the barrel of a wheel-lock, six inches from his nose.

'He forced her,' Bronheim says.

'Sir?'

'Forced her. In my billet. In my bed. This is justice.' He gestures with the pistol at the locked cell door. 'Not a word.'

Not a word indeed. It's a bad business this, bad all around, a rotten smell to it and no mistake. But no arguing with your colonel and no arguing with a wheel-lock pistol either, a weapon which by repute has a spring so powerful it'll go off if you as much as sneeze. The quartermaster pushes at the door – it takes a hefty push, which is a surprise, no trouble with it before, but it feels as if something is in the way of one of the hinges. The door scrapes open. A discarded length of rope writhes into sight around its bottom edge. There's more, hanging from the bars of the window. And unless the quartermaster is mistaken, what holds it there, as an extempore grappling hook, is the thigh-bone from his supper.

Otherwise, the cell is empty.

Bronheim's roar of fury sets dogs barking streets away.

*

No more than half-a-dozen streets away, scraped and breath-less, bare feet stinging as they strike the ground, Jack is doubling from alleyway to alleyway. *What I need now's another pair of boots.* A dog, hearing his running step, keeps pace with him, scratching and snarling the length of its garden fence. *Fuck off, you stupid mutt, it's me.* He knows this dog, its barking wakes them every morning. And here's the turning to their billet, and oh, thank Christ, its windows are dark. He peers inside and at once half-sees and half-hears, in the dark, the horses' heads swing round, their shifting bulk. *Shush!* he tells them, finger to his lips. Makes for the ladder to the loft – *now that is odd indeed.* Nobody at home.

Fine. Add a little thieving to the night's events, why not?

Five minutes later and feet still bare, he stops his wild search through the piles of kit. No-one here has boots that fit him, not even that old pair Hans has of his brother's. *Damn it, what's the rest of the world do, teeter round on little kitty-paws?* He holds up a shirt – one of Matz's, by the state of it – and rips it, neck to hem. Right. Bindings for him, bindings for Milano too.

Feet bandaged like a fucken lazar, he slides down the ladder again, holding his pack and with more ripped-up shirt to take care of Milano's hooves. This too takes longer and without a light is trickier than he'd thought; by the time he's satisfied the Holstein mare has edged up close, and she and Milano have their heads arched across each other's necks. 'What are you up to?' he asks, amused. 'You two saying goodbye?'

And it can't but help, of course, if Milano ain't the only horse they lose.

Moving quietly – don't want to alarm 'em, don't need any noise – he slips from horse's head to horse's head, ducking beneath their whiskers, undoing their ropes. Then picks up blanket, saddle and pack, and leads Milano out into the alleyway.

Leaves the door to the stables open behind him. Never knew a horse yet could resist an open door.

Up to the end of the alleyway, and still the town is sleeping. Not a light, not a moon, not a star.

When he looks back the last thing he sees is the gelding hack, poking its cautious nose around the open door.

It takes a good quarter-hour to get where he's headed, leading Milano all the way. The houses have grown smaller; were he riding, he'd be at head-height, in some places, with their sagging, weed-grown thatch. This is the other side of Grauburg, down by the West Gate, the poor end of the town. Every place has one. Those officers who don't get one hundred and fifty gulden a month lodge down here (Eickholz, for instance), these streets are where the infantry keep, or acquire, their women. Matz used to boast of escapades down here, romantic conquests – Matz, he thinks, with contempt. Well, that's one at least he won't miss.

And those others that he will?

Even less point dwelling on them. They all got along well enough before him, they'll get on well enough after he's gone. *Other people. You're not good with 'em. It's not for you. Get used to it.*

There's one plan: find Heinrich, get that name. Get that name, *kill* Heinrich. Find the other.

The town wall is lower round the West Gate, in less good repair; it ends up as the back to shacks and sheds. More importantly, those who pull sentry duty down here, instead of round with the gunners, facing the hills, get it because they ain't no fucken use (something else Bronheim might have found out for himself), either time-serving old lags who couldn't care, or tyros, novices, who haven't got a clue. They're not about to notice if one of those sheds serves as a stable for an hour or so.

He tries the door of one, and something falls to the floor inside it. The next has no door at all, and he can see night sky through its sloping roof. Can't have been used for years. Just about the right size, too.

'You,' he tells Milano, 'are going in there.'

Milano looks at him. It is an eloquent look.

'You heard me. Back up.'

He pushes Milano's hindquarters round, and backs the horse in. Milano settles, blows a sigh. Jack takes a step back. Nothing is visible of Milano other than the white points of his eyes. He steps inside the shed again, takes a double handful of Milano's tousled mane, and shakes it over the horse's face. Milano is now completely obscured. You could walk right past the black void of the doorway and never know there was a horse in there.

'Right,' he says. 'I'll see you later.'

Up on the walls, at this arse-end of the town, the first watch of the night has already deserted its post and is huddling at the braziers, blowing on its hands. Bertholdt is amongst them, trying to accustom himself both to the freezing conditions and to what he takes to be the banter of his peers, although that banter seems distinctly sour.

'Mind your sash, Herr Lieutenant *sir*,' as the coals in the brazier pop and settle.

'Yeah. Don't go singeing yer *tassel*.'

Maybe he'd do better checking on Heinrich's – no, his now – on his crew.

The braziers cast a deal of light as well as heat; all the same, on a night as dark as this, there's plenty of space between them for the curve of the walkway, the towering bastions, to disappear into blackness. Bertholdt, striding off, is within yards in darkness so complete he can't even see his feet. The next bastion looms up, adding its stony chill to the air, and hunched behind it, like sheep on a moor, the three boys. They turn, too cold and too depressed to do more than shuffle apart.

''Ere! Where's the other one of you? Where's Münster?'

'He went,' says the one with the face like a wasp.

'Went sodding where? Did I say he could go?'

'He went to 'ave a piss,' says the short, fat one, the gutser. And jerks a stiff, chilled hand in the direction of the next bastion along the line.

Bertholdt strides past them. 'Münster? Hoi, you, Münster, you there?'

'What d'yer want?' comes the exasperated reply.

'What are you up to?'

'What d'yer think?' Hans retorts, splashing his boots.

Even for Bertholdt, supervising the taking of a piss would be carrying discipline too far. 'Just don't be too long about it, d'you hear?' And he strides past.

Hans leans his forehead back against the stones. *Dearest Mutti –*

Well, things don't go so good for us no more, as you would know if you could see me now…

'Jesus!' exclaims Bertholdt, arriving back. 'What the fuck is *that*?'

What it is depends on where you are. For Milano, waiting patiently, it's a momentary wash of light across the shed's earth floor. For Eickholz, at his window – sleepless, lovelorn, moping over Gretchen (oh, how he adores her! Oh, how beautiful she is!) – it's a sudden flash on the inside of his eyelids, and a rumble, like thunder. When he opens his eyes, he's expecting to see rain.

For Bronheim, in the market square, surrounded by his startled guard, trying to make himself heard above the complaints of the householders woken by his bellowing ('I DON'T CARE IF WE WAKE THE WHOLE DAMNED TOWN! FIND THE LITTLE BASTARD, D'YOU HEAR?'), it's a shaking of the ground, then a meteor streaking overhead. For the sleepers in the tavern it's a very rude awakening indeed, to a room filling with smoke and the sound of the roof sliding off into the street. For Hans and Bertholdt, who have perhaps the best view of all, it's the darkness in the hills beyond the town erupting in a seam of fire. Then darkness once more, and a rumble as the echo of the first barrage rolls about the town; and then that seam of fire opens up again.

'Christ!' shouts Bertholdt. 'Christ, they're firing on us! Christ!'

They can hear shouts now, from further round the walls, and the barking of every dog in Grauburg. An extraordinary twittering sound, as a whole flock of sparrows comes out of the darkness and shoots across the walls between them. Then a church bell, tolling the alarm. Then another, bringing men tumbling from their beds into the streets. More shouts. Another rumble. The far curve of the walls round the East Gate is suddenly lit; their gunners now, replying in kind. 'Ho yes!' Bertholdt exclaims, exultant. 'Give it to 'em! That's the way!' And Hans, turning to say he knows not what, sees the watch-fire on the wall beyond Bertholdt change shape, as if the brazier had been kicked sideways. 'Bertholdt?' he begins, uncertainly.

Bertholdt, standing not two yards from him, has gone. Where he was, there is nothing. Hans is about to call his name again when something like the tap of a warning hand stops him. He takes a step back, back into the deep protective shadow of the bastion.

A clot of black is lowering Bertholdt to the walkway. Bertholdt is still moving. His legs are, anyway. The thing puts what might be its foot where Bertholdt's throat would be, and the movement ceases.

The thing steps forward, assumes limbs, a head. It's peering down over the wall. Hans, breath coming in tiny, terror-stricken spurts, does the same.

There are hundreds of men down there. Looking down on them is like looking down upon a swarm of beetle-backs; the ground is live with them, as far into the dark as Hans can see. They're carrying scaling ladders, passing them over their heads.

They're moving something up toward the gates. He can't make out what it is, but he can hear the squeak of wheels.

Oh Christ –

The man on the walkway is so close that Hans can hear his breathing, see the frosted breath puff into the air.

Oh Christ oh Christ –

A wavering lament from further down the wall. 'Hans!'

It's Stuzzi. 'Hans, it's all gone dark!'

'HANS!' All three of them together. The watcher has withdrawn his head. Footsteps coming toward him – *oh Christ oh God oh Christ –*

He takes a step back. Then another. The footsteps mimic his. Hans turns and sprints along the walkway, the timbers bouncing beneath his feet, head back, elbows driving down – 'THEY'RE COMING! THEY'RE COMING!'

Something has gone wrong with the air. It seems to have lost all ability to carry sound. It's being sucked past him, like water. It's like trying to run in water, against a turning tide. The timbers of the walkway are lifting like a rug. Something enormous is happening behind him. It sounds like the sea, sucking itself back before it falls in a mighty wave. The noise is getting louder, it's louder still, it's too loud – *God a'mighty*, Hans thinks, *Mutti, help me, this is it –*

So he turns to face it, whatever it may be, and finds himself facing a volcano. The West Gate has gone. In its place, a mouth of hell, a well of fire and flame, sparks rocketing from it into the sky, and from the dark beyond the gates, a roar of triumph: '*HACKAPEL!*'

Not coming, no. They're here.

This, Jack is certain of; a distinct, specific memory: turning as he heard the noise, and as he turned, it happened – every gap between the timbers of the West Gate filling with liquid gold, every crack and knothole shimmering. *What the hell?*

And then the gates had blown, those mighty timbers lifting like the edges of a curtain, and he had thought, *Yes, this could do it, this is big enough, this could kill me*, and there'd been a kind of acceptance of it, no point now trying to do anything, every problem solved at once.

It picked him up like a leaf, head tipping forward, arms outstretched, things dropping round him – spear-blades of timber, chunks of stone – and somewhere far off, a noise that was more a blow about the head than a sound, and left everything coming at you as if you were underwater.

After that, it's all a lot less clear.

He lies there. *Where am I?*

I'm upside down –

I'm upside down, and there's a lot of stuff on top of me –

And even more beneath. There's a strange taste in his mouth, like burnt toffee.

What happened?

He can feel his fingers, wriggling in grit. He tries to stretch his toes, and one foot hits something hot and sharp – *fuck!* – and as he pulls it back the pile of stuff beneath him shifts and spills him out. His head strikes cobblestone, and a length of lathes, still pinned together, slides over him like a sheet and hits him in the mouth. *Shit. Fuck.* He's getting angry and it clears his head; the clamour in the background loses its underwater quality and breaks up into individual shouts and wails of panic. He turns himself over, onto his elbows, and shakes his head, which feels different to how it should. One of his ears is blocked. He shakes his head again and as he does so the singing within the ear goes up by an octave into a high whine of warning: *you're going to pass out now.*

A blink of darkness. His forehead on his hands. His lips feel thick. The smell of burning on his fingers when he puts them to his nose.

A woman running past, clutching something wrapped in a counterpane. Two little feet protruding from it, bobbing as she runs. Then another, and this one is lopsided, holding her ribs. Then a man in a nightshirt, pulling two grimy wailing children, one by each hand. Then a man on his own, staggering. Then two together, holding each other up. He thinks of yelling for someone to help him when an old familiar taint wafts past, a smell that sticks its fingers up your nose and scratches the back of your throat with its nails – black powder – and his heart gives a kick like a horse. Now he understands. *Jesus Christ, they blew the gates.*

Now they run past in little groups – those hurt doubled up, arms crossed, holding themselves together; those unhurt all running alike, arms outstretched and wailing.

Go down, go deep, keep still.

And here come more, four, six, eight feet all at once, and unbelievably but unmistakably they're presaged by Matz's voice, shrieking, 'Run, run, run!' and first there's Matz, then Hans, then Stuzzi, and right at the back, Gunter, puffing to keep up, and behind them, oh yes, right on cue –

'*HACKAPEL!*'

Now the feet running past him are booted. Some thud so close he has to will himself not to jerk away. *Go down. You're dead, you understand? They tread on you, you're not going to feel a thing –*

As the booted feet run past, he counts them. Ten. Twenty. More. Losing count. He closes his eyes. *Go down, go deep, go deeper still –*

And finally the most beautiful quiet. Nothing but the crackling of flame, and the street slowly wreathing itself in smoke. Unobserved by anyone, the walkway is on fire.

He heaves himself up. All four limbs obey. *I'm alive*, he thinks. *I'm alive.* There's almost an urge to laugh. *They blew the gates and I'm alive.*

They blew the gates. They don't just want us out...

They want us dead.

Beyond where the gates were, the faint lights of torches, like the eyes of animals out there in the dark. The odd soft call. No need to hide themselves now.

And the other way, already the clash and riot of conflict. In his mind's eye he can see them: the infantry, tumbling from their beds, dragging barriers across the streets. The musketeers, clambering into position in the attics. And Bronheim and his officers – HQ at the house in the market square.

So that's where Heinrich will be.

So that's where you're headed.

He straightens his back. Steadier now. *The square.*

And not wherever-it-is, some alleyway nearby, from which he hears again that gleeful cry of '*HACKAPEL!*'

Oh, what is this? What is this thing, pulling at him? It's like there's some wretched beggar-kid down there, plucking at his hand, turning up its great reproachful eyes –

No. NO. Not the plan.

The cry again. '*HACKAPEL!*'

Oh God, he thinks, disgusted, *right, I'll do it, just bugger off, will you?* and sets off, following that gleeful cry.

A street of little houses. Window door, window door, window door –

'In here! In here!'

The man is right behind them. '*HACKAPEL!*'

In through a door, into a narrow hallway. Stuff all over the floor – shoes, clothes, a hat – no time to take any of it, barely time for the occupants to flee. Matz slams the door shut, shrieking, 'Hold it! Hold it!' and they pile themselves against it, bracing arms and legs. Above Gunter's panting and his own heart hammering against his eardrums, Hans hears the man go past, then back again.

'*HACKAPEL!*' The whack of axe blade into wood. '*HACKAPEL!*' It sounds like he's gone past them altogether, further up the street. Hans feels his legs fold up, slumps with relief against the door – and then from the room next door a splintering crash. The Hackapel is hacking his way into the house straight through its shuttered window. 'Up!' screams Matz. 'Upstairs!' So they run for the stairs because there's nowhere else to go, and then upstairs there truly is nowhere else to go, one room, that's all, a curtain on a rail across its doorway, a bed with blankets thrown back, just as the sleepers left it, a candle burning in a dish, and soon as he sees it Hans understands for sure that this room, with its bed, its flickering candle, this is where they're going to die.

They hear the bottom stair give a creak. Then the next up, and the next. As he draws closer, they retreat across the room. The curtain lifts – Hans, chill with terror, feels his shoulders touch the wall and the contact is enough to make him jump. There's a leather glove drawing the curtain aside. There's the bright eye of a pistol. Then the curtain's whipped back, rattling on its rail, and there he is – the enemy.

He's short, broad, flat of feature, heavy-set. But for a few subtle differences – a buff-coat of unusual length, some kind of emblem on the back of his gloves – he could almost be one of their own. Axe in one hand, pistol in the other. The man takes a step into the room, and looks as if he might be going to speak with them. The candle casts his shadow up the wall and Hans, watching the shadow, sees it raise the pistol. *I want a bullet*, thinks Hans, *I don't want to be chopped in bits. Did Wilhelm feel this?* Hans wonders, did he hear the hammer click, was there a moment when he realized what he'd done and then – and this truly is a moment full of wonder – he finds himself thinking *I'm going to know.*

Oh God, there's two of them.

A second figure behind the first, barging into him. The man staggers forward, the gun goes off – a flash, a cloud of smoke, that charcoal stink, a cake of plaster from the ceiling hitting the floor, and then this thing, this apparition, stalks into the room with the curtain-rail raised above its head. It's black as soot. Its hair is smoking. It might have come straight down the chimney. It might have come straight up from hell. All Hans can see are two glaring eyes and its teeth, bared, as it swings the rail into the back of their attacker's head.

Who drops the axe and goes down on his knees. The thing draws back the rail, and a whiplash of blood arcs across the ceiling. It swings again. Now the man is down flat on the floor. The thing leaps on the man's back, sitting on him, putting the rail under his chin and pulling back his head. The man's hands leave the floor. They're scrabbling at his chest. The thing moves its hands closer together on the rail and pulls again, gritting its teeth. The man's feet are kicking, banging on the floor. The thing on his back is snarling with effort. And there's a crack, almost as loud as the gun going off, and the man's hands fall away and his head drops forward, and the thing gets off the man's back, breathing hard, and its white eyes roll toward them.

'You might find,' it says, 'next time you're being chased, as it's an idea to keep QUIET.'

It bares its teeth. 'Well, fuck me,' the thing says (as they stand there, frozen). 'I think as I might get a word of thanks.'

Matz is the first to move. 'God a'mighty!' He points at the body on the floor. 'Is he dead? God a'mighty!'

'I fucken hope so,' says the apparition, grinning still. 'It'll make a hell of mess in here if I have to do that again. Yeah, all right, Stuzzi, that'll do,' as Stuzzi throws his arms about the apparition's waist and starts singing out its name – 'Jag! Jag! Jag!' And Matz, creeping closer, exclaims, 'Christ, mate, have you seen yourself?'

'Oh, this,' says the apparition, ruefully. It rubs a hand across its face, smearing the grime. 'I was at the gates. Well, I was right in front of 'em. You in one piece?'

'You killed him,' says Hans. At first he doesn't recognize the voice saying this as his, and the fact that the man is dead is so obvious he can't believe he's the only one to point it out. 'You killed him.'

Jag turns his head. His eyes are chill and hard. 'Yeah,' comes the reply. 'And now I'm going to have his boots. So you come here. You help me turn him over.'

It takes all of them to do it. The body is somehow twice the weight it might have had in life; the limbs flop, there is liquid in the mouth. Hans feels his stomach heave. 'God, Jag, how *can* you?' Gunter asks, as Jag, sitting back, pulls on the man's boots. The only reply is an irritated 'You got any idea how cold it is out there?' *Well yeah*, thinks Hans, *yeah, point of fact, mate, thanks to you, we have.* The jacket goes next, but as Jag hauls on the sleeve, something caught under the body scrapes against the floor, and they realize the man must have been wearing a sword. 'Wait up,' says Jag, pulling the sword free, then, wrapping his hand in the hilt, draws it from the scabbard.

It comes out with hardly a sound, the merest *shush*, like silk rubbed over silk. There's a crest stamped under the hilt, and the blade isn't grey, it gleams a soft and marbled blue, a blue like burning spirit. 'Jesus!' Jag exclaims, whipping it through the air. The blade sings, a weird, high, quivering note. 'That's Solingen! Solingen steel! By God, I never thought I'd get my hands on one of these!'

'You know how to use it?' Gunter asks.

The sword pauses in its song. 'You don't?' He stares at them. 'What, not *one* of you?'

They shake their heads. 'Sorry,' says Gunter.

Jag heaves a sigh, rolls up his eyes. 'Right,' he says. 'Hans, you're next biggest, after me. You take the axe. Matz, here, you take his pistol.'

'But it's been fired off,' Matz points out.

'I know it's been fired off. Hold it by the barrel, use the butt. Gunter, here, you take this,' and he pulls the blanket from the bed. 'If anyone comes at you, you throw that over his sword-arm. Then you grab his thumb and you just hang on. And Stuzzi –'

'Yes?' says Stuzzi, gazing up.

'Stuzzi, you just tuck in close by me.'

'Why? Where are we going?'

'We're getting out of here.'

Out they creep. The clouds have broken round the moon and the alley stretches away from them, empty as a stage. The houses leer down, top-heavy as tombstones.

A crackle of shots up ahead, then a strange flat *whumpf* and a change of colour in the sky. Somewhere in the street beyond, there's a house going up in flames. 'The Swedish,' whispers Stuzzi, voice a-tremble.

'Too damn right,' says Jag.

'We're behind 'em,' says Stuzzi, as if the full horror of this has just occurred to him.

'We're behind 'em, and we're staying behind 'em,' says Jag. 'Trust me, it'll be a damn sight safer than being in front.'

'But Jag—'

'Stuzzi, you do the same thing as everybody else, the same thing as happens to them'll happen to you.'

More shouting. Figures running past the end of the alleyway.

'But if they're ahead of us,' Stuzzi is asking, 'then how do we get out?'

'Bloody carefully,' says Jag.

One step, one alleyway, the next. They press themselves against the walls, bunch up where each alley meets the street, wait, wait, wait… then hare into whatever alley is beyond.

Another soft, flat *whumpf* from up ahead. 'Jag,' Hans hisses, 'Jag!' They're pressed against the long wall of a brewhouse; the smell of slops and piss could make you retch. 'Jag, mate, what are we doing? Where are we?'

'Back of the infantry billets. Near where Eickholz lodges.'

'But there's a plan? Jag, tell me there's a plan!'

'There was,' comes the answer. Jag is turned away from him, watching where the alleyway joins the street. 'It didn't have a place in it for any one of you.'

The scattered echo of more running feet. From somewhere in the street beyond, a sharp command.

'Best I can manage,' Jag is saying, 'is we work around to the East Gate, and find a way out there.'

'Right,' Hans agrees. 'That sounds just fine to me.'

'And if you happen to spy Heinrich, let me know. I'd like a word with him.'

Then from within the house, a confusion of bumps and yells. Footsteps pounding up a staircase. A shot, a cry, a fall, the slamming of a door, and then above their heads the face and torso of a man bursts from a casement window. The frame of the window is round his shoulders. He stares down at them, his face distorts, but before he can speak something pulls him back inside. There are five loud, distinct male shrieks, and at each one some new imagining, more ghastly than the last, rears up in Hans's head like a corpse coming out of its grave. Then more sounds from within the house, like someone moving furniture. The hole where the window was stays dark and blind.

Then a man comes out of the house to stand in the street surveying it, as you might a job well done. He's carrying something in one hand.

A thing untidy as a bird's nest, with its rope of hair. With its stalk of neck, like a cabbage, and its steady drip, drip, drip.

It seems to Hans that whatever it is normally keeps your bowels in your body has collapsed within him like a rotten floor.

A shout, from up the street, urgent and engaged. The man calls in answer. It's the first time Hans has heard Swedish spoken; it sounds incomprehensible, an organ with the organ-grinder turning the handle the wrong way. The man turns, he has his back to them –

– and there, in Jag's hand, the glimmer of his knife.

The man calls again. Then off he goes, trophy bouncing as he runs. Seconds later there's the sound of a door being stove in, and another burst of firing. '*Now!*' hisses Jag, and there they go, across the street, and into the darkness of the alleyway beyond.

Behind them, just visible inside the house, there's that familiar orange glow.

And Jag still has that knife of his, in his hand, bared and ready. Hans can't take his eyes from it.

It's like he's made of something different. Not the same as us at all.

And now Jag has seen Hans staring. 'I ain't leaving my bones here, Hans,' he says, softly.

'No,' Hans answers. 'Right.'

The alley before them peters out into a row of little sheds. A sudden grin. 'And I ain't leaving my horse here, neither.'

Here's Bronheim. He's not moved far.

'Colonel!'

Mannfred, grimy with smoke. Behind him, off the corner of the square, Bronheim can see the flashes of light from the musketeers, hear the shouts as his infantry engage.

'Mannfred!' He rises to his feet – no stray Swedish bullet is going to carry this far. The real fight must be a dozen streets away. He claps Mannfred on the shoulder. 'Make your report, man! Tell us, how many? What did you see?'

'Coupl'a hundred,' Mannfred replies, and doubles up, coughing. The fight may be a dozen streets off, but smoke is already wreathing its way into the square. Mannfred has taken in a lungful. Two.

Bronheim takes advantage of the pause to exclaim, 'Hah!' He looks about him. Here are his cavalry, came staggering from the tavern and running from their billets, slinging on sword belts, pulling on boots and jackets as they ran. 'You're sure of that?' The last to make it into the square had been Eickholz – still in his nightshirt, with his boots sticking out under the hem. 'You're certain?' Bronheim asks, as Mannfred straightens up.

'Sure as I'm here,' Mannfred replies. 'No, no, coupl'a hundred. Playing hard, by God, I'll give them that – they find a billet, straight in, hand to hand, and if we clear the place, they fire it. But, two hundred. The infantry can hold them.'

Bronheim senses the mood of his men altering. The first shock has left them; now they scent blood. 'The infantry? My friends – do we let the infantry take the glory?'

A chorus of 'No, by God!'

'Or do we save the day?' He raises his sword. A cheer in reply. 'To the East Gate! To the East Gate, and round, and fall upon their flank!'

The most extraordinary thing. The Swedish guns have ceased.

Here they are, Bronheim and his men, in sight of the East Gate, and no more fiery trails across the sky, no further shattering impacts behind them. All of a sudden, quiet as the Nativity. Bronheim signals to his ensign.

Work a way down the street. Tell me what you see.

He watches the man go. Twenty yards, fifty – at the crossing, the ensign pauses, lifts his hand, and waves. All clear.

Down they go. By God, they make a racket, down this silent street. The townsfolk must have took to their cellars, or be hiding under their beds. Not a soul.

And at the crossing, the ensign waits. Out comes the moon, silvering the street. And there at the end of it the East Gate –

– and the black and white of the land beyond the gate. And the darkness of the woods beyond that.

For a moment it is more than he can do to process this. The East Gate. Open. He is about to call for Bronheim when there's the tiny squeak of a window opening ahead of him.

The ensign looks up. He sees a figure at the window, raising its hand. Waving a greeting like a child would do, opening and closing the fingers over the palm.

And now raising its other hand. Holding a pistol.

Why would you silence your cannon?

Because your own men would be under their fire.

The ensign sees the firework leave the barrel and it's the last thing he does see, a finger of light pointing straight at him. His brain fires off a volley of incandescent images of its own, but it's a reflex only – there so instantly, gone so fast. His legs hinge forward. He pitches over, dead before he even hits the ground.

It might have been a signal. As Bronheim and his men scatter backward, diving for any cover they can find, a herringbone of shot bisects the street, criss-crossing from the houses on each side. Bronheim has bullets landing all around him, lifting little black lids from the frost-white ground. Those men at the edges of the group are caught so many times they're jumping back and forth before they fall. He shouts for Mannfred, 'Get them back! Take shelter!' and Mannfred turns to give the order, and as he does, something seems to lift him, like he's been run into from behind. The man to Mannfred's left lets out a cry, claws at his shoulder, then at his head, from which a wedge of purple has escaped, while Mannfred, hands flapping before him, brushes at the stain expanding across his chest, as if he thinks it could be brushed away. And now that view out through the gates is much less clear, for something – something – is filling the street with its mass. Its metal-edged mass, for as they come forward Bronheim can see the blades, the swords bared, the axes hefted overhead – and the one figure, in the lead. That beard, that plait of hair. And the men behind him, enough to fill the street, wall to wall. *They've tricked us*, Bronheim thinks, in wonder. *The West Gate wasn't the attack, the attack is here, now. They're before us. Up above us. Either side.* He raises his arm, and as he does so, realizes his side is wet with blood. He clamps the arm down. He shouts, 'Enric! Enric!' As he does he feels the blood soak into his waistband. God above, how quickly is he bleeding?

'Enric, gather them! Move them back!' He looks about. Of Enric, there is no sign at all. 'Enric!' Bronheim bellows. 'Enric, you coward! Where are you?' He rises on his tiptoes, looking over the heads of his men, and there, haring away down the street, Enric's shaved head, Enric running from them fast as his legs will carry him. 'Enric!' Bronheim bellows again. 'Enric, you bastard, come back here!'

And at a window fifty feet away a Swedish musketeer, less hurried than his fellows, takes a paper cartridge from his belt (another innovation, this), opens it with his teeth, tips powder and cartridge straight down the barrel of his musket and thinks, *Now then. Let's see what this can do.* There, that fellow, that one bellowing and roaring – how could he miss?

Kneeling, he balances its barrel on the windowsill. Squeezes the trigger, back, back, ba-a-ack… they're a novelty, firelock muskets, and none of them quite trusts that the burning fuse, coiled in its iron pincer by the stock, coiled like the smallest, deadliest of snakes, will somehow every time find the touch-hole – and fires. A single shot, a calligraphic flourish of smoke.

Bronheim, still bellowing, hears the shot that takes him; hears it come in like a hornet for the attack. Feels the course of fire it ploughs through his chest, feels those organs in its path implode. He comes to, to find himself propped against the wall of a house, the same chaos all about him, just as a second before, but all of it somehow changed. He wants to lie down, but someone has their arm in the way.

Eickholz. Kneeling with him, still in his nightgown. Bless the lad.

'Colonel! Oh, my Colonel!'

It's that note in Eickholz's voice tells him, clear as waking to the presence of a priest. There is so much to do, yet simultane-ously, so little of it matters. 'Find –' Bronheim begins. He has a sense of something lost. Oh, he so desperately wants to lie down. The fire in his chest will go out if he can only lie down, the wash of blood put out those agonizing flames. 'Find –' he says again, but find what? An image dancing in his head, light as a moth. He tries to seize it, but cannot. He slumps against the arm. *Find her*, perhaps he means to say, and perhaps he manages it too, for the reply comes, 'I will, I will! Oh, sir!'

His weight is too much. He's leaning sideways. His shoulder touches the ground. There is no further down than this.

'I will, I will! Sir! Do you hear me? Do you hear me? Sir!'

It's the last thing Bronheim does hear. And the last thing he sees is the frosted patch of pavement by his cheek, and his breath, melting a hole in it, then the cold sealing it across again. Black to white. Black to white. Black, to white. White –

SHE HEARD BRONHEIM leave their bed, she listened to him leave the room and lock the door, counted his footsteps down the stairs and then Gretchen had been out of that bed in a single bound. Hauled open the clothes chest and began dressing herself in everything within it – one pair of stockings, then another, her petticoats, her skirts... did he think she was simply going to lie there and wait? No, she's done with him, is Gretchen, she's done with them all. Time for a girl to look out for herself. Mummified and clumsy in her many layers, she'd knelt down at the door and gone to work on the lock. The din of the first cannonade made her do no more than redouble her efforts. The noises in the house, the shouts, the feet pounding down the stairs – what did they matter to her?

Then she'd smelled the smoke. But it was only when she'd sat back and seen how the air in the room was blueing with it that she'd begun to panic. Then she saw little fingers of it, tendrils, working their way in under the door. She put her ear to the lock. She heard the staircase outside creaking, but not as if it were bearing weight. She heard flame.

She'd backed away from the door, not thinking now at all, transfixed, rather, by the sight of the varnish this side of the door bubbling. Then a panel of the door had cracked. The edges of the crack began to char. Then it had cracked again and then, like it was dying, the door had fallen right into the room, and the room gave a great suck of air, like a gasp of horror at what was waiting outside it, and the fire that had been merrily devouring the stairs bounded through the doorway. It strung itself across the wall, and hurled itself at the bed-curtains, lifting them, sending them dancing like banners, straight up to the ceiling. The floor between the bed and door was nothing now but flame. It was reaching across the bed. It was coming for her –

Gretchen hurls herself at the door to the balcony. The door holds fast. She hurls herself at it again, and falls through it onto the snowy balcony, the heat of the fire on her arse. She looks up, and the whole façade of the house above her has flame at every window; flame like the tongues of dragons curling from under the eaves. She is transfixed. There are little lights dancing all around her. The ends of her hair are on fire. Then from the ground below she hears someone shouting, 'Jump, my dear one, jump! Jump down to me!' The rail of the balcony is at her back. She hears the voice again, 'Jump, jump!' She manages to get one leg over the balcony. Someone is down there, holding up their arms. Gretchen throws herself over, head first.

She opens her eyes. Her skirts are on fire. Someone is beating out the flames with handfuls of snow, then using their hat to flap air into her face.

It's that lieutenant. That one who's always making the sheep-eyes at her. It's Eickholz. 'My little love,' he's saying, 'my little love!' Now he's crushing her so tight against him Gretchen can hardly breathe. 'We must make our escape,' he's telling her. He's talking like he's on stage. 'Do you hear! We must make our escape! I will find us a way!'

Eickholz, this new Eickholz, equal to anything if he has Gretchen in his arms, starts pulling her away. And as he does, to his amazement, the finest, speediest mount in the entire regiment, that undeserving villain Heinrich's splendid mare, comes trotting through the smoke toward them.

FIVE BOYS, ONE HORSE; so close to the East Gate now that even Stuzzi could find the way. All the firing, all the noise has ceased. Nothing but silence, and moonbeams, and above their heads the movement of the sheets those citizens of Grauburg with the time to do so have hung from their windows. Of the people themselves, there is no sign at all. A crack of light escaping from a cellar, maybe; but that's it.

And the East Gate is just minutes from them. 'Jag, what is it? Why're you slowing down?'

'It's nothing.'

'Do you hear something? Is there someone behind us?'

'I said, it's nothing.'

On they go. Still he slows, and halts, and turns.

'Jag, mate, what is it?'

'Ah, the fuck with it.' His eyes close, then he straightens his back and gives a sigh. 'I'm going back for her.'

'Right then,' Hans hears himself announce, without hesitation. 'I'm coming with you.'

'I knew it!' Matz is so incensed he's hurled his hat to the ground. 'I knew this would happen! I sodding knew it!'

'I came back for you, didn't I?' says Jag, calmly, knotting Milano's reins under the horse's chin. 'And you I don't even *like*.'

'So what about us?' Matz demands, in the same furious hiss as before. 'You just going to leave us here? Leave us to be mopped up by the Swedish, that the plan?'

For a moment it looks like Jag is about to punch him. Instead he catches up Milano's reins, and before Stuzzi can protest, the reins are crammed into his grasp.

'There!' Jag says. 'D'y'see? I'm leaving Milano here. And no, Matz, no, I wouldn't come back for you, you fucken little maggot, not if I could leave you here, but you can be good and sure as I'll come back for *him*. That suit you?'

Back they go. Hans feels like he's in Ariadne's maze. Any minute they might meet the Minotaur. Come round a corner. Face to face. He hears Jag say, 'You're braver than the rest of 'em, that it?'

'No,' says Hans. 'Scareder. I ain't lettin' you out my sight.'

Some tiny something, falling against his face. Sparkling, like fireflies. He looks up. Then he shoots out a hand, saying, 'Oh my God, Jag, is that the marketplace? Is that them houses on the square?'

Those snapping, crackling sounds, they're not the sound of shots, they're timbers cracking in the heat. They're roof-tile splitting, plummeting to earth. The light ahead is yellowish. Jag's already broken into a run.

'Told you,' Matz is saying. 'He ain't half so smart as people think.' His voice is a furious whisper. 'He's mad, going back for her. Not in a hundred years 'ud she do that for him.'

Those rare times when the world makes sense to Stuzzi, it all comes at him in such a rush that he can't help voicing it. 'Why, it's 'cause he cares for her,' he says. 'And you ain't got nobody to care for you, have you, Matz? That's why you don't understand.'

And is astonished that Matz should shove past him so roughly, announcing, 'I ain't got to listen to this!'

Gunter shakes his head. 'You didn't have to say that,' he tells Stuzzi, sternly, then he too turns away.

Oh.

There's a horse, at a gallop, out there somewhere. Milano lifts his head.

So now here's Stuzzi, on his own.

No I ain't.

No, of course you ain't. You've Milano with you, and up there, where the alley turns, there's Gunter and Matz. You can make out their faces – smudges of white. They're talking. Maybe they're talking of you.

Don't care. No, why should you? Milano means Jag's coming back, and he's a good companion, is Milano, alert and watchful, with his ears swivelled forward and his lifted head. A snort. Is something there? Are you scared?

I ain't scared.

Nor me, says Milano, in Stuzzi's head, though he's snuffling the air and making grinding noises in his throat.

Something is there.

He hears the footsteps, then the growl. 'Who's that?' And first with astonishment, then with horrible delight: 'That you? My little flower?'

He retreats, then he grows angry with himself for retreating. Besides, you can't retreat far with a horse as solid as Milano behind you.

The footsteps come closer.

'That you, my flower? That my boy?'

Then the face. Grimed and striped with sweat, grimed even between the teeth.

'You've a horse. You've *his* horse.'

He feels the hands, over the reins. A sort of cry escapes him, an *ugh* of revulsion.

'Gimme the horse. Gimme the horse, you little shit.'

'No.' *Ugh.*

'GIVE ME THE HORSE!'

It's as if something else opens his mouth, forms the words for him. 'No,' he says. 'No, fuck you, you old bastard, *you ain't having him!*'

Too late. The heat, even behind the houses, is fierce enough to fight them. All four of those mansions facing the square are in flames, the first already fallen in, a ruin of glowing timbers and broken stone; all that fancy woodwork nothing now but fuel; and Bronheim's with the roof turning transparent even as they watch, the fire eating through it, revealing rafters, the interior bulk of the chimney, the chimney spouting sparks – too late. No matter how fast Jag runs, arm across his face, with Hans behind him – blown back for a moment by the heat, but then pressing on, reaching for Jag, trying to pull him back, calling out, 'Jag! Jag! Don't you see? It's too late! It's too late!'

In fact it seems to Hans that Jag can't be seeing much of anything at all, because his face is so rigid, as he stands there in the lane behind the house, as the chimney collapses and pulls the house down with it, it's like he can't even blink.

'Jag!'

'Jag!'

'Jag!'

He comes back to himself, with Hans shaking him.

He comes back to himself with the fire breathing into his face. There must be a prodigious heat, but he can't feel it.

And then running toward them, shrieking – no, not Hans, it's Gunter. 'Jag! Jag! Jag!'

Got it wrong.

'Jag, it's Stuzzi! Oh, come quick, come quick! Oh, *Jag!*'

Too late. Always too late.

*

It's all right now, it's all right. It had hurt, it had hurt a lot, but it's all right now. Now it don't hardly hurt at all. He looks up, smiling. Matz is there, kneeling beside him.

'Oh, Stuzzi, Stuzzi.'

Poor old Matz, he looks so bad. He looks like he could cry. Stuzzi would like to say something to make Matz feel better, if he could, but when he talks it's like the pain lifts its head. Best to stay quiet.

'Matz, get out the way.'

And here's Jag. Putting his arms about him. Trying to sit him up. No, don't, no, no –

And now Matz saying, 'Jag, just look at him! Leave him, leave him be!'

But being held is nice. Oh, he remembers now. 'Heinrich,' he says. Something makes him want to cry. 'Heinrich.'

His head is at Jag's breast. He hears the words come from inside. 'Heinrich. I know.'

'He took Milano.' A strange sort of hiccup forces its way up into his mouth, and brings with it the taste of blood. 'He hit me.' He's almost proud. And then there's that strange sensation again, as there had been before, of his inside being outside, of being somehow opened. They're all crouched round him, Hans, Gunter, Matz, and Jag, with one arm about his shoulders, the other cradling his head. He should feel so safe – if only it weren't for this strange feeling of everything slipping away. And wetness, under him. He lifts up his hand and stares at it. Oh. Hurt.

And perfect clarity. Clarity so huge, so whole, it's like he never properly understood anything before.

'I'm going to die.'

'Stuzzi, you are not going to die.' Jag's grip has tightened, as if that would be enough to stop it happening. 'You hear me? You are not going to die.'

'I am.' All of a sudden the tears are back. But they aren't real tears, not truly, he understands that, this has got so much more to it than them. He understands everything. 'I am. I'm going to die. And my mum and dad – they did love me.'

He closes his hand on Jag's arm. 'Oh—'

Everything leaving him. Feels like he's flying. Up from the alleyway, up over the roofs. There is the smoke from the market-place – *Oh*, thinks Stuzzi, *the poor town*. Then he thinks, *Why, that's us!* There is Jag, rocking back and forth, holding what he's holding, and the pain of it seems to hurl itself toward Stuzzi, jaws agape, to take a last bite at him – and it misses – and there, down in the market, there's Milano, with this ridiculous figure hopping about beside him, one foot in the stirrup, one on the ground. He sees the silly little figure fall flat as Milano pulls away, but now, coming over the hills, coming over the earth, is the sunrise, the dark and the cold all driven away before it, and there is Hans – good Hans, dear Hans – the only one to be looking up, and Stuzzi would like to tell him *don't worry, you know this all gets sorted in the end* because this is something else he understands, but he can't because here in all its warmth and majesty, here at last is the sun –

CHAPTER EIGHT

What's My Name?

'If you meet the enemie near his own quarter, and far from yours, you must resolve with a generous courage to go and charge him, though inferior in number; it being often seen that valiant resolutions are seconded with good luck.'

John Cruso, *Militarie Instructions for the Cavallrie*

ANOTHER DAWN, another place, a different day.

– Morning, Wilhelm.

– Morning, little brother. Finished, are you?

– Yup. Got the last of them fennel rolls in the oven, they're browning now.

– Ah. I like a taste of fennel, me.

I know you did, Will. I remember.

And he turns, wiping his hands on his floury apron. Good God, can this be Hans? Well, if you don't believe me, wait till he opens his mouth. That Westphalian accent of his is strong as ever.

'Tessie? You a-comin' down?'

'Coming, coming!'

Mrs Hans, the baker's wife. And no, she doesn't have dark ringlets, nor a face like a little cat. Her hair is blonde-ish, and respectably confined under a cap. And balanced on her hip, Miss Hans, the baker's daughter, two years old and stupefied with sugar from her morning pick of her father's labours – a sticky pastry in one hand, another, judged substandard, handed to her mother. Hans regards her fondly. 'What's she think of it?'

'She likes it,' Teresa replies. 'Don't you, duck?' And jiggles her daughter, who hiccups a little sugary saliva in reply. 'You should get another batch of them in, later on.'

The sticky pastry is cunningly woven into the shape of a double-headed Habsburg eagle, with raisins for its eyes. 'I'll do it now,' says Hans, and Teresa smiles at him, proud, as he goes back through the neat little shop, back to the heat of the ovens. He's not happy, her husband, unless every minute is filled. It had been the same when he'd proposed. She'd scarce known him a month, scarce learned his name. 'Look,' he'd said, 'we've got today, and that's all we've got. But you say yes, and we've got something more.' And the times being what they were, who could argue with that?

Hans bakes gingerbread men aloft on horseback, complete with hat and boots. He makes pastries in the shape of powder flasks, stuffed full of mincemeat; pretzels made of that soldiers' favourite, salt-raised bread, with the ends tied in and out, like the shape of the knot in an officer's sash. As each new regiment moves into town, Hans is first out on the streets, waiting for their standard to come by; before the men are even settled in their billets, the window of the soldier-baker's proudly displays their flag baked in double crust, inlaid with glossy cheese and snips of sausage. He does a roaring trade. Teresa has trestle-tables laid up in the street outside, and they're never empty. Hans knows two things about his clientele: first, that a soldier's always hungry; second, how lonely you can be, pitching up so far from home, and how small a thing can make you feel welcome. He remembers how lonely he was when he first pitched up here – fresh from his one and only leave back home, and raw with the understanding that he'd never fit in there no more, either. The baker's daughter and her friendly face was like the thing you swim to when you're drowning. He'd never really took to his new comrades, any case. The remnants of Bronheim's men got shared out round six other companies; Hans's new brothers-in-arms had never heard of Grauburg, and the story, once it got about, made him feel somehow ill-starred, a Jonah.

It's different now. The soldiers coming into town recognize him at once as one of their own. 'How'd you do that, friend?' (holding up some crisp, delicious simulacrum of a Saxon halberd, poppyseeds interlaced along its blade). 'You served, have you? Get away.' And fresh from his afternoon nap, Hans sits down with them and, with a little prompting, tells his tale. But it's no happy-ever-after, this, he warns his audience, and Tessie, still busy behind the counter as the dusk comes down, can tell when the tale is nearing its end because there's always one or two sat round her husband have to wipe their eye. It's Stuzzi's death that always seems to do it for them, and it's always the ones you'd think least likely, poking at their eyes the first. Soldiers. Was there ever a breed of men as sentimental?

'Now Jag –' (her husband is saying) '– Jag, he's holding Stuzzi and he's rocking back and forth with him, although it's plain and clear to all of us that Stuzzi's dead and gone. And I can't stand it, seeing him like that, so I kneel me down and sort of take the body from him, and we lay the poor lad on the ground together. Jag closes Stuzzi's eyes, gentle as a mother, then looks down at him for a moment, lying there, and then he says just one thing, he says, *Everyone*, real quiet and calm like that, *Everyone*, he says, and then he puts his head back and by God, if I never hear a man utter a cry like that again it'll still be too soon for me. It was half a roar and half a howl, and it goes banging off the walls – me, I'd got visions of the Swedish pausing in whatever murderous work they was about and asking themselves had they got werewolves as rivals here or what? – when like in answer to it there's this whinny, shrill and clear. And Jag is on his feet at once, and down the street, and we running after him, and he runs straight back to the marketplace – and it's only then I see he has that sword of his drawn as well – and Matz and Gunter and me, we're coughing in the smoke, which is so thick from the burning houses it has us three choking at once, but Jag don't seem to hardly notice it. He's yelling *Heinrich!* And then we hear Milano shrilling out a second time, and then there's Heinrich. Lo and behold.

'Man, I don't know which of us was more astounded. Him that we were there, or us that of 'em all, it should be God-damned Heinrich still in one piece. Well now, says Jag, and there's this glitter in his eye. Captain. Fancy meeting you.

'Well indeed, says Heinrich. And he looks about, like he ain't so sure what's afoot here, but he don't like the look of it so far. Well, my lads, my boys, says he. A sad day this, a sad, sad day. But they ain't done for old Heinrich yet.

'So we see, says Jag. And more's the pity. Jag's sort of circling round him – going one way, then back the other, like he's measuring the ground. Now make a road there, lads, old Heinrich says, and let me by. God willing, we shall meet again some day.

'Sure, says Jag. We'll let you by. Soon as you give me back my horse.

'Old Heinrich takes a grip on Milano's reins. Starts narrowing them piggy eyes of his. Now look here, boy, this horse is mine –

'That horse, says Jag, that horse ain't no more yours than we are. Now get away from him.

'You could see the veins start thickening up on Heinrich's scalp. Don't you cross me, boy, he snarls. You know me, I'll make you sorry –

'And then Jag says – he says –'

(And Teresa waits for the laugh, which always comes.)

'He says, Heinrich, you're a piss-head. And what isn't piss is wind. I have *shat* scarier things than you.

'Old Heinrich, he looks like he's ready to explode. I don't suppose he'd ever been spoke to like that in his life. You God-damned no-name piece of dust, he roars at Jag, you think you can take me?

'I'm God-damned sure I can, says Jag. And there's this *huge* grin on his face. And Heinrich gives a bellow and next thing he's drawn his sword, and he's slashing it about and swearing at Jag what he's going to do to him, and Jag lashes the Solingen sword out full-length, making it sing, and there we go. Jag and Heinrich, in a swordfight, right in front of us.

'I thought that Jag had clean gone mad, I truly did. Heinrich was twice his weight and twice his age and he'd had years of this – hacked his way round half of Germany, I have no doubt. He's got this big two-handed grip, and he's thrashing his sword about like he's felling trees. You think you can take me, boy? he's saying, you think you can take me on?

'Well as to that, Jag replies, circling round, I guess we're about to find out. And he sounds that merry about it, like he's a little kid. Let's see what you're up for, says he. And Heinrich gives another roar, and comes charging at Jag, with that sword of his coming through the air like it's going to chop the world in two, and Gunter's wailing and Matz is hollering, and me I don't know what I did, but the blade comes down – and when it does, Jag just ain't there no more. Fact is, as I remember it, he was moving even before Heinrich was. As I remember it now, he was moving soon as he saw the grip Heinrich had taken. All Heinrich's blade cuts through is empty air. Heinrich pulls up and there's Jag, still circling round him, still grinning, and untouched.

'Oh come, says Jag. Is that the best you can do?

'Heinrich roars and takes another swing, right to left this time. Jag dodges back – he's outright laughing now. My turn, he says. And he comes in, like he'll swing right to left as well, then he turns his wrist, and the blade kind of swivels in his hand – Heinrich's all over the place, don't know where it's coming from – and the tip of it catches Heinrich right under the ear.

'Jag steps back. It's like he's admiring his handiwork. Heinrich takes his hand from his head and stares at it, like he expects to find the ear lying there. Stings, don't it? says Jag.

'Heinrich goes back a step or two as well. He's looking kind of thoughtful. He does a couple of feints, and drops into a crouch, and then all of a sudden he goes in opposite and underneath to how you'd think, and you'd reckon with his weight and all as he'd be slow, but he's not. He's fast as a God-damned snake. There's this slash slash slash, this whirr of the blades – you ever see a real swordfight, the real true thing? 'Cause if you have, you'll know as you don't hardly see it, not at all, you hear it, more, and we hear this slash and crash and Heinrich's staggering forward, and Jag's turned on his toes – I mean it's like he's *dancing* – and that blade of his goes singing out, and now it's Heinrich has to dodge. Hasn't even got his breath back and Jag's in there again, gets a poke in at his shoulder, one at his head – like he was playing with him, do you see? And now Heinrich's slashing and cursing away, and Gunter and Matz and me, we're yelling our heads off, for by now it's plain to all of us, and doubly plain to Heinrich I should think, that this here no-name piece of dust is going to give him the fight of his life. And Jag's still got this great grin on his face, and all the time he's goading Heinrich too – Come on, fat man, he's saying, all that stuff. Come on, fat man. Let's see you sweat.

'Heinrich, he ain't even looking where he is no more, he's slashing away like a blind thing, don't care about nothing if he can just keep Jag off him. And he's blowing now, he's blowing hard, he can't keep this up much more. And the fight has took them over where the tavern was, so there's all this stuff strewed on the ground – bits of roof-tile, and the pegs that was holding the tiles to the roof when the tavern had a roof, and Heinrich gets summat under his foot, and turns it. Goes down on one knee. And Jag stands off, steps back, at once, like this is something as you just don't do, take advantage of a man who's down, and Heinrich gets back up, but now he's got this piggy bit of cunning in his eye. He circles, makes a slash or two, panting, and next lunge he makes, he's down again. And in that space he's made for himself, his free hand goes to his belt. Comes out with his knife.

'We're all yelling No! Jag! No! – for we can see Jag going in, sword aimed like a spear, and Heinrich with the knife ready in one great slash to open him up. And then *Wiedersehen*, Heinrich, we hear Jag say, and something comes into his eyes – I don't know what to call it, it was like something rising from the deep. And you can see, straight off, as he knew. He knew, if he stood off the once, Heinrich 'ud try the same damn trick again, and when he did, Jag had him. He throws that sword of his from right hand to left, like a juggler in a circus, and now his right hand's free he grabs Heinrich's sword-arm with it, shoves it wide, and in the same moment stamps down on the hand with the knife, and he's holding Heinrich there, pinned there, pinned and stretched like he'd planned this all along, and with his left hand, smooth as silk, he puts about a foot of Solingen steel straight into Heinrich's chest.'

The gasp from his audience. Like the laugh, there's always the gasp.

'Heinrich, he don't say nothing, not at first. Just gapes down at that blade, where it goes into him. Then Jag leans forward.

And this noise comes out of Heinrich like the air out a bladder. And the sword slides through him till him and Jag, they're all but face to face, and the blade of Jag's sword it's right through Heinrich and out the other side. Us three, we're stood there, froze. I don't think any one of us had thought this was possible. This was Heinrich, what had been the terror of our every waking moment for so long, and here he was, pinned like a louse. And Jag leans down toward him, and his hand goes to his neck, and he lifts out this little silver pendant that he wore. Holds it up, right to Heinrich's nose. Heinrich's goggling. Heinrich's like his eyes 'ud pop right out his head.

'Now you've seen this before, says Jag, don't tell me you ain't. He leans in a little more, and this same noise comes out of Heinrich, like a leak. You know where I got it? Jag asks next. I took it from my mother's hand. After that friend of yours had throttled her and strung her up. You know the man I mean. Him as killed my father, out in Picardy. You remember that little place in Picardy, don't you? So what's my name, Enric? And he jiggles the pendant up and down. I know yours, you see, says Jag. See if you can guess mine.

'This wheezing noise, it's coming out of Heinrich every breath. There's a little blood too, you can see it on his teeth. And now you know who I am, says Jag, all sweet and mild, you're going to tell me who that other is. He leans on the sword again. Charles the Ghost, Jag says. Tell me his proper name.

'Heinrich, he just sits there, on his heels, wheezing and goggling. Jag's getting impatient now. He says, Heinrich, I take my blade out, your lung will go as flat as if I'd stamped on it. You'll drown in your own blood, you understand? You'll go down to hell gagging on it. And then he stops. He peers in at Heinrich real close, and then he says, And that's what scares you, ain't it? That's the thing. And then he steps back, head to the side, and he says, I've got just three down there so far, waiting for me. How many you got, Heinrich, eh? And I reckon most of yours are little ones. Where are they going to be aiming their pitchforks first?

'Heinrich, you'd almost think as he was ready to start a-weeping. He's got this real blubbery look on his face, and then Jag leans in again, and he says, Y'know, Heinrich, maybe it ain't all over for you. Maybe if I take this out real slow, and we get you to a surgeon, what do you say? You reckon you might make it?

'And Heinrich, he's nodding his head and trying to mouth *yes, yes,* and Jag bends down again, and he says, What's the name? Tell me that first. What's his proper name?

'Heinrich says something. Jag bends in closer. Heinrich says it again. Jag straightens up. Carlo Fantom, he says. Charles the Ghost. That's him, is it?

'Heinrich's nodding, and now he's lifting his hands to where the hilt of the sword sits, in his chest. Please, he's saying. Please. And Jag is in a sort of circuit round him, like he's working his way to something big, and he's saying Carlo Fantom, Carlo Fantom, over and over, like he's testing the name out. Then he says, One more thing, Heinrich. Where would I start to look for him?

'Heinrich just shakes his head. Please, he says.

'You don't know where? asks Jag, and Heinrich shakes his head again. Jag's sort of behind him, so Heinrich has to look up and over his shoulder, and that's when I saw, Jag was holding that knife of his, ready to go. Well then, says Jag. What earthly fucken use are you to me? And with that, the knife goes bang, straight into Heinrich's throat, and this pipe of blood springs out of him and goes splattering all over the ground.

'Heinrich's hands go up, they're scrabbling at the hole, like he'd plug it with his fingers, but Jag has Heinrich's head in his grip, and he's pulling it back, holding Heinrich's throat open, and when it's that cold, blood *smokes.* They're stood there in this haze of it, Heinrich on his knees and Jag behind him, and Heinrich's hands are still a-scrabbling, but in this twitchy manner now, and everything about him is subsiding, like he's emptying for real. Weight back on his heels. Hands falling away. Jag lets his head go, Heinrich sinks a little lower, until the point of the sword stops him. And Jag goes round the front of him, puts his boot on old Heinrich's chest, and pulls the sword free, and Heinrich falls sideways, and that's it. That's old Heinrich, that's him dead.'

A pause. His audience exchange glances. 'And then?' asks one.

'Oh. And then.' And Teresa watches as her husband squares his shoulders. 'So, if I remember a-right, first thing Jag does is he leans on his sword and he hacks a gobful of spit on the ground. I can still hear Milano, capering about out of sight, and my first thought was how one of us ought'a go get him for Jag. I mean, it seemed like the least we could do. And I remember Gunter holding out his hand and saying It's snowing, in this little voice, all wonderment. And I remember turning my own face to the sky, and seeing how it was lightening, and realizing how this night was coming to an end at last, and feeling so thankful as the flakes landed on my face, and then hearing some little pop and flutter from behind me. And I turned to see what it might be.

'There was I don't know how many men stood behind us. They'd come in not from the West Gate, no (for we could hear that end of the fight still going on) – they'd come in from the East. And they'd got torches raised above their heads, and what I'd heard was the snow falling into 'em. I'd got just about enough time to work out who they were before they were down on us. I've got my arms twisted up behind my back and a pistol at my head before I've even got a scream out. I'm down on my knees on the stones, and Gunter and Matz are on their knees beside me, and the scariest thing of all is how I'm just not scared no more. Maybe there's something beyond terror, and I'd reached that. I've got all these big old peaceful thoughts inside my head – how we gave it our best, and at least this'll be quick, and how I'm sorry I ain't going to see my mother again, but even that don't seem to matter very much. Then there's this shout.

'This one man, this giant, he comes striding through the rest. He's got a cloak of bearskin, and his hair in a plait like a rope, and he's clapping his hands. This big, slow clap. Jag's still stood there, on his own, breathing hard, and this giant walks up to him, walks all around him, doing this big slow clap the while. And then the giant, he says summat I heard as Hauptmann, or Hartmann, but it weren't, of course. We'd have scarce knowed what such a thing was, back then, but it was *hard man* he was saying, and trying to say it in German, so as Jag would understand, and he's saying it sort of mockingly, but not entirely so, and then he snaps his fingers, and this boy comes to his side. Lord, that amazed me, that their army should have boys in it like ours. And the giant speaks a word to him, and the boy turns to Jag, and first thing he does is sweep Jag a bow, and then he speaks.

'This is our kapitan, Torsten Bjornson, he says. And this one – (pointing at Heinrich) – this one *mein Kapitan* knows. But wod *ist* you, hard man?

'Wondering who I'm fighting next, says Jag.

'The boy gives a sort of choke of laughter, and translates, and the man in the cloak he looks Jag up and down again, like he's thinking *Well, that's a pretty cool answer*, and he's impressed. He speaks to the boy some more, and now the boy points at us. And wod *ist* them?

'Mine, says Jag. My crew. The boy translates this back, and the man considers it, and through the boy, comes back with another question. Goot crew? the boy asks.

'You wouldn't think it, says Jag, to look at 'em now. Then the man says something more, and the boy goes, You want us to let them live?

'You could let 'em up, at least, says Jag.

'And the man gives a laugh and beckons to the soldiers holding us – up, up – and we're put on our feet again. There's another bit of chat between him and the boy, and the boy says to Jag, 'E ask, so, where you learn to fight, hard man?

'You tell him, says Jag, probably much the same kind of places as him.

'Now though we're on our feet, we're still ringed about by the Swedish, so we can't see much of what is going on, but it seems clear that the giant in the cloak and Jag, with this lad to translate, they're getting on something splendid. The man's squinting his eyes and sizing Jag up all the time, but whatever he's hearing, he likes the sound of it. Finally he moves off, and as he does, Jag catches my eye, and he gives me a wink. That gets me thinking, I can tell you. I almost don't want to trust it, for even at the thought my heart starts hammering, but what that wink says, it seems to me, is that maybe there's a chance we'll be getting out of this alive. And then the boy comes back, and he's pulling Milano with him, and he hands Milano's reins to Jag, and he gives another deep bow as he hands him over, and he says, I yam Zoltan. Your name, hard man?

'Jag, says Jag.

'Now here comes the giant again. He marches back to Jag, and there's this scrip of paper in his hand. Bit more chat, then Jag takes the paper from him, and he brings it over. The men ringed round us part to let him through. Here, says Jag, and gives the paper to me.

'What this? says I.

'That's a pass for safe conduct, says Jag. That's how you're getting out of here. Anyone stops you, you show 'em that. I'm going to need Milano, though – you'll have to walk.

'It's Matz who finds his voice the first. What about you? he says.

'Me? says Jag. Oh, I'm going with them.

'You're *what*? says Matz. And Gunter pipes up, But they're the enemy!

'Jag gives a smile. Not mine they ain't, he says. I ain't got but one enemy in the whole wide world, and he ain't here. And then he gives this merry, merry laugh, and then he looks at me again, and he must'a seen the shock on my face, for he says, Hans, this is war, it's how it works. Stay out the woods, stick to the roads, and the minute you don't need that pass, you lose it, understand? Have Gunter eat it. Don't let it be found on you. Be just like you, to do a thing like that. Then he pats my hand. You'll do all right, he says, I know you will.

'I'm holding that bit of paper, I look at it, and look at him, and I still can't believe it. I'm close to tears, I am. And then Jag ducks his face down close to mine and says, under his breath, Oh come on, Hans. Don't make a song and dance about this. I can't hardly take 'em all on for you, can I? It's me for you. That's the deal.'

And as Tessie watches, her husband's audience reels back. They always do.

'He did a *deal* for you?'

'What, and he went off with them? Your mate?'

'He went off with the Swedish? Fucken – pardon, missus, but holy *hell*.'

And her husband gives a shrug as always, and he says, 'That's how it was. His very words.'

'And you ain't never seen him since?'

'Never. Not hide nor hair. Last I saw of him, he was riding off across that square with them, sat atop Milano, with a sword of Solingen steel at his hip.'

'I ain't never seen a sword of Solingen steel,' says one, sounding despondent. 'Sixty thaler they cost, new.'

'Nor had I. And I ain't never seen another. And that suits me just fine.' And Hans leans back from the table, and crosses his hands over his belly. He understands the importance of giving an audience time to digest.

'Someone must know where he is,' says a voice, at last. 'Lad with a fire in him like that don't just disappear.'

'Oh, he would'a done,' says Hans. 'If that was what he wanted, and I reckon that it were. He was real good at covering his tracks, was Jag – so good you never even saw him do it. All that time, me thinking he was a Southerner? That was only because he wanted me to. Truth be told, we hardly knew a damn thing more about him when he rode away from us than we had that morning he rode in. Though I will say, if what he told to Heinrich 'bout his folks, if that was true, it made a deal more sense of him than he had made before. But otherwise –' and Hans shakes his head. 'You know in Swedish what Jag means? It means Me meself, that's what. It's not a name at all.' And adds, as an afterthought, 'Some part of me's still puzzled what they made of that.'

Someone has lit a pipe. 'That's proper sad, that tale,' the smoker says.

'*Ach*, well,' says Hans, 'that's how it was.' He flexes his shoulders. All things come to an end – the day, the labours of the day, each story winds down to its close. *It's how things are*, thinks Hans. It's how the world was made. Tessie will have their supper ready, and the little one will want a story of her own before she'll close her eyes. He rises, slowly, to his feet. 'I saw Gunter again. Walking up a street in Leipzig. He told me Matz had lost an eye in the hot stuff at Dessau Bridge.' *Poor old Matz*, thinks Hans. *Always convinced he'd strike it lucky some day.* 'But with Jag, not a word. And when something never happens, in the end you just stop looking for it. I'll tell you what, though,' he says, for he can feel his audience waiting. 'All these years, I don't think there's been a week, I don't think there's hardly been a day, when something hasn't brought him to my mind. And I ain't took a moment, sat, like here, and wondered. You know. Just what did become of him.'

CHAPTER NINE

The Edge of the World

'The Papists are on the Baltic, they have Rostock, Wismar, Stettin, Wolgast, Griefswald and nearly all the other ports in their hands... their whole aim is to destroy Swedish commerce and soon to plant a foot on the southern shore of our fatherland. Sweden is in danger from the power of the Habsburg, that is all but it is enough; that power must be met, swiftly and strongly.'

Gustavus Adolphus, King of Sweden

NOT A PLACE you'd linger, this, not any season of the year. The sea is never less than furious at finding its rampaging progress stopped; the land – the dunes – rear back in defiance and seem to mirror, with their wind-curved shapes and crests of stiff, salt, grass, those mighty Baltic rollers. Then there's the wind itself. This wind came out the Arctic, this wind first made landfall at Murmansk. Roared across

Lapland, down the Gulf of Bothnia, flying hail before it, yellow storm clouds in its wake. Barged its way to Stockholm, picked up the fleet there and whipped them before it like a child with a top, straight across the Baltic, straight to here. Usedom, they call this place, those few who call it anything at all: more sea than land, more sky than sea, and the wind on its coast never ceases, not even now, July. Why would anyone, tipped out their great ships at this desolate spot, be raising such a cheer?

But nonetheless, they are. This place does have its virtues. Usedom – this tiny island on the rim of Germany – is so damn far from anywhere that anything could come ashore here and it would be weeks before news of it reached inland. Make landfall here, you can make all the noise you like. Second, it has a beach like a shelf, a drop-off that puts thirty feet under your keel at once. Which is why that same fleet stands at anchor here, mere yards offshore. All you need do is load up your flat-bottomed transports and the wind does the work for you, carries your army to land. Near enough that the hardier souls can swim it, should they wish. Which is of course exactly what the hardier and most daring amongst them do, galloping their horses with wild cries straight across the deck and over the side, to land with a splash like a fountain; the horses gamely sticking their heads straight out the water, nostrils wide, and paddling off at once, and the riders scarce even dislodged from the saddle, riding their mounts as they paddle through the waves like an army sent by Neptune.

Not recommended for all, of course. Not, for example, this poor child here, being dragged from the water slack as seaweed. So sad, his bedraggled state, and in such contrast to his pretty clothes – that sky-blue doublet, and the matching cloak, with its arabesques of gold braid, whose weight had almost drowned him. And in such contrast, too, to the man dragging him up the beach through the surf, pulling him along by the scruff of the neck, something like (with the wrinkled leather of the man's own clothes, and his dripping whiskers) a walrus with its pup.

With his other hand, this same fellow leads his horse – a beast of impressive size, high-stepping ostentatiously through the waves as if it had as little patience with those unable to make it to the beach unaided as its master.

The man drags the boy to a group stood in a half-moon at the shoreline, their horses gathered behind them, the sea filling and swirling between the horses' legs. There are such groups as these, larger and smaller, forming all along the beach. Before those galleons turn about, thirteen thousand men will have disembarked here. The beach at midnight, in the light of the midsummer sun, will be pitted with the marks of booted feet, and corrugated with the lines of the gun-carriages. There will be twirls of smoke amongst the sand-dunes, the flap of flags. But no-one will see them, no-one will know. No-one but seagulls and mermaids.

And now, to the bleat of trumpets, those flags are being raised. What a noise each makes, as it's hit by the wind, and how various they are, and how many! That one with the ram, that's Gotland. The orb is Uppland. The standing goat there, Hälsingland. Every province in Sweden has rendered up its draft of young men. The cross there with the slash across its stem signals Muscovy – Russian irregulars, who have heard there is a new fight in the making, so why not? That flag with the white griffin, holding its sword, that is Livonian, from the eastern Baltic, those black-earthed lands that stand between Russia and the sea; Swedish territory now. There is the saltire of St Andrew, and those fellows standing round it, they are the Mackay – much prized as fighters, the plaid-bedecked Mackay, and let's not forget, it was their princess the Emperor drove from her Bohemian castle, all those years ago. Here are the Finns, naked-legged, leading their ponies to dry land, the Finns who by repute can cross rivers without fords, and summon up mists and tempests as they please. It would have to be some enemy could make one army out of all of these.

Immediately the flags are unfurled, the heralds present themselves. There must be fifty of them spaced along the long line of the beach, which is itself now solid with men. Soon as the trumpets are stilled, each herald unfolds a paper and begins shouting its contents to the wind. And each in a different tongue: Swedish, Finnish, German, Russian, English... as a means of communication, it leaves a lot to be desired, and within months of entering Germany this army will have discovered a handy argot of its own, which welcomes words thrown in from all. 'Rotwelsch' is what it's known as, this unholy cant, and civilians who hear it will report it as being so barbaric and obscene it must be what the devils speak in hell. And overlooking them all, up there on horseback, the man responsible for it all: barrel-chested, famously goggle-eyed, with the point of his beard jutting across his chest, proudly mounted on a chestnut stallion. The stallion is named Streiff, after its breeder; it has a pedigree long as its tail, a thousand-thaler price-tag, and a mien of such imperturbable superiority you'd almost expect it to stand listening with its arms folded too. The man on its back is Gustavus Adolphus, and he is King of Sweden.

The heralds, all having reached the same point in the proclamation, turn and doff their hats to him. The men on the beach raise another cheer. Let's go back to that first group, stood there in that half-moon at the water's edge, let's have another look at them.

They must have been some of the first ashore, these, for the wind has mostly dried their clothes and they've slouched into those easy ways of standing together you find in any group well used to one another's company. Elbow leaning on your neighbour's shoulder, say, or on the rump of his horse. A cavalry unit, with that many horses, and with that sort of cavalry insouciance about them too, even at their ease. The buff-coats are studded, the breeches fringed. The doublets have fancy linings. The hair is braided (sometimes the beards are too), the fingers be-ringed.

A swagger to them, even standing still. All save that poor boy, of course, who's now on hands and knees and emptying himself of a good deal of sea-water. He finishes, and turns a beseeching eye to the man stood above him. 'Forgive, Domini,' the boy begs. 'I have spewed upon your boots.'

'Kai,' says the man, looking down at him. The boy is twelve or so, that age when everything is awkward, while the man is maybe ten years older, and the horse stood by the man is old enough for there to be flecking on its muzzle, and grey streaked through the curls of its mane. 'Kai,' the man says, 'you're a disgrace.'

'Yes, Domini,' the boy agrees.

'Who's that up there?'

The boy takes a breath. 'That is my King.'

'That's so. Not mine, but yours. Who has brought you all a-ways here, so you can show him you're a hero.'

'Yes, Domini.'

The boy is struggling to his feet. It is only when he stands that you realize quite how tall those men around him are. Quite how savage-looking too. The one who dragged the boy to shore in particular: he's a sort of Nature's 'prentice-piece, put together as if to demonstrate just how ferocious two eyes, a mouth and nose can be made to be, with jagged teeth and warts across his face like stars across the sky. His portrait has been burned into the back of his buff-coat, and is carefully studded, to match where the warts sit on the original. The two stood by him might be twins, each with hair bright and white as a candle-flame, and the backs of their coats do indeed show the Gemini; two naked boys holding hands. Their coats also bear, down the sleeves, small uneven fields of tiny crosses. Which signify? Best not to ask. Stood by them one whose head is wholly shaved, other than a topknot of hair thick and long as his horse's tail. This has been dyed carmine, and so too is the tail of his horse. They are not – there's nothing retiring about this group, let's put it like that. The man – the 'Domini' to whom he had been speaking

– leans toward him, and as he does, the boy seems to shrink back into himself. A very new recruit.

'So next time you're going to spew,' the man says, 'do it in your hat.'

'But I have not my hat, Domini,' the boy replies, blinking nervously. 'The sea has swallowed it.'

The shouting heralds, the roaring sea, the screaming sea-mews. The man gives the boy a pitying glance. Hard to say which has less colour in them – the man's eyes, or the Baltic. He turns to his neighbour. 'Remind me, what was it we brought him for?'

This next is rather more human-looking than the rest. In fact he's positively handsome, with his dark hair and eyes, and as he speaks the flash of white teeth through his full-winged moustaches – or he would be, did he not look quite so miserable. 'Don't speak with me,' he says. 'This is Germany. This is the worst place on earth. Germany *eats* men.'

And the other laughs. He's a deal less showy than the rest, in fact compared to them he's downright shabby. An ancient buff-coat, burled with scars (its only decoration); boots tide-marked with much riding in the wet, even before the sea got to them. He says, 'Have your moan, Zoltan, you old woman.'

The boy is watching, his gaze twitching from one speaker to the other.

'I liked Poland,' Zoltan begins. 'Poland was simple. Poland made sense. This war –' The wash of a wave against his legs. Zoltan rises on his tiptoes to keep it from pouring down his boots. A snort of laughter from that white-haired pair behind. One of them reaches forward, touches the first man on the arm. 'Domini,' he says. The heralds have paused again, more cheering is required, and suddenly that name, that *Domini*, no longer sounds so childlike and naïve.

'The glory,' Jack says, lightly, once the cheering's done. 'The glory, Zoltan.'

'This war is crazy,' Zoltan says, stubbornly. 'We march into Germany, we are going to *die*.'

'No we ain't. Of course we ain't. You think I'd let that happen to you?'

A final burst of cheering. The flags have been furled. In their place, a mighty battle-standard – the field of blue, the yellow crowns – pointing straight into Germany, stiff as a signpost in this wind. The figure on the chestnut stallion has turned about. Zoltan feels his heart give a last whimper of despair. But now he sees Jack has lifted something from within the neck of his shirt, is holding it up so it twists upon its chain. The silver wolf.

'God's name!' Zoltan exclaims. Despite his forebodings, he can't help but smile. 'You don't think he's still out there? After all this time?'

'Oh, he's there,' Jack answers. His eyes have narrowed, like he's taking aim. 'Trust me. I can feel it in my blood.'

'Does your blood also tell you how we go about finding him?' Zoltan asks, amused.

'We don't. He'll find me.'

Bafflement. 'Why would he do that?'

'I'm a loose end.' A mighty grin. 'And there's nothing he hates more than that.'

The silver wolf turns in the wind: west… west-south-west… south.

'*Hallå*, Deutschland,' says Jack, softly. 'How good to be back.'

Acknowledgements

WRITING A BOOK begins as such a solitary experience. There's no-one but you, the author, all alone save for that cast of thousands in your head. Then as the writing extends, and the book takes shape, stage by stage, an ever-widening circle of folk from the real world become part of it too. When what you are writing turns out to be three books, rather than one, it leads to an awful lot of people to thank.

To begin with, Nick Marlowe, who allowed me to pillage both his knowledge of seventeenth-century military history and his library; and Mark Getlein who walked me through the seventeenth-century Louvre and the geography of Concini's assassination. As always, researching any kind of book at all would have been impossible without the wonderful British Library and its patient and dedicated staff. I spent many happy hours there, fossicking about in the underbelly of seventeenth-century history, and in the galleries of the British Museum, the V&A and Tate Britain; in Berlin's Gemaldegalerie and its Deutsches Historisches Museum; and in the Rijksmuseum in Amsterdam and the Metropolitan Museum of Art in New York, who I must single out for special mention here. Their open-access policies, placing so many images in the public domain, not to mention their ever-flexible search engines, became so much a part of my researches that they flowed over into the finished book which, I hope, will be all the richer and more immersive for readers now as a result.

Then there are my first readers, who were so generous with their enthusiasm and support, who read early drafts and were kind enough to ask for more, and who kept reminding me about that itch, and sending me back to scratch at it again.

Chief among these is Jenny McKinley, but also Colin Walsh and John Stachiewicz, Lucinda Hutson, Lee Ripley and Joe Schick (the best story-doctor you could ask for); Joyce Hackett, Barry Isaacson, Kit Maxwell, Tom Morgan, Kathy Rooney and Lydia and Rich; and my precious girlfriends – Lucy, Liz, Pru, Susan, Penny, and Kate K and Kate P.

Sara Bailey and the Richmond writers were invaluable as guide and companions in helping to shape and polish and shape and polish again; and for unstinting assistance in navigating the world of social media, Anita Chapman and Frances Wilson. I also have to proffer heartfelt thanks to Evan Fallenberg and Xu Xi, creators of the International MFA at the Vermont College of Fine Arts, and to the 2019 students of the MFA; and to Barbara Schwepcke, Harry Hall, and everyone at Haus and the Gingko Library for providing a writer with friendship, interest and encouragement as well as that most precious of commodities – gainful employment, but not too much of it.

King-size thanks, as ever, are due to my agent, Chelsey Fox, and to Charlotte Howard, of Fox and Howard, for bending the rules as I hopped the fence from non-fiction to fiction, and to Philip Gooden, for road-testing *The Silver Wolf* as an external reader; and more of the same order of magnitude to the team at Allen & Unwin, especially Joe Mills for the sensational cover design and Jeff Edwards for the map that brings the world of *The Silver Wolf* to life; Ed Pickford for the beautifully constructed page design; Tamsin Shelton for copyediting what became those same pages and Liz Hatherell for proofreading them with such sharp eyes; to Kate Straker and Sophie Walker for shepherding the book out into the world with such creativity and care; and above all to my virtuoso editor, Kate Ballard. Publishing teams such as that at A&U don't come along every day, and I am truly grateful.

Lastly, in the place of honour, the other essentials every writer needs: an understanding family and a paragon of a partner who completely gets it too. Thank you.

What lies in store for our hero?
Read on for an exclusive early extract from Book Two
in the Fiskardo's War series, *The Dead Men*.

July 1630–October 1631

CHAPTER ONE

Ghostland

'It seems we have another little enemy to fight.'

Ferdinand II, Holy Roman Emperor

N OW – WHERE were we? On an island, it turns out, though one so lightly separated from the rest of Germany and by tides so low and amiable, there are places a man might ride from island to mainland without his horse even wetting its belly. Among the conscripts also tumbled out here, out the great galleons and the flat-bottomed transports, the hundred or so tumbled into his tender care reveal themselves as the sons of fisher-folk from the Stockholm archipelago, who seem delighted to find the country they have just invaded so very similar to home.

Two hundred transports. Thirty-six galleons. Thirteen thousand men. The island of Usedom has been overrun. It takes two days to unload them all, by which time the supplies they brought with them have already been consumed, but what would an army be without the odd little oversight such as that?

Forage, he tells them. He feels himself inhabiting this new role of their captain as he says it. Lesson number one: use your wits, use what you know; you're fishermen, so you go fish. To add to the unreality of it all, they've made this landing in July, so it's past midnight, yet everything – his hands, the lads chasing fish through the shallows, the water itself, the sky above – is all the same fluttering, pulsing cornflower blue.

On the other bank, far off, dark and spiky as a crown of thorns, Wolgast and its fort, in silhouette.

The boy, Kai, sits down beside him (it being an ensign's duty to be as constantly about his captain as a shadow), in that splendid suit of blue and gold, now so sadly watermarked from its adventures on arrival here (and shrunk too, he notes, about the boy's limbs), and starts some tale of childhood days and long white nights at some summer house in the archipelago, and how his nurse would bring him treats from the table of those banqueting out on the terrace below. The sons of the fishermen gawp at him as if he had just fallen from the moon, and snigger behind their hands. Kai, gamely attempting to emulate the other men in the company, had gone plunging straight over the rail of the galleon, just as the rest had done, and the weight of gold thread on his jacket had nigh-on drowned him. The episode has already become one of the favourite tales of this company and its landing, embroidered and embellished at each handing-on. Now one of the fisher-lads, deftly throwing a fish onto the sand, calls out mockingly, 'Has 'e brung 'is little silver spoon?' and, in some presumption of agreement, slides his own gaze up to that of his captain, sat there on the bank with Kai beside him.

He thinks, Not *the* company, *mine*. He takes a narrow prospect of the josher. He thinks, *I know you. Cock of the walk since the day you were born.*

And so because this is his company, because he is its captain, and because years back, there had been another boy, also younger, bullied, loyal, he stands up. 'You – name?'

The answer comes back, 'Ulf. Ulf of Torsby!'

He crooks a finger. The lad approaches, splashing up the bank.

He lowers his head, and as he does so, Ulf of Torsby shrinks into himself a little. Kai is not the only one about whom tales are told. 'You speak to any man in this company in that tone again,' he says, 'you will regret it. Is that clear?'

Ulf of Torsby hangs his head. 'Yes, Kapten. Sir.'

Little bastard. All the same, it's Ulf of Torsby had the balls to crack the joke, to catch his eye, and on returning to those others in the stream, it's Ulf of Torsby is being given the commiserating pats on the back.

Meantime, Kai – Karl-Christian von Lindeborg, of Castle Lindeborg in the county of Uppsala, no less – gets stiffly to his feet, as one does when one is young as this and one's pride is tender. 'I too can forage,' he announces, and off he goes, those shrunken breeches rising up above his kneecaps at each step.

A shout of laughter from behind him. Zoltan, Ziggy, the Gemini, the Executioner are hunkered in the dip there, and Zoltan, it transpires, has been composing his will. Now Ziggy has taken it over. 'Item,' he hears Ziggy declaim, at full volume, 'item, my boots. Which I leave to the cheese-makers. Item, my fine moustache, which is to be put upon a string and made into a diversion for the cat. Item, my cock and balls, which are to be stuffed and varnished, and given to the artists, to use when next they must depict a god!'

They are all of them still half-deaf from the thump of those Baltic rollers on the island's eastern side. His hair feels thick with salt, the skin on his face made tight with it. Here though, here, facing the mainland, the thump and boom is distant. There are cottages; there are little farms – all deserted now, of course. The population of Usedom, such as it was, has taken to its boats and fled. Instead, here and there across this open landscape, there are regimental flags, battle standards, snapping in the wind. Messengers, galloping back and forth. The peep of bugles. The far-off bellow of an order, blown past them on the wind. *So this is what I have*, he thinks. *My Praetorians, the sons of the fisher-folk, and the boy. My company. Amongst those thirteen thousand men, this is all that is actually mine.*

He folds himself back down again, there on the bank among the salt-grass. On the horizon, Wolgast waits. Either it has one more day to live, or they do. His hand goes to the pendant at his breastbone, the silver wolf, scratched and niello'ed now with age, but still the only compass he has ever had, or ever needed, come to that. Grace alone, faith alone. *Gott mitt uns.* We'll see.

This war, this German war, is twelve years old. It has already swallowed the armies of Duke Christian of Brunswick, and of the Danes. It has chewed its way through the troops sent by the Dutch and English. It has sucked in regiment after regiment of Emperor Ferdinand's soldiers, and those of his cousin the King of Spain, picked its teeth with their bones; and still it goes on. And every one of those armies, Catholic, Calvinist or Lutheran, claimed God was with them too. *And now us,* he thinks. This army: this army of the Lion of the North, His Majesty Gustavus Adolphus of Sweden.

He keeps it to himself, but it seems to him God is an unreliable ally.

Kai returns. He returns with a round flat basket over one arm, and with a little old man and a little old woman, like the figures on a weathervane, bringing up the rear. There being a lady now present, Zoltan and Ziggy get to their feet. The Gemini and the Executioner also being present, the little old woman tucks herself in behind her husband at once. He hears Kai telling them, in flawless German, *'Don't be afraid. Here is my company, these are its officers. This is our captain.'*

He goes forward. 'Kai, who are these?'

'Herr Tessmann, Domini,' the boy replies. 'And his wife Frau Tessmann. Bette.'

He sees Frau Tessmann give the boy a fond quiet glance. Frau Tessmann, he thinks, is a grandmother.

'They have a little house and farm,' the boy continues, pointing back beyond the trees. And then, swapping back to Swedish, They wished to see us. He lowers his voice, glances at the Gemini, adding, They had heard all the Swedish had white hair. They wished to see if it was true.

And indeed Frau Tessmann, from behind her husband's shoulder, is now peering at the Gemini, with their candle-flame white hair, and tittering softly to herself.

And tails and horns, Kai continues, abashed.

'Tails and horns?' He laughs, switching to Deutsch again, holds out his hand. 'That would be me. Fiskardo, Herr Tessmann. Jack Fiskardo.'

Herr Tessmann takes the hand in both his own, which are soft and dry with age, and pumps it, as farmers do. Frau Tessmann removes the cloth from the top of the basket. Inside, there are duck eggs, layer upon layer, nested on straw. Astonishing bounty. 'Kai!' he says, amazed, and the boy's face flushes up with pleasure.

I said that we would pay, he admits.

'Indeed we will pay. Herr Tessmann, how much for these fine eggs of yours?'

Herr Tessmann removes his cap, scratches his head, looks up at him from a daring angle, and announces that these eggs will be four pfennig the dozen.

Pay him five, he tells Kai. Five a dozen, and we'll take them all, and we want sweet butter to cook them in, too.

He raises an arm. This may be the one and only time anyone went foraging armed with no more than good manners, he thinks, and returned with such a result. This army, even with its thirteen thousand, might be ludicrously short of men, they may be altogether out of cash (so rumour has it), they may, in fact, be marching on nothing but faith and earnest promises, but this morning, his company at least has –

'Breakfast!'

Clams, flounder, shrimp, the odd dozy herring, all chopped and fried together; a certain amount, it must be said, of seaweed and sand; the eggs piled on top, yellow as the butter and as soft. His whole company, sat around him on the ground, filling their stomachs (filling the dip in the land too). 'I must admit,' says Zoltan, 'this is by no means as revolting as I feared.' He raises his spoon in acknowledgement to the Tessmanns – still watching, still apparently fascinated that these men from the north should do anything as commonplace as eat. 'But it is a strange thing,' Zoltan continues, lowering his voice, 'all their neighbours are fled. Why are they not gone too?'

'Herr Tessmann says they are too old,' Kai answers, seriously. 'He says they fled before, but not again. And Frau Tessmann fears to leave their animals.'

'You speak good German, Kai,' he says, and the boy flushes up again.

'My tutor was from Heidelberg.'

'Your *tutor!*' Zoltan exclaims, with a bark of laughter. 'Of course!'

Kai continues, 'It seems the greatest shame we must make war against his people.'

Puzzlement, on Zoltan's part. 'Your tutor, he was a Catholic?'

'No indeed!' The boy sounds shocked to his core. 'No, he was of God's true faith, of course.'

'Then we make war *for* him, not against him,' Zoltan points out.

'I think we make war *on* him,' Kai says, quietly. 'On all these people. They will be lost beneath our boots.'

He hears himself ask, 'Where is your tutor now?'

'Magdeburg. He and his family, they are in Magdeburg.'

Magdeburg is one of the few cities to have made those earnest promises of support. It is surrounded, unluckily, by many that have not.

He looks at the Tessmanns, how they hold onto each other in the wind, the little old woman with her hand in her husband's, like a bride. He stands up. 'Ulf!'

'Yes, Kapten!'

'Take a dozen of your friends, put a guard upon the Tessmanns' farm, and if any other company comes sniffing round, you tell 'em Fiskardo got there first.'

A mighty grin. 'Yes, Kapten. Yes, Domini!'

Domini. These names keep attaching themselves to him. *Fransman*, the Frenchie, is another. The *Främling*, the stranger, a third. *Oooshtiana*, a fourth. Tomorrow, who leads the forlorn hope? Oooshtiana. Why do they call you that? Kai had asked. He'd sounded as if he was contemplating taking offence, that perhaps being part of an ensign's duties too. (Don't ask me, he'd told the boy. I was older than you before I knew such a thing as an ensign even existed, and I never in my life imagined I'd end up with one.)

'Trzciana,' he'd explained, spelling it out. 'In Poland. A battle, a year ago. It's where I was made captain. By your king.'

And the boy's eyes grew wide.

'Your king has a habit of hazarding himself,' he'd continued, explaining. 'Getting too close to the fire. He had four Cossacks after him, but I had Milano.' And he points to where the horses wait in their usual patient line, heads down, doing whatever a horse does to get some sleep under the midnight sun. 'And I was first, and he was fastest.'

They say Gustavus Adolphus lost his footing as he came ashore. Stood up, clutching handfuls of Germany in each fist, gave thanks to God for putting it so easily within his grasp. It's a good job Lutherans do not believe in omens.

Wolgast. More flats, more shoals, more sand. More heath, more scrub, then stands of birch and pine, and a field thigh-high with grain, grain tangled like hair, sprung from last year's unharvested crop. He and Zoltan pick their way along one edge of the field, through a forest of green bracken almost as high as their heads, and along the other, the Gemini do the same.

He indicates the two white-blond heads, bobbing in and out of sight. 'Think we should have them dye their hair?'

Zoltan is elbowing aside stems of bracken that are thick and sturdy as cane. 'I think we should have left them where we found them, that pair of freaks,' he hears Zoltan mutter in reply.

'What, in a pit, in Poland?' In a pit in Poland, villagers gathered round it, stones in their hands. Neither of the Gemini has ever offered an explanation as to why, but it don't take much to work one out. 'The dew falls on us all,' he informs Zoltan, and gets as expected a snort in reply, and then Zoltan comes to a dead stop, pointing to the ground at their feet.

There is a corpse laid there, right in front of them. What was once a man: the skin now a suit of leather, loosely rolled about the bones, the bones at wrists and legs protruding, white as chalk.

'Germany,' says Zoltan, under his breath, as if no more need be said.

He crouches down. The front of the skull is blackened, the face consumed. Whoever killed this one did so by putting their head to a fire. He tries to remember the last time a corpse – any corpse – made him do anything other than speculate who might have killed it. This part of Germany has had armies marching through it ever since the war began. This same war in which he did his growing. Now here he is again; a veteran at twenty-four.

And then a shout from the far side of the field. He stands. The Gemini are pointing to the fort, and there is the garrison from the fort, racing away, taking flight like game.

Well. That was easy.

Forty-odd miles to the west, Wollin, another town, another fort, and that too falls without a fight. Plenty far enough inland by now for the sound of yawping seagulls, as they push through woods, farmsteads, fields, to have been replaced by the alarm-cries of songbirds. The next is Stettin – the beachhead at Usedom two weeks and seventy miles behind them, moving down the banks of the river Oder as down a road. Once again, they are ordered to be the advance guard, the forlorn hope. Where do these orders come from? Kai wants to know. 'Åke Tott,' he replies, as Åke Tott's messenger turns his horse about, departs. 'General Åke Tott. In the wars in Poland he knew my old commander, Torsten the Bear.' Below Tott, General Baner; below Baner, Colonel James King, a Scot, one of many in this salmagundi of an army; below King, any number of lieutenant colonels, other captains – an entire farmyard full of both cockerels and pecks.

'They put us at the front because they know as we can do it,' Ulf of Torsby declares. Ziggy – their horse-master as well as the resident clown (every company has one) – describes Ulf as riding like a sack of cabbages, but the life of a soldier seems to be suiting him. Ulf has developed the habit of starting the day by practising swinging his sword above his head as if he were casting a net. Not a few times, his comrades have started the day diving to the ground to save their necks. As *Kapten*, he hesitates to point out to Ulf that the other reason to put them at the front is that their loss would be a nothing: supposedly there are another forty thousand conscripts on their way, while Zoltan is Hungarian, the Executioner by birth a Muscovite; Ziggy's family are Bohemian refugees and, as for the Gemini, God knows where they call home. And he himself is either the *Fransman*, or the *Främling*, the stranger, just as always. And Colonel James King, he suspects, knows, likes, trusts, none of them. Torsten the Bear had a reputation, a wild man of the woods; and then –

Well. If you were Colonel James King, and found yourself with this oddity among your captains, this man who by repute is proof against any weapon made of iron or lead or steel, who wears the token of a hard man about his neck, wouldn't you put him at the front, too, just to see what happens?

Stettin is in sight. He sends Ziggy up a tree with the spyglass. 'I see the castle,' comes the report, shouted back down, and then, 'By Christ, they're off again! That's the garrison! On the run! The people are on the walls!'

He thinks of some of those little places they came through in Poland. He asks, before he can stop himself, 'Are they alive?'

They are indeed. There is a pretty little meeting outside the walls, between Gustavus Adolphus of Sweden and the Duke of Pomerania, who (as these things turn out) are brothers-in-law. Duke Bogislaw looks sick and tired, King Gustavus buoyant as ever. Meantime, Oooshtiana and his forlorn hope are sent to flush out any mad-for-glory snipers that might by some chance have been left behind.

They come into the city from the east, Stettin's castle rearing up before them like a land-berg. The walls behind them may be full of folk and noise, but the streets before them are empty as if the plague had just come through. Over the rooftops an Imperial flag, the Habsburg eagle, trapped on its broken pole, mopping and mowing as if bewailing how it has been forsook, flaps and beats above them, leading them on. Schooled in terrifying monosyllables by the Executioner, those sons of the fisher-folk are getting the knack of this most pleasingly, this chequerboard game of feints and darts down the streets, and now there's a gatehouse, so they ease the gate open, wary, and there beyond is one of the castle's many courtyards, and there within it an entire commissary-worth of supplies: half-laden wagons, barrels of beef, crates packed with bottles, chickens hanging from a rack, sacks of bread, wheels of cheese, hams, dried herring, all of it abandoned in confusion. Ulf and his fellows stand at its centre, turning round and round, some-where between delight and disbelief. He tells them, 'Fill your packs and fill your pockets, do it now,' and out the corner of his eye sees Kai approach something the size and shape of a catafalque, shrouded in canvas; sees the boy lift the canvas back, spring away, and go straight down on his arse, skittering back across the ground on heels and elbows, with a cry of 'Holy *GOD!*'

Two animals: huge, spotted, snarling; prowling left to right. A pair of leopards in a cage. His men surround them, all amazed. The Executioner hunkers down, peering in, and one of the animals backs up, squats down, pisses itself. It's the male. The female, hackles in a crest, swipes at the bars of the cage with a paw that makes the metal ring. *There's a moral there*, he thinks.

And then behind the cage, there's movement; there's a man, crouching down, seeking to hide himself behind the barrels and crates, then scurrying for the gate. The Gemini catch him with ease; lift him up under the arms and pin him against the wall. The man wears a buff-coat like theirs, but the strangest pair of breeches in harlequins of yellow, green and red. 'Quinto del Ponte!' the man shrieks, pointing at his breast, 'Quinto del Ponte, Quinto del Ponte!' He seems to think he will need dumb-show before they understand this is his name.

'*E chi o che cazzo è Quinto del Ponte?*' he asks, and the man does a splendid job of apparently going limp with relief, and replies, '*Sono il servitore del generale Wallenstein.*' I am the servant of General Wallenstein. These beasts were a gift from him, to the Emperor.

He finds he still remembers just enough Italian to ask, You are their keeper?

Del Ponte nods.

He looks across to the animals' cage. There is a bowl in it, broken, dry; and a single bone, licked down as the sea licks a stone. *Their keeper my arse.* He turns back to del Ponte and says, So now you can join us, and make them a gift to a king.

Del Ponte demurs. No, no, I am nothing. No soldier. Please, you may keep the beasts, but please, you will let me go.

He leans in. Does Del Ponte speak German? Soon find out.

'You know what His Majesty Gustavus Adolphus of Sweden would say to that?'

Del Ponte, glancing from him to the Gemini and back, shakes his head again.

'He'd say, you're with us, or against us, friend. So which is it to be?'

Night falls, only of course it don't. The leopards, sated on chicken, with a bucket of water let gingerly into their cage through its cunning little door, lie on their sides, bellies heaving with content. He and Kai lean over the cage and chat.

'Why do they keep running away?' the boy asks. 'The Emperor's army – why do they not stand and fight?'

'They're stretching our lines,' he replies. 'The only place from which we can reinforce or resupply is the beachhead back on Usedom. The further we get from it, the faster, the better for them. General Wallenstein is no fool.'

The leopardess, beneath them, gives a stretch to all four legs, then all four of those mighty paws, toe by taloned toe, and opens her eyes as if their conversation is of interest.

Kai, looking down at her, asks, 'What will become of them?'

'They will go to Stockholm,' he says. 'To the Djurgården, I would think. A whole island for them to range about on.'

Kai looks mournful. 'Poor beasts,' he says. 'They are so far from home.'

As are we all.

'Master Ponte says they are worth five hundred thaler,' the boy continues, in a marvelling tone. And lo, at the boy's words, there is the man himself, still in that outlandish costume, sidling into view. Something prompts him: extend the conversation. Let Master Ponte come up if he will.

'When I was much the same age as you,' he begins, 'I helped disembark a horse worth double that and more.'

The boy's eyes widen once again. Everything seems new to Kai, the boy spends his days agog. 'A horse worth so much?'

'So I was told. The Buckingham mare. She was being shipped to Stockholm too.'

And here is Master Ponte himself, ducking his head in greeting, hands steepled together in supplication. '*Buona sera, buona sera.*' And then in German, 'My friends.' He comes closer. 'I am intrigued,' he begins. 'You speak Italian, Kapten. Excellently, if I may say so.' An ingratiating smile. 'A man who speaks Italian is as rare in these climes as – well, these.' A hand waved over the cage.

It comes to him that Quinto del Ponte's costume is exactly what a man would wear if he wished not to be taken seriously. 'Yet you are here,' he replies.

'Ah, yes. My business takes me everywhere. *Il mondo è il mio mercato*, as they say.'

'Sadly you are at the limits of my Italian, Signor del Ponte,' he says, 'as you are at the limits of your own range.'

'Ah, so.' Hands in the pockets of those harlequin breeches. 'But yet I am intrigued. How is it that you speak Italian at all?'

'An old acquaintance. When I was first a-soldiering in Germany.' And then just to see, he adds, 'Another trader, like yourself. One Tino Ravello.'

Quinto del Ponte's face congeals instantly, a response so swift even a dissembler as practised as this one can't hide it. The boy, Kai, eyes darting from one to the other, aware something has happened here, but nothing like fast enough to work out what.

'Well then!' del Ponte declares. 'I believe I know the man. Or I have heard the name, at least.'

'Indeed? How small this great world can be.'

Del Ponte waits a moment, rocking on his toes. 'Then my curiosity is sated. I bid you *buona notte*, Kapten.'

The leopardess watches him go.

'He is a little strange,' says Kai, uncertainly.

'He is a *lot* strange. I think we keep a careful eye upon him.'

'But he knew your friend,' Kai points out, as if this must be proof of good character.

'He knew the name, sure enough. But the Tino Ravello I knew was an intelligencer, a spy. And I strongly suspect our Signor del Ponte may prove to be the same.'

The leopardess is on her feet. She lifts her head – her head that is both chamfered and square, and as if pulled from the mass of her body between the finger and thumb of her creator. He lays his hand to the top of the cage, feels the heat of her breath, her whiskers stiff as salt-grass. The blood and ivory of the inside of her mouth. Then she yawns, and the yawn extends into a yodel of complaint, of feline huff; with just enough of a growl to it so you know to pay it due heed. *You remind me of someone*, he thinks.

All these shades, all these echoes, all these ghosts, a whole land full of them, all a-waiting. His hand lifts to the silver wolf.

And only one that matters. *Where do you wait for me, you son of a bitch? What stone are you hiding under now?*